Except for historical personages, all characters herein are fictitious. Episodes of the novel are based on historical events, but dialogue and the actions of fictional characters, as well as deeds imputed to historical personages, are the invention of the author. The dialogue pertaining to the court-martial of Maj. Littleton Waller is based closely on excerpts from official trial transcripts in the National Archives.

LYFORD Books
Published by Presidio Press
505B San Marin Dr., Suite 300
Novato, CA 94945-1340

Library of Congress Cataloging-in-Publication Data

Saunders, Raymond M., 1949–
    Fenwick Travers and the forbidden kingdom : an entertainment / Raymond M. Saunders.
        p.   cm.
    ISBN 0-89141-480-0
    1. Americans—Travel—Philippines—Fiction. 2. Soldiers—United States—Fiction.   I. Title.
PS3569.A7938F45   1994
813'.54—dc20   94-9750
                                                                    CIP

Typography by ProImage
Maps by Joe Purvis

Printed in the United States of America

Fenwick Travers
and the
FORBIDDEN
KINGDOM

An Entertainment

RAYMOND M. SAUNDERS

LYFORD
Books

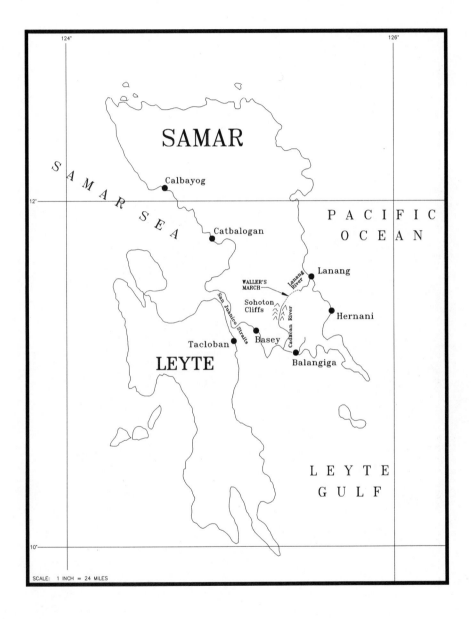

124°

SAMAR

S
A
M
A
R
S
E
A

Calbayog

12°

Catbalogan

PACIFIC
OCEAN

WALLER'S
MARCH

Lanang
River

Lanang

Sohoton
Cliffs

San Juanico Straits

Cadacan River

Hernani

Tacloban

Basey

LEYTE

Balangiga

LEYTE
GULF

126°

10°

SCALE: 1 INCH = 24 MILES

1

Manila, Luzon
December 1900

"Captain Travers?" asked the veteran sergeant who clambered up the gangplank of the steamer as soon as it had docked.

I nodded and he drew himself to attention and saluted. "Sergeant Markley, sir. Company C, 9th Infantry. I was sent to escort you to headquarters."

"The Ninth? Why, that's my old regiment, Sergeant."

"I know, sir," said Sergeant Markley. "The Ninth's been here in Manila since we returned from China."

"I see. Well, just let me get my things and we can get on our way."

Sergeant Markley waited as I went to my cabin and gathered my bags. I was in the Philippines, all right. President McKinley had been true to his word on that score. He had said he needed a good man to help put down the rebel bands in these parts and capture their leader, Emilio Aguinaldo, and I was his choice. Lucky me, I thought bitterly. All my attempts to dissuade McKinley, Roosevelt, and the host of War Department functionaries who greeted me upon my triumphant return from Peking had been for naught. I was the designated fair-haired boy, the one who would set matters straight in this fetid backwater of empire, and that was that. I had time for no more than a brief, yet oh so sweet, sojourn with lovely Alice Brenoble in New York after my return from China, and then I was Asia bound once more.

Alice had been distraught at my sudden departure, as was her uncle, George Duncan. After three years of waiting for me during the Cuban campaign and the Boxer Rebellion, she had yearned for some quiet time alone for just the two of us. Perhaps I felt guilty for all the misery that she had endured on my behalf, or perhaps I genuinely loved her; whatever the reason, Alice and I became engaged before I left once more for the mysterious East. Promising that we'd be wed upon my return, I had left her heartbroken yet hopeful by the pier when I sailed.

As for her Uncle George, his sorrow at my departure had nothing to do with affection. He needed a rugged young gunslinger to settle his labor disputes, and he thought I was just the fellow. Despite my reservations about being sent to the Philippines, I was heartily glad to be beyond his clutches.

Thus it had been with mixed feelings that I made landfall in Manila Bay aboard the transport SS *Boston* shortly after dawn on a day that promised to be blazingly hot. I had watched with a sense of foreboding as my steamer made half speed past the imposing green heights of the Bataan Peninsula, skirted the island fortresses of Corregidor and El Fraile, passed the navy yard at Cavite, and dropped anchor at Manila near the mouth of the sluggish Rio Pasig.

The Spanish city of Manila was spread along the low, swampy shore like a crescent hugging the bay. Manila's most noticeable feature was the Intramuros, the walled inner city that loomed above its otherwise flat surroundings. All about the Intramuros lay the native hovels of the Filipinos, palm-thatched nipa huts built on stilts to keep out snakes and high water. As the steamer docked, my nostrils filled with the dank smell of decaying matter.

Here, I told myself, fever lurked. To ward it off, I resolved to resume the alcohol regimen I'd perfected in Cuba: a half bottle of spirits per day, rain or shine. Oh, I'd be nearly inebriated most of the time, to be sure, but at least I wouldn't have the sweaty shakes that had felled thousands of other poor sods in the Tropics.

I returned to the deck with my bags and handed them to Sergeant Markley, who hefted them with ease and led me to the gangway. As we disembarked, the gravity of the military situation on Luzon became apparent. Medical orderlies began hauling a steady stream of soldiers on stretchers aboard the *Boston*. All around on the dock lay dozens more men waiting to be embarked. Here and there I could see bloody bandages bespeaking combat wounds, but the vast majority of soldiers had the glassy-eyed stare of fever victims. It was Cuba all over again.

"See anybody you know?" Sergeant Markley asked lightly.

"No, thank God," I quavered.

I followed Markley to a donkey cart by which stood a drowsy Filipino. Markley loaded my bags into the cart, told the driver to follow along, and then marched away from the quay into the teeming center of Manila. In this manner we headed up a slight incline that led to the Intramuros. Along the way we passed rows of vendors in tiny open-air stalls who hawked everything from fried snake to pickled monkey brains. The street noise was deafening, and the smells rising in the morning heat beggared description. I held my breath lest I gag, and hurried after Sergeant Markley.

At the gate of the Intramuros lounged a corporal and two privates, rifles stacked. They eyed the flow of traffic entering and leaving, rising from their wooden benches only when an officer passed. They scrambled to their feet as I approached.

"Welcome to the islands, sir," hailed the corporal, rendering a salute as he spoke. He was savvy enough to spot a newcomer when he saw one, and his voice carried a tone more of condolence than of welcome.

"Glad to be here," I answered ruefully as I returned the salute, bringing a barely suppressed smirk to the corporal's face.

"All quiet, Corporal Lawless?" asked Markley as we passed.

The corporal nodded. "Quiet as you could please, Sergeant Markley."

The walls of the Intramuros, once the military center of the Spanish government in these islands, were a full ten feet thick. We'd be safe in here, I told myself, but then I noted with concern that the Filipinos got by the sentries easily, many of them leading burros laden with wares.

"Peddlers," said Markley, noticing the direction of my worried stare. "Filipinos have a way of burrowing into garrison life like you wouldn't believe. They do the laundry, cook the meals, and shine the boots. Why, a private can live a decent life here on his army pay and still have a greenback or two left at the end of the month to spend on the whores."

"All the same," I muttered, "it would seem safer to keep the natives beyond the walls."

Sergeant Markley merely shrugged, knowing that the wall had yet to be built that could keep out a Filipino intent on commerce. Once we were inside the Intramuros, Sergeant Markley pointed to a large limestone edifice on the far side of the wide interior park. "The adjutant's office is right across the plaza, sir," he said. "You need to report in there, and the adjutant will see to it that you're settled in."

Nodding, I paused to take in the scene before me. The central plaza evidently served as a parade ground. It was big enough to drill an entire regiment at one time. On three sides it was bounded by sturdy stone barracks interspersed with various storerooms. On the fourth side, opposite the gate through which I'd entered, were the administrative offices.

Soldiers relaxed on the wide wooden verandas of the barracks, obviously resting after their morning drills. You see, I knew from my time in Cuba that military exercises in the Tropics were always conducted in the cool of the morning. One knot of soldiers gathered around a fellow with a banjo, and together they sang lustily the song that was all the rage:

O Dewey was the morning
Upon the first of May
And Dewey was the Admiral
Down in Manila Bay;
And Dewey were the Regent's eyes
Them orbs of royal blue
and Dewey feel discouraged?
I dew not think we dew.

Everywhere Filipinos swarmed about the soldiers, seeing to their myriad needs. This buzzing domestic activity gave the plaza the air more of a great open market than of a military post. It was clear that the natives treated the place as an extension of the street markets I had passed on the way up from the quay.

I turned to Markley. "Very well, Sergeant. See to my things, will you?"

Markley nodded and I set off toward the adjutant's office. I had gone no more than ten paces, however, when all hell broke loose.

"Hey, stop them!" rang out an American voice.

I turned to see a group of perhaps fifteen Filipinos, dressed in typical Luzon peasant garb, boiling through a doorway onto the plaza. What the dickens was the matter? I wondered as I watched this scene unfold. As they ran, one tall Filipino, his face shaded by a conical straw hat, suddenly thrust aside the blanket draped across his shoulder. The barrel of his rifle glinted in the morning sun.

"Jesus, he's armed!" gasped Sergeant Markley from behind me; but before he could give the alarm, the Filipino fired. A pursuing American collapsed with a bullet in his heart.

At the crack of the rifle, all activity froze in the plaza. Then bedlam erupted. Filipinos raced for cover as soldiers poured out of the barracks, most of them unarmed. The band of attackers, now bent on escape, headed straight for the gate where I was standing.

Sergeant Markley dropped my bags and reached for his pistol—only to discover that he was unarmed. I had only my saber, which I drew from its scabbard, and then the Filipinos were on us.

"Run for it!" cried Sergeant Markley, ducking out of harm's way as I lashed out desperately at our attackers.

I managed to drop one Filipino with my saber before the tall leader slammed his rifle butt into my chest. As I sagged painfully, I grabbed for the fellow's feet, determined to prevent the Filipinos behind him from trampling me into the dust in their haste to be off.

My strength was enough to trip up the leader; he stumbled, dropping a rolled-up parchment to the ground. With the speed of a born athlete, however, he caught his balance, grabbed the parchment, and delivered a savage kick to my ribs as I lay sprawled on the ground.

With Sergeant Markley and me now out of the line of fire, the sentries at the gate leveled their Krags at the onrushing Filipinos. They loosed a volley, dropping three of the attackers, but before they could work their bolts to fire again, the Filipinos were on them. Bolos—the wicked fighting weapons of Luzon, having the general size and weight of a Cuban machete—flashed in the heavy air.

The Americans went down to a man, Corporal Lawless decapitated and the privates mortally wounded. In the melee, the tall leader lost his straw hat, revealing an emerald-hued silk turban wrapped about his head. Then suddenly the struggle was over, and the attackers escaped into the crowded streets beyond the gate.

It happened so quickly, I could scarcely believe the carnage my eyes had just witnessed. I rose shakily as Sergeant Markley scampered over to the fallen sentries. He grabbed a Krag, relieved one of the fallen men of his cartridge belt, and bellowed grimly, "Let's go get 'em."

Soldiers from the barracks were rushing to the gate, many of them now armed, and all of them looking to join the chase. "Which way, sir?" one asked me. It became clear that I was expected to lead the pursuit.

"I, er, that is . . . ," I stalled—more than willing to let the raiders be on their way—when another officer appeared. I took one look at him and blinked.

Could it be? "Charlie? Charlie Hobart?" By God, it was! Then I remembered that Charlie had been banished to Manila when the 9th Infantry was sent to Peking.

"Fenny!" hailed Hobart. "By God, I didn't know you were here."

Pleasantries would have to wait, under the circumstances. Instead I demanded a bit shrilly, "Charlie, what the hell's going on here?"

"*Ladrones,* Filipino bandits," he replied tersely. "They just hit the paymaster's office. They got a few stacks of dollars and an old map that was in the safe. I don't know why they wanted the map, but our job now is to make sure they don't get away."

Then Hobart noticed the silver captain bars on my shoulder. A look of surprise registered on his face; I was now a grade ahead of him, although we had both graduated from West Point together. Hobart apparently was not fully acquainted with the honors and advancement heaped upon me as the result of my China exploits. "Are you coming, Fen . . . er, that is, sir?" he faltered awkwardly.

Under the eyes of the expectant soldiers, I had no real choice in the matter, you see. I could either join the pursuit with as much good grace as possible, or be branded a lily-livered shirker for the rest of my stay in these damned islands. Silently cursing Markley for getting me into this predicament, I muttered glumly, "Lead on," and added irritably, "and call me Fenny, damnit."

Then we were off on foot, with Sergeant Markley leading the way, there being no cavalry nearby to take up the chase. We were guided by a trail of overturned kiosks and irate merchants whom the fleeing raiders left scattered in their wake. From up ahead came a steady chorus of shouts as the escaping Filipinos shoved their way through the narrow, crowded streets. The hunt quickly led from the heart of the city onto a hard-packed carriage road that followed the bank of the Rio Pasig toward the interior of Luzon.

"They're heading for the hills," called Markley, redoubling his gait from a slow trot to a medium run. We held this doggedly determined pace for a mile, passing through the suburbs of Manila and then past stately plantations that dotted the riverbank. One mansion loomed above the others, and I huffed to Hobart, "Charlie, what's that place?"

"Malacanan Palace," panted Hobart in reply. "MacArthur's headquarters."

Why, that could only mean Gen. Arthur MacArthur, the commanding general of the Division of the Philippines. This was just great, I thought forlornly. Rebel patrols were able to shoot their way into the heart of Manila and then trot away past the commanding general's headquarters in broad daylight. President McKinley had been right when he told me that matters in these islands needed drastic attention.

Under different circumstances, I might have stopped to admire Malacanan Palace. It was several stories high, with an intricate facade of distinctly Moorish flavor. A delicate red-tiled roof set the place off to perfection. Excepting the digs of Tzu Hsi back in the Forbidden City, of course, it was one of the most unique buildings I had yet seen in the East.

I had had time for no more than a cursory look at the place, however, when suddenly I caught sight of a flash of green on the road ahead. Then the scurrying forms of our quarry came into view.

Sergeant Markley stopped and shouldered his Krag. He drew a careful bead and fired. A Filipino sprawled in the dirt; then the others redoubled their speed and were gone from sight once again.

The sound of the shot drew an instant response from the direction of the palace. The honor guard, a squad of black regulars, ran down the drive from the palace, rifles at the ready. Leading them was a gray-haired sergeant major. Behind him was a sturdy corporal of the guard.

It was the corporal who instantly drew my attention. He was a strapping six-footer, with the seasoned look of a veteran who had seen his share of fighting. That rugged face seemed awfully familiar somehow. Then it hit me. By God, it was Henry Jefferson from Elm Grove!

2

"Henry!" I cried, genuinely glad to see him. The two wound stripes on his sleeve told me that he had done some hard campaigning since we last met in the wild deserts of Arizona. The crossed rifle insignia on his collar bearing the numerals of the 25th Infantry indicated that Henry was still with his old regiment.

Henry stopped, his face registering pleasure and surprise. "Suh" came the stiff reply, but from the twinkle in his dark eyes, it was obvious that he was equally tickled to see me.

Hobart brought his posse to a halt with an upraised hand. "Do you know this man, Fenny?" asked Hobart.

"Yep, and so do you, Charlie," I replied. "Henry here once poled your barge to St. Louis."

Hobart gazed narrowly at Henry. "Why, yes, now I recognize him. He's the one who ran off the same day you . . . er . . . well . . . that is, I recognize him all right."

That was all the time there was for greetings, for the foe was fast receding. Hobart hurriedly outlined the situation to the sergeant major, who immediately put Henry's squad under Hobart's command and then ran back to the palace to turn out the rest of the guard.

"Forward!" ordered Hobart, and we were again off at a trot. Beyond Malacanan Palace, the surroundings grew more rural. The road narrowed to no more than a rutted cart track on either side of which rice paddies spread toward the horizon. We had covered nearly five miles now, and most of the soldiers from the Intramuros were reaching the limits of their endurance. Hobart was unsteady on his feet, and my breath was coming in labored gasps. The black regulars were fresh, however, and it was they who finally brought us in sight of the fleeing foe once more.

The fugitives were ahead on the road where it passed between flat rice paddies. At a command from Henry, his squad halted and commenced to lay down a withering fire that dropped two Filipinos in the dirt. The others immediately split into four groups; two broke for the rice paddies to the right and two to the left. On the left the paddies were not particularly wide, and were bounded on their far side by a high earthen dike. Beyond the dike I could make out treetops, telling me that over the dike there was probably cover and therefore a likely escape route.

As for the right side of the road, the paddies in that direction were wider. Beyond them were tall stands of cogon grass.

"If they reach that grass, they're gone," gasped Hobart, now thoroughly blown. It was then that the sound of hoofbeats from behind made me turn. The swarthy sergeant major was galloping down the road at the head of another squad of black regulars. They were all mounted on mules, and strapped to the side of one snorting beast was a Colt machine gun.

The reinforcements pounded to a halt and dismounted just feet from where I stood. The sergeant major barked out his orders. In a blur of motion, the new arrivals set up the Colt, loaded a magazine, and trained the gun on the bandits fleeing to the right of the road. Then the Colt roared.

A shower of lead ripped into the Filipinos, blowing an arm off one unfortunate wretch and dropping the others into the fetid paddy waters. Immediately the second group on the same side of the road stopped and raised their hands. They had seen enough.

"Take them in!" ordered Hobart. Sergeant Markley and a few privates trotted off to do as he bid.

The Colt was now aimed toward the paddies on the left side of the road. The two groups of Filipinos fleeing in this direction had diverged even farther apart. I could see clearly that one band was being led by the rascal in the emerald turban. He had found a footpath of raised earth that headed in the direction of the high dike. His group, consisting of three men including himself, was sprinting along while the other group, a knot of four men, mucked laboriously through a paddy.

"Let's go!" wheezed Hobart. Henry nodded, ordered a private to lead off, and then followed with the rest of his squad and Hobart in tow. There was nothing for me to do but to follow. As we ran, the Colt roared, and the lagging group disappeared in a hail of spray kicked up by flying bullets. When the Colt fell silent again, I counted four bodies floating in the paddy.

Now we gained the footpath and were in hot pursuit across the paddy after the three remaining natives. As we ran, the men on the Colt adjusted their aim to where the footpath intersected the dike. They worked hurriedly, for the Filipinos, spurred by the roar of the Colt, were making amazing speed. The leader in the green turban reached the dike and flew to the top with his men on his heels.

The Colt spoke again, and a huge cloud of mud and debris exploded near the top of the dike. On we ran, our eyes fixed on that point, but when the dust settled we saw nothing. If the bandits had been hit, their bodies had fallen on the far side of the dike.

We were so intent on the pursuit that we failed to notice the spot in the footpath where none of the escaping natives had trod.

"Yiii!" screamed the lead soldier as his foot slid into a pit lined with slivers of bamboo.

"Foot traps!" yelled Henry, motioning the soldiers to halt. Hobart and Henry were pulling the writhing fellow from the pit when the bandit in the green turban reappeared on the top of the dike, his Mauser shouldered. He fired once—the range so close that he couldn't miss—and a soldier slid into the paddy water with a bullet in his head.

In an instant, I realized we'd blundered into a killing zone. The Filipinos had probably expected pursuit, and this was a site they'd preselected to make a stand. I knew that even with the Colt to back us up, we'd all be dead unless we did something quickly. The specter of extermination galvanized me into immediate action. I did what I did best in such circumstances—I ran like the dickens! Leaping and bounding like a singed deer in a forest fire, I headed smartly for the rear, only to feel a second bullet graze the crown of my hat. By God, the son of a bitch had me in his sights! There was no way I could make it across that exposed paddy.

Now completely possessed by terror, yet unable to stop running, I turned on my heels once again and darted right back toward the shelter of the dike. As I flashed past Hobart, he cried out anxiously, "Fenny, where are you going?"

"Arghh!" was my reply, for rational speech was beyond the capability of my fear-crazed brain. I was in a one-man stampede, you see, and I had no idea where it would end. Some ingrained survival instinct prodded me to seize the Krag dropped by the soldier who had blundered into the foot trap as I flew past Hobart. Then I was scampering straight for the dike, chambering a round as I ran and bellowing like an elk in rut. Somewhere deep inside me, I had formed the determination that if the turbaned fellow was going to kill me, then by the blazes I was at least going to take a couple of shots at him in return.

I clambered to the top of the dike, screaming and grimacing like a drunken Comanche, only to find that my attacker had disappeared. Throwing myself down, I peered fearfully over the crest. Beyond was a swamp and a narrow creek leading into a tangle of mangrove trees. I couldn't see the foe, and I concluded that they were hunkered down at the bottom of the dike, just beyond my line of sight. Well, I figured, my faculties slowly returning to me, if the bandits were down there, they couldn't shoot me, right? That meant that now was the time for me to skedaddle. Determined to do just that, I clumsily heaved my weight about on the narrow crest, rather like a fat spider trying to turn around on a slender twig.

It was then that I hit the mud. The far side of the dike, sheltered from the morning sun, was slick with dew. My legs lurched out from beneath me, and suddenly I was sliding downward toward the killers lurking below. Desperate to stop, I reached out for a clump of grass or anything that would arrest my sudden descent, but the surface of the dike was completely bare!

"God Almighty!" I yelled, hurtling downward with the speed of a toboggan on ice. I zoomed right into the Filipinos crouched at the bottom of the dike, bowled one over, and then crunched headfirst with sickening force into something hard. Stunned, I blinked away the stars to see a *banca,* the native canoe of Luzon, pulled up on the bank of the creek. Despite the blow, I was coherent enough to realize that my Krag had kept going straight into the water. I was completely unarmed!

Groggy, I rolled to my back, only to be trampled by two of the foe as they bolted into the *banca.* Then green turban was above me, a wicked weapon in his hand. It was a long knife like a bolo, but strangely different.

The razor-sharp, double-edged blade was delicate and wavy, not blunt and heavy like that of a bolo. I shuddered at the thought of the horrible wound that wavy blade could inflict. When my assailant raised his awful weapon for the killing blow, I realized I had but an instant to live.

Without conscious thought, I brought my boot up into his crotch with a speed born of desperation. My enemy gasped and collapsed into the *banca,* the force of his fall propelling the craft into the stream. His men began paddling furiously, and in an instant they had disappeared around a brush-covered bend in the stream and were gone.

From the far side of the dike, I heard Hobart call, "Fenny? Are you all right? We're coming over! Can you hear me?"

I was about to answer when I noticed something in the mud near my head. It was a parchment. By God, it was the map the raiders had stolen from the paymaster's office! My kick had caused the character in the green turban to drop it.

What was so special about a rumpled piece of parchment that the Filipinos were willing to risk their lives for it? I wondered. I reached out for the parchment and closed my hand around it.

For a second I pondered what to do with it. For any other officer, the proper course of conduct would have been unquestionably clear. The parchment should be returned straightaway. I was no ordinary officer, however—a fact I'd demonstrated amply during my looting spree in China. Besides, this paper didn't look like government property to me. It looked more like war booty, which happened to be my stock-in-trade.

I hastily tucked the parchment inside my tunic and croaked hoarsely, "It's okay, Charlie. Come on over. I've run them off!"

3

Of course I said nothing about the map to Hobart as he detailed the sergeant major and his men to collect the bodies. I bade farewell to Henry and promised to look him up during my tour; then Hobart and I borrowed two mules and rode back to Manila. We reported to the adjutant, an elderly, overweight fussbudget named Major Kingsbury, whose pasty face told me he hadn't seen field duty in decades. Kingsbury, ensconced behind his desk, beamed like an approving headmaster as

Hobart detailed the rapid response to the sudden raid. A crowd of staffers gathered about at the telling, all nodding approvingly as Hobart recounted the deaths of nine foemen and the capture of three others. Only the escape of the leader and the failure to recover any of their loot detracted from the incident.

"You say the leader wore a green turban?" queried Major Kingsbury.

"That he did," confirmed Hobart.

"And he had a strange-looking bolo, too," I added.

"Strange looking?" asked Kingsbury. "In what way?"

"It was wavy," I replied, "like a snake slithering along the ground."

Now the portly old major stroked his double chin thoughtfully. "A wavy knife, eh? And a turban to boot?" Kingsbury, a self-proclaimed expert on the native cultures in the islands, was silent a moment before pronouncing, "You must have seen a Moro. You see, turbans just aren't worn by the Tagalogs."

"The who?" I interrupted.

Here Hobart eagerly leaped at the chance to exhibit his slender knowledge of the Philippines. "The Tagalogs," he repeated. "They're the dominant tribe in southern and central Luzon. Almost all of Emilio Aguinaldo's troops—he's the *insurrecto* chieftain, you know—are Tagalogs. They're the most civilized group in the islands."

"I see," I said.

"As for the wavy sword, that could only be a kris," continued Major Kingsbury.

"What's a kris? And for that matter, what's a Moro?" I asked, perplexed.

Major Kingsbury, although he hadn't stirred from within the sheltering walls of headquarters since his arrival in Manila, didn't hesitate to chuckle condescendingly at the extent of my ignorance. "Yes, I suppose all this must be confusing. I'll take the second question first. The term *Moro* was applied by the Spanish to the Muslim inhabitants of the southern islands of the Philippines. It's what the Spanish called the Moors in Africa, who were also sons of Allah. When the dons discovered Muslims here in the Tropics, well, they just used the same name, you see. As for what a kris is, why, it's the weapon of the Moros— one, I might add, which is particularly well suited for mayhem."

"I've heard a little about the Moros," chimed in Charlie. "They're a race of pirate heathens, right?"

"Only partly right, Lieutenant," Major Kingsbury corrected him pedantically. "Yes, they're pirates, I grant you, but Muslims aren't exactly heathens. Followers of the Prophet have a religion every bit as detailed as ours. They can be quarrelsome, however. Moros would as soon kill a Christian as look at one. A thoroughly nasty breed they are. But even as villainous as the Moros are, there's one particularly odious fellow who stands out from the pack." Here Major Kingsbury gazed directly at me. "What's more, Captain Travers, he's known for wearing a green turban."

"And who is he, sir?"

"Surlang" came the clipped reply. "A bloodthirsty hellion who's murdered and raped his way around the Sulu Archipelago for the past decade. He generally infests the waters between the Philippines and Borneo. Rumor has it that he was once a captain in the guard of the sultan of Jolo, but he got too ambitious for his own good. Started taking slaves and plunder from among the Christian Filipinos but neglected to turn over the proceeds to his master, the sultan."

"Slaves?" I asked, curious.

"Yes, slaves, Captain. You see, the Moro way of life revolves around slave raiding and fighting, and Surlang is a past master of both. When the sultan turned him out, Surlang went into business on his own in a big way. The Spanish dons were on his trail for years but never succeeded in taking him, unfortunately."

Here Major Kingsbury paused and shook his head. "You know, though, it just doesn't make sense. The Moros generally have no truck with the Christian natives of Luzon, and besides, the Sulu Sea is hundreds of miles from here. No, it just doesn't add up. It may have been Surlang you saw, but I'd be inclined to pass off his presence as no more than an opportunistic raid, nothing more. He's probably halfway to Jolo as we speak."

"I'm certain you're right, sir," chirped Hobart.

For my part, I held my tongue. I wasn't as certain as Kingsbury on that score. Only Surlang among the bandits we'd chased had carried a kris or worn a turban. That meant his followers were not Moros. I was convinced that there was more to this tale than any of us fathomed at the moment. What had occurred was more than an "opportunistic raid."

Major Kingsbury, however, did not sense my doubts. Instead he beamed anew at Charlie's concurrence, and declared with finality, "I think so, Lieutenant Hobart, and what's more, I think that because of the efforts of both of you young gentlemen, there has been a satisfactory ending to this whole affair. And I must say, Captain Travers," he added warmly, "I'm very pleased to see that your actions live up to your reputation. We've all heard what a first-rate job you did in China."

I fairly preened at this. "Oh, sir, it was nothing, really," I replied with a suitably modest smile, drinking in the compliment with gusto and ready to play the role of conquering hero to the hilt. And why not? I figured. Heroes were usually tapped to be generals' aides, right? In two campaigns against determined foes I had yet to see a dead general, so I figured that a billet as a general's aide would put me close enough to the flagpole to be safe.

"Nothing, says he!" guffawed Hobart. "I'll have you know, Fenny, that quite a few officers from the 9th and 14th Infantry have been through this office upon their return from the Boxer Rebellion. I've heard all about your actions at Hsiku Arsenal and the Tatar Wall outside of Peking. Why, for a while there, it seemed every dispatch from General Chaffee's headquarters mentioned the intrepid Lieutenant Travers. Although I had no idea until we met today that you'd been promoted to captain, I say it's well deserved." Here Hobart turned to the others gathered about, addressing them as a body: "Gentlemen, meet a real soldier!"

In a second I was surrounded by the backslapping staffers. They insisted on telling me what a splendid fellow I was, with fat old Kingsbury being the biggest backslapper of them all. "Look out, Aguinaldo!" laughed a florid Signal Corps lieutenant, whose rosy complexion seemed to come more from performing bacchanalian devotions in the officers' mess than from duty in the field. "Now we have a real tiger to set on you!"

I smiled bravely at this and gave my mustache a fierce tug. If these boys were convinced I was a hero, well, who was I to disabuse them of the notion, eh? I was busy exchanging manly handshakes with all comers when Hobart mentioned, "Oh, there's something else for you here, Fenny."

He handed me a buff-colored envelope bearing the emblem of a major general, a red banner with two white stars emblazoned on it. "This came from General MacArthur's aide. It's an invitation to the general's New Year's Eve ball tomorrow night."

"A ball?" I queried, surprised. Then to impress Hobart I added sternly, a faraway look in my eyes, "They didn't have many of those on the north China plains, you know."

"I'm certain of that, old man," replied Hobart quietly, no doubt thinking I was manfully suppressing horrible memories of the savage fight against the heathen Boxers. "But that's all the more reason why you should definitely attend. General MacArthur wants to see you, Fenny."

"And since it's the New Year's Eve ball," added Major Kingsbury with a knowing wink, "I expect there'll be some very lovely ladies in attendance."

"Ladies?" I grinned. Now, that cast a whole new light on MacArthur's invitation. "You know, Charlie, maybe a little party would be just the thing to help me forget the Boxers."

Everyone laughed at this. "That's the spirit!" Hobart cried, clapping me on the shoulder. "Listen, the rest of the day is going to be a loss, but the Army-Navy Club is only two blocks away. What do you say we go lift a few in honor of the Long Gray Line?"

"Now you're talking, Charlie," I concurred heartily. "Lead on!"

The Army-Navy Club was a former officers' mess from the Spanish colonial era. It was a fine old structure, with high ceilings, wooden fans, and rattan furniture everywhere. We bellied up to the bar, where the white-liveried steward, a taciturn little Filipino with a badly pockmarked face, casually sauntered over to be of service. We ordered drinks, downed them, and ordered another round.

Watching the languid motions of the steward, I began to wax philosophical. "You know, Charlie, I was just noticing how, banditry aside, nothing seems to happen in a hurry in the Tropics."

Our fresh drinks arrived and Hobart swallowed deeply from his. "That's true when you're speaking of the natives, Fenny. The Filipinos do seem to move two paces slower than ground sloths. But General MacArthur—well, he's nothing but greased lightning. He relies on light, fast-moving columns of infantry and cavalry to fan out into the brush and keep the *insurrectos* on the run. He's succeeded in scattering the larger guerrilla bands and pushing them back into the remote hills. Now he's laying plans for the final defeat of Aguinaldo and his remaining holdouts. Why, there's not an *insurrecto* alive today who'd dare to show his face within fifty miles of Manila."

"Except those fellows we just ran off," I reminded him sharply.

Hobart was unperturbed by my barb. "Oh, don't judge MacArthur's progress by today. The Filipinos have banditry in their blood, so I wouldn't say that those were necessarily Aguinaldo's forces we tangled with. No, Major Kingsbury was right. They were just a bunch of freebooters hoping to make a payroll heist. I'm glad that all they escaped with was a few greenbacks and an old map."

I disagreed with Charlie. What we had witnessed was not the act of a few local thugs. No, it had all the earmarks of a military action complete with a well-conceived escape plan. I thought once more of the parchment tucked in my tunic. I needed time to study it alone. That map had cost the lives of nine men, and I wanted in on the secrets it held. In the meantime, however, I intended to relax and enjoy my first day ashore in more than a month.

"Well, here's to MacArthur, then," I said, raising my glass. "May all his efforts be crowned with success." The sooner the war was over, of course, the sooner we'd be free to exploit these monkeys in peace. That, in turn, meant I could be on my way back to civilization and sweet Alice.

"To MacArthur!" chorused Hobart. We drained our glasses again and ordered refills. When they came, Hobart continued, "Say, Fenny, have you heard the news about Joshua Longbottom?"

"Can't say as I have, Charlie," I answered. I hadn't seen Longbottom since our march to Peking after he'd done his best to get me captured during the assault on the Native City at Tientsin. "He hasn't run off with some dance-hall floozie and gotten a dose of the Manchu pox, has he?" I asked with a laugh. It would have served the bastard right for trying to cut me loose in a horde of sword-wielding Boxers as he had.

"Oh, not Longbottom," Hobart assured me. "He's so straitlaced he'd never take any improper liberties. No, nothing like that. In fact, it's quite good news. After China, Longbottom returned to Manila. He's in town now, on MacArthur's staff."

"Well, here's to Longbottom then," I toasted again. I was in a good enough mood to toast the devil himself, you see.

"No, no, Fenny, that's not the news," Hobart hastened to explain. "The news is that he's been confirmed permanently in the rank of captain, just like you. He was breveted in China after Captain Harris was killed, you know."

"What? A permanent captain? Why, that means he's been promoted years ahead of his peers!" I exclaimed, flabbergasted. I knew he'd been breveted, of course. A brevet promotion just means filling a space until an officer of suitable rank comes along and displaces you. But a permanent promotion like mine was unheard of so quickly. Ordinarily a lieutenant in the infantry could expect to wait ten years to be considered for the permanent grade of captain. Longbottom had made it in half that time, which meant that he'd caught up with me!

"Right you are, Fenny," agreed Hobart. "It was a reward for bravery in the face of the enemy. He went for help when the Ninth got pinned down before the walls of Tientsin."

"What?" I sputtered. "Are you telling me that insufferable prig Longbottom got promoted for that fiasco? Well, I'll be damned. Why, I was with him, and all I got was a thank-you for a job well done and a pat on the back. I'm the one who eventually led the Ninth out of the trap. Longbottom just wandered around lost all night!"

Hobart was taken aback at this outburst. "You were there too, Fenny? And you went for help also? Why, I had no idea. . . ." Hobart trailed off here, a note of awe in his voice.

"Of course I was there, Charlie. It was a day I won't soon forget," I spat, in a foul humor now. But then I thought, what the hell, why not let bygones be bygones? If the army wanted to make Longbottom a captain, well, that was its business, as long as he stayed out of my hair. So I calmed down with an effort and growled with grave finality, "Never mind, Charlie. Memories of China tend to get me all worked up, you see."

For a second Hobart could say nothing, the impact of sitting so close to what he thought was a true hero stealing his tongue. When at last he was able to master his emotions and speak once again, he fairly blubbered with choked admiration. "Oh, Fenny, you are quite the paladin, more than anyone realizes. I only wish"—here he stopped and dabbed at a patch of moistness in the corner of his eye—"I only wish that Colonel Liscum could have lived to learn the full extent of your deeds. God rest his soul!"

"God rest his soul," I seconded perfunctorily, quickly taking another drink from my glass. Liscum, the irascible former colonel of the Ninth, had expired in China when I deserted him under fire. I had no doubt that had Liscum survived the campaign against the Boxers, he would have had me summarily drawn and quartered. In fact, I was sure he was spinning in his grave right now at the unadulterated drivel Charlie was mouthing.

Hobart sniffed, took a deep breath, and said earnestly, "What a lion you've become, Fenny!"

I gave a stalwart smile at this. "Go on, Charlie, I did no more than any of the others who went to Peking, and I daresay a great deal less than most." Truer words were never spoken, of course.

"Don't josh me, Fenny," countered Hobart, not to be put off by my apparent soldierly reserve. "You weren't mentioned in all those dispatches for nothing. You're a hero, Fenny, even if you won't admit it to yourself!"

The Filipino bartender appeared once more. Hobart laid out some silver and called for another round.

"Let me get that, Charlie," I insisted, my relief at being ashore after a long ocean voyage making me uncharacteristically generous. I fumbled at my tunic pocket when what should peek out between my buttons but the edge of the parchment I had purloined. I hastily tucked it out of sight.

"What's that, Fenny? A love letter from a mandarin belle?" asked Hobart drolly.

Hobart was so damned gullible that I couldn't resist toying with him a bit. I smiled slyly and leaned close to his ear. In a stage whisper I announced dramatically, "No, it's a secret map, Charlie, like the one that pesky Moro made off with today. It could change the course of the war, you see, so keep it under your hat!"

"Go on," Hobart retorted in a tone that told me he half believed me, the dolt. "That's not true, is it?"

I merely gave him a sly wink. "Suit yourself then, Charlie. It's a love letter, okay?"

Tired of being trifled with, Hobart changed the subject and we soon got down to some serious imbibing. Despite Hobart's company I managed to have a rollicking good time until dawn.

4

Manila, Luzon
December 31, 1900

The following day in my quarters at the Army-Navy Club, I had time to examine the parchment. I opened it carefully and immediately saw that it was ancient, at least a hundred years old. When I spread it flat on my bed, I saw that Hobart had been right. It was a map, all right, depicting a group of islands, and it had various legends around the border written in Spanish. The parchment was faded and stained in places, but all in all it was a perfectly serviceable map. I was able to distinguish the outline of Luzon, the main island in the Philippine archipelago. Beneath that were the lesser islands of Samar, Negros, and the large island of Mindanao, the home range of the Moros. Ocean currents were clearly marked on the map, and various margin notes seemed to contain nautical information about tides and such.

A line ran across the map from right to left, or, using the cardinal directions printed on the map, from east to west. The line went more or less directly to the northeastern coast of Mindanao, and then stopped. At that point a Maltese cross and the words *Jesus Maria* were drawn on the map. I surmised I was looking at a ship's chart of some sort, but beyond that, the map was Greek to me. Frustrated, I put it away and prepared for MacArthur's ball.

Hobart arranged for the houseboys to clean and press my tropical white uniform and to polish my shoes to a glowing sheen. I dressed carefully, strapped on my ceremonial saber, and then gingerly folded the aged parchment, tucked it into the pocket of my tunic, and patted it reassuringly. Thus prepared for the evening's festivities, I stepped outside the club, where Hobart awaited me in a coach he'd hired.

We quickly left the Intramuros and crossed the Rio Pasig on one of the ornate bridges the Spanish dons had built before we'd booted them out. We skirted several dilapidated barrios on the far bank, where sad-looking children of mixed Malay and Chinese blood glanced at us as we passed. The road then opened a bit, and before long we were approaching Malacanan Palace.

We presented ourselves for admittance to the honor guard of the 25th Infantry drawn up under the palace's huge portico. The same ramrod-straight sergeant major was present. He insisted on inspecting our invitations even though he'd accompanied us on the pursuit of Surlang just the other day. Some people went completely by the book, I realized, and so I idly admired the beautifully landscaped gardens that descended all the way to the river's edge as the sergeant major carefully studied our invitations.

"Very good, sir," he snapped briskly when he was satisfied. "Please proceed."

Behind the sergeant major was Henry Jefferson, again serving as corporal of the guard. I smiled as we passed, but Henry merely stood at stiff attention. We passed through a portcullis and joined a stream of guests flowing through a polished marble corridor of breathtaking beauty, lined on either side by liveried footmen. Then we proceeded up a bank of steps into the grand ballroom.

The festivities had already started by the time Hobart and I arrived.

An orchestra of enlisted men was well into a stirring waltz, and the floor was alive with swirling couples, ladies in flowing gowns and officers in their tropical whites. The attendees were almost all military, I saw, with a smattering of diplomatic types easily identifiable in their tuxedos. Also present, of course, were the obligatory foreign military attachés, but none I recognized.

"Perfect timing, Fenny. The receiving line's just finishing up, so there'll be no waiting," said Hobart, nodding toward a serried rank of military dignitaries and one enormously fat civilian. This huge fellow sported a tuxedo so large it looked like one of those black tents favored by the Saharan Bedouins.

"Who's the civilian?" I asked.

"Judge Taft," answered Hobart, eyeing the rotund jurist who dabbed at his face constantly with a handkerchief in a vain effort to staunch the torrent of perspiration flowing down his jowls. "He's been sent over as a sort of adviser on government affairs to MacArthur. There's no love lost between those two, I can tell you."

Hobart led me to the end of the receiving line, where we waited to be ushered into the general's presence. At the very front of the line, as was customary on such occasions, was an aide. This minion was in charge of determining the names of the guests as they appeared before him. He then passed each name down the row of assembled notables and ultimately to MacArthur. When we arrived, the aide had his back to us. Then he turned and I found myself staring into the unforgettable mug of Lieutenant Colonel Quinlon!

"Quinlon, by God!" I exclaimed in shock, and then, feeling Hobart's alarmed gaze upon me, added numbly, "sir."

To my surprise, Quinlon did not immediately try to throttle me; instead he smiled as cheerily as you please and chirped, "And if it isn't the renowned Captain Travers himself." Then the old blowfish seized my hand and pumped it vigorously. "It's been a long time, bucko."

Was this some type of ambush? I wondered anxiously. I pulled my hand back quickly should I need to go for my sword. After all, the last time I had seen Quinlon was back in Old Havana when he had caught me in flagrante delicto with his daughter, Fiona. He had been so incensed that he had done his best to gun me down right then and there; it was only to his ineptitude as a marksman that I owed my survival. Surely he would never forgive me for what I had done, I thought. Yet to my complete amazement, I was wrong.

"Relax, lad," smiled Quinlon. "What's done is done. I'll not be holding a grudge against you. I'm sure but for me barging in on you and Fiona the way I did, you would've done the right thing by her, at least eventually."

All this was going right over Hobart's head, of course, but then he was used to being in the dark about a lot of things. Besides, I was too busy concentrating on the signal that Quinlon was sending to be concerned about Hobart's confusion. If I'd heard him right, Quinlon was offering me a graceful way out of an embarrassing situation. But why? I knew instinctively that a Tammany creature like Quinlon would have morals as flexible as a ballerina's limbs, but even he had to have some nonnegotiable taboos. I rather thought that seeing his daughter disrobed and seduced in broad daylight would be one of them. Apparently I was wrong on that score too.

"Er, sure, that's right," I stammered. "There was never any doubt about it, Colonel. It's just that things were so, er, rushed that day, if you recall."

Quinlon smiled again, his leprechaun-bright eyes belying the fact that if he'd been half as good a shot as the worst private in a normal infantry company, I'd be a dead man today. "And I've heard some fine, fine things about you, lad. Why, the stories that were a'coming back from China made me proud to know you. You're a credit to the regular army, lad."

I watched him carefully for some hint of sarcasm, but there was none. Incredibly enough, the wizened old boghopper had come completely around regarding me, and now I was fully back in his favor. He'd probably figured that my stock was rising and that I might be in a position to help him somehow, so he had belatedly decided that Fiona's bout of fellatio with me was no more than the healthy play of a love-struck couple.

Greatly relieved by this turn of events, I felt expansive. "I'm flattered, sir," I breathed thankfully. "You do me great honor." But now I was curious as to how a broken-down old politician like Quinlon, who had finagled a commission in his waning years, had come to be on this receiving line, and in a position usually held by a senior aide at that. My curiosity piqued, I put the question to him directly.

Quinlon cackled and slapped his thigh in response. "Why, don't you know, Travers? It's on the great general's staff I am! Yesirree, I'm one of his trusted confidants."

I couldn't believe it. Quinlon? On the staff of General MacArthur? If this was true, then it was no wonder that the *insurrectos* had survived for the past two years. With bumblers like him at the helm, this uprising would probably last for another fifty years. I didn't trust myself to respond to this bit of news, so I swallowed hard and forced myself to change the subject.

"You mentioned Fee. I trust she's well?"

"That she is, lad. That's the darling colleen whirling about out yonder." He nodded his head toward the dancing couples. I turned to see Fiona floating lightly across the floor—in the arms of Joshua Longbottom! Now there was a match made somewhere other than in heaven, I thought wickedly.

But then the receiving line lurched forward and Quinlon gestured for Hobart and me to move along, saying, "Gentlemen, the Boy Colonel"— this being MacArthur's nickname for having attained that rank as a mere youth of twenty years in the Civil War—"awaits."

Hobart steered me past all the lesser luminaries, who shook my hand and clapped my shoulder, and led me before MacArthur.

"General MacArthur, this is Captain Travers," announced Hobart, presenting me.

"Ah, Travers," rumbled MacArthur. "I've heard a great deal about you, all of it good."

"I'm honored, sir," I answered, giving a little bob of the head to show I was suitably impressed. MacArthur scrutinized me sternly, seeming to take my measure, and as he did I studied him closely in return. He was a tall, heavyset fellow whose girth looked painfully constricted by the gold sash about his massive waist. He wasn't as portly as Pecos Bill Shafter, the rotund general who led the invasion of Cuba back in '98. Since MacArthur was close to six feet tall and carried his weight rather well, I would have described him as substantial rather than obese. He had a commanding visage, with a shock of iron gray hair parted down the middle, and he wore pince-nez glasses. All in all, I decided, he looked like a larger, more intelligent version of Teddy Roosevelt. It was his stormy, sea green eyes, however, that drew one's attention. Those orbs were piercing, the searing gaze of a fighting leader who would brook no nonsense. And they were fixed right on me.

"General Chaffee has kept me apprised of your exploits in China, Captain. He says you're one of the finest field soldiers he's ever seen, and I happen to set great store by his opinions."

"That's awfully kind of him," I said, beaming.

"Kind? It's no such thing," snapped MacArthur. "Chaffee knows, like any good commander, to be on the watch for the young eagles coming up, Travers. He's thinking of the army, son, not you."

"Uh, of course, sir," I floundered in reply, feeling like a fool and looking for some way to end this interview. But MacArthur wasn't done with me just yet.

"I've received instructions from Washington about you, Travers," announced MacArthur, adding meaningfully, "from the White House, in particular."

"Oh?" was all I could muster in response to this.

"Yes," continued MacArthur. "I've been advised to employ you in a position suited to allow you free rein in our campaign against Aguinaldo. Rather extraordinary instructions, I must say, rather like those given regarding a general, not a captain."

It was clear that MacArthur was not pleased about having Washington dictate how he was to employ a captain under his command. I sensed the meddling hand of Roosevelt in all this. But MacArthur was astute enough to realize that none of this was my doing. "Be that as it may, you'll be assigned to my headquarters until you get your feet on the ground. After a few months in the islands, you may have some useful suggestions."

I detected a note of doubt in MacArthur's voice, but I was too elated at the prospect of tarrying in Manila rather than being rushed off into the hinterlands to take offense.

"Yes, sir," I answered.

Now Hobart unexpectedly piped up. "Sir, shouldn't Captain Travers be assigned to a combat unit? We can always use experienced officers in the fight against this bandit Aguinaldo and his *insurrectos*."

MacArthur gave Hobart a look usually reserved for a puppy that soils a carpet in the parlor. "Lieutenant Hoadley, isn't it?"

"Hobart, sir," Charlie corrected him. "I've been in your headquarters for a year."

"Yes, of course," growled MacArthur dismissively. "The fact is, Lieutenant Hobart, I rather agree with you in that regard. The current troubles are a golden opportunity for any young officer to get a command under his belt, maybe even an independent column. Why, my youngest son, Douglas, would give his eye teeth if only he could get out here to the islands before this shooting match is over."

All of this was dangerous talk to my thinking, so I was relieved anew when MacArthur added with finality, "But all that is neither here nor there. Captain Travers has been marked as headquarters material and there he shall stay, I'm afraid."

With that, MacArthur turned to his next guest and we were dismissed. Hobart led the way to the bar on the far side of the ballroom, where a steward served us each a glass of wine. I'd no sooner taken a sip than an alluring distaff voice caught my ear.

"Fenny, you cad, you've been hiding from me all evening."

Startled, I turned. It was Fiona! She was looking more ravishing than ever. "Hello, dearest Fee," I greeted her. Feeling a nudge at my elbow, I added, "This is Charlie Hobart, a classmate of mine from West Point."

"Ma'am," squeaked Hobart with an awkward bob of his head. I suspected that he'd never gotten so much as a sniff of a vixen as comely as Fiona before, and now he was quivering like a diviner's rod over an underground stream.

"You heartless boy," Fiona chided me. "You never wrote after Havana. Not one line."

"It wasn't because I didn't want to, Fee," I parried, the devil in my eye, "it's just that there wasn't time to get your address before I left."

Fiona laughed impishly at this, blushing as she did. From what I could see, it looked as though both she and her pater were willing to let bygones be bygones, and who was I to stand in the way of sweet reconciliation? "Would you like some wine, my dear?" I suggested.

"Not on your life," Fiona scolded me playfully. "You think you can get me tipsy and then take advantage of me. You, sir," she said, leaning forward a bit to give me an unobstructed view down her majestic cleavage, "are no gentleman."

I smiled broadly. And you, Fee, I thought, are no lady, and we both know it. But before I could resume the verbal swordplay, we were joined by yet another familiar figure. It was Captain Longbottom.

"Fenny," fluttered Fiona, taking Longbottom's arm, "I believe you know my fiancé, Joshua Longbottom."

"Your fiancé?" I gasped, taken aback. "I had no idea, Fee. How could this be . . . er . . . I mean, uh, congratulations to the both of you," I stammered lamely. My mind raced—where had they met? It had to be here in the islands, for Fiona hadn't known Longbottom in Cuba, and she had never been to China: That meant they'd gotten together only since Longbottom's return from China, some four or five months ago. A true whirlwind courtship, I thought, and totally unlike Longbottom, whom I'd never known to do anything impulsively.

"Why, thank you, Fenny," replied Longbottom with the air of solemnity he perpetually affected. I knew, however, that beneath his pompous facade he was so elated he could have burst with glee. "It means a lot for me to hear you say that. Fee told me that you and she were acquainted back in Tampa. But despite your friendship, I was certain that you'd be pleased to hear the news."

So that was it! Longbottom was using Fiona to spite me. He'd failed to rub my nose in the mud back in Tientsin, so when he stumbled upon Fiona here in Manila and learned from her that we had been close back in Tampa, he had quickly put together a scheme to get between us. As for Fee, she needed shelter from the storm, so to speak. Her father wouldn't be able to look after her for too many more years. Longbottom, on the other hand, was a young officer with a future. He had been promoted early and appeared to be a rising star in the army, so Fee knew she could do much worse. Well, well, I laughed silently, Longbottom has truly outdone himself this time.

"Pleased?" I said, smiling. "Why, my dear Longbottom, I'm positively delighted."

"I'm gratified to see you taking this so well, Fenny," he replied, looking as smug as a cat with its paws around a saucer of cream.

I merely smiled anew, but Charlie coughed nervously and Fiona stepped in to relieve what she perceived to be embarrassing tension. "I am so looking forward to being an army wife. I think it'll be ever so exciting."

Just let her spend a week at Plattsburgh Barracks washing clothes in an icy stream and she'll be singing a different tune, I thought, but instead I averred, "Fee, I'm sure you'll illuminate the lives of all the officers of any post to which you go."

Fiona looked at me quizzically, and then, catching my double meaning, giggled. I turned to Longbottom and extended my hand. "You're a lucky man, Joshua."

Longbottom puffed himself up afresh and took my proffered hand, savoring his supposed victory. I had to bite my lip to keep from laughing out loud, for this self-centered hypocrite thought he was on top of the world. Oh, he had an enviable service record, all right, and his early promotion to captain, like mine, marked him as one of the army's brightest young prospects. Now he thought he'd cut out the perfect wife from the herd. She was nominally a "brat," the child of a soldier, and thus a woman who could be expected to understand the ways of the service. Moreover, she was undeniably beautiful. Yet best of all, she had once belonged to me, and now Longbottom had stolen her away, or at least so he thought.

The joke, however, was on Longbottom. If he thought he had what it would take to hold down a wildcat like Fiona, he was sadly mistaken. "Joshua," I inquired politely, "would you allow me the great honor of your betrothed's hand for the next dance?"

"Why, of course, Travers," he replied condescendingly, satisfaction evident in his calculating eyes. He positively relished watching me so near to what he thought I could no longer have.

"Fiona," I said, addressing her with a courtly bow, "may I have the pleasure?"

Fiona smiled coquettishly and took my arm. We paraded to the center of the floor, and when the music commenced, I waltzed off with her.

5

"I can't believe it!" I exclaimed to Fiona as I whirled her across the floor. "Marrying Longbottom, of all people. Fee, you'll wear him out in the first week!"

Fiona said nothing, but merely smiled up at me sweetly, arching her neck and raising her bosom delightfully as she did. My gaze lingered on those soft globes; wouldn't it be lovely to see them swinging free again, I thought dreamily.

"Tell me, Fee," I asked as we capered about, "do you love Longbottom?"

"Not yet," she admitted straightforwardly, "but I imagine that will come in time."

This caused me to snort, and Fiona eyed me puckishly. "Oh, and I suppose you find that hard to believe?"

"To the contrary, my dear. I believe that you could love any man, given the proper incentives," I replied merrily.

She looked miffed at this, and for a second I thought I'd gone too far. But then she gave me that delightful smile of hers and laughed, "Oh, Fenny, you're such a devil!"

"I've never denied that, Fee. In fact, I wouldn't mind raising a little hell this evening, if you follow me." I gazed at her meaningfully.

For a moment a look of hesitation flashed across her face, only to be quickly replaced by one of passion. The music increased in tempo now as we swept across the floor, and I tightened my grip on her. "When?" she whispered.

"As soon as you can manage," I answered. "I'll be down by the river," I added, nodding my head to the far side of the ballroom, where a line of French doors led to the gardens and the darkness beyond. "I'll be waiting."

She said nothing, which alarmed me not a bit. I knew the Fiona of old, and I knew that there was nothing she'd like better than one more spirited roll in the hay before consigning herself to the staid marital bed of Joshua Longbottom. Then the music ended and everyone stood about applauding the musicians.

"That was delightful," I said with a bow.

"Not half as delightful as our next dance will be," she promised enticingly.

I offered Fiona my arm and escorted her back to where Longbottom was locked in earnest conversation with Hobart. "Gentlemen," I announced, "I'm afraid I'm a bit winded. Not only have you been able to land the prettiest girl in these islands, Joshua, but she's also the friskiest dancer. I congratulate you again, sir!"

Longbottom, of course, reveled in this drivel. "You're most gracious, Travers," he sniffed, taking Fiona's arm in his. "But if you gentlemen will excuse us, we really must make the rounds now." Hobart and I bowed to Fiona as they marched off to be seen by all the exalted personages Longbottom thought mattered in his scheme of things.

"So you know Lieutenant Colonel Quinlon?" asked Hobart when they had gone.

"Yes. We met in Tampa when I was with V Corps getting ready for the invasion of Cuba back in '98," I replied, then added, "He was a slippery old rogue and a damned poor soldier, too. He proved that while leading the 71st New York Volunteers at the Battle of San Juan Hill."

"You're right about that," agreed Hobart. "The tale of the 71st's cowardly conduct is common knowledge in the army. The whole skulking regiment was sent home in disgrace soon after the Spanish surrender. When Quinlon arrived here from Cuba, his career was all but over. He was a laughingstock, or at least he was until Longbottom showed up."

"How's that?" I asked, my interest kindled.

"Well, once Longbottom started to make a run at Quinlon's daughter, everyone took notice of the old geezer. After all, despite Longbottom's faults, he is one of the most promising young captains in the army, and he is on MacArthur's staff—no small honor that. So I think that Longbottom took matters in hand a bit. Quinlon had been in charge of the warehouses over in Cavite across Manila Bay, handing out mess kits to the troops departing for China. Suddenly he was summoned to Malacanan Palace and placed on MacArthur's staff. It was a stunning reversal of fortune, and the old gnome actually seems to be doing well in his new role. MacArthur's using Quinlon in political matters, mostly coordinating with the local hacks and keeping the damned *gugus* pacified. . . ."

"The who?" I interrupted, confused.

"The *gugus,*" repeated Hobart. "It's what the troops call the natives. As I was saying, Quinlon pacified the *gugus* with doles of rice and farm tools. Seems that the colonel's a natural at the job."

He damned well ought to be, I mused. Especially since the old ward heeler had spent most of his adult life perfecting the art of distributing spoils in New York City for the Tammany Hall machine. I had to shake my head in amazement, though, for in a bizarre fashion Quinlon actually owed his resurrection to me. If it hadn't been for Longbottom's desire to spite me, Quinlon would have rotted away in obscurity, and Fiona would never have had her chance to break into the ranks of the army's blue bloods. I smiled at the thought of this; it was as though Fiona owed me, and in a short while I intended to collect!

"Well, that makes things much clearer, Charlie, thank you," I said. Then, finishing my wine, I added, "I see some familiar faces from China across the room. I think I'll go visit with some old pals. Excuse me, won't you?"

"Okay, Fenny," said Hobart. "But don't be gone too long. There are others here you need to meet. I'll come and find you in a while."

"Sure, do that, Charlie," I said absently and sauntered away. Once I was certain I was out of Hobart's sight, I hurried through the French doors and out onto a wide veranda overlooking the Rio Pasig. Couples were gathered in the shadows, but no one noticed my passing. I descended a stone staircase onto the manicured lawn and made my way down gardened terraces until at last I stood by the river. I stepped into the shadow of a huge palm tree and waited. After some minutes I saw another form flitting through the shadows. It was Fiona.

"Over here, Fee!" I whispered.

She came to me and flew into my arms. "Fenny, my love!" she cried throatily.

Emotional little puss, I thought as I planted a wet kiss on her ruby lips. Fiona responded eagerly.

"Where?" she breathed, looking about in the moonlight.

"How about right here?" I suggested brightly.

"No, Fenny," she protested. "Not on the grass. I'll have to go back inside and I can't have grass stains all over my gown."

"Of course, dear, of course," I agreed hastily, searching about for a suitable spot to do the deed. A few feet away was a low stone wall, and behind it was the blackness of the Luzon jungle.

"Over here, Fee," I whispered, taking her hand and leading her to the wall.

"What have you got in mind?" she asked, looking dubiously at the wall.

"You'll see," I promised, lifting her by the waist and setting her facedown across the wall. Since the wall was quite thick, Fiona could lie comfortably athwart its width, with her feet dangling several inches above the ground.

She finally got the idea. "Oh, Fenny, you wicked boy!" she giggled.

"Bear with me now, Fee," I cautioned. So saying, I raised her gown over her shoulders, wrestled her hoops aside, and drew down her pantalets; her firm white buttocks glowed dreamily in the brilliant moonlight. I carefully hauled my saber to the side, freed my throbbing manhood, and slowly eased it into the honeypot between Fiona's parted thighs.

"Ahhh!" she sighed heavily as I slid home. "I've missed you so, Fenny!"

"And I you, dearest," I seconded, as I set to work and began to rock her gently, my hands greedily massaging her supple rump.

"Oh, harder, harder, Fenny!" she urged.

"Certainly, my dear," I puffed happily, beginning to be driven now by my mounting pleasure.

"Oh, oh, oh!" Fiona began to caterwaul as I hit my stride and really began to ride her.

"Shhhh!" I hissed. The last thing we needed was for her wailing to attract the notice of some strolling partygoers. She quieted down immediately, and I closed my eyes to enjoy the gallop.

Then to my disbelieving ears came a voice. "Senor, I have come for the secret map."

My eyes flew open! Who the hell . . . ? With a gulp, I realized that I was staring down the barrel of a leveled Mauser. My saber would do me no good now!

"What?" I gasped, shot through with fear and pleasure at the same time, for Fiona, oblivious to the fact that we had company, continued to buck along mightily beneath me.

"The map, Senor!" the apparition repeated. "I want it!" In the moonlight I saw that I was confronted by a thin fellow of above-average height for a native who was peering at me from beneath a green turban. Large gold earrings dangled from his ears, giving his determined face a devilish cast. It was his eyes, however, that held my attention. They were dark and empty of both fear and pity. By God, it was the dreaded Surlang, right here at Malacanan Palace!

And what was more, he was not alone. In the shadows nearby lurked other Filipinos, dressed in the Luzon fashion. These must be Tagalog guerrillas, I realized. One stood at Surlang's elbow. He was a slim little fellow, shorter than Surlang and sporting a weather-beaten pith helmet. This hombre had no weapon that I could see, and from his demeanor I could sense that he was altogether a milder sort than the fierce Moro. In fact, he looked more like a college professor than a battle-hardened guerrilla.

As if to nudge me out of my shock, Surlang hissed again, "Give me the map!"

"You must be mistaken," I stammered. "I have nothing of the sort!" Then it hit me—the Filipino bartender in the Army-Navy Club! That fellow must have been an *insurrecto* informer. Of course! And I had foolishly taunted Hobart about having a secret map right in front of the bastard. Oh, God, how stupid of me! Beneath me Fiona suddenly became still; her sense of hearing had evidently returned to her.

Surlang said nothing. Instead he reached across the wall, unbuttoned the top pocket of my tunic, and drew out the carefully folded parchment!

"Now wait a minute, friend," I protested. "That's mine and you can't just take it! Why, it's . . . it's not fair!" I sputtered in outrage, pawing at him in a futile effort to retrieve the precious document.

The Filipinos backed away to avoid my awkward swipes, and Fiona took advantage of my movement to roll aside and spring up from her compromising position beneath me. "Oh, my God, Fenny!" she gasped. "Who are they? What do they want?" she demanded, heedless of the fact that her gown was still north of her hips and her pantalets dangled ludicrously about her ankles.

Surlang gave a violent nod in the direction of his mild-mannered companion. "Look on the face of Aguinaldo, yanquis," he sneered viciously. Then the bolt of the Mauser slid home. "And die!" he added coldly, snapping the Mauser up to his shoulder and drawing a bead right between my eyes!

Those eyes nearly popped from my head. Why, I was not five feet away from the legendary Aguinaldo, right here in the heart of MacArthur's seat of power. The honor of the occasion dimmed somewhat, however, as Surlang's finger tightened on the trigger.

But before I could beg for my life, Aguinaldo spoke. "No, amigo," he said to Surlang. "There is no need to kill them, especially the lady."

Just then Hobart called through the night. "Fenny, where the hell are you?" He blundered onto the scene before any of us could react. "What's going on here?" he demanded.

He was never to know; the Mauser exploded with a single shot, its muzzle flash splitting the night. Hobart pitched over dead on the meticulously cut grass.

I dove for cover behind the wall, leaving Fiona standing alone and screaming at the top of her lungs.

"Call out the guard!" sounded from the veranda. "Bring torches!" called another voice.

Surlang hesitated, glared after me furiously, and then fled with Aguinaldo and the others following on his heels.

In an instant, the lawn was covered with armed men searching for intruders. Once I was certain that Aguinaldo was safely off, I shakily took up the hue and cry while Fiona hauled up her drawers, smoothed down her gown, and promptly broke into hysterics.

"Oh, Fenny, this is awful!" she bawled, great tears coursing down her cheeks. She held out her arms to be comforted, and I hugged her obligingly, patting her back absently. But my mind was racing. There'd be time for gnashing teeth later; what was needed now was action. That bastard Surlang had my property, and I wanted it back. His presence here had confirmed my suspicions that the map held secrets of great value.

Soon a crowd gathered about us, and an officer threw a cape over poor Hobart. Longbottom appeared and took Fiona in his arms. Then MacArthur himself was there. "What the hell happened here?" he demanded of me, still puffing from his run down the steps.

I told him the tale that I'd hastily concocted. Hobart had gone out alone. I'd asked Fiona to help me find him, since I didn't know my way around the palace gardens. We'd stumbled upon Hobart just as he fell in a rebel ambush. Fiona nodded vigorously at every word, looking amazed at the rapidity with which I reconfigured reality.

MacArthur heard me out, and then rumbled, "That damned Aguinaldo!" He glanced down at the still form of Hobart. "Hoadley was a good boy, no Robert E. Lee, mind you—"

"Er, that's Hobart, sir," I interrupted him.

"That's what I meant," continued MacArthur, unfazed. "No genius, but a fine boy all the same. If I've said it once, I've said it a thousand times—Aguinaldo must be taken!"

"Sir," I declared with all the solemn dignity I could muster, "I volunteer to capture Aguinaldo."

MacArthur studied me a moment. "Nonsense, Travers. You've just gotten to these islands, son. There are more experienced hands available to take care of this business. And besides, Washington's made it quite plain that you're to be put to work in a high staff position."

You damned old fool! I raged inwardly. I was going to get that stinking bandit Surlang—and with him both Aguinaldo and the map—with or without MacArthur's permission. "Sir, I insist!" I pressed in a tone not normally used by a captain to a two-star general. "That's my friend lying there," I said hotly, pointing to Hobart's stiffening corpse, "and, by God, no little brown monkey's going to do that and get away with it!"

This did the trick. MacArthur gave me a look of paternal understanding and nodded. "I see, son. If that's the way you want it, then you have my blessings, and Washington be damned. I'll have orders prepared assigning you to the 20th Kansas Volunteers. The commander of that regiment is Brigadier General Frederick Funston, who also commands the Fourth District of northern Luzon. He's been given the mission of bringing in Aguinaldo—dead or alive."

"There's something else, sir," I added.

"Then out with it, Travers," prompted MacArthur.

"I need a striker, sir," I said, a striker being an enlisted orderly assigned to an officer. "I request that Corporal Henry Jefferson be assigned to me. He's with the contingent from the 25th Infantry that's assigned to guard the palace." I knew that I would need a guide through this hellish land, and Henry's two wound stripes told me he probably knew his way around the Filipino backcountry.

MacArthur assented readily. "Then you shall have him."

"Thank you, sir!" I said, snapping MacArthur my crispest salute to seal the deal. MacArthur returned the salute and then lumbered off into the night, and I turned to watch some troopers carry Hobart's lifeless body back to the palace.

6

San Isidro, Central Luzon
January 1901
Henry and I found General Funston's headquarters in the remote barrio of San Isidro, one of the sleepy hamlets that dotted the heavily populated plains of Nueva Ecija Province in central Luzon. When we arrived, Funston was sitting on a camp chair in the shade of an open-sided nipa hut, poring over reports at a desk made of discarded ammunition crates. In the distance somnolent peasants prodded listless carabaos, the water buffaloes of these islands, through placid paddies crowded with emerald-hued rice shoots. Above the carabaos droned thick clouds of black flies, the insects compelling the beasts to flick their ears and slap their tails in endless torment.

To the north of San Isidro, beyond the edge of the rice paddies, the trackless cogon grass extended for hundreds of miles before merging into the impenetrable forests of the northern highlands—the Cordillera Central in the middle of Luzon and the Sierra Madres along the northeastern coast. On the horizon, barely visible in the haze of the midday heat, were other hamlets, so-called amigo villages, which were nominally pacified by day, but which at night offered aid and comfort to the elusive guerrilla resistance. As I viewed this dispiriting landscape, it was easy to see how Aguinaldo had managed to elude capture for so long.

"Captain Travers reporting, sir!" I said with a practiced salute, one that proclaimed I was no greenhorn, by God, but which at the same time communicated that I was sage enough to approach a general, like any stray mongrel, warily until its disposition was known.

"It's about time!" Funston spat acidly, not bestirring himself to return my salute. Perplexed by this reaction, I dropped my hand slowly as Funston eyed Henry suspiciously. Funston, a brigadier of white Kansas volunteers, appeared to have little regard for black regulars. Evidently unimpressed by what he saw, Funston gave a little snort in our general direction and returned his gaze to the papers he was perusing. Uncertain about what to do in the face of this less-than-effusive greeting, I removed my hat and took a seat on a decrepit camp chair in the corner.

Sweat was cascading off my brow, for the heat of the Filipino sun at midday was brutal, but I sat silently while Funston pored over his papers. Finally, he set them aside and looked up. "MacArthur told me you were coming, Travers. He didn't say anything about your bringing along a darky, though." He bobbed his head in the direction of Henry, who, used to such pointed insults in his army career, remained standing at parade rest near the hut's entrance. "Nonetheless, glad to have you," Funston continued, his face devoid of the slightest indication that such was the case.

"Glad to be here, sir," I replied with equal candor.

Funston was young for a general; I pegged him as being about forty-five. Surprisingly, he was a runt of a fellow—barely five feet four. He had short reddish hair with a close trimmed beard and mustache. I'd taken the trouble to find out a bit about him while I was in Manila. It seems that Funston was a maverick who had first come to public notice as a fiery but uncouth soldier of fortune in Cuba, fighting for the Cuban *insurrectos* back in '95 against the brutal regime of Madrid's General Weyler. Funston rose to the rank of lieutenant colonel in the service of the *insurrectos,* but he was captured, brutally interrogated, and eventually returned to the United States, largely through the good offices of the U.S. counsel in Havana, Fitzhugh Lee, son of the late "Marse" Robert Lee.

Yet Funston was nothing if not a fighter, and a mean one at that, so it was understandable that when war was declared he had hurried to Tampa to put himself at the disposal of General Shafter. But Funston's peppery, unpredictable nature, coupled with the fact that he was a volunteer instead of a regular, had gotten Shafter's nose out of joint. The long and the short of all this was that Shafter refused to give Funston a role in the Cuban invasion, and Funston returned home in frustration to his native Kansas. There matters might have rested but for the fact that this bloody affair in the Philippines had begun to demand increasing drafts of manpower. Eventually Funston managed to wangle the command of the 20th Kansas Volunteers and had gotten called into the game.

In Luzon, Funston had quickly acquired a reputation for employing unorthodox means to defeat guerrilla bands. He reinforced his Kansans with parties of savages from the non-Tagalog groups scattered throughout northern Luzon. These mercenaries, dubbed the Filipino Scouts, were hardy beasts who hunted down their Tagalog enemies in exchange for food and Yankee gold. The Filipino Scouts, like their counterparts, the Apache Scouts, who were used to great effect by the United States to hunt down Geronimo, quickly became so successful that they were recognized as one of the most potent weapons in the war against Aguinaldo.

Whispered rumors in the Army-Navy Club also had it that another of Funston's pacification techniques was the water torture. A suspect would be thrown onto his back and pinned to the ground by troopers. Then water was allowed to trickle down his throat, and if he spat it out his nose would be pinched shut. Eventually, despite the wretch's best efforts, his stomach and intestines would swell with water until he became a misshapen figure of a human. If the unfortunate suspect chose to remain silent, the water would be forced out of both ends of him by a sturdy trooper stomping on his belly. It was an extremely effective interrogation technique, to be sure.

As for Funston himself, it was said that he was utterly fearless in combat, but it was also said that he enjoyed killing people, and as I watched him rise from his desk and approach me, his cold blue eyes told me that there might be some truth to the rumor. In his sweat-stained khakis with his Colt slung low on his hip, Funston looked more like a hired gun than a general in the U.S. Army.

"I hear you have some experience in irregular warfare," Funston said, almost accusingly. Not waiting for me to answer, he continued, "I hope that's so, Captain, because you'll need it out here. When I first came to these islands, I was like you are now—damned ignorant and hopelessly confused about where to get started. . . ."

I could see that he was launching into a prepared welcome to the islands speech reserved for newcomers, but I hadn't come here to listen to his yarns. No, I was here at the personal direction of General MacArthur, and I had a writ valid throughout the length and breadth of Luzon. What was more, I had stolen property to recover, and the sooner the better. So I interrupted Funston's soliloquy as delicately as I could by inquiring mildly, "General, this is all fascinating, but before you go on, could you perhaps tell me if you have any idea where this fellow Aguinaldo might be right now?"

Funston stopped in midsentence and gawked, not quite believing that he had heard me correctly. In his book, a mere captain never interrupted a general—for any reason. Infuriated by what he viewed as my insufferable gall, he took a few gasps of air, as though unable to find his tongue, then pointed savagely at a map propped upon an easel in the far corner of the hut. "Somewhere in there, damn your impudent hide!" he roared.

My eyes shot to where his finger was pointing at the Sierra Madre mountain range, which ran the length of the coast of northern Luzon. Why, that was thousands of square miles of territory, I realized in despair. Seeing that I was now out on a weak limb, and not being certain how to get back, I compounded my error by stammering, "Er, it would be most helpful, sir, if you could be a mite more specific."

Funston glared at me furiously, pure malice blazing forth from those blue eyes. "Of course it would be helpful if we knew exactly where Aguinaldo was, Travers!" he exploded. "But the gentleman hasn't exactly cooperated with us on such matters, you know!"

"I understand completely, sir," I quailed before this onslaught, desperate not to antagonize this volatile little bantam any further. Unfortunately, it was too late; Funston had taken all of my sass that he could stand.

"The hell you do, you little peckerwood!" he ranted, on his feet now. "You don't have the foggiest notion of how many times I've thought I had that stinking weasel Aguinaldo cornered, only to have him slip out of the net at the last moment. Each time he's gotten away, he's been able to raise another band of cutthroats to follow his orders. A bridge blown there, a sentry's throat slit here. But he never dares to stand and fight—no, that's not the bastard's style. Just raises enough of a stink to get in the papers and make us look like complete fools! Look out there at those damned *gugus* peacefully tending their crops, Travers," he demanded, pointing to the bucolic vista outside the nipa hut. "Do you think they give us the slightest bit of help in capturing Aguinaldo? No, by God! He's goddamned Robin Hood to 'em! That's why they call him *el presidente,* for Christ's sake!"

Funston's face was now as red as his hair. In his rage I feared he would do harm to either me or himself, so I sat perfectly still, not daring to utter another word lest I drive him to further tantrums. Henry followed my lead, his eyes fixed straight to the front so as not to catch Funston's glance. In the few minutes I had been in the general's presence, one thing had become abundantly clear: Funston's efforts to capture the elusive Aguinaldo had come near to unhinging his reason.

As though sensing my doubts about his sanity, Funston suddenly fell silent, took several deep breaths, and after a monumental effort, regained his composure. When his countenance had faded from a dangerous scarlet to a more amenable pink, he continued tautly, "Of course, we have been making some progress against the *ladrones*. They can't collect taxes from the peasants with any regularity. Also, Aguinaldo's strength has dropped off sharply in the past year, and there's been no report of his operating near Manila for months."

What? I thought. No report of Aguinaldo operating near Manila? Hadn't anybody told Funston about poor Hobart the other night, or the raid on the paymaster's office? Then I realized that the answer was no and I knew why: This was not the sort of fellow to whom one willingly told bad news. I for one was not going to let the cat out of the bag, especially in view of the fact that this lunatic was armed. Instead, I gently steered the conversation to future plans for dealing with Aguinaldo.

"Well then, sir, if you've got the *gugus* confined to the backcountry, what's your next step?"

"I intend to continue doing what I've done since I got here, Captain," he responded firmly. "I'll send small columns against the enemy wherever they appear. I'll slash 'em and slash 'em until they're killed or they give themselves up."

Despite my better judgment, I observed warily, "But sir, isn't that exactly the sort of strategy that Aguinaldo has been able to elude all these months? Isn't it time for a different approach?"

To my surprise, Funston didn't erupt. Perhaps he had vented all his fury in his last outburst, or maybe he no longer thought I was worth the energy it took to savage me. Whatever the reason, his only response was to snicker and demand sarcastically, "Like what, sonny?"

"I don't know at the moment," I admitted, never having been too handy with solutions to problems. I specialized in causing them, you see. "But I'm certain that something will occur to me."

Funston gave me an appraising look that said he didn't think so, then he went back to his makeshift desk, sat down, and started reading. This interview was obviously over. I waited for some sign to withdraw, but there was none. With an uncertain little waggle of my hand that passed as a farewell salute, I rose and crept from his presence. Henry followed silently on my heels.

Outside I stood gazing at the depressing hovels of San Isidro. With a sinking feeling I realized that this vermin-infested pigsty would be my home until I managed to bring Aguinaldo to ground. I had no idea how I would do it, but I meant to succeed even if I had to personally put out a snare on every damned trail on Luzon!

7

For weeks following my assignment to Funston's headquarters, nothing of importance transpired. I tagged along at Funston's heels wherever he went, trying to learn as much about Aguinaldo's tactics and whereabouts as possible. I quickly learned that Funston's days consisted of sifting through reports he constantly received from various intelligence operatives he'd planted all over Luzon. He sat for hours trying to assemble these scraps of information into some comprehensible picture of Aguinaldo's intentions, but too often these tidbits were so scrambled or out of date as to be completely useless.

I began to suspect that the blame for Funston's inability to bag Aguinaldo did not lie totally with the incomplete intelligence reports he received. A great deal of the problem lay with Funston himself. After months and months of analyzing these reports without success, Funston had become sloppy and missed little details. Therefore I began to sift through the intelligence reports once Funston had finished with them. It was no small task, I can assure you, for it seemed as though Funston had an agent in every barrio on Luzon. I cleared out a little space in the corner of a nearby hut for my purpose and set to. To my surprise, Henry sat down at my side and started reading intelligence reports too.

"Henry," I said at the sight of him scanning a communique, "just what the blazes are you doing?"

"Why, I'm reading, Fenny, just like you."

"Don't pull my leg, old friend. I know for a fact that there was no school for the colored at Elm Grove. You don't know how to read."

But rather than being abashed at my assertion, Henry merely beamed happily. "Oh, but I do know how to read, Fenny. Back in Fort Grant in Arizona there was a school for the Apaches, remember?"

I thought for a moment and then slowly nodded. "Yes, yes, I remember that. It was run by the officers' wives, as I recall. But what has that got to do with you?"

"I was one of the students." Henry smiled. When the expression on my face told him I had my doubts, he went on. "It's true. When I wasn't on duty I slipped in the back door and took a seat. Soon the white ladies gave me a primer of my own and let me join right in. I was in Fort Grant over five years, Fenny, and when I left, I could read and write just fine."

"Well, I'll be damned!" I exclaimed. I knew that Henry was a good man to have by my side in a fight, but until this moment I had never for an instant thought he had an ambitious bone in his body.

With that he went back to the document before him, and from the intense expression on his face, I had no doubt he was comprehending everything written on it.

And so we passed the days, elbow to elbow, going through the papers discarded by Funston. Things were looking less than promising, however, until one clear morning late in January when the flies weren't as bad as usual. Henry pulled a dog-eared sheet from the pile before him and turned to me. "Have you already read this, Fenny?"

I perused it quickly. "Yep. Nothing important."

Henry shook his head slowly. "I wouldn't be so quick on the draw, Fenny. Read it again."

He held the paper out to me and I scanned it. Then I read it again, only this time more slowly, for now the light was beginning to dawn. "Hot damn!" I gasped. "Of course! You're absolutely right, Henry. I should have seen the significance at once."

Excited now, we rose and hurried into Funston's hut, for although the general had a mean streak as wide as a buffalo's backside, and all the natural charm of a grizzly bear with an abscessed tooth, this news would brook no delay. Funston was in but seemed inclined to ignore us. Having no time for his games at the moment, I spoke right up. "Have you seen this, sir?"

Irritated, Funston took the paper from my hand and glanced at it. "Yes, of course. That was a letter from Aguinaldo we seized last week. We also captured the courier, a vile little *gugu* by the name of Cecilio Segismundo. The letter's addressed to one of Aguinaldo's chieftains, a blackguard named Lacuna who roams central Luzon. It asks Lacuna for reinforcements. There's nothing new there, Travers; Aguinaldo's always begging for reinforcements from his supporters.

Between disease and battle casualties, he's usually hard-pressed to keep a creditable force in the field."

Here to my utter amazement Henry spoke up. "That may all be true, suh," he insisted, "but if you carefully study on this message, it tells Lacuna where to send those reinforcements."

Funston was silent; he, like me, had missed that part of the message. Yet he still didn't see the beckoning opportunity, so I picked up from Henry now. "It says to send the reinforcements to a town called Palanan." I rose and went over to the map on the easel. After a few moments of searching about, I found the place. "Ah, here it is," I said, pointing to a spot about five miles inland from the eastern shore of northern Luzon, along the bank of the Palanan River.

"I know where Palanan is, Travers," snapped Funston, mortified at having let such an important fact slip past him. "It's also known to be one of Aguinaldo's most secure bases."

"But doesn't this letter suggest something to you?" I pressed.

"Not really," retorted Funston testily. "Like I say, I've seen dozens of similar messages since I've been here. Why, back in '99 I intercepted a message that Aguinaldo was holed up in Tarlac, over on the Lingayen Gulf, awaiting reinforcements. MacArthur stormed ashore within days and took hundreds of prisoners and mounds of booty, but Aguinaldo was long gone."

Once again Henry waded in, undaunted by the fact that he was addressing a general. "But wouldn't Aguinaldo act different, suh, if he was approached by reinforcements rather than the enemy?" he prodded.

"Of course he would, you fool!" seethed Funston. "Wouldn't you?" He stamped his feet in anger at both of us and muttered something about damned fool niggers and equally foolish West Pointers—he'd read my file, you see—and I could see that it was only a matter of moments before he tossed us both out on our ears.

This outburst put Henry off, so I again picked up the burden of persuasion. "Of course I would, sir," I assured Funston. "And that's exactly what I'm suggesting."

But Funston wasn't with us yet. "Just what the hell are you trying to say, Captain?" he demanded hotly.

"That we send reinforcements to Aguinaldo," I replied brightly. Henry nodded his head vigorously in agreement.

Funston's eyes bugged out of his head, and for a second I feared he'd draw his Colt and start blazing away. "What? Have you both lost your goddamn minds? You nincompoops!" he roared, advancing menacingly on us. "I've seen some strange cases since I've been in these islands, Travers, but you and your corporal have got 'em all beat by a country mile. Just how in tarnation can we bag Aguinaldo by sending him reinforcements?"

"Sir, hear me out," I pleaded with a passion rare in me except when I'm trying to steer some comely gal into my bedroll. "Corporal Jefferson and I have got a hunch that we can use this message to get our hands on Aguinaldo at long last."

Something in my voice convinced Funston to let me have my say, for he backed off a pace and looked at me uncertainly. "Okay, Travers, let's hear your pitch. But if it's as scatterbrained as I expect it'll be, I want the both of you packed and on the road for Manila by sunset."

"Very well, sir," I replied. "First, I need to know if there are some villagers hereabouts who are opposed to Aguinaldo and kindly disposed to us."

"Well, I don't know what that has to do with anything," growled Funston, "but there are tribes on Luzon who were loyal to the dons when they held sway here. I mostly use the Ilocanos when I need auxiliaries, but they're all out on patrols to the west of here. There's another band I call upon once in a while, though. They're the Macabebes, named after their village in Pampanga Province. Savage fellows, they are. The dons gave them special privileges in exchange for an agreement that they'd help keep the majority Tagalogs in their place. The rumor is that the Macabebes are really the descendants of Mexican Indians brought to these islands centuries ago to serve as mercenaries. Whatever the truth of the matter, the arrangement worked fine, since a Macabebe would as soon gouge out a Tagalog's eyes as look at him, they being hereditary enemies and all. I suppose the Macabebes would suit your purposes, Travers."

"Excellent," I said. "I propose that a force of the Macabebes be sent to Aguinaldo as so-called reinforcements. We'll send a message to him, forging this fellow Lacuna's signature to it, telling Aguinaldo that help is on the way. Then we'll march our Macabebes right into Aguinaldo's camp and seize the bastard." Henry nodded his head again in agreement.

"Simple as that, eh?" sneered Funston.

"That's right, sir," I countered confidently.

"Travers, you've a lot to learn about this war," sighed Funston, shaking his head at what he took to be my hopeless density. "It's more than two hundred miles from here to Palanan, straight across the heartland of the Tagalogs most of the way. Don't you think they might notice a company of Macabebes ranging through their country, and don't you think they might bring this state of affairs to the attention of Aguinaldo? He'll see right through your ruse, Travers, and melt into the jungle long before you get to Palanan. And even if you escape the Tagalogs, once you get into the mountains you'll have to cross the territory of the Ifugao, the Kalinga, and worst of all, the Igorot. They're all savage headhunters who would like nothing better than to throw you and your Macabebes into a stew pot."

Headhunters? By God, I'd had no idea that our expedition would cross the territory of headhunters. After several minutes of awkward silence, I was about to withdraw the whole plan when Henry spoke up.

"They won't be discovered if the Macabebes go by sea, suh," Henry observed calmly.

"Go by sea?" echoed Funston, not grasping Henry's scheme.

But in a twinkling I saw Henry's reasoning, and it was magnificent. "Yes, go by sea!" I agreed excitedly. I walked over to the map, inspected it carefully for a few moments, and then announced, "We'll slip off under cover of night and sail south across the Sibuyan Sea, through the San Bernardino Strait, and then up the east coast to Casiguran Sound. We'll land our party under cover of night, and strike north through the Sierra Madres to Palanan. From the map, there appear to be few villages in this hill country. The odds of detection should be low. Once we're near Palanan, we'll send Aguinaldo a message that his reinforcements are in the neighborhood. That'll ensure that he's on hand to greet us. Once we're actually in Palanan, of course, he'll see the trap, but then it'll be too late; he'll be in the bag. Right, Corporal Jefferson?"

"Couldn'a said it no better myself, suh," agreed Henry.

"But all of this is nonsense, Travers," scoffed Funston. "We can't just send a herd of natives into the jungle to capture Aguinaldo. They'll bolt as soon as they're out of our sight. By God, they'll need white officers to have any chance of success."

"Oh, they'll have white officers, all right," I assured Funston.

"Now see here, Travers!" fumed Funston. "You're making no damned sense at all! How can we send white officers along with a column that's supposed to be coming to reinforce Aguinaldo? That would give away your whole ruse."

"No, it won't," I explained patiently. "You, I, several other officers, and Corporal Jefferson, of course, will be in the column. Our cover will be that we're prisoners that the reinforcements captured and are now taking to Aguinaldo. To keep from alarming Aguinaldo as we near his camp, we'll even attempt to have a message sent ahead saying that the column will be bringing in American prisoners when it arrives."

Funston considered all this noncommittally, rubbing his bristly beard thoughtfully. Then he began nodding his head, slowly at first and then more vigorously. "It might work," he allowed. "A long shot, to be sure, but it might work."

Thinking of the lost map, I redoubled the pressure. "It may be a long shot, but by God, it's your only shot. You've chased this bastard all through these islands for years and caught nary a peek at him. Well, I'm offering you a plan that'll catch him flat-footed. Besides, look at it this way. If you nab him, you'll be up for another star, and maybe even the chance to secure a commission as a regular. On the other hand, if Aguinaldo slips away again, you're in no worse shape than you are right now."

This appeal struck home, especially the part about possible advancement. "It just may work at that," Funston again acknowledged, looking more ambitious than at any time since I'd arrived. Then he made his decision. "By Christ, Travers, we'll give it a go!" Rising to his feet, he declared with finality, "I'll see to raising a suitable herd of Macabebes." With that he shoved his hat on his head and left.

8

We immediately got busy. First, Henry found a trooper in the 20th Kansas who was literate in Spanish, the lingua franca of these islands. I then had the trooper sworn to secrecy on pain of never being returned to Kansas from Luzon and set him about drafting up a convincing reply to Aguinaldo's call for reinforcements. My missive stated that Aguinaldo's message had been understood and would be obeyed. Specifically, he could expect a column of reinforcements to arrive in Palanan within the month. Later that same day I gave the reply to Funston, who approved it and then arranged to have it carried to Aguinaldo through our network of operatives.

A short two weeks later Funston had assembled all the players needed for our upcoming charade. The gunboat *Vicksburg,* a three-masted steam frigate that normally patrolled Lingayen Gulf, was moved into Manila Bay to ferry our force to the far side of Luzon. That had taken a bit of staff work, but fortunately Major Kingsbury, a master of paperwork, had come through. He had rather liked Hobart for some reason, perhaps because officious drones have some sort of natural affinity for one another. Whatever the reason, Kingsbury was prepared to move heaven and earth to avenge Hobart's death, and he soon overcame all obstacles the navy placed in our way to secure the gunboat.

Meanwhile, a company of about a hundred Macabebe scouts was raised under the leadership of one of their tribal chieftains, a brute named Bustos. As noxious a fellow as you would care to encounter, Bustos was short and squat, with jagged scars from past confrontations all over the crown of his head, and a gaping socket where he'd lost an eye some years back in a head-hunting raid on a neighboring tribe. When he was feeling polite, he'd cover the socket with a red bandanna, but when he was out of sorts he uncovered his horror for all the world to see.

As for his men, they were howling savages right out of the Stone Age, who filed into Funston's camp clad in breechclouts and beads and carrying bolos. They stank to high heaven, and though I wouldn't have thought it possible, the density of flies in San Isidro actually increased once they arrived. With them came two American officers, brothers named Oliver and Russell Hazzard, who commanded these heathens when they were on campaign as American mercenaries. To round out the American presence, Funston included two lieutenants from the 20th Kansas—his nephew, Burton Mitchell, and Harry Newton.

In addition to the Macabebes, Funston also enlisted the services of a certain Senor Segovia, a Spaniard who had somehow been brought over to the American side in the war against Spain and who now served in Funston's intelligence network. Just how this change of heart had occurred was never made clear to me, but rumor had it that Funston had once put Segovia to the water torture and that Segovia was forever after in fear of that treatment. How true this was, I never knew, but for my money Segovia gave every appearance of being a rogue for hire by the highest bidder. He was young, in his midtwenties I'd say, with a sly face that reflected the calloused heart beating within his breast. I sized him up quickly: Segovia was a greasy backwoods renegade, an archetypal squaw man. I had seen his type before, flitting about the fringes of Arizona's frontier society when I had been posted to Fort Grant. I knew that Segovia would be loyal only as long as the gold held out, and then he'd be gone. I only hoped that Funston had not paid the varmint in advance.

Segovia's role was to act as guide and interpreter; he spoke flawless Tagalog, which would be handy if we encountered any *insurrectos* on our trek. He also spoke the barbaric Macabebe tongue, at least well enough to keep us informed of any rumblings in the ranks. Discontent among these heathens was a distinct possibility, since they were being marched into the heartland of their ancestral foes, and if they were taken they could expect to be tortured and killed. Under such circumstances, it would be wise to be alert to any last-minute cases of cold feet among them.

Funston had other reasons to suspect the reliability of his Macabebes. In his negotiations with Bustos, it rapidly became apparent that the brown bastards were completely money mad. Funston's initial offer was a flat four dollars per man for the duration of the raid, with a handsome bonus to Bustos upon our safe return no matter how the affair ended. But Bustos, a hard-bitten trader of pigs and goats, balked at what he perceived to be slave wages.

"No gu! No gu!" he grunted through his thick nose, which was decorated with an enormous gold ring through the septum. "Thi' mooch!" he demanded, rapidly opening and closing his hand four times to indicate twenty dollars per man. Through Segovia, Funston tried to haggle with Bustos, but the stubborn aborigine stuck to his guns. In the end Funston agreed to the twenty dollars per man, mainly because Bustos made the very valid point that a lower price would only be acceptable if the Macabebes were merely being required to rove their own territory and slaughter any stray Tagalogs they chanced upon. This, of course, was the time-honored method of warfare on Luzon. But what the Americans wanted was a planned offensive, an unheard-of maneuver for the Macabebes. For such a deviation from customary norms, a premium should be paid, argued Bustos. Eventually Funston agreed to the savage's demands, since the Macabebes were his sole option. But he slipped in a proviso: Bustos would collect his personal bonus only if the expedition succeeded. It was classic American free enterprise at work; give the monkeys a stake in the outcome and they were certain to bust their guts trying to get Aguinaldo into the poke for us!

Further to his credit, Funston himself provided a couple of novel twists. First, through the tender offices of the Macabebes, he arranged for Segismundo, Aguinaldo's captured courier, to be politically "reoriented" so that he agreed to accompany the "reinforcements" back to Palanan and allay any fears that Aguinaldo might have upon the column's approach.

Then to further assuage *el presidente*'s fears, Funston dragooned into the expedition another recently captured rebel who'd taken an oath of loyalty to the Americans. This was a fat pig of a fellow named Hilario Talplacido. Hilario was known personally to Aguinaldo, and to the best of *el presidente*'s knowledge, Hilario was still in arms against the Americans. Funston calculated that having Hilario and Segismundo in the van, both of them trusted confederates of Aguinaldo, should still *el presidente*'s natural suspicions. Furthermore, Hilario had traveled to Palanan many years previously and would be invaluable as a guide to assist Segovia. And there was one final reason for bringing Hilario along. Other than Segismundo and me, he was the only person who knew what Aguinaldo looked like.

On the appointed night, Funston gathered his forces on a little-used quay near Manila's docks. Just visible through the gloom over Manila Bay was the *Vicksburg,* a dark hulk with all her lights dimmed to avoid detection by prying eyes. The Macabebes had been decked out in the traditional peasant garb of the Luzon plains: white cotton trousers with loose shirts of matching material and wide-brimmed straw hats. Each carried a razor-sharp bolo strapped to his side. They also carried a mixture of Krags, Mausers, and battered Remingtons so that they would look the part of a patriotic band of poorly equipped rustics rallying to the banner of their folk hero.

Despite the careful planning, there were last-minute hitches. As the *Vicksburg*'s whaleboats glided up the Rio Pasig and lay alongside the quay, Henry and I walked through the Macabebes to supervise the embarkation, only to happen upon Bustos trying to lead a gigantic sow into one of the whaleboats. His way was blocked by a huge American tar, whose rolled-up sleeves revealed a massive pair of forearms completely covered with lurid tattoos.

"Now just where th' hell do ya think you're going with th' pig, Chief?" demanded the sailor, addressing the proud aborigine as though he were a pacified reservation Indian.

"Go big *banca!*" grunted Bustos in reply, pointing to the distant *Vicksburg.*

"Oh, no," sneered the American. "You're out o' yer mind if you think you're hauling that filthy beast aboard a man o' war. Why, you're damned lucky th' captain's agreed to let you on board, ya filthy nigger!"

Bustos was not certain what the tar had said, but he apparently discerned from the tone that the message was not a pleasant one. Even in the faint light I could see Bustos's hand edging toward his sheathed bolo.

The tar saw it as well, for with a blur of motion he whipped out a double-barreled derringer and leveled it in Bustos's scowling face. "If you so much as fart, Chief, you'll wake up in th' happy hunting grounds, and I'll send yer damned swine along right behind ya!"

"Hold on, there!" I cried, moving between the two antagonists. "We've got our hands full catching Aguinaldo without fighting amongst ourselves as well."

Just then Funston and the Spaniard, Segovia, joined us. "What the hell's the problem here, Travers?" Funston demanded irritably.

"It's Bustos," I explained. "It seems he wants to bring that damned sow to war with him."

"Tell him the pig stays," Funston snapped at Segovia.

Segovia spoke rapidly to Bustos in the Macabebe tongue. Bustos gibbered back heatedly, then stood with his arms folded, glowering at the tar, who never lowered the derringer.

Segovia shrugged and turned to Funston. "It's no good, General. He thinks he must bring food with him to the land of his enemies. Otherwise, he believes he will starve."

"Goddamn!" swore Funston. "I can't believe this! I'll go to hell before I let this baboon turn the most important operation of this whole goddamned war into a swine drive!"

Despite Funston's fulminations, it was clear that Bustos would not be swayed. We had a full-blown Mexican standoff, and we hadn't even weighed anchor yet. I struggled to think of some way out of this impasse but came up dry. I looked imploringly at Henry for some assistance.

Fortunately, Henry had an idea. "Maybe if food's the problem, the chief here might like some of the grub we're packing along with us," suggested Henry mildly.

His smile let me know exactly what he meant. Yes, of course—that was the solution! Turning to Funston I asked excitedly, "General, what kind of rations are you bringing along?"

"Why, the usual," he replied. "Hardtack and canned beef. Why?"

I ignored his question. "Segovia," I ordered, "run down the way and fetch me a can of that beef."

The Spaniard did as he was told, and when he returned I held the can up to the moonlight and read the label. "Aha!" I exclaimed. "It's just as I thought! This stuff was canned back in '96."

Henry nodded his head. "It's the same tripe that the army fed the troops in Cuba back in '98, suh. That's what made me think of it."

"Travers, what's the goddamned point here?" demanded Funston, his patience with me and Henry at an end.

"Watch," I said confidently. I borrowed Segovia's skinning knife and hacked off the top of the tin. Then I skewered a slab of the noxious meat on the blade and passed it under Bustos's ringed nose. The savage sniffed tentatively, paused, then with the speed of a hungry leopard snatched the knife from my hand and gulped the meat down in a single swallow. After a few seconds, he belched loudly, then grabbed the tin from me and gobbled the rest of the contents as we stood watching him.

"Good God!" whispered Funston. "He actually likes that filth!"

"Yep!" smiled Henry. "It's that good old 'embalmed beef' from Tampa, the stuff that Congress investigated after the war. The boys always said it tasted like long pork"—human meat—"so I figured a cannibal like Bustos would naturally take right to it."

The standoff was over; Bustos set the pig loose and with a great squeal it fled into the night. Then he turned to his waiting tribesmen and began caterwauling at the top of his lungs. With an immense roar they took to the waiting whaleboats. The crews shoved off into the turgid river and we were away. As the stars twinkled above them, and American seamen strained at the oars, the Macabebes sat happily on the cases of embalmed beef and chanted war songs all the way to the *Vicksburg*.

9

The voyage itself went smoothly, and after seven days we heaved to just over the horizon from Casiguran Sound on the eastern coast of Luzon. After nightfall, the *Vicksburg* steamed quietly shoreward until she was close enough to launch her boats. The sea was running a mite high for a landing, but those same waves ensured that there would be no Tagalog fishing boats abroad this night.

The Macabebes, who had never been beyond sight of land before, cowered on the bow, terrified. They were joined by Henry, who was deathly afraid of the open swells since he couldn't swim a stroke. "Damned jackals," spat Funston. "Whipped by a high wind! Let's hope to God that we don't have to fight our way into Palanan with this bunch."

Amen, I seconded silently. With a great deal of cajoling and main force furnished by the tars, who were only too happy to heave the savage Macabebes and Henry off their vessel, we got our expedition to the beach. There we quickly scrambled for the edge of the jungle. From our landing point, Palanan was about thirty miles northward along the coast and then inland a few miles. We dared not go any closer with the *Vicksburg* lest the smoke from her stacks frighten Aguinaldo and cause him to flee before the trap could be sprung. We quickly arranged ourselves into an order of march consistent with our cover story: Hilario, Segismundo, and Segovia at the head of the column as the commanders, then the Macabebes as the reinforcements, and then finally we white officers and Henry, attired in ragged enlisted men's uniforms to better play our role as prisoners.

When all was ready, we set off and marched brazenly into the nearby barrio of Casiguran, where our cover worked like a charm. The headman came out to greet Hilario and Segovia, and then we were all wished godspeed by the assembled villagers and waved along the rugged track to Palanan. We walked until nightfall but barely covered three miles, so uneven was the path. The coastline was formidable: One seemed to be either walking straight up or straight down, and the way was continually barred by huge boulders and gaping chasms.

As the sun set, Funston called the exhausted column to a halt. The tired men fell out along the way, and Funston staggered up to where I lay and sat down. "I had no idea the trail would be so punishing," he gasped when he was able to talk. "This is going to be much more taxing than I ever reckoned." I caught something more than fatigue in his voice; I also detected fear. The appalling topography had clearly unnerved Funston.

I was so winded that all I could do was nod. When I managed to catch my breath, I wheezed, "How much food do we have?"

"Enough for two days," answered Funston. "Looking at the map, I thought we'd be in Palanan tomorrow. But in this country, we're spending most of our time walking up and down rather than straight ahead."

I nodded my agreement. "If we can't make any better time than we did today, there's no way we can get to Palanan in less than four days."

"Yep," Funston agreed uneasily. "It's clear already that things will be tight in the vittles department. Spread the word to have the men conserve food as much as possible." From the nervous way he eyed me, I could see that he was having second thoughts about this wild goose chase. To be truthful, I was having my doubts too. Sitting in this jungle surrounded by gibbering savages would make any sane man wonder if the end was worth the effort. But then I thought of what a genuine treasure map could mean to me: Wine and women would be mine in endless abundance. The alternative—a life of useful toil—was so repugnant to me that I dismissed the thought out of hand, and once more steeled myself for the campaign.

"Cheer up, sir," I urged. "If we ration the food, we've enough to last us to Palanan. Once we're there, we can empty the enemy's larders while we wait to rendezvous with the *Vicksburg* for the return trip. If we run short, we can always live off the land for a day or two, eh? Never say die, right?"

Funston glowered disdainfully. "Travers," he fumed, his anger rising in the face of my feckless optimism, "if we run out of grub, those Macabebes will disappear faster than loose change in a Cuban saloon and we'll be stranded. We'll be high and dry, understand?"

I gulped and nodded.

"Good," seethed Funston, "because if that happens, we'll all be dead men. No ifs, ands, or buts about it. And all because I let myself be buffaloed into this scheme by a wild-eyed captain and an overeducated nigger, neither of whom possesses the brains he was born with!"

"Now, sir, don't get all down in the mouth. . . ." I began to soothe. The last thing I needed was Funston becoming a croaker on me and turning us back toward Casiguran.

"Don't patronize me, you pipsqueak!" roared Funston. "I'm starting to hate the smell of this whole thing, and I'm starting to hate the sight of you! We're going forward, but only because we really have no choice now. But if this raid gets mucked up, Travers, I'm going to hold you personally responsible."

Then he stomped off for a fitful sleep. I gave him enough time to drop off, and then decided it was time to go see Segovia about that map. Was it really worth risking the chance of getting killed? I needed the answer to that question pronto, so after blundering about the sleeping column for some minutes, I at last found Segovia wrapped in a dirty blanket on the side of the trail.

"Segovia," I whispered, giving him a shake.

The Spaniard woke with a start. "Is it time to go, Senor?"

"No, no, I just wanted to ask you something."

Wary of Americans, Segovia narrowed his eyes. "And what might that be, Senor?"

"What do you know about old Spanish treasure maps?"

Segovia shook his head, as though he were having trouble hearing me. "Treasure maps, Senor? What does that have to do with chasing Aguinaldo?" He observed me carefully, half wondering whether my reason hadn't already been unseated by the rigors of the trail.

"I know it's an odd question, but just humor me, will you? Would there be old Spanish treasure maps lying around these islands for any reason?"

Segovia slowly nodded. "*Si*. There is always talk of treasure maps in these parts, Senor. Centuries ago, when the Spanish Empire was in its glory, Manila was the center of the galleon trade."

"What was the galleon trade?" I probed, my curiosity thoroughly aroused.

"It was the richest trade in the world at the time, and it was all based in Manila. From China would come silk and porcelains, and from the southern islands spices. From Japan would come pearls and fine swords. In exchange for this, the Spanish would ship silver from their mines in the New World. The silver would be exchanged at Manila for the goods of the East, and then the galleons would sail back to Acapulco on the coast of Mexico. In this way the treasures of the East would find their way to the courts of Europe while the silver of the New World would find its way to the mints of the Orient."

I knew instantly that Segovia spoke the truth, for I had seen with my own eyes the mints of China. The horde of silver in Peking had been beyond belief. "Then there would be treasure maps charting the routes of these galleons?" I pressed.

"Perhaps," replied Segovia suspiciously. "The truly valuable maps were those that located the spot where a treasure ship sank or went aground. The waters around these islands are often swept by typhoons, and many of the galleons were lost. For those that went down in the open seas, of course, there is no hope of recovery. But some went aground on reefs. Wrecks found near to shore have been salvaged from time to time. It is difficult work, but the native pearl divers are quite capable of recovering cargo that is many fathoms deep."

"Have you ever heard of a galleon called the *Jesus Maria?*" I asked quietly.

Segovia let out a low whistle. "All children from these islands have heard of that ship, Senor. The *Jesus Maria* was supposed to be the richest galleon that ever sailed from Acapulco. She sank in a typhoon near the coast of Mindanao, but no trace of her was ever found. It is said that in her hold was a king's ransom in silver."

In an instant I realized why Surlang had coveted the map. The Maltese cross I had seen pinpointed the wreck of the *Jesus Maria*; it was right off the coast of Mindanao! Surlang must have joined up with Aguinaldo for the necessary muscle first to steal the map from the paymaster's office in the Intramuros and then to recover the ship's cargo. Each party to the recovery would have his own motives. For Aguinaldo, there would be cash to buy weapons for his beleaguered independence movement. After all, hadn't Funston said that Aguinaldo was having difficulty raising taxes? As for Surlang, the sunken *Jesus Maria* would represent filthy lucre, the goal of all true pirates. With a fortune in silver, moreover, he might even be welcomed once more in Jolo by his master, the sultan.

"Well, that was most interesting, partner," I said, rising. "I think we ought to get some shut-eye now."

"*Si,* Senor," agreed Segovia, who stared at me with searching eyes as I withdrew into the shadows.

I woke before dawn, my face a bloody mask from the savage assault of mosquitoes that had penetrated my netting in the night. The first sound to come to my ears was Funston cursing a blue streak. "I'll hang the bastard who did this! I'll lynch the son of a bitch personally!"

Instantly I was on my feet and racing to where a cowed Segovia and Hilario were vainly trying to deflect Funston's anger. Henry quietly appeared at my side after I arrived. "What's wrong? Have we been betrayed?" I demanded, raw fear clutching at my guts.

"Worse!" fumed Funston. "Those damned Macabebes gobbled half the food while we slept! A good part of the tinned beef and all of the rice! We'll be on quarter rations for the rest of the trip!"

Henry and I exchanged worried glances. "Oh, my God," I blurted, "we'll starve!"

"Travers, shut up!" ordered Funston. "I don't need you to tell me we're in a hell of a fix."

Obediently, I fell silent, stunned at the enormity of this blow. Several feet away stood Bustos, silently scratching his distended belly. Suddenly he belched loudly and then scurried off as Funston glowered at him, blue eyes filled with fury.

"Segovia, get the column moving," ordered Funston. "Tell the scouts to keep an eye out for any provisions along the way as we march."

And with that we moved out. With food scarce the exertion of the trek became unbearable, and before noon I was exhausted from hacking at the *bejuco* vines that seemed to reach out and grasp my legs at every step. The freshwater from the *Vicksburg* in our canteens was soon exhausted, and in the tropical heat we were forced to slake our thirst in the small rivulets that crossed our path.

If anything, the trail we followed seemed even more precipitous than the day before, and our pace slowed to a crawl. Just as the sun reached its zenith and the heat soared to almost a hundred degrees, the column halted. From the van I heard Funston's voice in excited discussion with someone. Realizing that something was afoot, I hurried forward.

"You flea-bitten varmint!" an angry Funston was bellowing at Hilario, who cowered behind Segovia for protection. "What the hell do you mean telling me the trail is gone?"

Again both Segovia and Hilario quailed before Funston's wrath. "But, General," beseeched Segovia, "it's true; look for yourself!"

I took it all in at a glance. Segovia was absolutely right: The trace suddenly and inexplicably vanished. Before us loomed a solid wall of green vegetation.

"But you two are the guides, by Christ!" raged Funston. "You're supposed to know your damned way through these parts!"

Now the quaking Hilario spoke up in a trembling voice and babbled in a mixture of Spanish and Tagalog, with Segovia rapidly translating. "He says this trail was open on his last trip to Palanan. He swears by the holy Madonna."

"Damn," I muttered fearfully. "Now what do we do?"

"Take a guess, sonny," retorted Funston angrily.

"Go back?" I ventured hopefully, my appetite for this adventure now all but gone.

"No, you fool! We'd die of starvation on that beach at Casiguran Sound long before the *Vicksburg* came for us!" said Funston scathingly. "That's why we're going forward."

"Into that?" I asked tremulously, pointing at the looming curtain of green before us. Even Segovia, who had steadfastly played the toady to Funston thus far, looked dubious at this proposal.

But as I said, Funston was a fighter. He had apparently recovered his nerve from the previous evening, for he brushed aside all doubts. "You're damned right, Captain. We're going into that. Use your brains a minute, no matter how painful that might be. The fact that the trail is overgrown tells me that nobody has approached Palanan from this direction for quite some time. And that tells me Aguinaldo has no scouts posted in this direction, and therefore we won't be detected by the bastard until we're so close that it's impossible for him to slip away!"

I nodded numbly: One didn't need to be an old hand in these parts to know that hacking our way through that impenetrable jungle meant serious, serious trouble. But if Funston felt the same way, he didn't let on.

"Segovia," Funston ordered, "set the men to work in groups of five with bolos. Each group works twenty minutes, then falls to the rear of the column and the next group takes over. Everyone works, including the white officers."

Here was a damned preposterous idea, I thought. It wasn't right for white men, officers at that, to work like common laborers when we had the heathen Macabebes to do our bidding. After all, what were we paying the little buggers for if we couldn't drive them like cattle? Oh, I instinctively recognized Funston's motivation: He wanted us officers to lead by example and thus encourage the Macabebes onward. What he should have remembered, however, was that they were acclimated to this hellish place and we were not. Hard work in this heat would wear us down in no time, but Funston had made up his mind. As inane as his order was, I decided not to draw his ire again by challenging him directly.

We labored through the day, and when night fell we were exhausted to a man and ravenously hungry. Ominously, nothing edible in this wilderness had yet been found, and to compound our travails the insects had become so insistent that nothing could keep them from our necks and faces. I watched fretfully as Funston checked his map in the fading light. "Fifteen miles," he said quietly, and rolled over and went to sleep.

Fifteen miles! Was that all we had covered? At such a slow rate, it could take us more than four days to reach Palanan. I shuddered silently and hunkered down for some shut-eye.

The following day, our third, was the worst yet. Now hunger was starting to tell and fever was gripping Funston, me, the other officers, and even some of the Macabebes. Henry, thank God, bore up well. As a result of my fever, when it came my turn to wield a bolo at the head of the column, the physical exertion was pure hell. Sweat coursed off my brow and all my remaining strength ebbed from my aching limbs.

Strangely, as I and the others wilted under the strain of the march, Funston seemed to become stronger despite his fever. He was everywhere in the column, calling out, "Press on, men!" here and, "Forward, boys!" there to the now dispirited and sullen Macabebes.

We passed yet another day in hell and then late in the afternoon of the fourth day, when I'd been called to the head of the column to hack at the jungle for the tenth time, I finally balked at taking the bolo.

"I can't possibly!" I protested to Funston. "These filthy savages we've brought along are used to hard labor in this heat. Such work ought to be left to them; it's crazy to wear out your officers by using them as beasts of burden!"

"Take this bolo," ordered Funston angrily, "and set to work! I'll not have a sniveling quitter in my command!"

"But, sir! We'll all be dead soon if you don't let us rest!" I protested to no avail, for Funston thrust the bolo into my hand and propelled me forward to face the brush once more.

"The next time you try to evade your duty, Travers," vowed Funston, "I'll double your time with the hacking party!"

There was no point in further argument, so I reluctantly took the bolo from his hand, and Funston marched off to the rear of the column. Halfheartedly, I began to whack away at the unyielding vines in front of me. After several minutes, my less-than-enthusiastic demeanor drew comments from the four Macabebes working with me. I couldn't understand their lingo, but I surmised that they were complaining, if you can imagine such effrontery, about my lack of zest for the job. How dare these insolent brutes complain openly about a white man and an officer! I raged to myself.

"What's the matter with you sidewinders?" I snarled, only to draw back quickly when two of them squared up to me with bolos at the ready.

"Hold on, boys, hold on!" called a voice from behind me, and then Henry was suddenly between me and the savages. He had spotted the confrontation and rushed to head off what promised to be a fatal encounter for me. "Just settle down, you hombres, easy now," coaxed Henry, calming the Macabebes with the soothing tones one used to placate growling dogs. The savages didn't understand Henry, but his black skin and obvious goodwill stayed their attack a few precious moments until Segovia could hurry forward.

"*¿Qué pasa?*" demanded Segovia.

"It's these damned savages!" I complained bitterly. "They seem to think I should labor as hard as they do."

"Out here, Senor Travers, that is very much the case," said Segovia curtly. He turned to the Macabebes and jabbered to them a bit in their incomprehensible tongue. Mollified somewhat, they gave me murderous looks but then returned to their task.

Satisfied that the danger was past, Segovia rounded on me. "You will not do such a thing again, Senor, *comprende?* You will work as hard as the Macabebes, or I will not be able to protect you from them. You are making them start to wonder about this raid. They are not happy."

"Don't tell me it's my fault that these critters aren't happy—" I began to remonstrate, only to be cut off by Funston, who had heard the uproar and hurried forward once more.

"Silence, Travers!" he ordered. Despite my sense of outrage at these damned insolent natives, and at Segovia for taking their side, I didn't want to try Funston with his dander up. I shut my mouth. "I've heard all I want to from you." He stood on tiptoes and thrust his bearded face into mine. "This is the second time in ten minutes you've started a ruckus, Mister. If you do it once more, you can rest assured I'll convene a general court-martial to deal with you. Is that clear?"

I nodded angrily.

"Good!" snapped Funston. "Then pick up that bolo and get back to work."

"But I can't," I protested. "I'm exhausted from fever; I must have some rest."

Here Henry mercifully stepped in. "I'll do the rest of the captain's shift, suh," he volunteered to Funston.

Funston didn't like it, but he could tell from my haggard expression that I was near the end of my tether. Reluctantly he agreed to Henry's proposal and then spat disdainfully at me, "Now get to the rear and stay there until I call for you!"

10

Obediently, I slunk off, at least outwardly chastened. Thereafter I tagged along silently as we painfully hacked our way forward. It was clear that any benefit I had hoped to glean from this expedition was now offset by the very real possibility that Funston would see me in chains at journey's end. The time had come to start thinking very seriously about how to escape this fiasco with a whole skin.

Actually, I had already taken a major step toward ensuring my survival. Although Funston had threatened me with extra labor, my row with the Macabebes had so unsettled both him and Segovia that he decided it would be better if I were kept completely away from the scouts. Moreover, in a fit of idiocy, Funston decided that he would take up the slack by working both his and my shifts with the bolo. Soon I could hear him calling to the others in encouragement, "Come on, boys, if I can do the work of two men, you can do the work of one!" Whether his theatrics did anything to bolster the morale of the Macabebes is doubtful, but I do know that the respite gave me the strength to continue onward.

The extra burden on Funston, however, quickly wore him down. The fifth day came and went with no end of our trek in sight. We halted in oppressive heat in the midst of a tangled rain forest that gave no hint of ever yielding to us. The column sank to rest on rotting vegetation and in a stupor of exhaustion ate the last of the meager rations.

Funston's fever, aggravated by his strenuous exertions, was now flaring high. "Wha' s'matter wi' ya mens?" he demanded blearily of those around him, sounding like a drunken sailor on shore leave as his faculties slowly succumbed to the fever. "S'only another few miles! . . . A few miles!" And then he collapsed.

In the growing dark, I could see Segovia shaking his head in discouragement. The hungry Macabebes were silent as they rested, and even the other American officers and Henry were unnerved by the realization that things seemed to be going hopelessly awry around them. There was no indication that we would reach Palanan soon, and our strength was diminishing so fast that even if we did get there we would likely be too weak to fight any rebel troops we might find.

Dawn exploded noisily over us as flocks of parrots, resplendent in plumages of red and iridescent green, called raucously down to us from their nests in the trees above. Through a gap in the jungle canopy I saw a majestic Luzon eagle soaring above us on its ten-foot wingspan. I had heard that these huge raptors preyed on monkeys, which they pulled screaming from the trees. I wondered if the eagle also had a taste for the flesh of weakened men and shuddered involuntarily at the thought.

Soon we were on our feet, pale and drenched from a nighttime downpour. Funston was so weak that he had to be supported by two Macabebes. Although he fought to retain command by babbling, "H'up and at 'em, boys. For Kansas!" it was Segovia who now gave the order to move out.

I noted with alarm that even Bustos, despite his contingency-fee arrangement, was now giving way to defeatism. He greeted Funston's fevered ravings with a look of dark malevolence. I knew enough about this savage's ways to realize that this could only mean Bustos had decided the effort was no longer worth the reward—and that spelled trouble for us all! Soon there would be a mutiny, and all the Americans as well as the Tagalog turncoats, Hilario and Segismundo, would be cut down. Segovia, I guessed, would side with the Macabebes in a pinch.

So I began to hang back even farther from the column, nervously fingering the few grains of rice I'd been able to hoard before the Macabebes plundered our provisions. I planned to let the column slip out of sight and then turn and follow the cleared path behind me to the coast. Once there I could find a fishing village and beg for food.

By midday, only the last few men in the column were visible to me. Among them was Funston, who had sunk so rapidly that now he was reduced to crawling along on all fours. He had become such a burden to the weakened Macabebes that Segovia had decided to let him fend for himself. The Hazzard brothers and the other white officers, themselves in the throes of fever, were unable to help their leader. Now in extremis, Funston crawled back to where I plodded along behind the others.

"Travers, for God's sake give me a hand!" he called piteously, stretching out a wasted arm to me.

I shrank from him with revulsion. "I can't help you," I protested, pulling back from him as he grasped at my trouser legs. "I can barely go on myself."

That seemed to satisfy the loon, for he grew calm and then said dreamily, "Yes, 'course. Every man mus' stan' on his own feets. . . . His own feets."

I could see that Funston was slipping off into a delirium from which he was not likely to return. Ahead the column rounded a curve in the track and disappeared from view. The time had come to slip away at last!

"That's right, General," I said soothingly to the demented figure crawling along at my feet. "Everyone must make it on his own. Now be a good fellow and totter off by yourself and just leave old Fenny alone, okay? There's the good fellow."

Lulled by the sound of my voice, Funston sat on his heels and rocked his head back and forth, as though listening to some strange music within his skull. Slowly I backed down the trail, all the time calling softly, "Now you just stay there, General, and I'll fetch some help. You'll see, I promise."

Of course I'd sooner have insulted a fully armed Manchu than render aid to the flagging Funston, for if he survived he would likely be the chief witness at my court-martial. With him gone, and if I survived the trek back to the coast, I could explain away everything. Funston, I'd claim, succumbed to hostile natives, or maybe wild animals. Oh, have no fear, I'd spin a whale of a yarn.

As I turned to bolt, I called softly once more to Funston, "I must be off now, General. You stay put like a good boy and I'll be back with help!"

Funston sat there with an inane expression on his face and tears began welling up in his eyes. "S'long, son. G'bless ya!"

I turned and began walking down the path as quickly as I could when suddenly a squad of Macabebes came running up on me from behind at full tilt, seized me roughly, threw me to the ground, and before I could resist, pinned my hands behind my back.

"I didn't mean it!" I squealed. "I was coming back, honest to God I was! It's not what it seems!"

Then Segovia was among them, and as he grunted orders the Macabebes produced cords and began binding me. "Don't let them do it!" I cried to Segovia. "I can explain everything!"

"Silence!" commanded Segovia, holding his finger to his lips. "A Tagalog is here!"

"Whaaa . . . ?" was all I could manage before a stranger appeared and Segovia silenced me with a savage kick to the ribs.

"Oooff!" I grunted, and then lay there silently as Segovia and the stranger, who looked like a simple unarmed peasant to me, carried on an animated conversation in Tagalog. As they gibbered back and forth I could make out references to *el presidente* and *los americanos,* and I realized that we'd somehow blundered near the camp of Aguinaldo and that this fellow was one of *el presidente*'s lackeys. I just prayed that Segovia hadn't decided to switch sides and give up Funston and the rest of us to the *insurrectos.*

It quickly became apparent, however, that Segovia was still on our side, at least for the time being. "You will remain tied, Travers. I have told my amigo here that you, the general, and the others are prisoners of war. *¿Comprende?*"

I nodded my head warily in confirmation. As we hoped, our newfound companion had been expecting the arrival of reinforcements, and in a few moments the lot of us were moving once more, with Funston being borne now by the stronger of the Macabebes. As I hobbled along the best I could, I had to admit that we *americanos* were certainly convincing in our roles as woebegone prisoners. Like myself, my companions were bound, and all of us looked much the worse for wear from our jungle odyssey.

Abruptly the jungle began to thin. We entered an area of rude cultivation and soon came upon a tiny village, called Dinundungan by our guide. There a collection of short, Negrito aborigines stood before thatched huts and watched us with feral eyes. On a lance stuck in the ground in front of one hut was a bleached human skull.

These, I quickly learned, were the primitive Negrito mountain dwellers of the Sierra Madres cordillera. They cared little for either the Tagalogs or the Spanish, and were rumored to be quite fierce if they saw an opportunity to take a head or two. Our "guards," the Macabebes, herded us to an area apart from the huts and gestured for us to sit. Then my heart stopped, for into the village strode two fully armed *insurrectos,* fighting men from the looks of them, who glared at us Americans with pure hatred!

Segovia, Hilario, and Segismundo hailed the emissaries from Palanan, and as the *insurrectos* prattled away, Hilario and Segovia answered right back as friendly as you please. I could tell things were going well when the *insurrectos* produced some rice balls to share with the "reinforcements." I listened in on this palaver as best I could and heard enough to learn that Palanan was only some three miles distant over a flat, wide footpath. After extended conversation, an arrangement of some sort was worked out with the emissaries, and then Segovia sauntered over to me.

"It has been decided that you, the general, and the other *americanos* must remain here in Dinundungan. Aguinaldo has given orders that the yanquis may come no farther toward Palanan. *El presidente* is one very careful hombre, no? I will take the column onward to meet and capture him."

"But you can't leave us here!" I protested in a whisper. "What about these savages?" I demanded, nodding to the nearby Negritos. One of them pointed at me at that very moment and smacked his lips, exposing teeth filed to sharp points. I gave a shudder and exclaimed, "Next to them, the heathen Macabebes are citified dandies, damn your eyes! They'll roast us alive if you leave us here hog-tied like this!"

Segovia laughed. "Be calm, Travers. The Negritos are children of the forest. Believe me, they are more frightened of you than you are of them."

"I don't see any fear in their eyes!" I insisted. "All I see is hunger; those bastards are going to make a meal of us, I tell you!"

"Travers, you must understand the Negritos the way I do. They eat only foes killed in battle and only after elaborate rituals that take days to perform. They do not have the time to eat you properly, trust me. Besides, it looks as though this band is obedient to *el presidente*. He probably trades food and supplies with them. Just be thankful to the Madonna that there are mainly Negritos here and not many Tagalogs, who might sniff out our ruse, *si?*"

That calmed me down a bit. But then I remembered something: How was I going to get my map back if I was trussed up here while Segovia and the Macabebes were in Palanan rounding up *el presidente?* If the Macabebes didn't panic and lose their quarry, they were more likely to kill Aguinaldo than capture him. And what about Surlang, by God? I was the only one who even realized he was the real target of this expedition, and he too might be killed accidentally by rampaging Macabebes. With Surlang and Aguinaldo dead, I might never recover my precious property. No, I would have to go to Palanan no matter what Segovia said!

"Segovia," I whispered, carefully looking about to see that none of the Americans were within earshot, "I've got to go with you to Palanan. I know that General Funston would have insisted on going if he was . . . er . . . well, rational, you know. But since he's under the weather, as it were, it's proper that an American officer go in his place. Since I'm the most fit"—and I was, you see, for I was the only one who had not been physically broken by hacking at the jungle with a bolo—"it should be me. There should be an American officer in on the capture, eh? You can smooth it over with Aguinaldo's men, can't you? Tell them that there can't be any harm in bringing just one of the prisoners to Palanan now."

"No, Senor," replied Segovia firmly, shaking his head vigorously. "The order to leave the *americanos* here comes from Aguinaldo himself. I cannot disobey without raising great suspicion. No, you must remain here."

I could see that further argument would be a waste of time, so I lay back with a great show of resignation, hoping to convey to Segovia that I saw the wisdom of his logic and would abide by his decision. Meanwhile, my mind was searching feverishly for a way to get to Palanan with the Macabebes.

"Travers, do not be so sad. Everything will be fine, I promise you. I must tell you, I am surprised that you want to go to Palanan. Along the trail I thought that you were frightened of Aguinaldo. I see now that I was wrong."

I said nothing, hoping that Segovia would take my silence for stoic acceptance. He did.

"Soon, amigo, we will have the fox at last!" he promised, giving me a pat on the head as though I were a favorite retriever. Then he sauntered off to where Hilario stood jabbering with our Tagalog visitors.

Blast his impudent soul! I raged as Segovia left. He seemed too damned cocky about leaving all us Americans here in Dinundungan and rushing on ahead to meet *el presidente*. I smelled a rat here, and I was determined to let nothing foil my plans to seize that rogue Surlang.

Soon orders were shouted out, and the Macabebes formed into a column behind Segovia and marched off toward Palanan. The Negritos bound our feet roughly and deposited us inside their rude huts to await news of our fate. I was pushed into a hut with Henry and Funston, who was still raving deliriously.

"Wha's goin' on?" he asked faintly, his tongue lolling from his mouth and his glassy eyes unfocused.

"Shhh!" I hushed him urgently. "You've got to be quiet, you fool. We don't want to rile these beasts," I said with a nervous glance through the entryway of the hut. Our Negrito captors lounged about just outside with wicked-looking javelins at the ready.

"Aguinaldo, where's Aguinaldo?" Funston murmured softly.

I was surprised that he was able to recall the purpose of our mission, but then Funston was nothing if not dogged. "Don't worry, General," I assured him quietly, "you just rest here and I'll bring Aguinaldo to you."

This seemed to mollify Funston, for he nodded happily and dozed right off. But how the hell was I going to get free? "Henry," I whispered, "we've got to break these bonds. I don't trust Segovia. We need to be with him when he meets Aguinaldo."

Henry nodded and looked about hastily. In the center of the hut was a cold fireplace, bordered by rocks, some of which I noticed had split, probably from the heat of cooking. "The rocks," he whispered.

Yes, that was it! The sharp rock edges would do quite nicely. I wiggled clumsily over to the fireplace and positioned my hands so that my bonds were over a sharp edge, then I began sawing. After ten minutes of determined work I felt one thong snap and then the bonds fell away. I rubbed the circulation back into my hands and then set about freeing my feet. In seconds I was unbound, then I untied Henry. It was time to set out after Segovia and Hilario!

I cautiously poked my head out of the hut. Only a few children and their completely naked mothers remained in the village. They were some distance away by a stream, beating tubers into fibers with heavy cudgels as they laughed and giggled amongst themselves. The armed men I had seen earlier were gone; I surmised that they had wandered off to hunt the main course for the day's meal.

I looked back at Funston trussed like a swine on its way to market. Now, I'm not normally the softhearted type, and God knows I had no warm thoughts toward Funston, but he looked so thoroughly wretched lying there with his hands bound behind him and his feet yanked clear to the small of his back that I decided to cut his thongs and let him stretch out a bit. There'd be no harm in that, since he was unconscious and he'd make no fuss until after I was gone. I cut his bonds and rolled him over on his back. Concluding he looked as comfortable as he was likely to get under the circumstances, I slipped out of the hut and crept to the nearby brush.

After a minute's interval, Henry too stole from the hut and joined me on the edge of the clearing. There we paused to listen for any outcry at our departure. There was none, so we circled around the village until we intersected the trail that the Macabebes had taken for Palanan and set off in pursuit.

11

Hunger and fever had taken a fearsome toll on me, and despite my best efforts to make speed, the most I could manage was a stumbling lope. Fortunately, the way was flat, and with Henry's help I was able to make reasonably good time under the circumstances. After a half hour of labored shuffling, we caught sight of the rearmost of the Macabebes. We pushed in among their startled ranks and indicated with sign language that we wanted to borrow straw hats and cotton tunics to conceal our features. There was nothing we could do about our towering stature other than to bend our knees and stoop our shoulders. Once properly attired, we blended into the mass of the Macabebes and lumbered along in a bent-over posture, looking for all the world like two giant Filipino hunchbacks.

We marched on a mile or so like this when the country opened up even wider than before and we left the jungle completely behind. Then before us I saw a swift flowing river with sandy banks and on the far side a collection of neat huts amidst carefully cultivated fields. "Palanan!" grunted Bustos, pointing across the river.

Many *bancas* lined the riverbank. The Macabebes began piling into these and shoving off for the far shore. Henry joined them while I pushed through the crowd to the *banca* occupied by Segovia, Hilario, Segismundo, and their Tagalog guides. Just before the *banca* shoved off, I clambered aboard and seated myself directly behind Segovia. "Howdy, amigo," I whispered softly.

"*¿Qué?*" asked Segovia, startled. When he looked over his shoulder, his eyes flew wide and his mouth fell open in shock. "Travers! Madonna, what are you doing here?" he hissed. "I ordered you to stay back with the others—"

"I don't take orders from you, partner," I growled back harshly. "And you're forgetting just whose show this is. I'm the one who dreamed up this circus. I'm going into Palanan with you, amigo, and if you don't like it I really couldn't care less." I had taken all of this dago's posturing I could stomach. In any event, there was damned little he could do about me at the present.

Segovia shrugged his shoulders and rolled his eyes heavenward in silent supplication, no doubt beseeching the deity to spare him from the consequences of my stubbornness. As we approached the far bank, the whole village turned out in welcome. Fifty *insurrectos,* all armed, formed up in a single rank to salute us as we landed. I held my breath; if they suspected treachery, they could mow us down while we were crammed in the *bancas.* It would be a massacre.

Then the prow of our *banca* crunched into sand and we were there. Around us other *bancas* gained the shore at the same time, and the Macabebes scampered ashore and formed into a rank facing the *insurrectos.* An order was barked in Tagalog, and with a heavy metallic crash the *insurrectos* presented their arms in a salute to their bogus *compadres.* Their commander saluted us elegantly with his saber, and stepped forward to deliver a flowery welcome speech.

But Hilario stepped forward first, orating urgently in Tagalog. I immediately knew what was up—the varmint was selling us out! He intended to save his skin at the expense of the *norteamericanos.* Stunned, I looked at Segovia, who gazed at me and smiled serenely, as did the other Tagalog, Segismundo. It was as I had suspected; Segovia had intended to double-cross us all along; he must have been a double agent! Funston had been hoodwinked by this shifty Spanish polecat!

The *insurrecto* commander stopped in his tracks, nonplussed by the tale that Hilario was suddenly pouring out to him. It was at this instant that we were joined by another figure from the village—one in a green silk turban. It was Surlang, on hand to greet the American prisoners, no doubt. He had not taken ten steps before his eyes found mine and he froze, every nerve taut with alarm.

But before Surlang could utter a word, and before Hilario could make himself completely understood, the jig was suddenly up! From the far bank came the strains of a familiar melody:

> O Dewey was the morning
> Upon the first of May
> And Dewey was the Admiral
> Down in Manila Bay . . .

As one, the assembled host turned to gaze across the river at the source of this tune. It was Funston! He was up to his thighs in the river, singing madly at the top of his lungs. And behind him were the Hazzard brothers and the others, clearly identifiable as Americans. The Hazzards were pushing a *banca* into the stream, obviously intending to cross over. My mind sized up the situation in an instant: Funston must have come out of his stupor long enough to free the others and then set off after me.

My gaze swung back to the *insurrectos* before us. Their commander looked from Hilario to Funston and back to the massed Macabebes. He smelled the trap! A ripple of suspicion went through the rank of *insurrectos* behind him, and slowly they began to level the barrels of their rifles at us. That's when Surlang began caterwauling in his heathen Moro tongue that nobody present other than himself could understand.

Segovia and Hilario were suddenly frozen with fear. Only old Bustos was uncowed, scowling openly now at his hated ancestral foes. Gunplay was only a second away, and I was unarmed; there was not an instant to lose!

"Get out of my way!" I screamed, breaking from the Macabebes and running headlong through the rank of the astonished *insurrectos*. I dashed for a pile of logs directly to the rear of the *insurrectos* and threw myself behind the protection it offered.

My charge threw the *insurrectos* into confusion. Henry saw the opportunity I'd created and bellowed, "Now's the time, boys! Fire!"

The Macabebes understood; in one fluid motion they leveled their pieces and let fly a volley at point-blank range. Twenty *insurrectos* fell dead or wounded in the dust, while the others ran screaming in fear, all the fight gone from them.

With Tagalogs falling everywhere like wheat in a hailstorm, I shouted to the Macabebes, "After 'em, you flea-bitten beasts!" The Macabebes drew their bolos and obeyed, howling after the fleeing Tagalogs like demons from hell.

I popped to my feet and pounded after them. As the fighting surged through the dirt streets, I noticed Hilario, Segismundo, and Segovia at my heels, afraid of being alone in the midst of the Macabebes now that their duplicity had been exposed.

"You've got to find Aguinaldo and that Moro!" I roared at them. "Do you understand?"

"We understand," replied Segovia, bobbing his head submissively, acknowledging that I was firmly in control. He made a great show of looking into a few huts, but I could see that his heart wasn't in the search. No doubt he'd been bought by the *insurrectos* and wanted only for Aguinaldo to slip off unharmed.

Then I spied Bustos nearby. "Bustos," I called, "tell your men to catch Aguinaldo! You savvy, damn you? Aguinaldo! Catch him, pronto!"

Bustos nodded his blunt head and roared out a command over the din. Around me the Macabebes began to chant, "Aguinaldo! Aguinaldo!"

They'd gotten the idea, all right. The Macabebes pushed all the way to the far side of Palanan, where their sudden high-pitched yipping told me that they were onto something! I ran toward the sound of the exultant war cries, with Hilario and Segovia still dogging my every step. A knot of Macabebes had surrounded a solitary figure whom they were now pummeling into a bloody pulp. "Aguinaldo," one of them assured me with a gap-toothed grin as I pulled their quarry from them the way a hunter would pull a torn fox from a slavering pack of hounds.

I seized their victim roughly by the throat and ripped the straw hat from his head.

"It's Aguinaldo!" crowed Hilario in Spanish. "You got him, Senor!" Hilario slapped me on the back, and the Macabebes beamed with immense pride.

The only problem was that it wasn't Aguinaldo; I was staring into the pockmarked visage of the bartender from the Army-Navy Club, the one who had overheard me talking to Charlie Hobart and who had tipped off Aguinaldo about my secret map!

"Goddamn your lying hide, Hilario!" I raged. "This isn't Aguinaldo and you know it!"

I threw the terrified bartender to the ground. "But, Senor, I swear on the grave of my ancestors, this is *el presidente,*" insisted Hilario, pointing at the cowering bartender.

"Shut up, you bastard!" I snarled, cracking him hard across his fat face, which instantly reduced him to bawling like a chastised child. Segovia stepped back to give me a wide berth, wanting no part of me with my dander up. I turned on the crestfallen Macabebes. "You fools!" I ranted. "Aguinaldo's escaped you! He's walked away from right under your damned noses!"

The Macabebes got my message, and they too backed away like whipped dogs. Now Henry joined us, and I was wondering what to do next when a sudden flash of movement caught his eye. While we were distracted with the bartender, two figures had slipped from the village and were making a beeline for the cane fields beyond. One was wearing a pith helmet and a khaki uniform. The other wore a green turban!

"Fenny, look'a there," called Henry, pointing at the escaping figures.

My eyes followed his finger. "Surlang!" I bellowed, springing off to give chase, the Macabebes instantly following.

The fugitives, within twenty feet of the safety offered by the vast expanse of sugarcane, sensed the pursuit. With the agility of a cat, Surlang whirled to face us. As I closed on him at a dead run, I saw the same intense eyes that had stared at me from the shadows on New Year's Eve at Malacanan Palace when I'd been robbed of my precious map.

Surlang, determined to draw blood, slid his wicked kris from its sheath at his side and poised himself to strike as soon as the first foe stepped within slashing distance of his razor-sharp blade. Instantly I realized that if I hesitated, I was a dead man.

"Yaaa!" I screamed, and with a desperation born of fear, I charged straight in as if to deliver a crushing football tackle. Surlang, determined to take this *norteamericano* to paradise with him, braced himself to lop off my head as I bore in. Instead, I dove for the ground just as I entered his range.

"Eee-yiiii!" screeched a Macabebe who had been right on my heels, unable to stop as I hit the ground. The poor wretch ran right into the bright flashing blade that had been meant for me. Instantly I was up and after Surlang, but the wily Moro seized Aguinaldo, now paralyzed by fear, and threw him in my path.

Deciding that a bird in the hand was better than one in the bush, I grabbed Aguinaldo and unleashed a veritable rain of blows to his head. The fury of my assault, coupled with the fact that I was nearly half again his size, drove *el presidente* to the ground. Although he had a bolo, he never attempted to slash me, or indeed gave any hint that he even knew how to use his weapon. Stunned by my assault, he dropped the useless bolo from his hand, and in seconds the remaining Macabebes were in the fray, pinning him to the ground. A few went off in pursuit of Surlang, who flew into the cane fields with the speed of a deer.

Surlang was gone, but maybe, I prayed, he had entrusted the map to Aguinaldo. "Where is it, you bastard?" I demanded, leaning over and snarling in his face.

Aguinaldo looked at me blankly, so I roughly tore through his clothing as Henry, Segovia, and Hilario looked on puzzled. I damn near tore the uniform from his body before I concluded that the map I sought was not on his person. Angrily, I seized Aguinaldo by the lapel and shook him violently. "Where's my property, you little pile of horseshit?"

Aguinaldo, with maddening self-composure, merely smiled up at me. It was more than I could bear. Crazed beyond restraint, I grabbed Aguinaldo by the front of his tunic and commenced to pound him against the ground as a mastiff might worry a captured rabbit. It was a punishing thumping, which might have killed a less resilient man. Aguinaldo's body slumped and his eyes rolled up in his head; he was out cold.

Then Henry seized my wrists. "Fenny, Fenny, have you gone loco? You can't kill him. It'll be the end of your career. You'll be throwing everything away!"

Something he said must have gotten through at last, for I finally stood back, gasping from my exertions, eyeing my fallen enemy with burning hatred. Now Segovia stepped in, swinging back to the American side once more.

"Captain Travers, the corporal is right. *El presidente* is much too valuable a prisoner to General Funston and General MacArthur to be killed!" He gave some hurried orders to the Macabebes, who quickly trundled Aguinaldo off toward the riverbank where the main party was now assembling.

"Damnation!" I swore. "After all this effort, I come up with nothing!" I was beside myself with frustration, and Segovia was eyeing me warily lest I now attack him for spiriting Aguinaldo away from me. Beckoning to Hilario and Segismundo, he hastily retired with them in the wake of the departing Macabebes and Henry.

My strength suddenly evaporated. The chase through the village, the assault on Aguinaldo, all on top of my fever and lack of food was too much. My head began to spin violently and I staggered about uncontrollably until I lurched to the edge of the cane field and collapsed into the green stalks. I rolled about deliriously when suddenly a vision swam before my eyes. It was Surlang's ivory-handled kris. To my fevered eyes, it seemed to come alive and slither toward me like a huge snake, flicking a hideous blue tongue as it advanced.

"Make it go away!" I whined feebly as I desperately tried to crawl out of harm's way. Now the kris-snake coiled itself and loomed over me, preparing to strike. I knew that when it did, I would die.

"Oh, no," I whimpered and put my hands over my face in stark terror.

Then the nightmare vanished as Bustos appeared at my side, smiling down at me like a benevolent ogre and patting his stomach. "Bustos eat Aguinaldo, *si?*"

I looked up blearily at the old man-eater: "Sure, go ahead, partner," I answered dreamily and then passed out.

12

Manila, Luzon
April 1901

Slowly my mind rose above the haze that enveloped it. My eyes opened and focused; I was in a small, clean room and lying in a proper bed all made up with fresh linens. Perplexed, I struggled to raise myself to a sitting position but found I was too weak to do so.

Then the door opened and a white-clad nurse strode into the room. She beamed solicitously at me and warbled gaily, "Captain, you've come to! How marvelous! Doctor, oh, Doctor," she called through the door, "Captain Travers is coming around!"

"Where am I?" I managed to croak.

"Why, you're in the fever ward in Manila." The way she stood there looking at me with her eyes all agog, you would have sworn I had just risen from the dead. I got the distinct impression that she had not expected me to recover.

A doctor joined us, on his shoulders the silver leaves of a lieutenant colonel. "Ah, Captain Travers," he said, "it's so good to see you rallying at last. We were very concerned about your condition."

"What about my condition?" I rasped through a throat that felt like the inside of a salt mine. I couldn't remember how I'd gotten here, or anything else for that matter.

"You fell deathly ill on the Funston expedition. After that bandit Aguinaldo was taken, you were carried by native bearers on a litter from the interior of Luzon to the coast. There you were taken on board the *Vicksburg* and transported here. You've been here more than a month. Since you showed no sign of improvement, it was decided that you should be evacuated to the United States. A change of climate was deemed to be the only thing that might save your life, you see. But now, obviously, that prognosis is all changed. It looks as though you'll pull through just fine."

What? I thought. I had been unconscious for a whole month? The very thought of such a close brush with death chilled me for a moment. But then vague memories began coming back, and forgotten concerns began pushing themselves to the fore of my befogged mind. First, the map. I remembered that it was the whole reason for the expedition, from my viewpoint, and that Surlang had escaped my clutches at the last moment. Then I recalled my conduct on the march and wondered whether Funston planned to do anything about it.

"General Funston . . . ," I said in a whisper.

"He's fine, Captain," the nurse assured me. "He was in the fever ward until just last week. You should know that the whole time he couldn't speak highly enough of your valiant efforts, and I understand he vowed to see that General MacArthur bestows a commendation upon you."

Then his fever must have been a whopper, I concluded, hugely relieved.

The doctor added, "General MacArthur himself has been following your condition, Captain. He's ordered that he be notified of any changes. In light of your recovery, I expect that he may pay you a visit."

The doctor was right. Before the day was out the general was at my bedside, with his aide, Joshua Longbottom, in tow.

"Travers, by God, you did it!" MacArthur hailed me, pumping my limp hand vigorously. The old boy was wild with excitement at the Aguinaldo coup, but I could see that Longbottom was cool to the whole development. It put me one up on him, since it was obvious that no feat remained to be done in these islands that could match my achievement. So as weak as I was, I allowed myself a grin of self-satisfaction at Longbottom's discomfiture.

"This has absolutely changed the political reality of the rebellion, Travers," glowed MacArthur triumphantly. "Since Aguinaldo was taken, he's signed an oath of loyalty to the United States. I've had that oath posted in every barrio on Luzon. The *insurrectos* have laid down their arms by the thousands. We can send columns into villages that were armed camps only a few months ago. Why, Judge Taft and I both agree that it's time to institute civilian rule in the northern regions of the archipelago."

All this was very fine, and I nodded along like an attentive toady at every word from MacArthur, but the truth was that my map was gone and the sport of the thing just wasn't there for me any longer. Besides, my mission for President McKinley was now complete. Shouldn't I be shipping out for the States soon? I was about to ask exactly that when MacArthur got to the point he intended to raise with me.

"The doctors have assured me that you're likely to experience a complete recovery, Travers. That's excellent news, because the army needs you more now than ever before."

At first I wasn't sure I heard him right. "I don't follow you, sir. If I understood you correctly, you just told me that the war is all but over."

MacArthur shook his head. "Only part of it, son. The action has merely shifted south. True, I now consider Luzon to be secure. But a few of Aguinaldo's diehards have slipped south to the island of Samar, in the Department of the Visayas. Samar is still in a state of insurrection, I'm afraid. And farther south beyond Samar is the Forbidden Kingdom."

"The Forbidden Kingdom? What's that?"

MacArthur turned grimly to Longbottom. "Tell him," he ordered.

"It's what the Spanish called the island of Mindanao, the home of the largest concentration of Moros. There are other Moro groups, to be sure, scattered throughout the islands of the Sulu Archipelago from Mindanao to Borneo, but the fiercest and most powerful are definitely the Moros of Mindanao. In the interior of the island is a large lake, called Lake Lanao, and around its shore reside Moro clans that have resisted Spanish expansion for centuries. The clans are grouped under local lords called *datus*. A *datu* holds sway over his own fortified village, called a *cotta*. In turn a *datu* owes allegiance to a greater lord, or sultan. A powerful sultan may hold sovereignty over an entire region, called a *rancheria*. These sultans do not recognize American power, and any advance into the interior of Mindanao is likely to be bloody."

Here MacArthur spoke again. "As Captain Longbottom stated, the Moros aren't confined only to Mindanao. Although their military power is there, the great political and spiritual leader of the Moro race is the sultan of Jolo, a disgusting little degenerate by the name of Jamal-ul-Kiram."

The sultan of Jolo, did MacArthur say? Why, that was Surlang's old boss! Now I listened attentively as MacArthur continued.

"Although his prestige is great, his sultanate isn't. Jolo's just a small island across the Sulu Sea from Mindanao. But tiny or not, Jolo has remained unconquered through the centuries, and the Mindanao Moros looked to the sultan of Jolo for guidance. So as you can see, there are still any number of hornet's nests to attend to in these parts."

I knew it was hopeless, but I asked the question anyway. "If the Moros are so hostile, why not simply ignore them and content ourselves with our gains here on Luzon? It saves us the trouble of having to put these Moros on a reservation, doesn't it? Why not leave well enough alone?"

Longbottom winced at my denseness, but MacArthur was more kind.

"That won't answer, son, and the reason is good old-fashioned politics. You see, Mindanao and Jolo and the other southern islands are close to Borneo, which is a Dutch and British stronghold."

"So?" I still didn't grasp the point here.

"So," continued Longbottom for MacArthur, "if we don't fill the power vacuum left by the Spanish in Manila, someone will. Don't forget, Admiral Dewey had to drive off a German fleet that was casting covetous eyes at these islands after his victory in Manila Bay."

MacArthur nodded at this and added, "You see, Captain Travers, leaving the Muslim islands to themselves just won't do. We need to get busy down there, and the sooner the better."

"Er, begging your pardon, sir, but just what do you mean by 'busy'?" I asked warily.

"I'm assigning you to headquarters for the Department of Mindanao-Jolo at Zamboanga on Mindanao. You're to report to Brigadier General George W. Davis, commanding. I'll instruct him that your mission is to explore ways to approach the Moros with an eye toward a peaceful accommodation with them that involves the establishment of American garrisons throughout the Forbidden Kingdom."

Staggered, I sank back on my pillows. I was off to Zamboanga in Moroland? By God, I could hardly pronounce the place, let alone pick it out on a map. And as for effecting peaceful contact with foreign cultures, well, my record in that regard was a trifle weak. I generally shot my way into and out of strange places, and my sojourn to Moroland was not likely to be much different.

MacArthur, however, was pleased as punch by the notion of sending me south. He clasped me by the shoulder. "Take your time here and recover your strength, Travers. Call on Captain Longbottom for anything you need. Decide when you're ready to go, but remember, the sooner you're on your way, the better I'll feel."

As he turned to leave, he remembered something. "Oh, yes, Travers. Here's a card for you from Aguinaldo."

"Aguinaldo?" I exclaimed, puzzled.

"Yes, *el presidente* himself," chuckled MacArthur. "He and I have started to get along famously, you see. Oh, I had imagined him to be some sort of pitiless brute, but once you get to know him, he's a likable enough fellow. I told him I was going to visit you, and he insisted on sending along his felicitations."

MacArthur handed me the card. "Uh, tell him I appreciate his kind thoughts," I murmured uncertainly, wondering if Aguinaldo had mentioned to MacArthur that I had nearly beaten his brains out during his capture. Apparently not, for MacArthur was all smiles as he turned to take his leave once more.

Then it was my turn to remember something. "Sir," I called out, "if I may have one more minute of your time. There's something about the capture of Aguinaldo I wanted to raise with you. I'm afraid somebody's contribution might get overlooked, you see."

"Eh? How's that?" queried General MacArthur. "There's you, General Funston, and the other four officers. Who else deserves credit other than that?"

So I recounted the tale of Henry's exploits, of how he had hatched the scheme to catch *el presidente,* and how he had faithfully stood by me each step of the way until we had bagged our quarry.

This took General MacArthur aback. "I read the report of General Funston, and those of his officers. None of them mentioned your striker. I don't understand how such a mistake could have been made, Travers. It sounds like this Corporal Jefferson is as fully deserving of recognition as all the officers involved."

"Oh, he is, sir, but as to how such an omission could have occurred, well, er," I hemmed and hawed delicately, "I'm afraid I know the answer to that."

"Then out with it, man," demanded General MacArthur.

"The fact of the matter is that Corporal Jefferson is colored. If you recall, he was detailed from the 25th Infantry to be my striker."

"Ah, yes, now I remember," murmured General MacArthur. That said it all; Henry would receive no recognition, because blacks rarely received recognition for military exploits. That was just the way things were in the army, you see.

MacArthur chewed on this tidbit awhile before announcing firmly, "Here's what I'll do, Travers. A citation for Corporal Jefferson is out of the question, you understand. He undoubtedly deserves one, but, well, it's politically impossible. The capture of Aguinaldo must be seen as a triumph of the white man over his brown brother. Having a black man on the same stage will, er, just confuse matters. The American public doesn't appreciate how complicated these things can get sometimes. That being said, however, there's nothing to prevent me from arranging a promotion for your valiant corporal. I'll see to it straightaway. Anything else?"

I hesitated. For a second I toyed with the idea of letting MacArthur know that Funston's chief spy and his Tagalog friends were all double agents, but I instantly dismissed the notion as foolhardy. An investigation would raise too many embarrassing questions and could possibly rekindle Funston's fuzzy memory. No, that sleeping dog would just have to remain where it was.

"No, sir," I responded cheerily. "There's nothing else I can think of."

"Well, if there is, you let Longbottom know."

I thanked General MacArthur profusely, and then he was gone, with Longbottom on his heels.

13

Fortress of Nuestra Senora del Pilar
Zamboanga, Mindanao
Department of Mindanao-Jolo, Philippine Islands
June 1901

Zamboanga was the end of the world. It sat on the tip of the Zamboanga Peninsula, which jutted out from the western flank of Mindanao proper. The town boasted a Spanish presidio with the impressive name of fortress of Nuestra Senora del Pilar, a customs house, a church, a small jail, and about a thousand torpid Malay and Chinese inhabitants, plus an American garrison. Despite its southern latitude, the town was healthy enough because it was situated so as to catch the fresh sea breezes that gusted in from the Basilan Strait. What's more, it was picturesque, with its unpaved streets lined with banana and mango trees, and for a Filipino town, I decided, it was altogether quite clean.

From Zamboanga, a chain of islands stretched away to the southwest. This was the Sulu Archipelago, which reached all the way to Borneo, a distance of more than two hundred miles. About halfway from Zamboanga to Borneo lay the small island of Jolo, the seat of the sultan of Jolo. To the east of the Zamboanga Peninsula, across the Moro Gulf, was the mass of the great island of Mindanao, with the mysterious Forbidden Kingdom hidden somewhere in its mist-shrouded highlands.

General Davis proved to be a genial professional intent on his task of bringing the Moros to heel now that the war against Aguinaldo was successfully concluded. He called me into his office the day after my arrival, set me at ease, and gave me to understand that he viewed me as something of a free agent who would best know how my unique talents could be used.

"Captain Travers, I've told General MacArthur that I've decided to make you my aide. He's agreed and thinks that would be the very best employment for you until you have time to get the lay of the land in my division."

"Why, that's most kind of you, sir," I said with easy good grace. A cushy billet as a glorified paper shuffler would suit me fine, thank you.

"Think nothing of it, Travers. You cinched the job by your intrepid action at Palanan." Then he changed the subject back to the Moros and suggested that I consult with another bright officer on his staff, his former adjutant general, Capt. John Pershing. "Pershing's the most experienced and gifted officer in the Mindanao-Jolo Department, Travers. He has a few thoughts about pacifying the Moros that I've told him to share with you. I'm sure you're raring to do all you can in that regard while you're with us, eh?"

"I'll get with Captain Pershing straightaway, sir," I promised General Davis in reply. You see, I had decided it wouldn't be advisable to bawl out that I viewed my assignment to Zamboanga as a clear breach of contract. Yes, a shoddy double cross, for I'd signed on only to get Aguinaldo, and I'd done my bit, by God. Everything thereafter was simply pure greed on the part of Uncle Sam. Davis clearly had no power to countermand what MacArthur had wrought, however, so I grudgingly decided to put the best face on things and muddle through as well as I could. Which meant that I was determined to hunker down safely in Zamboanga until my tour in these islands was up, whereupon I would sail for home, poorer but wiser. So if General Davis wanted me to go speak with this Pershing fellow, I would, but it would suit me just fine if the Moros weren't civilized for the next hundred years.

"Oh, and there's some rather ominous news I need to share with you, Travers," Davis added. "The Moros have been generally neutral toward us Americans, but lately there's been some bloodshed. Seems a pirate named Surlang—"

"Surlang, did you say?" I interrupted, suddenly attentive.

"Yes, do you know of him?" asked General Davis.

"I'm afraid I do, sir," I replied. In a cryptic and incomplete fashion I proceeded to explain the role Surlang had played in the raid on the Intramuros and how he had been spotted at Palanan.

When I finished, General Davis shook his head worriedly. "Well, it's too bad you couldn't bag Surlang on Luzon, Travers, because there's no doubt now that the devil's back in his home range. It seems that a Chinese pearling schooner was surprised at an anchorage thirty miles east of here. Her crew was massacred and then the vessel was stolen. A passing fisherman said the leader of the pirates wore a green turban, Surlang's trademark. Surlang's known as a vicious killer, and there's no telling the trouble he's likely to stir up with the other Moros. What's worse, our agents say that he's gathered a crew and is busy running guns from Borneo to the rebels on Samar."

"Samar?" I said. "Why, General MacArthur said that Samar was the last stronghold of the Tagalog rebels who had fled from Luzon."

"And he's right," affirmed Davis. "That's why this link between them and Surlang has me very worried."

"Is the island of Samar part of Moroland?" I asked.

"No, it's not. Oh, I realize this is a bit confusing, but you must understand that many of these islands are inhabited by culturally distinct tribes. Oh, they're all Malays, all right, but traditionally as suspicious of each other as Englishmen are of Frenchmen. The Moros, as you know, dominate Mindanao and the Sulu Sea islands. Samar, however, has its own tribes. Those tribes are nominally Christian but every bit as fierce as the Moros. They're called Pulajans, the fierce warriors of the interior highlands of Samar. On the coast of Samar are found the usual mixture of Tagalogs, Spanish, and Chinese. All of these are generally harmless. It's the Pulajans who are the backbone of the resistance. The danger that Surlang poses is that he is a link between the Pulajans and the Moros."

I nodded. "It's like the old saying that goes, 'The enemy of my enemy is my friend.'"

Davis nodded somberly. "As you can see, I have use for a talented young man like yourself, Captain. That's why I want you and Captain Pershing to put your heads together as soon as possible and think about ways to nip in the bud what I fear may become a very unpleasant situation."

He rose and called for an orderly. "Take Captain Travers down the hall to Captain Pershing," he ordered, "and when he's done there get him settled in." Turning to me, he said by way of dismissal, "Captain Travers, it looks like you have your work cut out for you here."

I found Pershing in a small alcove down the hallway from Davis's office. He rose and curtly gestured me to the single straight-backed chair available for a visitor. Then he spread a map on the desk between us, took a seat himself, and got down to business.

"Since you're new here, Travers, you better get to know the area
of operations," he announced in clipped tones. I surmised that Pershing
viewed me as a bit of an upstart, what with my sudden and unexpected
rise to captain, a rank it had taken him nearly fifteen years to attain.
So I was not surprised that Pershing was stiffly formal toward me,
and quite intent on letting me know that, notwithstanding my coup in
nabbing Aguinaldo, he considered me to be a greenhorn. After all, Pershing
had nearly two years in the islands under his belt, whereas I had barely
six months under mine.

"Here's the situation, Travers," explained Pershing, tapping on the
map with his finger. He pointed to the town of Iligan on the north
coast of Mindanao. "Iligan is to be a staging area for our move into
the Forbidden Kingdom. General Davis has told me that he intends
to give me command of Iligan, together with three companies of the
19th Infantry and two troops of the 15th Cavalry."

"That's nearly two battalions," I said levelly, amazed that such a
large force was being placed under a mere captain. Usually only senior officers were entrusted with important independent commands. I
had heard that Pershing was a favorite of General Davis's, but until
this moment I never dreamed how much so. "Why do you need such
numbers if your mission is to make peaceful contacts with the inland
Moros?"

"To build the road," replied Pershing.

"The road?" I asked, puzzled. "What road?"

"This one," he replied, tracing a route from the coast at Iligan due
south into the interior to Lake Lanao. "It will be a first-class road,
usable in all weather, and suitable for moving troops to any threatened point."

"Well, I don't claim to be an expert on the Moros, but won't building
your road into the very heart of Moroland ruffle their feathers just a
mite? What's more, I've been led to understand that they're rather rough
customers when they get riled. I mean, I heard the Spanish never made
any headway against them."

"You heard right," Pershing assured me. "There was an expedition
mounted by Spain against the Moros about ten years ago. The Spanish governor-general sent eight thousand troops from Iligan to Lake
Lanao to take this place right here." His finger rested on a small point
on the northern shore of Lake Lanao named Marahui.

"Marahui is the *cotta* of the sultan of Madaya, a fellow named Ahmai-Manibilang," Pershing continued. "He holds sway over the powerful Maranao tribe. The Maranaos are the premier military power on Mindanao. The Spanish believed that Ahmai-Manibilang possessed a valuable secret and they wanted it."

"Oh, and what was that?" I asked casually.

"A treasure map," replied Pershing.

Naturally, I was riveted to my seat now. "Er, what kind of treasure map?" I inquired as lightly as I could.

Pershing shrugged. "The details are vague, but my understanding is that a Spanish galleon went down on the coast of Mindanao hundreds of years ago, and the map marked the spot. The Spanish wanted that map and they went after it."

I cleared my throat carefully before asking, "Did they get it?"

"No, the Moros drove them back. But that's not the end of the story. The map disappeared about the time we Americans arrived, allegedly stolen by a Moro. They're notorious thieves, you know, even amongst themselves. It was rumored that the map was to be sold to Aguinaldo, but somehow it wound up in American hands."

"And where is this map now?"

"In Manila in some vault, or at least it was when I last heard of it."

I smiled shakily. "Then it's probably safe and sound, and someday, when the natives have been put into some semblance of order, we can get to the bottom of this mystery in a cool, methodical fashion."

Inwardly, however, I was raging. Clearly the map was the genuine article, for why else would the dons have mounted an expedition to capture it, and why else would Surlang have led that desperate raid into the Intramuros to recover it? More than ever I yearned to lay my hands on Surlang and throttle him until he told me what he'd done with my precious map!

"My thoughts, exactly," agreed Pershing, and then he glanced with concern at the sudden sweat on my brow.

"Just a bit of fever that's still with me," I explained as nonchalantly as I could manage.

"I understand, Travers," he said. "I still get the chills from my own bout of malaria in Cuba."

I mopped my brow with a handkerchief. "Tell me, Pershing, if the Spanish couldn't conquer the Moros with eight thousand men, won't your little road-building scheme be endangered by the fact that you'll have only a fraction of those numbers under your command?"

Pershing gazed at me with steely eyes. "It's possible, I suppose. But I've already discussed this with General Davis, and I told him that in my opinion there's a major difference between us and the Spanish."

"And that is?" I asked.

"We're not on a treasure hunt, Travers."

"We're not? I mean, we're not, of course, you're right. We're here to, er, that is we intend to, er . . ." Then I stopped, for I hadn't the foggiest notion of what our intentions were toward the Moros if it wasn't to rob them blind.

Pershing, oblivious to my dilemma, said flatly, "We're here to bring civilization and the rule of law to these benighted islands."

"Ah, of course, the rule of law!" I said, beaming. "It was right on the tip of my tongue."

"We're going in for the long haul and we're willing to be patient," continued Pershing. "Once the Moros see we have their best interests at heart, they'll gradually welcome us. The trick will be to win them over a clan at a time, nice and gently. We'll gain a toehold and then ease ourselves into their midst."

Pershing's scheme was about as practicable as slipping one's foot into a boot with a sleeping scorpion nestled in the toe, but that was his problem, not mine. "And what do you expect of me?" I asked brightly.

Pershing surveyed me coolly, and I saw the answer in those flinty eyes before he uttered a word. What he wanted was for me to stay as far from the action as possible; the planned pacification of Moroland was to be his show and his alone. Special emissary of MacArthur or not, I was not to upstage Pershing in his glory.

"You could be most useful to me by becoming thoroughly familiar with the Moros. They come into Zamboanga to trade occasionally, and when they do I always find it helpful to strike up a conversation with them. Stay here at headquarters absorbing the Moro culture for the time being, and when I have need of you at Iligan, I'll send for you."

I nodded, quite content to stay far from harm's way. "Whatever you say, Pershing."

At this reply Pershing looked surprised, and I instantly realized he'd expected an argument from me about being cooped up at headquarters. Prepared for a row, he was caught off guard by my ready compliance. "Well, good, good. Yes, very good," he managed awkwardly.

I was smug in the face of his astonishment. "Yes, I think it'll work out all around that way, don't you? Besides, as the general's new aide, I should be available whenever he needs me, don't you agree?"

"Oh, yes, certainly. Absolutely," he readily concurred, and then his face clouded as he remembered something. "Hmmm. General Davis did mention to me that he had decided to make you his aide. That presents a bit of a problem, I'm afraid."

Now my smile turned frosty. "A problem? What sort of problem, Pershing?"

"Oh, not a problem for you, Travers," Pershing assured me hastily. "A problem for someone else. You see, up until your arrival it was more or less understood that General Davis's new aide was to be a certain officer due in from Manila. He arrives today, in fact. A Captain Longbottom. Do you know him?"

I nodded. "I know him well." Too well, in fact. I digested this information quickly. Longbottom hadn't mentioned a word to me while I lay in the hospital about coming to Mindanao. I racked my brain for the meaning of this development and concluded that with the capture of Aguinaldo, Longbottom had decided that the southern theater was the place to be for further advancement. My assignment here must have prompted him to prevail upon MacArthur to send him to Zamboanga forthwith.

"Oh, you do? Well, I hope this situation doesn't get too sticky," fretted Pershing, and then explained when I looked at him quizzically, "I'm afraid this Captain Longbottom was under the impression that the aide position was already his."

"Ah, now I see your difficulty," I said, just barely managing to keep a note of glee from my voice. Wouldn't Longbottom be green with envy when he learned that I had edged him from a general's aide billet! Ah, I thought complacently, there's nothing quite so satisfying as having what someone else desperately wants. Then I shrugged. "Well, we must simply serve as best we can wherever we're assigned. Captain Longbottom will simply have to adjust, eh?"

"My philosophy exactly," agreed Pershing. "It's like I've always said, just do the best you can sawing the wood in front of you. If you do a good enough job, people will notice."

This caused me to bite my lip, because it was well known throughout the army that Pershing had pulled every string he could to get assigned to Cuba, and then had done the same thing to get here to Mindanao.

Oblivious to his own hypocrisy, Pershing continued. "Since you're an acquaintance of his, you can help me in welcoming this Longbottom fellow, Travers. He's due to arrive at the quay by steamer in a short while. I understand his wife will be accompanying him."

14

"Fee's married? And coming here?"

Pershing studied me anew. "You know Mrs. Longbottom, too?"

I nodded. "Oh, we go back a long way. Tell me, if Longbottom's not going to be the general's aide, what's to become of him?"

"He's being assigned to one of the companies of the 9th Infantry on Samar. There's still some tension with the natives there, you know."

"General Davis mentioned that."

"Things could get hot there soon. That's why most of the 9th Infantry Regiment has been posted there over the past few months. You hail from the Ninth yourself, don't you, Travers?"

I nodded again. "Yes, I do, Pershing. I last served under those colors before the walls of Tientsin." This last I added with a stern look in my eyes, fully aware that Pershing had missed out on the Boxer expedition, to his everlasting chagrin.

"I've heard about you there and at Peking, Travers," he said, somewhat enviously if I wasn't mistaken.

"Will Mrs. Longbottom accompany her husband to Samar?" I asked casually.

"No, that's not possible," replied Pershing, taking up his hat and heading out the door with me in tow. "The conditions on Samar are total bedlam, completely unfit for a white woman. She can remain here in Zamboanga or she can return to Manila or the United States for that matter. The decision is quite up to the Longbottoms."

As I hurried along I contemplated the delightful notion of an unchaperoned Fiona sharing this garrison town with me. The possibilities were so intriguing that I was fairly salivating as Pershing led me to the docks.

When we arrived the pier was empty. After a short wait a tiny smudge of smoke appeared on the horizon, and soon the smudge grew into a ship that plowed slowly into port and lay along the quay with a loud thud. A horde of Malay crewmen lashed the vessel to the teak pilings and dropped the gangplank, and soon passengers flowed down to the dock.

Fiona disembarked on the arm of Longbottom, who saw me and smiled broadly. She waved and called, "Yoo-hoo, Fenny! Guess who's here?"

"Why, the sweetest wife in these islands?" I suggested, bringing a dour look to Longbottom's face.

"No, silly," cooed Fiona. "I don't mean me. I mean your fiancée, Alice Brenoble."

"Alice?" I fairly stammered. "In the Philippines? Where is she? Manila?"

"No, right here in Zamboanga." Fiona turned and pointed to the rail where stood a vision of loveliness in white taffeta with luxuriant auburn hair streaming from beneath a beribboned sunbonnet. The sea breeze rose and the woman's skirts stirred, outlining a magnificent figure beneath the fabric.

"Alice!" I exclaimed, and then I was up the gangplank and she was in my arms.

"Fenny, my love!" cried Alice. "I just had to come to you. Uncle George protested, of course, but I wouldn't be stopped. I just had to be near you."

"Alice, dearest," I sighed, giving her a lingering kiss. Then I remembered Pershing, who eyed this public display of affection from the dock with profound distaste. Under his baleful glare, I regretfully withdrew from Alice's tender embrace.

"Alice, my sweet, I had no idea you were coming to the islands."

"But I telegraphed, Fenny," she insisted. "Last month. Didn't you receive my wire?"

That would have been while I was still in the fever ward in Manila. Her wire had completely missed me. "No, no, I didn't, but all that matters is that you're safe and sound and with me. Here, let me help you to disembark, dear, and then we'll get you settled in. We have a great deal to catch up on, don't you agree?"

She caught the devilish glint in my eye. "Oh, I couldn't agree more," she purred. I gave her my arm and she gave me hers, a perfectly formed limb of alabaster that immediately started my mind thinking about how long it had been since I'd seen the rest of her. I paraded Alice down to Pershing, whose eyes flew wide at this exquisite vision of female charm advancing upon him. White women were few and far between in Zamboanga, you see, and even if the place had been packed with them, Alice was a rare beauty. For a moment I thought Pershing might faint, but he recovered manfully and, doffing his hat, even managed a stiff bow.

"A pleasure, ma'am," he breathed hoarsely when I'd made the introductions, and the five of us set off into the town. Pershing took charge of Longbottom and marched him off to see General Davis. It would be there that he received the news about his assignment to Samar. With

Longbottom taken care of, I steered Fiona and Alice toward the quartermaster's office to see about lodgings.

The quartermaster, a young shavetail named Lieutenant Callen, rose like a shot as we entered his office, anxious to be of service to the two ravishing creatures on my arms. I explained their needs as Callen dutifully listened.

"Mrs. Longbottom will be no problem, sir. We can put her and her husband into a vacant hacienda on the edge of town. As for your fiancée, Captain, the best I can do is to arrange for a room in the convent."

"The convent?" I laughed. "Why, that would be perfect, don't you agree, Alice?" I asked with irony in my voice.

From the passionate look in her eyes, I could see that she had a more private arrangement in mind, but being too genteel to discuss such things in front of strangers, she said nothing.

Fiona caught her look, however, and insisted, "Nonsense. Alice won't stay in a convent. She came thousands of miles to see you, Fenny, and the two of you should have time alone." She turned to the lieutenant and asked, "How big is this hacienda? Is there room for Miss Brenoble there too?"

Lieutenant Callen nodded. "Yes indeed, ma'am."

"Good," said Fiona firmly. "Miss Brenoble shall stay there with us. Have her things sent along with mine."

That settled the matter, and I set off to spend the rest of the day showing my fair companions the sights of metropolitan Zamboanga. As we strolled, I could contain my curiosity no longer. "Tell me, Fiona, how long have you and Alice been acquainted?" I also wanted to ask how much she had told Alice about the two of us, of course, but I would just have to piece that picture together as best I could.

Fiona's grin told me she was half tempted to let me twist in the wind a bit longer, but Alice spoke up to relieve my anxiety. "We only met on the steamer, Fenny. Dear Fiona saw me all alone and came over to see if there was anything I might need. Imagine my surprise when I learned that we both knew you!"

"And mine," added Fiona impishly, but when Alice threw her a quizzical glance she beamed brightly, causing Alice to smile in turn.

"Of course, I told Fiona all about our engagement," continued Alice, "and she was amazed. Fenny, I don't think Fiona believes you're the marrying kind."

"Well, I am," I laughed nervously. "There are a few things about me that Fiona doesn't know."

"Not many," she shot right back, and then gave such a honeyed smile that Alice giggled.

"Oh, you two must have some stories to tell about each other," Alice said merrily.

"Oh, that we do," Fiona assured her.

This was getting too damned ticklish for me. Desperate to change the subject, I could only manage a lame "Well, well, imagine that. My two favorite lady friends just happening to cross paths like that in the middle of the Pacific. It certainly is a small world." Damn small, I thought to myself shakily.

We were down by the harbor now, where we just happened upon a group of sullen Moros waist deep in the water fishing. What was unique was that they used no nets or lines. Instead they produced a large tuber, rather like a tulip bulb, and began hacking off slices of it with their krises. Then they tossed the pieces into the water all about them. Soon gasping fishes bobbed to the surface, seemingly drugged.

"What's that bulb?" I called to the Moros in Spanish.

At first they ignored me, and only when I repeated the question three times did one of the brutes deign to look my way. "*Bobo*," he spat, and then went back to his fishing.

"Petulant beasts," said Fiona, pouting disdainfully.

"I agree," I said, "but you must admit they're clever. They've apparently stumbled upon a plant that paralyzes fish and allows them to scoop up catches with little effort. Very impressive indeed."

We went along our way, and when the shadows grew long I steered my charges to the hacienda. When we arrived I found that the enterprising Lieutenant Callen had set a crew of Filipinos to work on the place. We crossed the threshold to find that supper was on the stove, the table was set, and a houseboy was pouring wine into glasses for our enjoyment.

Just then Longbottom joined us, his duties done for the day. I noted with satisfaction his clouded countenance.

"Joshua?" inquired Fiona with some trepidation. "Is there a problem?"

Longbottom fought to retain his composure and managed what he thought passed for a gracious smile in my direction. "I wouldn't call it a problem, my dear, but I will allow it is a surprise. It seems that I'm not to be General Davis's aide after all." Here he glared at me, unable to completely hide his fury. "The general informed me that he has already selected Fenny here for that position."

"Oh, Fenny, how wonderful," said Fiona, beaming, but then she recovered herself and stammered, "that is, I see."

"Joshua," I blurted, feigned astonishment all over my face, "I assure you this is news to me. General Davis didn't breathe a word of any of this when I saw him."

"Then where will you be assigned, Captain Longbottom?" asked Alice. In her innocence of military matters, she was only barely able to perceive that Longbottom had been dealt a loss, and I a gain, in some inexplicable manner.

The beautiful smile with which Alice accompanied her interrogatory made even Longbottom put his disappointment aside. "To Samar, Miss Brenoble. I'm to command a company of the 9th Infantry, my old regiment. They're in the field against some diehard insurgents, it seems."

"How wonderful," breathed Alice, her exquisite bosom rising enticingly. "That must be every officer's dream, to command troops in the field."

Longbottom peeled his eyes away from Alice's breasts long enough to smile and admit, "I suppose you're right at that."

"Then, here's to Joshua's new command," I toasted, raising a glass from the table. Before the others could follow suit, however, there was a knock at the door.

"Oh, that must be Captain Pershing," said Longbottom.

"Pershing?" I asked with a raised eyebrow.

"Yes. I invited him to share our first meal on Mindanao, and he graciously accepted."

Oh, I bet he did, I smiled. He had been clearly entranced by the presence of Alice, and Fiona too, and must have been overjoyed at Longbottom's invitation. I was right; when Pershing was admitted by the houseboy and seated after a graceful bow to the ladies, I could sense he was hungry, but not for food.

Once we were all settled, Pershing raised his wineglass with a flourish and said gallantly, "Ladies, welcome to Mindanao."

Fiona smiled and Alice replied ever so gently, "Thank you, Captain."

Pershing smiled hugely at Alice and dug into his meal with gusto. We all followed suit, settling down to a delicious repast of delicately broiled fish, something called a *taraquito* by the houseboy but which tasted like pompano to me. With the fish we had spiced rice and exotic vegetables that were completely foreign to my palate.

As we ate, Longbottom by his fawning manner made it very evident that he viewed Pershing as a comer and a fellow to be cultivated, which explained why Pershing had been invited to dinner on Longbottom's first night in town. Pershing, for his part, responded affably to Longbottom and positively warmly to the ladies. Sensing he was spreading it on a bit thick with Pershing, Longbottom turned to Alice.

"Tell me, Miss Brenoble—" asked Longbottom, only to be sweetly reprimanded.

"Alice, Captain. Please call me Alice."

Longbottom gave a courtly nod of the head. "Then Alice it is. Tell me, Alice, where did you and Fenny meet?"

Longbottom's expression was still that of an attentive host, but I could sense the tension lurking beneath his polished exterior. After all, he had wed Fiona thinking she was my heartthrob, and he was more than a little annoyed to find out after the fact that I had a creature as lovely as Alice stashed in the wings. Not only had he been outmaneuvered for the aide job, but there now existed the possibility that he had also been buffaloed into a quite unnecessary marriage.

"We met in Arizona, Captain," Alice replied rapturously, giving me a look of pure adoration that caused Longbottom's eyes to crinkle at the edge and Fiona to force a leaden smile.

"Please, call me Joshua," insisted Longbottom with that same forced conviviality.

"Well, Joshua," Alice obliged, "when I met Fenny in Arizona he was just a common soldier in the cavalry. Whoever would have thought back in those days that he'd become an officer?"

I could read Longbottom's thoughts: I wouldn't be an officer now if only he'd had the foresight to run me out of West Point and save himself the aggravation of having me as a perpetual thorn in his side. He pushed that bitter thought to the back of his mind and replied carefully, "Oh, I imagine that even then Fenny must have shown certain flashes of potential." He said it so sincerely that I knew the effort caused him immense pain.

"Oh, he did," gushed Alice, who then proceeded to regale the company with the hoary tale of Pedrolito the Yaqui outlaw, and how he met his demise at the business end of my gun barrel. That had been a fateful shot all right, setting me down the road to a military career and also delivering the lovely Alice into my lecherous grasp.

"How exceptional," drawled Longbottom, the laudatory note of his voice just a bit overplayed. "Yes, I would definitely classify that incident as evidence of future leadership promise," he mouthed for Alice's benefit. He would have been even less impressed, of course, had Alice remembered to mention that I gunned down Pedrolito as he was riding away from me with his back turned.

Pershing, however, was genuinely taken with Alice's tale, and I saw him eyeing me appraisingly over his wine. "So, you're an old cavalryman, Travers?" he mused. "I did some time on the plains myself with the 6th Cavalry. What was your regiment?"

"The Seventh, Pershing. Garry Owen and all that."

"To the cavalry, then," proposed Pershing, and another toast was drunk by all.

Fiona, however, was bored by tales of the dusty frontier. She had a more pressing concern on her mind and she laid it right on the table. "Tell me, Alice," she asked with a sugary little girl simper, "how long will you be in the islands?"

The point wasn't lost on me; now that she and I were together in Zamboanga, Fiona was fairly itching to resume the torrid romance we had resurrected in Manila the night poor Hobart was killed. I surmised that Longbottom was proving to be as much an officious drone in married life as he was in his professional pursuits. The intriguing aspect of Fiona's situation as far as both she and I were concerned, of course, was the plentiful free time she was likely to enjoy in Zamboanga occasioned by Longbottom's unswerving devotion to duty.

Alice, on the other hand, was a problem for Fiona. It was evident that Alice wouldn't let me out of her sight while she was in town, and it was further evident that I was prepared to pay Alice the closest attention for as long as she desired.

"Oh, that's all to be decided, Fiona. My Uncle George, George Duncan of New York . . ."

"*The* George Duncan?" interrupted Pershing, impressed anew. Pershing admired men of power and wealth, and despite George Duncan's many failings, he possessed both those qualities in spades.

Alice nodded. "Yes. Have you heard of my Uncle George, Captain Pershing?"

"John, please," he insisted.

"Very well, John," agreed Alice gaily.

"Yes, I have heard of Mr. Duncan, Alice. I understand he's one of the major political powers in New York." Not only did Pershing like men of power, but he also liked people close to men of power. By dint of my intimate relationship with Alice, that group included me, and I could see that I had risen considerably in Pershing's estimation since this evening began.

"Well, my Uncle George is prepared to support an extended stay, and I really can't bear to be apart from Fenny any longer. It seems he slips away as soon as I get him into my grasp, and now that I have him near me, I want to hold on."

This was all a bit much for Fiona, who was squirming in her seat now. Fortunately, Longbottom had a thought to impart to Alice before Fiona could get catty. "Well, I suppose there'll be plenty of opportunity to catch up on old times for you two, but I must say, a garrison town like Zamboanga is hardly the place for a refined young lady like yourself."

"Why, Captain Longbot—that is, Joshua," countered Alice melodiously, "certainly it can't be dangerous with so many brave soldiers around to protect me. Isn't that so, John?"

Pershing smiled chivalrously at her, his gaze lingering on the swell of Alice's white bosom. Pershing was a fellow who admired pretty women and didn't bother to hide it, you see. Yet despite the fact that he was clearly taken with Alice, he was a tough realist at heart, and he didn't mince words when he answered.

"Captain Longbottom's got a point, Alice. It's hard to ensure your safety. These natives are a truculent race. Oh, the Chinese and the Malay traders in town are no threat, and even the Christian Filipinos are generally harmless. But one must take the greatest care in dealing with the Moros hereabouts. They're Muslims, you know, and one can never tell when one might turn *juramentado*."

"What the devil is that?" asked Longbottom, perplexed.

"*Juramentado* is a wicked custom in these parts. When a disgruntled Moro warrior wishes to go to paradise, he dresses in a white *jubba*, or robe, and straps on a kris."

"But how does dressing in white get anyone into paradise?" asked Fiona.

Pershing smiled. "That's merely the preparatory phase, Mrs. Longbottom. The important act is that the *juramentado* kills a Christian."

"Oh, my goodness," quailed Fiona, paling considerably.

"Will any Christian do?" I asked, now fascinated in a morbid way.

Pershing nodded. "Usually. You see, the word *juramentado* comes from the Spanish word *juramentar,* which means a person who has sworn an oath. The *juramentado* swears on the Koran to kill a Christian, usually the very first one he encounters. Sometimes, however, he sets upon a preselected victim. If he succeeds, his religion tells him he will be in paradise immediately upon his death, so he's quite willing to die in the act."

"How ghastly." Fiona shuddered anew.

Pershing shrugged. "It's in the Malay blood, Mrs. Longbottom, and the Moros are of Malay stock. All Malays are known for flying into bloody frenzies and killing whoever might be at hand. Such a killer is called an *amok* and is said to have a bad head. In a way, a *juramentado* can be thought of as simply a very focused *amok.*"

"Oh, come now, Pershing," protested Longbottom tentatively, not wanting to be disrespectful but also not wanting to be the foil for some tall tale, "you're dramatizing all this a bit too much, don't you think?"

Pershing was unperturbed. "Not at all, Longbottom. When we relieved the fortress of Nuestra Senora del Pilar from the Spanish, the garrison was overjoyed to see us. They had been penned up within those walls for years, fearful to walk the streets of Zamboanga because they knew they'd be hacked to pieces by *juramentados.* And even those Moros who don't go *juramentado* are dangerous. No Moro can rise to the rank of *datu* without killing men. They're a bit like outlaws on our own western frontier, in that regard. They even notch their guns, so to speak."

"Eh, how's that?" I queried.

"If you have a chance to look at the blade of a kris, Travers, look near the very tip. You'll see little holes bored out there and then filled with copper. Every copper filling represents one life the kris has taken."

Now Alice too gave a little shiver. The dangers of Zamboanga were becoming more apparent to her. As for me, however, I was still curious. "I don't get it, Pershing. Why, if the dons were penned up by *juramentados,* do we have the run of the place? I mean, we go wherever we want in this town, Moros or no Moros. Right?"

Pershing nodded. "So far, Travers. You see, the Moros are still sizing us up. They fought the Spanish for centuries and couldn't dislodge them, but we showed up only a year or so ago and ran the dons off quite handily. So the Moros are still uncertain about us; they feel we have big medicine, but familiarity is bound to breed contempt. Besides, there's something about us that sticks in their craw."

"Oh, what's that?" pressed Longbottom.

Pershing smiled. "It's our attitude, Longbottom. We act like we own Moroland, and indeed, we intend to make the place our colony. That's a problem, you see, because we base our claim upon Spain ceding the Philippines to us after the Spanish-American War."

"True enough," replied Longbottom, "but I don't see how that's a problem."

"Oh, it's a big problem," Pershing assured him. "Spain never conquered the Moros. At best they clung to a few small coastal garrisons like Zamboanga. The Moros never submitted to Spain, and in fact held the Spanish in contempt. So when we showed up on their doorstep waving our treaty with the dons, the Moros realized that the Spanish sold us something they didn't own. That, Longbottom, spells trouble in my book."

The silence that greeted Pershing's pronouncement was broken finally by Longbottom. "I suggest that both you ladies take Captain Pershing's information to heart and not wander too far from town," he admonished.

"That's good advice," seconded Pershing.

Fiona nodded dutifully. "I'll be sure to stay close to the soldiers, John," she promised, and despite her fear managed to give me a meaningful look as she spoke.

Dinner was at an end, and we all retired to the spacious veranda. We men lit up some of the excellent Manila cigars proffered by the houseboy and sipped brandy while Pershing regaled us with tales of the Sulu Sea far into the night. He spoke of Moros and the wonders reported to exist deep in the recesses of the fabled Forbidden Kingdom.

"The Moros are fiends in combat, gentlemen," he assured us gravely. "They held off the might of the Spanish Empire for centuries, and now they're plotting to fend off us Americans. I'll tell you one thing about the Moros," he said portentously, leaning forward in his chair for emphasis. "They're warriors to a man from what I've seen. They do nothing but loot, kill, and—excuse me, ladies—rape. They'll deign to fish and hunt, but they view all other forms of useful activity as being beneath them. That's why they hold slaves. Their slaves till the land and perform all their drudgery for them."

Longbottom chuckled nervously at this. As much as to steady his own nerves as to soothe the ladies he insisted, "Come now, Pershing. We crushed the resistance on Luzon, didn't we? I'll wager that we'll do the same thing on Mindanao and Samar in short order."

"I hope you're right, Longbottom" was Pershing's retort. "Nonetheless, in my opinion the Moros are the fiercest fighters we've encountered since we conquered the Apaches."

Coming from an experienced campaigner, this was a damned serious viewpoint. I had served in Arizona and had fought side by side with a little Mescalero hellion named He Listens. I knew what the Apaches were capable of, and if the Moros were only half as warlike, we were in for a dreadful struggle in Moroland.

"Is there nothing the Moros fear?" I asked, failing to keep the alarm from my voice.

Pershing sat back in his rattan rocker and took a long pull on his cigar. Exhaling, he replied, "Yes, Travers, there is."

"And? What is it?" asked Longbottom hopefully.

"Nothing human," Pershing said flatly. "The Moros are in dread of the spirits of the night, probably because they have so much blood on their hands that they have an abnormally pronounced fear of ghosts and such. What really gives 'em the shivers, however, is the *bal-bal*."

"The what?" queried Alice with trepidation.

"The *bal-bal*," repeated Pershing. "It's their word for werewolf. The *bal-bal*'s supposed to be a creature with a man's shape except that it's got wings. According to legend, it seeks out corpses and feeds on their livers. The Moros are so in dread of the *bal-bal* that they will evacuate whole islands if they think the *bal-bal* is on the prowl."

"Damned silly superstition," Longbottom responded with a forced laugh. The rest of us were silent, for Pershing's chilling tales stopped all conversation for a minute or two.

Then Alice cleared her throat delicately and changed the subject by inquiring what flowers might be found around Zamboanga. That mercifully set everyone off on a general discussion of the indigenous flora. Once free of the depressing topic of the Moros and werewolves, the banter soared again, and it was nearly midnight when Pershing and I rose to take our leave and Longbottom and the ladies turned in.

Not an hour later I was back at the shutters to Alice's room. I tried the latch and found it was undone. Silently I slipped into the chamber where Alice waited for me under gossamer sheets. I drew back the covers to find her completely naked and thoroughly aroused.

"Fenny," she sighed passionately as I slid into bed beside her. "I wasn't certain if you'd come."

I kissed her firmly on her upturned lips, and gave her breasts a sensuous squeeze of homecoming. "Wild Moros screaming for my blood could not have kept me away, my love," I assured her truthfully, and then set about the pleasant task of giving Alice a night of tropical delight she could treasure forever.

15

The following morning I awoke to the normal routine of outpost life. Reveille sounded shortly after dawn, followed by a hearty breakfast in the mess hall, after which the troops were turned out for morning drill. I joined a cavalry squadron for saber practice and worked up a respectable lather sabering straw men as I galloped past them at the charge. After drill, the troops were marched back to their barracks for various details. We officers descended on the headquarters building to push papers across the desktops until the day was sufficiently advanced to allow us to go to the officers' mess and commence our daily carousing.

At headquarters I met Longbottom returning from a meeting with the division adjutant. "Things are a bit tense in Samar, Fenny," he said. "I've been ordered to leave this afternoon."

"This afternoon?" I said gleefully. Then, controlling my joy, I added sternly, "What damn bad luck, Joshua. I mean, why, you just got here yesterday."

Longbottom nodded briskly. "I'm afraid that's the way it is. There's shooting going on all over Samar, and experienced officers are at a premium at the moment. I'm off to pack my things and say good-bye to Fiona. Watch out for her while I'm gone, won't you?"

"You have my word on it," I assured him truthfully, and in a fit of sudden good humor, I insisted on seeing him off. I accompanied Longbottom to the hacienda, where Fiona took the news of her husband's immediate departure rather well. Since Longbottom's things had never really been unpacked, packing took no time at all. With the help of a carabao cart sent around by the adjutant, we got Longbottom and his things to the dock. There he gave Fiona an awkward farewell kiss.

I could see that after nearly a month of marriage, women—his own wife included—made him nervous at close quarters. Then he was off to faraway Samar.

It was all I could do to stop myself from dancing a jig as his ship disappeared over the horizon. With Longbottom away, it was time for me to play. I quickly settled into a delicious routine. I took all my meals in the company of my two devoted companions, exchanging double entendres with Fiona and furtive gropings under the table with Alice. Then I whiled away the hours after supper until it was time to retire, when I would creep into Alice's room and spend the night frolicking until shortly before dawn.

It was a thoroughly satisfactory arrangement, but I soon found that the girls wanted to make some slight adjustments. As was the practice in the Tropics, all activity halted during the hours from approximately eleven in the morning until four in the afternoon. This was siesta time, and it had quickly become my practice to spend siesta with Alice and Fiona. On reaching the hacienda the Monday after Longbottom's departure, however, I had no more stepped into the drive than out popped Fiona and Alice attired in long bathing suits and carrying robes.

I ogled the broad expanse of exposed calf that greeted my eyes. "Just where do you two think you're going dressed like that?" I asked with a lecherous smile.

"To the beach, silly," Alice laughed blithely. She pointed to the surf in the distance. "The water looks lovely, and we even packed a lunch for you to eat while we go wading."

She waved a picnic basket in my general direction, and Fiona chimed in, "Yes, lovely cold mutton from last night and a few bottles of ale. All that plus you get to see two girls frolic in front of you while you enjoy your meal."

"That does sound tempting," I breathed, licking my lips and not from hunger. I was on the verge of taking them up on their offer when Pershing's admonition came back to me. "I don't know," I demurred. "These waters can be treacherous, and you remember Pershing's warning the other night."

"Yes, but there's no danger in the broad daylight," insisted Fiona. "I'll tell you what," she said, pointing to a nearby sentry post. "Why don't you fetch along some guards with rifles, and they can watch over the three of us. What could be safer?"

"Well, I suppose that might be satisfactory," I allowed slowly. I was swayed not so much by Fiona's cajoling as by the sight of her and Alice stamping their feet in the sand imploringly, which caused their soft breasts and buttocks to jiggle appealingly.

"Pleee-ase!" they begged in unison, jumping up and down so enticingly that my reason was crashingly overborne by their beckoning femininity.

"Oh, very well," I capitulated good-naturedly, and marched over to the sentries. I arranged for two off-duty privates to follow at a respectful distance, their Krags slung and their eyes open.

In this fashion, the three of us with our protectors ventured out onto a deserted strand of pristine beauty. The sand was a dazzling white, and beyond the surf the dancing sea was a breathtaking shade of azure. The water was so clear that I could see brightly hued schools of fish playing in the shallows. We found a sturdy cabana, no doubt built by the former occupants of the hacienda, and I sat down on a wooden bench to have my lunch.

Alice and Fiona gamboled in the water as I ate my mutton and savored the bottled ale. The two guards sat on the sand and took in the placid scene. Just beyond the surf, fishing boats passed on their way into Zamboanga harbor with their catches. It was altogether a scene of uninterrupted beauty and tranquillity. In fact, it was all so peaceful that I dozed off, only to be awakened by laughter and good-natured cursing from the direction of the sentries.

I opened my eyes to see a slender native sporting gold earrings and a proud demeanor. He was jabbering away with the sentries. What the devil is that fellow up to? I wondered idly, noting the cloak of vivid scarlet silk slung over his shoulders. The bright cloak and the garish gold earrings dangling from his distended earlobes marked him as a Moro. He held a tray of baubles before the faces of the soldiers for their inspection. I sized up the native as an itinerant peddler, desperate to sell some trinket to the soldiers in exchange for hard Yankee cash.

I turned my gaze back to Fiona and Alice, who were splashing each other and running about in the surf like a pair of schoolgirls on holiday. They're getting on famously, I thought approvingly.

I lifted my gaze to where a large square-rigged pearling schooner passed not a hundred yards farther out just beyond the breakers. A few of its crewmen stood at the rails, leering at the playful white women.

I can't blame the poor devils, I thought to myself with amusement.

Fiona and Alice were each quite an eyeful. I grinned as I took in the sight of their lithesome forms flitting about the shoreline when suddenly a comment made by Pershing jerked me back from my reveries.

What was it he had said? Then I remembered his words: "The Moros are warriors to a man from what I've seen. They do nothing but loot, kill, and—excuse me, ladies—rape. They'll deign to fish and hunt, but they view all other forms of useful activity as being beneath them."

I quickly glanced back to the sentries. The fellow before them was acting the part of a peddler, not a warrior. If Pershing was right, then this was obviously one Moro in a million, or else something was amiss! I began to rise to my feet, a feeling of dread suddenly upon me. Just as I did, the pearler abruptly altered course, swinging its bow directly for the beach.

"What the blazes is going on?" I blurted aloud, dropping an unfinished bottle of ale into the sand. At that moment, the scarlet cloak slipped from the shoulders of the peddler, revealing a robe of pure white. At the same time, he drew a razor-sharp kris and swung it over his head. The blade caught the sun and gleamed murderously before it bit into the skull of the first sentry.

"*Juramentado!*" I bellowed, and slapped leather, only to remember that I was not armed. I ran toward the sentries instead, shrieking hysterically in alarm. The first sentry was down, his brains spilling on the beach. The second sentry seized the swinging kris, stopping it mere inches from his own skull. He struggled to hold the raging Moro, whose face was now contorted in such a paroxysm of hatred that it resembled a monstrous mask. His eyebrows were shaved until nothing remained but a thin line, and his teeth, black from chewing betel nut, were filed to sharp points. From his mouth ran the blood red saliva of a betel addict, giving the Moro the look of a demon from hell thirsty for human blood!

Although the frightened sentry outweighed the Moro by at least fifty pounds, I saw that he could barely hold his assailant at bay. "He has to be on opium!" cried the soldier, eyes bulging with fear as the Moro forced the wicked kris toward his neck. "Kill him, Captain! Kill the crazy bastard!"

"How?" I screamed in reply, since the soldier's Krag was slung across his back, and there was no way I could unsling it while he was locked in combat with the Moro.

"The other rifle, you idiot!" gasped the desperate wretch, bobbing his head wildly at the Krag lying in the sand by his dead companion. "Shoot him!"

I lunged for that rifle. Immediately the Moro, seeing his dilemma, redoubled his effort against the soldier in his grasp. The Moro loosed one hand from his kris and commenced bashing the soldier's face ruthlessly. Then he took the poor fellow by the throat, picked him up like a rag doll, slammed him down to the sand, and fell on top of him.

"Oh, Christ! Shoot!" pleaded the beleaguered soldier through the blood now bubbling from his nose and mouth. I seized the Krag, blew the sand from its chamber, worked the bolt, stepped back from the struggling pair, and leveled the weapon at the Moro.

"Don't miss, for God's sake," implored the private, and then the Krag roared.

The Moro stiffened as the blast tore a great chunk of flesh from his rib cage between the hip and the shoulder, splattering him and the stunned soldier with gore. That shot should have killed any human, but to my utter astonishment the Moro only turned his head and grinned up at me, his mouth a gaping red gash. As the blood spurted from the immense hole in his side, the Moro jerked his wrist suddenly from the soldier's grasp, and raised his kris high.

"Oh, no!" screamed the terrified private. Before I could squeeze the trigger again, the kris flashed. The soldier raised his arm to ward off the blow, only to see his hand lopped from the wrist as cleanly as if removed by a surgeon's scalpel. He let out a howl and rolled piteously away across the sand. Gaining his footing, he scampered off yowling, with his bloody stump spewing a geyser of blood with each beat of his heart. Then the Moro turned on me.

"Damn your heathen hide," I swore. The fiend rushed on me with the speed of a maddened leopard. The Krag roared again, the high-power bullet catching the *juramentado* just under his jaw and blowing the skull clean off his shoulders. Instantly the headless corpse collapsed to the sand, and the kris fell harmlessly at my feet. Enraged by the carnage wrought by this wild man, I stepped back and emptied the remainder of the magazine into the quivering corpse for good measure.

It was only then, after the ring of the muzzle blast had left my ears, that I heard the faint screams over the roar of the surf. In shock, I turned to see Fiona being hauled from the surf by a Moro in a *vinta*, the outrigger canoe of the Sulu Sea. Another Moro in the rear of the *vinta* was busy binding Alice's hands and feet. Then I saw a stout hemp line running from the deck of the schooner to the *vinta*. Once Fiona was seized, the crew hauled on the line and the *vinta* shot over the waves to the side of the schooner, where the hapless captives were manhandled over the rail.

"Stop!" I yelled helplessly. Overcome with shock, I leveled the Krag at the Moros, but remembered it was empty. Damning myself for a fool for wasting ammunition on a corpse, I frantically pulled out cartridges from the Mills belt of the soldier with the split skull and loaded them one at a time into the Krag. With only three cartridges in the magazine, I decided that would have to be enough.

I looked up. The schooner had come around, her bow pointing for the open sea and the west wind filling her sail. Then she began picking up speed. I fired once, and the crewman at the wheel on the open deck dropped over the rail. For an instant the wheel spun, but a second crewman sprang for it and brought the bow back on course. I aimed for the new helmsman and was about to squeeze off my next shot when something obscured my line of sight.

I looked up from the sight to see Fiona and Alice! They had both been bound and gagged and were being used as human shields by a tall Moro holding a kris to Alice's neck. That Moro wore a green turban. By God, it was Surlang!

I lowered the Krag impotently. "I'll follow you, Surlang!" I vowed at the top of my lungs. "There's no place in these islands you can hide. I swear I'll get you!"

And then the schooner drew away, became a dot on the horizon, and disappeared.

16

"Gone? What in God's name do you mean they're gone?" demanded General Davis.

"Exactly that, sir," replied Comdr. Ogden Henderson of the U.S. Navy who stood before him. General Davis, myself, Commander Henderson, Pershing, and the rest of General Davis's staff were at dockside the day after Fiona and Alice had been abducted. As soon as I had run gasping to headquarters to report the terrible attack, a search had been launched along the coast of Mindanao for a hundred miles in either direction, and the telegraph wires had hummed with messages to all garrisons to be alert for news of the missing American women. Henderson, who commanded the small group of oversized, steam-driven cutters that conducted the hasty search, had just sailed back to Zamboanga to make his dismal report.

"As you know, sir, there are only two large vessels in the area of the Sulu Sea, and my few cutters. That being the case, our search was necessarily limited, but all indications are that the pirates have escaped successfully."

"But to where?" demanded General Davis. "Surely the presence of two white ladies on a Malay pearler must have attracted notice." His eyes roamed his staff for answers. None were forthcoming—until Pershing spoke up.

"My guess is that Surlang's headed for the Sultanate of Jolo in the Sulu Archipelago to sell the ladies."

"What?" exploded Davis. "You can't be serious."

"Oh, but I am," affirmed Pershing. "Slavery is as endemic in these southern islands as polygamy. A *datu* normally has several wives, and a sultan—that's any *datu* who lords it over a region and has several lesser *datus* as vassals—loses face unless his harem is the size of an infantry platoon. Everything about this incident tells me that Surlang seized the ladies for the slave trade."

Now Colonel Baldwin, Davis's senior commander, a cantankerous and beribboned fighter from the Indian Wars, spoke up. "That's madness, Pershing. He'll never get away with it. Why, if any *datu* or sultan in these parts had the gall to buy white ladies, we'd torch his *cotta* and flay all his damned warriors to boot."

Pershing was silent at this, merely exchanging a look with General Davis, who in turn shook his head with resignation. "There are limits to our power in this region, Colonel Baldwin," said General Davis quietly.

"Limits?" I echoed uncomprehendingly. What the hell was going on here? Wasn't General Davis prepared to follow the trail of Surlang to the ends of the earth if necessary to rescue two fair specimens of American womanhood?

The answer, put simply, was no. "Yes, limits," repeated General Davis firmly. "Although I'm the commander of the Mindanao-Jolo Department, my actual control extends only to the immediate region of Zamboanga and Iligan. Beyond that, the Moros do pretty much as they please. I don't have the force necessary to provoke a war with them, even over this abduction."

"Why, let me have that battalion you're settin' aside for Captain Pershing, then," challenged Colonel Baldwin. He placed a meaningful emphasis on the *captain,* and I realized instantly that there was bad blood between these two. Baldwin quite rightfully questioned placing such a force under Pershing, when he, Baldwin, a seasoned fighter and senior officer to boot, was woefully underemployed in the middle of a horde of savages who obviously needed a good old-fashioned thrashing.

There was a murmur of agreement from the assembled officers at this, but Pershing merely stood silently. He was General Davis's fair-haired boy, and he knew it. He and Davis were in agreement about the present limits of Uncle Sam's power in Moroland, and between them they had decided that tact, not martial power, was the way to a successful pacification of the touchy Moros. Giving Baldwin a fighting command under such volatile circumstances would be in Davis's view like waving a red flag in front of a bull.

"But what about Alice and Fiona?" I demanded, a note of desperation in my voice.

"We'll get them back if we find them on the seas or in a region not squarely under the control of a major *datu* or sultan. But if they've been sold, as Captain Pershing suggests . . ."

"Then they stay sold?" I asked incredulously.

"No, of course not," snorted General Davis. "What I'm saying is that under such circumstances, we will be forced to rely upon diplomacy to secure their release."

Diplomacy? With rampaging heathens who had split one man's skull and lopped the hand off another in order to go to paradise? The notion was so ridiculous that it didn't bear consideration. There was only one thing that would recover Alice and Fiona from their Moro slave masters, and that was brute force. It was obvious, however, that Davis wasn't ready to hear such talk, so I asked cautiously, "What plans does the navy have, sir, to continue and perhaps broaden the search?"

Davis looked at Commander Henderson, who was clearly sympathetic to my plight. "As I said, we have two major vessels near at hand. They'll continue the search for the next few days. After that, they'll have to return to their regular stations farther out in the Pacific. The cutters can linger longer, perhaps another two weeks, but they simply can't range as far as the larger cruisers. That means they are necessarily confined to the shallower coastal waters."

I pondered this and said stonily, "Then Fiona and poor Alice have about two weeks."

Silence from all around met this pronouncement. It was then that Pershing asked, "How can the army assist the navy, Commander Henderson?"

Henderson considered this and then answered, "Any such help will necessarily be limited by the fact that your men are not seamen."

"What about serving as sharpshooters and lookouts?" I suggested. "We could put small platoons aboard the cutters to serve as boarding parties if any Moros are found."

Henderson nodded as he entertained my proposal. "I suppose that would work, especially if we find the schooner in question. The more guns available, the better, I say."

"Then I'll make a company available for sea duty forthwith," snapped General Davis. Glancing at me he added, "Captain Travers will command. My staff will assist in any manner that might be productive." Colonel Baldwin stamped his foot at this, completely left out of the game again. I, on the other hand, nodded in satisfaction; at least being at sea would make me feel as though I were doing something useful.

"One caution, gentlemen," added General Davis, addressing Commander Henderson and me. "As many of you know, Captain Pershing is being detailed to Iligan to command the operation aimed at penetrating the Forbidden Kingdom. I do not want the effort to capture this outlaw Surlang to jeopardize that mission." He gazed at me purposefully before continuing. "That means if there's any gunplay, I don't want it near the Lake Lanao region. If Surlang goes there for refuge, by God, it's refuge he'll get. Also, I don't want any incursions into the Sulu Archipelago, especially the domain of the sultan of Jolo."

Pershing added his voice now to General Davis's. "The sultan of Jolo is the nominal head of all Moros, even the ones deep in the interior by Lake Lanao who have their own sultan, Ahmai-Manibilang. Although Moros fight amongst themselves all the time, by tradition they all look to the sultan of Jolo for leadership. If the sultan should proclaim a holy war against us, a jihad, I rather think that every fighter in Moroland would rally under his banner."

I clenched my jaw, for I was quite willing to make war with every *datu* within a thousand miles if that's what it took to get Alice back, but with a visible effort I looked at General Davis and said crisply, "I understand Captain Pershing's point, sir."

Silently, I vowed to kill Surlang wherever I found him—no matter what General Davis or Pershing said.

The following days were filled with frenzied preparations. Three cutters were assembled in Zamboanga's harbor. The flagship of this makeshift flotilla was the *Jackson,* a forty-five-foot craft. With the *Jackson* were the *Emerald* and the *Monterey,* each of these being but thirty-five feet in length. An understrength company refitting from an extended patrol on Leyte was detailed for the search mission. Its acting commander, a Lieutenant Vicars, and his first sergeant, a grizzled veteran named Sergeant O'Bannion, seemed eager enough for the chase. The company was given hasty training by the cutter crews in the fine art of staying out of the way on a vessel at sea. Then ammunition was drawn, rations were issued, and the troops were moved aboard.

I took command of the first platoon aboard the *Jackson,* which was fitted with a pair of Colt machine guns, one mounted amidship on each rail. The second platoon was placed aboard the *Emerald* under the command of Lieutenant Vicars, and the third aboard the *Monterey* under Sergeant O'Bannion. In all I had fifty-nine soldiers, a force I reckoned to be quite capable of taking Surlang, assuming we ever found him. Once the troops were settled, steam was raised, and the cutters set off on their search.

Before embarking, however, I had made some special arrangements. Knowing that I could use all the knowledge of these islands available to me, I wired Manila and requested that two individuals be detailed to Zamboanga for the duration of the operation. The first was Henry. There was nobody I wanted close to me in a tight spot more than him, and right now I was facing the biggest challenge of my life. If I failed, Alice and Fiona were doomed to lives of bondage.

The second person I requested was my favorite man-eater, Bustos. He was a despicable old pagan, all right, but I figured I might need someone who could think like a blood-crazed Moro, and Bustos fit that bill as well as anyone alive. The request had been approved by Davis and gone all the way up the chain to MacArthur's successor in command, Gen. Adna Chaffee. MacArthur had pulled up stakes by now, you see, changing over the command on July 4, 1901. Not surprisingly, in view of how well Chaffee and I had gotten along in China, upon seeing my name he approved the request.

Thus three days out from Zamboanga, the *Jackson* hove to alongside a ferry outbound from Manila. The *Jackson* tied up to the ferry on a smooth sea, and two familiar figures appeared at the rail. The first was now-Sgt. Henry Jefferson, who waved upon seeing me, threw his pack over to the cutter, and then clambered aboard and gave me a snappy salute.

The second figure had no pack, or even a uniform for that matter. Nor did he have a pig. The gold ring in the nose was there, however, as was a fierce grin when he caught sight of me.

"Bustos eat Surlang?" demanded Bustos with a low growl, and leaped aboard. With my expedition now complete, I set off in search of the hated Moro pirate.

17

The search began with no clear plan, because we had no knowledge of Surlang's whereabouts. He could have been anywhere in the Sulu Sea as far as we knew, but I figured that he would be bold enough to still show the flag in the waters around Mindanao. In fact, I fully expected him to tweak our noses as soon as a suitable opportunity presented itself. With this in mind, the flotilla headed north until we sighted the Cagayan Islands, then cruised east until we saw the distant hills of Negros, and then headed south along the coast of Negros until we sighted Mindanao once more.

At Tagolo Point, we headed our bows west, coasting along the shore of Mindanao in a loose formation. Zamboanga was now a hundred miles ahead. If we reached it with no sign of Surlang, I was not sure what to do next. It was becoming depressingly clear that the Sulu Sea was an enormous blue universe containing countless thousands of islands. After stopping at a dozen villages on our travels and being met by silence and sullen stares from Muslim villagers, Commander Henderson finally corralled me for a heart-to-heart talk.

"Captain Travers, this is hopeless," he said. "If we proceed to traipse around this sea in a random pattern, we'll never corner Surlang."

"He's right, Captain," agreed Henry, careful to remain properly formal in the close confines of the cutter in sight of the other soldiers. "We can spend the next ten years searching each of these tiny villages."

They were right and I knew it. In my rage at the seizure of Alice
and Fiona, I had lunged into action—any action—just to overcome the
feeling of powerlessness I felt in the wake of their abduction. "We'll
go on to Zamboanga," I insisted. "If nothing shows up by then, we'll
try something different." Just what that might be I had no idea, and I
was hoping we wouldn't get to that point when the lookout cried out,
"Vanderhoven Plantation off the port bow, sir! Looks like the place
has been torched!"

We signaled the *Emerald* and the *Monterey*, and the flotilla steered
for shore. As we neared I saw the ruins of what had once been a stately
colonial manor perched on a grassy knoll with a path that led down
to a sturdy waterfront dock. No boat rode at anchor there, and the fields
of cotton that stretched inland behind the manor were deserted.

"This looks bad," muttered Commander Henderson. "The Vanderhovens
were Dutch settlers from Java, and they knew how to take care of
themselves. Looks like they got hit with a force they couldn't contain."

The *Jackson* docked while the rifles from the *Emerald* and *Monterey*
covered her. At a signal, my platoon accompanied by Henderson scrambled over the rail, rifles at the ready, and with Henry and I in the lead,
we advanced up the hill. What we saw there was not pretty.

"My God! It's a massacre!" gulped Commander Henderson, his bile
rising at the carnage before our eyes.

I nodded. The body of what I took to be the late Mr. Vanderhoven
lay spread-eagled and staked down in the ruins of the manor. From
his charred remains, he appeared to have been naked and mutilated
horribly. At his side, another corpse was staked down in a similar manner.
From its long blond hair, I assumed I was looking at the remains of
Mrs. Vanderhoven. Protruding from her skull was a heavy battle-ax
of some sort. The Vanderhovens had been ripped apart as if by demons, and I could only hope for their sake that death had released them
quickly from their suffering.

Bustos grunted and pulled the ax from the corpse's skull. "*Patok*,"
he grunted.

"That's a Moro ax, all right," said Sergeant O'Bannion, who had
disembarked and come up behind us. "They use 'em to kill pigs and
prisoners."

I looked at Bustos. In pidgin Spanish I asked, "How long ago all
of this?" indicating with my hand the destruction all around us.

Bustos squinted as he looked around, studying the pieces of decayed flesh scattered about and the buzzing horde of flies before he replied, "Four day, maybe three."

I nodded and turned to Henderson. "This was undoubtedly Surlang's work. He must have sailed east along the coast of Mindanao after he took Alice and Fiona, rather than heading off to Jolo as Pershing thought. The beast stopped here to have a little fun while we were off the coast of Negros, then slipped past us before we gained the Mindanao coast again and began our sweep to the west. I say we should put about and search east along the coast of Mindanao until we find him."

Henderson didn't look enthusiastic at this. "If we do that, what's to keep him from putting farther out to sea, maybe on some dark night, and slipping past us to the west again? I mean, we can play this cat-and-mouse game forever in these waters."

"Then we can spread the cutters out, have each one range along on its own in a general eastward direction and hope that one of them gets lucky."

"Then we can't support each other," objected Commander Henderson. "From what we've seen here," he said, indicating the ruins around us, "Surlang's band is quite capable of fighting. When we find them, we'll need all the guns we can bring to bear."

Henry nodded his agreement at this while Bustos scratched his genitals and hefted the bloody *patok* appreciatively, no doubt thinking of all the uses he could make of it.

"Then what do you suggest?" I demanded, looking from Commander Henderson to Henry.

Henderson was stumped and shrugged his shoulders. Henry, however, had an idea. "We need to do two things, Captain. First, we need to just forget about spreading the cutters out with no communication between them. We ought to pull them all into some central location instead. They can be spread out a little, but close enough to concentrate if we catch the scent of Surlang."

Coming from anyone else, I might have taken offense. But Henry had shown me he had a head on his shoulders, so I merely said, "And what's the second suggestion?"

"That we realize that most of the natives in these islands wouldn't tell us if Surlang was hiding in their midst. They may not like him, but they absolutely hate us. We're infidels, and worse, invaders. There are folks, however, who will be glad to help us."

"Who might that be?" asked Commander Henderson, desperate for some guidance in what promised to be a futile search.

"The Chinese sailors in these waters," answered Henry.

"The Chinese?" said Henderson, dubiously.

"Yes, suh," explained Henry. "They're just like the Chinese in Manila. They want to ply their trade in peace. That makes 'em our natural partners. The Chinese visit all these ports, and they have no love for Surlang or any other pirate. We should stop their ships in areas where Surlang might be on the prowl. Then we see if they have any news for us. If we get lucky, Surlang's trail might suddenly get real fresh. If it does, we pull the cutters together and spring on him quick-like."

I pondered this. It made sense, a hell of a lot more sense than the mindless search we were presently pursuing. "Where do you think we should concentrate our boats?"

"Let's go back aboard and look at Commander Henderson's charts," Henry suggested.

I nodded and instructed O'Bannion to get a burial detail together to inter the unfortunate Vanderhovens. Judging from the buzzards circling overhead, there would be more bodies to find: probably those of the laborers missing from the cotton fields. O'Bannion saluted and set to work as we returned to the *Jackson*.

As we neared the *Jackson,* two of the sailors had taken advantage of the layover to doff their uniforms and dive into the crystal waters. Bustos, trailing along behind us, also noticed them. He grunted ominously in Spanish, "Bad water. Bad water here."

"What's he saying?" asked Henderson.

"He says bad water," I replied with a shrug. "Must be some superstition of his, I suppose," and thought nothing more of it.

Once aboard the *Jackson,* Henderson spread the charts and we all pored over them. I surmised that map reading was another skill Henry had acquired since our days together in Arizona, for he studied the charts intently. Then he asked me, "Didn't you tell me that Surlang was involved in running guns?"

I nodded. "Yes. He's reportedly involved in a thriving trade between Malay arms dealers in Borneo and the insurgents on Samar."

Henry rustled through the charts until he located the one showing the waters around Samar. He ran his finger from the Sulu Archipelago past the northern shore of Mindanao. Off this shore was the Bohol

Sea, a small body of water some two hundred miles long and fifty miles wide. In fact we were almost on the western edge of it at the moment. The Bohol Sea was essentially a strait separating Mindanao in the south from the islands of Negros, Cebu, Bohol, and Samar to the north. Of these islands, Negros was the most westerly—and closest to the Sulu Sea; Samar was the most easterly. At the far end of the Bohol Sea, between Leyte and the extreme northeastern tip of Mindanao, lay the Surigao Strait. From the chart, it appeared that the Surigao Strait at its widest was no more than twenty miles across. "Here," announced Henry. "If Surlang visits the south coast of Ṣamar, he must pass through this strait. We should concentrate here."

I looked to Commander Henderson, who studied the chart with interest. "What Sergeant Jefferson is saying is true, unless Surlang takes a more northerly route and visits Samar by passing through the Visayan Sea." He traced a route north between Negros and the island to its north—Panay—and from thence eastward through the Visayan Sea to the west coast of Samar.

"That could be so," I allowed. "However, when my fiancée was taken, Surlang was coasting along the shore of Mindanao. Moreover, the killing of the Vanderhovens shows that Surlang was still hugging the Mindanao coast as recently as perhaps three days ago. No, I think all of this is evidence that his usual route is the southerly one." I paused as I considered my options and then said firmly, "We're going to the Surigao Strait."

When the Vanderhovens were buried along with six of their laborers, and Henderson had said a few words from his Bible over their graves, we set off. After a day and night of steady sailing, the small flotilla was on station in the narrow strait just off the town of San Juan on the south shore of Leyte. There we established a procedure. The cutters would scatter within an area of ten square miles, hugging the opposite shores as much as possible along deserted beaches, but visible to each other through telescopes and able to communicate with semaphore flags. When a likely sail was sighted, the *Jackson* would move to intercept, while the *Emerald* and *Monterey* kept their distance, watching carefully for any semaphore signals that might announce news of Surlang.

For a day and a half, this routine produced nothing, other than uncomprehending stares from local fishermen. Then, on a searingly hot afternoon, a large sail was spotted. It was scalloped along the edges in the Chinese fashion.

"A junk," said Henderson, studying the distant vessel through his telescope. "A large one."

"Let's go," I ordered.

The men hastily sprang into action, loading magazines and taking positions between meal bags filled with sand, which were arranged along the rails to act as parapets. As we closed on the junk, she made no attempt to run. Instead she hauled down her sail and stood to. A figure hailed us from the foredeck.

In broken Spanish, a Chinese sailor called, "Doctor! Do you have doctor?"

"Looks like they've seen trouble," said Henry, pointing to bullet holes in the ramshackle cabin rigged on the aft deck and the splintered gouges in the mainmast.

The helmsman laid us alongside the junk, and Henry and I went aboard. "No, we have no doctor," I said in Spanish. "What's the trouble?"

"Moros" came the reply. "Big trouble. Big fight. We have two dead and three wounded." He pointed to the cabin, which was really no more than a lean-to. Inside I could see three prone figures swathed in bloody bandages. Their soft moaning drifted to my ears in the stifling heat.

"Where were you attacked?" I demanded.

"Off Taytay Point" came the reply. "Last night."

I called over to Commander Henderson. "How far is Taytay Point?"

He consulted his charts and called back. "Twenty-five miles ahead along the coast of Leyte."

I turned to the seaman. "Did any of the Moros wear a green turban?" He had trouble with the question, so I pointed to my head and then to the distant shore. "Green," I said. "Green on head, *comprende?*"

"Ah, *si*, Senor," he replied, once I made myself clear. "One Moro, he wore green on head."

It was Surlang, all right! By God, he was only a night's sail away!

"Were there any white ladies on the Moro ship?" I demanded.

The Chinese sailor took a moment to digest this. "No" came the answer. "I see no ladies there."

Did this mean Surlang had disposed of his captives? I wondered. Or had they merely been below decks and out of sight? The answer to these questions could only be found at Taytay Point.

"Henry, let's get the bastard," I said grimly. We returned to the cutter and sent over whatever medical supplies we could spare to the thankful Chinese. By then our excited semaphores had drawn the other cutters to our side, and at a signal from Henderson we all turned our bows into the Surigao Strait and raised steam.

18

Taytay Point, Leyte
July 1901
We traveled through the night at half speed, careful to avoid the many shoals that dotted this waterway. As dawn unfolded red and expectant over the Pacific, the verdant foliage of Leyte became visible off the port bow. A narrow finger of land projected into the strait from the Leyte shore some two miles ahead.

"That's Taytay Point," Commander Henderson said grimly.

"Get ready," I said to Henry, who passed the order to the platoon, and then by semaphore to the other cutters. The metallic snap of rifle bolts being worked suddenly filled the still air. Here and there could be heard the sound of bayonets being sharpened on whetstones. The soldiers knew the mettle of their foe, and everyone expected it to be a fight to the finish.

Even I fingered my revolver nervously, a Colt single-action army pearl-handled beauty. It was my personal sidearm, a booming .45-caliber man stopper—not the polite little .38-caliber-issue popgun. After having seen that *juramentado* withstand a point-blank shot from a Krag, I wanted all the firepower I could get in any fray with Moros.

As we neared Taytay Point, we saw nothing. "Take her around the point," I said to Henderson. "Let's see what's on the other side."

He nodded at the helmsman, who guided the *Jackson* to the tip of the point, careful to keep clear of what looked like an extensive reef that paralleled the shore. As we rounded the point, I saw it.

"There she is! It's Surlang!" It was the same pearling schooner that had snatched Fiona and Alice. The Moros saw us immediately. The schooner swung about so that her bow pointed for distant Samar, her anchor chain was quickly hauled in, and then she was off.

"After her!" ordered Henderson. Sailors seized coal shovels and threw open the grate to the boiler. Then they shoveled like madmen, giving the *Jackson* every bit of power she had. Behind us the *Monterey* and the *Emerald* did the same. The air was filled with black smoke and the chase was on.

Two things became clear very quickly. First, the flotilla would soon overtake the lumbering schooner, since the Moro craft was just too low in the water to make its escape from the swift cutters. Second, somewhere along the way Surlang had acquired another craft, for there was a small ketch being towed on a line behind the schooner.

I pointed to the ketch and Henderson nodded. "I recognize it. It's the Vanderhovens'. He's using it as an away boat, I imagine."

We chased the pearler for an hour, all the while angling to get within rifle shot distance. I borrowed Henderson's telescope and studied the deck of the schooner anxiously. Although Surlang was much in evidence screaming at his crewmen and lashing them with a length of cord whenever they flagged, there was no sign of Alice or Fiona. I could only hope that they were somewhere below deck and that they were unharmed.

We closed to within a half mile, extreme rifle range, when suddenly our quarry altered course. The schooner swung about hard to port and ran for the coast.

"She'll go up on the reef!" cried Commander Henderson. We all watched in anticipation of a ship-wrenching collision when suddenly the schooner went hard to starboard and dropped anchor, resting securely against the dangerous underwater reef.

"Eh? What's this?" asked Henderson, perplexed. "She's gone dead in the water."

"Moros no give up," Bustos muttered gravely.

I knew he was right, for the ketch swung empty behind the schooner. One of the Moros showed himself briefly with a musket and fired into the ketch, immediately sinking it. Clearly our quarry was not planning on using it to make their escape. These hellions wanted a fight, and only prayed to take as many of us with them as possible.

Henderson signaled the *Emerald* and the *Monterey* to hang back in support; the *Jackson* was going in. "Helmsman, head straight for her," ordered Henderson. "Clear the Colts for action," he added.

That cheered me immensely; I'd seen what the 6mm Colts could do, you see. Yes, they were just the thing. We'd stand off a few hundred yards and riddle them with lead. Why, in no time at all Surlang and his crew of cutthroats would be bleeding cadavers. I smiled broadly as crewmen ran for the Colts and hauled off their canvas tarpaulins. Magazines were loaded, chambers cleared, and the heavy barrels sighted as we rapidly approached the schooner.

I watched it as we closed. Up on the mast was a knot of crewmen—snipers, probably. On the deck I could make out a parapet of rice sacks. "They're going to fight, Commander," I sang out blithely. I wasn't worried, you see, not with the firepower we were bringing to bear. "But I can't see the captives. If they're on board, they're probably below deck. We can't fire into the hull."

Henderson nodded. "Open fire," he ordered. "Grazing fire across the deck only."

The two Colts instantly fired, stitching neat patterns of hot lead into the rice sack parapet. Several Moros were pitched lifeless to the deck, but the others hunkered down and weathered the storm. "Give it to the little bastards!" I whooped with a wave of my revolver. "Let's teach 'em a little lesson about crossing old Uncle Sam."

I was at the rail now, bravely shaking a fist at the Moro craft for the benefit of the troopers all around me and generally looking the part of a fire-breathing fighting man. There was no sign of any defense from the enemy. Even if there had been, I was sure the Colts would finish the job straightaway. In fact, I was just muttering in a stage whisper about how I'd love to get my hands around a damned Moro's throat when Henderson unexpectedly bellowed, "Prepare to board!"

I turned in stupefaction amid the chilling sound of bayonets being snapped in place on rifle barrels. Board? What in the blazes for? Weren't we just going to pick the vermin off from a safe distance? The stern look in Henderson's eye as he stood near the wheel, however, told me no, that wasn't the way he fought sea battles. Straight at 'em, that was his style, with everyone going over the rail with cutlasses swinging.

I was damning my luck at having inadvertently thrown in my lot with a latter-day John Paul Jones when the whine of a bullet passed near my ear. "They've got Mausers!" I fairly yipped, ducking as I did.

This was a damned unpleasant development. The thought of Moros armed with modern weapons, in fact, cast such a sinister pall over this whole engagement that I was all for pulling away at once. I stammered out that very thought to Henderson, who stolidly shook off my unsolicited advice. "Never let up when the foe's dead in the water," he insisted.

"But at the very least we need to silence those snipers!" I whined, eyeing the masthead of the schooner, which was fast looming over us as we closed at nearly ramming speed.

Thankfully, Henderson agreed. "Port gun!" he ordered. "Fire on the crow's nest."

"Aye, aye, sir," acknowledged the gun chief. The barrel of the Colt was elevated and sighted, and the big gun barked again. Thin shrieks reached our ears, then two bodies came spinning down from the top of the mast to crash on the deck below.

"Good shooting," said Henderson grimly.

Now the *Jackson* was a hundred yards from the schooner, and we could see the Moros' rifle barrels protruding over the rice sacks.

"Get ready!" Henderson shouted. "Take her in by the port side. Board with your men at my signal, Captain Travers!"

Numbly, I nodded as the platoon crouched tensely behind the sandbags on that rail.

"Fifty yards!" called the helmsman.

Then the Moros showed themselves! There were at least twenty warriors, half of them armed with good Spanish Mausers and the rest with single-shot muskets. They loosed a volley into the *Jackson* that splintered the port rail with the sound of a hailstorm beating on a roof.

"That's heavy fire, Fenny," muttered Henry, at my side.

Then the *Jackson* lurched wildly. "The helmsman's been hit!" cried a sailor.

"Keep up the fire," yelled Commander Henderson, lunging for the wheel, determined to guide the cutter in himself.

The Colt on the port rail roared anew, trying to keep the Moros down. The starboard gun, masked now that we were going in by the port side, fell silent.

I had made up my mind: I wasn't boarding the Moro craft. I had seen what incensed Moros could do, and I'd be damned if I would put myself in danger when the sensible way to finish this brawl was with hot lead at two hundred yards. No, by God, boarding parties had gone out with tricornered hats, and that suited me just fine. If Henderson wanted a melee, well, he could damned well lead the way himself. Just leave poor Fenny out of it, thank you.

With my mind made up, I was about to holster my revolver when there was a sudden crunch of wood. Henderson had succeeded in his design—he'd laid us alongside the Moro craft. The force of the impact, moreover, was so tremendous that it threw me bodily over the rail. I landed athwart the pile of rice sacks that the Moros had constructed as a parapet. I shook my head to clear it and realized I was all alone!

Petrified, I shrilled, "Let's go, men! Get over that damned rail!" I was on my feet gesturing wildly as Henry leaped over and then Bustos, then a few troopers on their heels. I stepped to the side, to make it easier for them to move to the front, you see, when a Moro krisman materialized before me.

"Moros!" I yelped, and fired my Colt. The Moro lurched backward, and then Bustos was at my side with his *patok* raised. He swung viciously, and the heavy blade spun the Moro back to the deck, dead.

Now the rest of the troops were surging aboard the schooner, and it was hand-to-hand combat with no quarter asked or given. Krises flashed and Krags roared. Soldiers plunged bayonets into screaming Moros, then fired their rifles to clear the struggling victims. Bustos laid about with his *patok,* fighting with demonic fury as he howled his bloodcurdling war cry.

"They're giving ground!" exulted Henry, and indeed the Moros were being forced from the shelter of their breastwork. They didn't run, however, but instead contested each foot of the now blood soaked deck.

In the heat of battle, I had yet to catch sight of Surlang. I knew in my bones that the day would not be truly ours until he lay dead at my feet. "Surlang!" I shouted over the din. "Where's Surlang?"

By way of an answer, a burst of machine-gun fire erupted from the dilapidated cabin on the aft deck of the schooner. One soldier went down, riddled with lead. Fortunately, the first burst of fire forced the barrel of the hidden Maxim gun to rise, for the next burst was high, riddling the schooner's mast and the furled sail.

I took stock of the situation in a flash. The Moros had guessed we would come straight at them, and had foreseen that we would push them back from their parapet by main force. With cunning forethought, Surlang had secreted the Maxim gun in the aft cabin to sweep the contested deck with a point-blank shower of lead just when we thought we were on the verge of victory. I saw the Moro gunners struggling to depress their barrel to finish their grisly job, and I realized we had only seconds to live.

"Get back over the rice bags!" I cried.

Before the Moros could depress their barrel, the boarding party with me in the van scampered behind the bullet-riddled barricade of rice sacks.

"Take out that gun!" ordered Commander Henderson, seeing our plight from his post on the *Jackson.* The gun crew on the port Colt immediately snapped to. They sighted on the cabin and fired a burst.

"Did you get them?" I called to Henderson. Being at the helm and slightly elevated over the deck of the schooner, he had a better view of the action than I, hunkered down as I was behind the friendly side of the rice-bag parapet.

"I can't tell—" he began to say when a sudden return burst from the Moros answered the question for me. Their fire hit the port Colt, wounding the crew and blowing the barrel from the weapon.

"The Colt's out!" cried Henry.

The Moros, elated by this sudden turn of events, now increased their fire between shrill cries of victory.

"They've got us pinned down!" I raged.

"What about the other Colt?" asked Henry.

I nodded. "It's our only hope."

"Let's go," he said, rising.

Let's go? I thought, taken aback. Why, I hadn't intended to volunteer for anything—especially anything that exposed me to fire. I tried to tell Henry exactly that, but he was already scampering back over the rail of the *Jackson,* just before a hail of fire filled the air at that very spot.

Damn, I thought morosely as I watched him run. Now the Moros will know just where to aim. All the troopers were eyeing me, expecting me to emulate Henry's intrepid example. Seeing no way that I could gracefully pass, and half mad with fear, I tensed for a leap, and then I was off. The Moro Maxim gunners, thinking they were seeing a general retreat, were ready. As I rose, they fired, and my life was spared only because at that very moment I slipped in a pool of blood and dropped like a stone to the deck. The bullets went high as I thrashed through the rickety rail and fell into the small gap of water between the vessels.

When I came up, I saw my danger: I would be crushed if the two ships slammed together. Desperate to save myself, I dove deep and swam under the *Jackson.* Just as I went under the keel, a slender shape skirted past my line of sight.

Was that a shark? I wondered nervously. No, it was too damn small. In fact, it didn't even look like a fish, but rather more like an eel. Not wishing to tarry in those depths a moment longer than necessary, I kicked out hard for the starboard side of the *Jackson*. I broke the surface of the water and blubbered, "Get me out of here!"

A sailor crouching by the rail blinked once, then tossed down a rope. I hauled myself up to the deck, then scuttled on all fours to where Henry was working feverishly at the Colt.

Shaken and near shock from my narrow escape, I was in no mood for any further foolishness. Henry, however, was just warming to the task at hand. "Let's pull her out of her mounting," he urged. "We'll manhandle it to the port side, raise her up over the rice bags, and fire her into the Moro cabin before they can duck."

"That will never work, Henry!" I protested. "A Colt's made to be fired from a mounting. The thing will run away from us. We won't hit anything but air."

Henry was undeterred. "We'll be firing from point-blank range. We can't miss, I tell you. It'll work if they don't suspect what we're up to." With the help of the second gun chief, Henry got the Colt off its mounting, and with me in tow made his way to the port bow of the *Jackson,* being careful to stay low the whole way.

He pointed to a sturdy tar nearby. "You're our new gun mount."

Henry handed him an empty meal sack he found lying on the deck, told him to face about, and then placed the heavy barrel on his shoulder. "Wrap the sack around the barrel and then hold it on your shoulder as tight as you can. Fenny, you and the chief lift the Colt so I can concentrate on aiming. When I count to three, we'll all stand. Then I'll aim and fire. You all hang on, and I'll try to empty a magazine into the bastards before they know what's up. Ready?"

I wasn't, but the others nodded grimly.

"Okay, on three," said Henry firmly. "One, two . . . three!"

We stood as one. Immediately I saw that we were directly abreast of the Moro gunners. Their eyes came around in astonishment at the destruction suddenly looming before them. In an instant, however, they recovered and started swinging the Maxim barrel our way.

Then Henry fired. The Colt chattered angrily and a cloud of hot lead sprayed into the Moros, blowing heads from torsos and limbs from bodies. In an instant it was over; the cabin was in shreds and the gunners lay in a mound of gore.

"After them!" I cried exultantly, and with a great hurrah the platoon went over the disputed parapet again. I threw down the Colt and followed them, anxious to search Surlang's body as soon as the soldiers butchered him. Once over the rail I poked into the cabin. Other than the dead gunners, however, it was empty. I glanced toward the bow of the schooner, where several troopers were cautiously raising the hatch to the hold. "Anyone in there?" I called to them.

A soldier peered in. "No, sir," he replied. "Just a few sacks of rice and some barrels. That's it."

"Where in tarnation is Surl—" I started to say, when I was interrupted by Henry.

"There he is!"

My eyes followed Henry's pointing finger. Making their way across the reef were four Moros pulling a *vinta,* the same boat used to snatch Alice and Fiona! What was more, one of the Moros wore a green turban! By God, they had lulled us by plainly showing the empty ketch. All the while Surlang had been making his escape in the hidden *vinta!*

The fleeing Moros were in water up to their hips, and had about seventy yards to go until they reached the relative depths of the lagoon on the far side of the reef. From there, they could reach the shore and escape our grasp. The cutters couldn't follow, since they couldn't get across the reef, and the small boats of the cutters were lashed down to their decks and so not readily available to give chase. What was worse, there were two figures seated in the *vinta.* They were bound and hooded, and they were very definitely female!

Now Surlang's plan became crystal clear. He had laid his vessel alongside the reef fully intending to make good his escape while his crew held us off. It was a brilliant plan formed in rapid response to a hopeless situation. As much as I damned Surlang for being a bloodthirsty killer, I had to admire him as a first-rate tactician.

"After them!" I bellowed, leaping across the rail of the schooner in pursuit. By God, that was my future livelihood fleeing for the shore. In a flash Bustos, Henry, and five soldiers followed. We splashed for the reef, gained purchase, and slogged off after our quarry. It immediately became clear that walking across a reef was no easy matter. Our feet encountered tangles of coral branches that tripped us and reduced our advance to a slow wade. We were closing on the Moros, however, since the *vinta* held them to a pace even slower than ours. We had to catch them before they reached the lagoon, and I could tell it would be a close run thing.

Surlang must have been calculating along the same lines, for suddenly he barked out an order. One of the Moros turned back toward us, unslinging a Mauser from his back as he came. As we slithered and fell forward, I yelled, "He's the rear guard! Watch out!"

This Moro advanced to a spot about thirty yards behind his retreating leader, then stepped up on some underwater object. Now he was only about knee-deep in water, and had a firm platform from which to pepper us.

"Uh-oh, here it comes!" warned Henry, then the first Mauser round zinged among us.

The soldiers stopped and fired back, but between the current rushing across the reef and the lack of any footing, nobody could draw a bead on the Moro. Our Krags barked, but the shots went wide of the mark. Of even greater concern to me, however, was the fear that a wild shot might hit the captives.

A Mauser bullet kicked up a splash not an inch from my hand. That was enough for me. I was already wading for the rear when I bleated out over my shoulder, "Pull back! Back to the *Jackson*."

Just how we would do that without being gunned down to the last man was a question that had just crossed my mind when the Moro marksman suddenly gave out a shriek and slapped at the water around him.

"What the hell . . . ?" I wondered aloud as the fellow threw down his rifle and raised one foot.

Then I saw it: A huge serpent was hanging from the Moro's foot, its body pale white with startling black stripes from head to tail.

Now Bustos was gibbering in Spanish and flailing wildly in retreat. "Snake! Bad snake!" he grunted as he struggled.

By God, that was what I'd seen under the *Jackson!* It was why Bustos had said these were bad waters. They were the home of poisonous sea snakes!

The shrieking of the Moro stopped suddenly and he clutched his chest, then toppled into the water, dead.

"Let's get out of here!" I bawled in fright. The men needed no encouragement, for Bustos's antics had thoroughly unnerved them. We splashed hurriedly back over the reef, looking fearfully beneath the surface as we went. Oh, the snakes were there all right, for now we could see them plain as day in the crystal waters. Most hung off, alarmed by our wild blundering about, but one or two pressed in for quick strikes. Our heavy boots and trousers saved us, protection that the hapless Moro lacked, but the chance of a lucky bite on bare skin was too terrible to contemplate.

Kicking off snakes as we went, we reached the schooner and scrambled aboard, thankful to be alive. Only then did I look back for the *vinta*. It had reached the lagoon, and now the Moros were pulling for the shore.

How had Surlang and his followers passed unharmed through that tangle of serpents? I wondered angrily. Either he was exceedingly lucky or else he knew something about the angry reptiles that we didn't. It was Bustos who found the answer.

"*Bobo*," he said, pointing to the deck of the schooner. I looked where he indicated and saw shredded vegetable matter of some kind, and then remembered the Moro fishermen back in Zamboanga's harbor.

"Damn, that's it!" I exclaimed. "Surlang spread *bobo* around him in the water to stun the snakes. They must have recovered quickly, however, and by the time we got among them they were full of piss and vinegar."

Looking up, I saw that the Moros were still within rifle range, but the wily Surlang had resorted to another of his tricks, this time one that I recognized. He had the captives placed between the rowers and us. We could only fire on the Moros by killing the objects of our rescue. By God, stymied again!

It was then that a soldier sang out. "Holy Jesus, look at this!"

A crowd was gathered around the hatch to the cargo hold. Commander Henderson had crossed over from the *Jackson* and he too was staring into the hold. He was suddenly pale under his tropical tan. "What a monster," he shuddered.

I stepped across the bodies littering the deck and looked into the hold. What we had thought were rice bags weren't. They were shrouds. Here and there a hand or foot extended from the fabric. Bloodstains were everywhere, and from one sack a hank of long black hair spread across the filthy deck of the hold.

"My God, they're women!" I gasped.

Bustos was there now, and he nodded impassively. "Captive slaves. Surlang kill them. This is the Moro way."

"Stave in the barrels," I ordered.

A sturdy tar seized a bolo and dropped into the slippery hold. With a few quick slashes he tore apart the bindings holding a lid on one of the barrels. Then he pulled off the lid and peered in.

"Rifles, sir. They look like Spanish Mausers."

19

Commander Henderson gave the order that the unfortunate victims of Surlang's wrath be buried at sea, and then commanded that the schooner be burned to its waterline. When these somber tasks were done, the flotilla set a course north by northwest along the coast. The lookouts were instructed to find a channel through the reef. When one was found Commander Henderson passed the cutters through it, then doubled back to the south to find the spot where Surlang had gone ashore. When the lookout spied the deserted *vinta* half covered with some hastily gathered palm fronds, he cried out and we heaved to. The anchors went down with a splash and I hastened ashore with Henry, Bustos, and one squad.

Bustos's practiced eye scanned the jungle around the deserted *vinta* and pointed into the dense foliage. "Trail go there."

He led the way into the jungle with us close behind. The path was narrow, and we had to fight off clinging *bejuco* vines at every step, but after three miles the track merged with a wider trace that paralleled the coast. This was evidently a byway frequented by the tribes of Leyte, for it had the look of constant use. We picked up our pace now, breaking into a slow trot for another two miles. We were jogging along as quietly as we could manage when suddenly Bustos raised his hand and pointed. "There" was all he said.

The squad halted and trained their Krags at the spot on the side of the trail indicated by Bustos. I nodded at Henry, who advanced carefully, his Krag at the ready. With his barrel he pushed aside some huge plant leaves.

"Holy Moses!" he exclaimed and jumped back.

"What is it?" I demanded, stepping forward, my revolver cocked.

"More murder," shuddered Henry with disgust. I looked into the brush where he pointed. It was the two captives Surlang had used as shields. They lay on the dank earth, still bound and hooded. My God, had Alice and Fiona met their fates here in this hellhole? My heart suddenly froze in my chest, and in a shaking voice I called for a knife and slit one hood. The face of a very pretty Malay woman came into view. The other victim too was a Malay.

Relieved and repulsed at the same instant, I raged, "What did he do with Alice and Fiona? The bastard knew that we were after them, and that's why he killed all his captives except these two. He tricked us into holding our fire, and then when he had no further use for them, he killed them."

"We're tracking a mad dog," gasped Henry, clearly shaken.

"Moro make bad enemy," observed Bustos unnecessarily.

"How far ahead are they, Bustos?"

The Macabebe squinted at the trail and seemed to even sniff the air. "Maybe half a sun," he replied.

Half a day, I realized. "How long before we catch up with them?"

Bustos grinned hideously. "Never, *Capitán*. Moro no have women now. They move through jungle like spirits. They gone."

That was it? Gone? Vanished like wraiths into this green hell? I was furious beyond words, but there was no point remonstrating with Bustos. After all, he knew the Moros better than any of us.

"Bury them," I ordered tersely, pointing at the bodies.

When the women had been laid in their miserable shallow graves, I announced: "We're going back to the *Jackson*."

Once aboard, I called a council of war. "Commander," I said to Henderson, "we've used up most of the two weeks you allotted, and I don't know what my next move should be. With Surlang loose on Leyte, there's no telling where he might be. A whole army could plunge into that jungle and not catch him for years."

Commander Henderson patted my shoulder sympathetically. "Captain Travers, as far as the two weeks goes, don't fret on that account. I can always, er, well, extend the availability of the cutters. These boilers are always breaking down, and one never knows when a disabled cutter will limp back to port."

I got his point. "Thanks, Commander," I replied morosely. "But even with more time, I don't have a clue where that Moro will go from here."

It was Henry who spoke up in the gloomy silence. "That's why you brought him," he said, pointing at Bustos, who had lopped the top off a tin of beef with his *patok* and sat gobbling his food with no apparent concern in the world. "Ask him where Surlang is off to."

I shrugged. Why not? "How about it, Bustos? Where will Surlang go?"

Bustos looked up and belched. "Surlang go where he can kill white man. He hate you now. *Mucho* hate." Then he went back to his repast.

"Well, that was a big help," I muttered.

"Maybe it was," said Henry slowly. "If Bustos is right, Surlang isn't just running away. He's heading for the place he feels he can do us the most harm."

"And that is?" I queried.

Henderson answered. "Why, that would be Samar. That island is the most restive in the whole Philippine archipelago right now. Things have only recently simmered down to the point of a low boil. You see, before his capture, Aguinaldo sent one of his generals to Samar, a Tagalog named Vicente Lukban. Right now Lukban's lying low because his forces have been hounded mercilessly about the island by the 9th Regiment. The rebels are low on food and arms, but they're capable of murder on short notice. I'd hate to think what could happen if a firebrand like Surlang was on hand to stir up the embers."

"I suppose all that's so," I said slowly, "but don't forget that Surlang is stranded here on Leyte without his schooner or his crew. How can he cross to Samar?"

"Easiest thing in the world," countered Henderson, unfazed. He unrolled his chart of Samar and pointed to where it abutted the island of Leyte. "The two islands are separated only by the narrow San Juanico Strait. A *vinta* could make that passage even in rough seas, and there are thousands of *vintas* on Leyte."

I studied the chart. Beyond the Surigao Strait, the channel opened into the broad Leyte Gulf, which formed a great bay bounded on the west by Leyte and on the east by the southernmost part of Samar. At the northernmost extension of Leyte Gulf the waters narrowed into the San Juanico Strait, as Henderson had said. One glance at the short distance across San Juanico Strait told me that Surlang would indeed be able to cross over to Samar almost at will. That realization deepened my gloom.

"Then what do we do?" I asked, dispirited.

Now Henry spoke. "If I'm right about Surlang heading to Samar, we'll know in short order."

"Oh? How?" I challenged him.

"Soldiers will start turning up dead" was his answer.

I looked from Commander Henderson to his chart. "Take us here," I said, pointing at the port of Tacloban on the east coast of Leyte, just across the San Juanico Strait from Samar.

Commander Henderson nodded his approval. "Tacloban's the headquarters of General Smith, the general in charge of Samar. It's also the headquarters for the 9th Infantry and the supply point for the pacification of Samar."

I knew all that already from Pershing's briefings back in Zamboanga, of course. I motioned with my head to Henry and Bustos and merely said, "We can hole up there until Surlang surfaces. You take the rest of the company back to Zamboanga."

"And what shall I tell General Davis are your plans, Captain Travers?" he asked.

I thought for a second. Surlang had despoiled the peace of my idyllic situation in Zamboanga. He had carried off not one but two ravishing American beauties, both of whom were romantically inclined toward me. Worst of all, he had my damned map. "Tell General Davis that I intend to stay on Surlang's trail until I run the varmint to ground," I snapped.

20

Tacloban, Leyte
September 1, 1901

Henry was absolutely right: Surlang announced his presence on Samar in a big way. As planned, we had gone to Tacloban and found that place well suited indeed for our purpose of monitoring events on Samar. It turned out that the 9th Infantry had strung telephone wire from Tacloban to the forward garrison at Basey on Samar. The wire ran right beneath the San Juanico Strait by underwater cable. We had been in Tacloban no more than a week before that wire brought the news we had been expecting.

A patrol had been sent from Basey to inspect the telephone lines. On its way back to the base, the patrol had been ambushed by the fierce Samar highlanders, the Pulajans that General Davis had told me about. At least two Americans were killed.

"Let's go," I said tersely to Henry and Bustos. I arranged passage across the strait on a military ferry to Basey. Like all the other coastal towns on Samar, Basey was no more than a decrepit trading enclave clinging to the flank of an untamed island. Samar was shaped like one of the conch shells that littered its beaches, a gigantic shell 130 miles long laid on the ocean bottom so that its broad end faced north and its narrow, tapered end faced south. Like a conch, Samar had no level surfaces. Instead the land soared from the narrow coastal strip to a forbidding highland mountain fastness completely covered with primeval forests and perpetual mists.

Samar's ruthless topography in turn dictated its population mix. On the coast, depending on seafaring for a livelihood, were Chinese and Tagalog merchants, a governing class of mixed Spanish-Tagalog ancestry, and a mass of overworked and underpaid mixed-blood Visayans. Immediately inland, the rugged interior was the home range of aboriginal Visayans, a group linguistically and culturally apart from the coast dwellers. It was among the mountaineers that the insurgents found safe haven from the Americans, just as they had from the Spanish before them.

At Basey I reported to Lieutenant Colonel Foote, the commander of the 2d Battalion, 9th Infantry. With him was Joshua Longbottom. Spying me, Longbottom spoke first.

"Travers, where's Fiona?" he demanded. "Have you found her yet?"

I cleared my throat, unaware until this moment that Longbottom had gotten the news of his wife's abduction.

"No, there's no news about her, I'm afraid," I replied lamely. I was not quite up to telling Longbottom that I'd gotten within sight of Surlang off Taytay Point, only to have the devil slip away. Fortunately, I was rescued from this uncomfortable pass by Lieutenant Colonel Foote, a trim fellow with a confident gleam in his eyes.

"Ah, Captain Travers," said Foote with a smile. "Welcome back to the Ninth. Your China exploits are still a legend in the regiment, I'll have you know."

I smiled distractedly. "Why, thank you, sir." It was always good to be praised, of course, but China had been a long time ago, and I had more urgent matters to tend to than swapping war stories with an evident admirer. "I'm here on the trail of the renegade I think caused the death of your men."

Lieutenant Colonel Foote looked quizzically at Longbottom and then back at me. "Whatever can you mean, Travers?"

Longbottom, however, got my drift. "The telegraph that informed me about Fiona mentioned a bandit named Surlang. Is he here on Samar, Travers?"

I nodded. "I think he came ashore about a week ago. He's on the warpath, Longbottom, and we need to find out where he's going from here and then cut him off."

None of this meant that I intended to take on Surlang personally, you see. No, indeed, for what I planned was to get Bustos within ax range of Surlang before the outlaw had gathered too much of a following. From what I had seen of Bustos wielding his *patok* in the Taytay Point fight, the Macabebe would be more than a match for Surlang.

Lieutenant Colonel Foote had the information I needed. "The Pulajans went south. We followed their tracks and blood paths for some distance, and there's no doubt about it."

I decided it was time to learn about Surlang's new allies. Turning to Foote I said, "Tell me about the Pulajans. What motivates 'em? How do they fight?"

He shrugged. "Their motivation? From what I can see, they just flat hate us, Captain Travers, just like they hated the dons and all other foreigners. The Pulajans are rough mountaineers. They've allegedly been Christianized, but it's only skin deep. They rally around their war chiefs and medicine men. When they fight, they use bolos like the Tagalogs. And, oh, how they fight."

"What do you mean?" I pressed.

"They wear little amulets given to them by their medicine men. The amulets are called *anting-antings*. They think their charms make them invincible against bullets, and that belief makes them fearless in battle. Their bravery, plus their costume of red breeches and tunics, covered all over by a white cape, makes them an awe-inspiring sight."

Amulets? Medicine men? This all sounded depressingly familiar and I said so. "Why, it's like the Boxers all over again with all this talk of charms and magic."

Longbottom nodded, for he too recalled the futile talismans worn by the Chinese during our march on Peking. Lieutenant Colonel Foote also agreed but added, "Don't forget, Captain Travers, we mowed down the Boxers by the hundreds, just like we'll do to these damned Pulajans."

Foote was right regarding the Boxers' charms being wholly useless. My .45 Colt alone had sent a passel of howling Boxers off to meet their ancestors, and I rather suspected that the *anting-antings* of the Pulajans would also fail to make their gullible wearers bulletproof. No, the natives' trinkets would not save them. The real problem was the hard fighting we'd have to endure until the point sank in.

Yet I was prepared to wade hip-deep in blood—other people's, of course, not mine—if that's what it took to lay my hands on Surlang, so I asked impatiently, "What's the nearest garrison to the south, Colonel?"

"Balangiga, some forty miles down the coast," he answered. "The track through the interior is nearly impassable, though. If you're right about this fellow Surlang heading in that direction, I wouldn't expect him to reach Balangiga for at least two weeks, or maybe even a month."

I didn't agree. Foote simply didn't know Surlang; that demon had just traversed the daunting mountain chains and dense jungles of Leyte, crossed to Samar, and organized an insurrection—all in little more than a week. I was certain that he would continue to move like greased lightning, and I didn't have time to educate Foote on the brute's speed and determination. All I said was "I request transportation to Balangiga, sir, and the sooner the better."

Lieutenant Colonel Foote looked at Longbottom. "That should be no problem. Captain Longbottom is going there to take over Company C. You can leave together when the next transport is available."

"When will that be, sir?" I inquired anxiously, not wanting Surlang to have too big a lead on me.

"I can't really say. It depends on when Company C decides to send a boat this way for supplies and mail. It could be tomorrow, or it could be two weeks from now."

As things turned out, it was nearly three weeks before Company C got around to sending for its mail. Those three weeks were an eternity to me, not knowing if Fiona and Alice were dead or alive, and all the while certain that Surlang was out in the wilderness plotting further bloodshed and destruction.

Basey was not without its attractions, however. As I idled around the headquarters waiting for transportation, my eye fell upon a lithe Filipina drawing water from a well. I watched her strong brown body draw up the bucket, and despite my fondness for Alice, I felt the unmistakable pangs of arousal. The point is made if one understands that the distaff garb on Samar consisted of a tightly wrapped sarong that showed the hips and breasts to exquisite advantage, the whole effect being crowned with a slit up the side clear to the buttocks. What was more, the gals on Samar were intriguingly fetching and, unlike their sisters on Mindanao, quite open-minded about dalliances with foreign officers.

I sauntered over to this comely siren and doffed my Stetson. "May I give you a hand, Senorita?" I asked with a flashing white smile.

She eyed me only a moment before smiling. "*Si,*" she answered, not at all shyly. Her brown eyes had a mischievous sparkle and her tawny skin was smooth and unblemished. You've stumbled upon a gem, Fenny, I congratulated myself. I hauled up the bucket and poured the water into the urn she had brought along for that purpose. With her urn filled, the lovely miss balanced it expertly on her head and turned to go.

"Hold on," I urged. "Er, perhaps I might have a drink of your cool water, *si?*"

She turned, and stood there with a delicate hand on a rounded hip. "I think you have earned a drink, *Capitán.*" Her Spanish was fluent, suggesting that her family was of some substance hereabouts. She poured the clear liquid into my cupped hands and I drank deeply.

"Ah, many thanks," I gulped. "To whom do I owe this welcome refreshment?"

Her warm brown eyes looked straight into my blue ones as she spoke. "I am Lenai Jacosalen. I have not seen you in Basey before, have I?"

"No," I agreed. "I am new to your lovely island. But I forget my manners. I am Fenwick Travers. It is a pleasure to make your acquaintance."

"Fenwee?" she asked, puzzlement on her lovely countenance.

I chuckled as her sweet lips struggled to get out the proper sound. "*Si,* that's perfect."

Lenai didn't think so, though. "I shall call you *capitán*. The American *capitán.*"

She could have called me George Washington had she wanted, the only important thing being that Lenai and I were soon chatting like old friends. I walked her down a dirt lane past flocks of scrawny chickens and an occasional hog to her home, where I met Senor Jacosalen, a pudgy little character who apparently had earned a living collecting taxes for the dons and aimed to do the same thing for the next thirty years for Uncle Sam.

If Lenai's pater wasn't thrilled to see an American officer sniffing after his offspring, he hid it well enough. Over a cup of the fiery home-brewed palm wine, I got to meet the rest of the clan. It was a pleasant enough day, and when I retired to my billet for the evening, I had a firm notion of how to spend my time while I waited for the boat to Balangiga.

And so when on a quiet September morning a proa, one of the indigenous coastal lighters of Samar, slipped out of Basey and headed south through Leyte Gulf, I was on board wistfully wondering when I might once again return to Basey and the sweet favors of Lenai.

With me were Henry, Bustos, and Longbottom. The proa was under the command of 1st Lt. Edward Bumpus, one of the platoon leaders of Company C. He was an amiable fellow who liked the notion of detached duty at Balangiga but detested both the village and its unpredictable inhabitants. Bumpus told us quite a bit about Captain Connell, his commander. Connell was of a mind that the way to win the allegiance of the Visayans was to treat them fair and respect their customs. Damned poppycock, insisted Bumpus, and for my money, I agreed. After all, how would we have reacted if a boatload of Visayans showed up in San Francisco armed to the teeth but promising to let the citizens parade about on the Fourth of July and not to heave them in the calaboose unless they got a trial? Would the good burghers greet their brown conquerors with open arms and vows of fidelity? Not very damned likely, and neither was it probable that the Visayans would submit to us without a good reason for doing so. So far, Bumpus said, we hadn't given them one.

We had smooth sailing south along the coast of Samar and reached Balangiga in the late afternoon. The town was situated where the Balangiga River emptied into a narrow bay, which in turn emptied into Leyte Gulf. The proa entered the bay and sailed up the river about a hundred yards to where a rickety quay jutted out into the murky water. No sooner was the proa lashed to the quay than I went ashore with Henry and Bustos and took the lay of the land.

A few listless children, completely naked and burned a dark shade of mahogany by the tropical sun, watched us as we disembarked. Bumpus had not overstated the sorry state of Balangiga. Next to it, Basey was a veritable metropolis. The village was a backwater of dilapidated nipa huts that had sprung up around the few mold-covered structures erected by the Spanish. Balangiga was laid out in more or less a grid pattern, with a large Catholic church right near the quay. Between the church and the river was a two-story convent. The convent, which abutted the church, had been converted into a hospital on the lower level and sleeping quarters for the American officers on the upper level.

The landward side of the church opened onto a large plaza. There conical tents had been erected to serve as guard posts and prisoner detention centers. Among the tents wandered herds of pigs, rooting and excreting freely. Overlooking this scene of rustic slovenliness, near the entrance to the church, was a tall bell tower.

Across the plaza from the church was an old Spanish courthouse, or tribunal as it was termed. It too was a two-story structure, the upper level of which had been converted into a barracks and an arms room. The lower level housed a mess hall and the office of the native chief of police.

On the far side of the tribunal from the church ran a dusty street generally parallel to the river. In an open yard along this lane stood Company C's field kitchen, which could be reached by a wide wooden staircase that descended from the upstairs barracks in the converted tribunal. Scattered about near the field kitchen were more open tents, where the troops apparently took their meals when they didn't want to be crammed into the tiny mess hall.

Beyond the field kitchen stood large multifamily nipa huts. Since the barracks over the tribunal could not house all the troops, these large nipa huts also had been converted into barracks. The rest of the village consisted of tiny, single-room nipa huts used by the natives.

No sooner had I gotten oriented than a handsome captain of infantry strode up and introduced himself. "Hello, I'm Captain Connell. Captain Longbottom, I presume?"

He extended his hand, so I shook it. "No, I'm Captain Travers. That's Longbottom on the proa."

Captain Connell looked at me quizzically, so I explained about the brazen kidnapping and the pursuit of Surlang, the fight up the coast at Basey, and how I thought that Surlang was coming this way. Then Longbottom joined us and introductions were made again. Connell offered to put the two of us up in the convent. "It's not much, but it will keep the infernal Samar rains off your heads. Your men can bunk with the troops," he added, referring to Bustos and Henry.

Connell called to a corporal to have our things carried to the convent, and then he took us for a tour of his encampment. First stop was at the office of the mayor, or alcalde as the locals called him, one Pedro Abayan. Present with Abayan was the native chief of police, a dark-complected rascal named Sanchez, whose height bespoke Visayan blood. With flitting black eyes, he seemed to size up us newcomers. Connell made the introductions. These two luminaries shook our hands and solemnly assured us that our coming was the highest honor ever accorded them in their benighted lives. There were more handshakes at this and then we took our leave.

As we went, Connell boasted, "I've established rather good relations with Mayor Abayan, and I've even extended the hand of friendship to the local padre. These villagers are pretty devout Catholics, so I figure that one way to win their allegiance is by displaying respect to the good father."

Connell stopped and pointed to a group of shawled senoras approaching the town from the fields. "See there? Those women are on their way to church for some feast day or another right now."

Following Connell's finger, I saw several groups of women, all of them unusually bundled up for Samaran gals, who tended to show quite a bit of skin. As they passed through Connell's checkpoints, the sentries waved them on, but they stopped any men with them to search for weapons.

"Yes, religion means everything to these people," continued Connell. "That's why I make it a point to attend mass weekly with them. I suggest you do the same, Captain Longbottom."

Longbottom waggled his head vaguely, as though he might consider this, but as for me I had to bite my tongue to keep from snorting aloud at such tripe. Bumpus had been right about Connell. From what I'd seen so far in the Philippines, Americans didn't win the allegiance of any of these natives. They had no desire to be our willing servants, and at best we formed no more than uneasy truces with them based on mutual fear. If Connell thought otherwise, then I had grave doubts about him being able to grasp the threat that the approach of Surlang posed.

"Er, how long have you been here with your company, Captain Connell?" I asked, suspiciously eyeing the villagers we passed. These latter squatted on their haunches in circles smoking huge cheroots as they watched their trained fighting cocks ripping themselves bloody, but they rose and bowed respectfully as we neared. They appeared tame enough, yet who could really tell what thoughts lurked behind those dark eyes?

"I've only been here a few months, Captain Travers," responded Connell. "Colonel Foote wanted to secure this end of Samar while his other companies seized the east and west coasts. There's been little fighting, thank God, and we've had no serious incidents."

"Oh?" I asked lightly. "If you've established such good relations with the populace, can you tell me what's going on over there?" I pointed across the plaza to where a large number of native prisoners were lolling beneath a canvas awning under the watch of some bored soldiers.

"Oh, them." Connell smiled. "That's just a measure I felt was justified. There have been a few attempts to steal rifles, and I told Abayan that I'd not stand for it. I ordered him to have Sanchez bring in the young men from the surrounding area. I plan to hold them here for a few days just to establish the notion in their minds that we mean business. In the meantime, we can use the labor to clean up the area and beat back the encroaching jungle. The Filipinos are rather untidy, you know. They toss all their trash out the windows of their nipa huts and there it lies until the monsoon washes it away. Dreadful sanitation."

Apparently, though, Connell's civic works program was not pressed too energetically. Most of the prisoners sat about on their brown backsides. One or two were on their feet, wandering about the plaza hacking halfheartedly at the numerous weeds all about. A chill ran through me as I watched them, for they did their hacking with bolos.

It was as I thought: Connell had damned little experience with fighting natives. He clearly believed everything in his precinct was under control and that he was surrounded by jolly yokels all quite content to be under the protection of a benevolent Uncle Sam. With Surlang on his way, this realization hardly warmed the cockles of my heart.

Longbottom, predictably, saw nothing amiss in Connell's attitude; he gave a satisfied nod as if to say he concurred that all was well in Balangiga. "Well, if I'm to take over this company, Captain Connell, why don't you introduce me to the chain of command. I've already met Lieutenant Bumpus, of course, but I'd like to meet the first sergeant and platoon sergeants."

"Then let me lead on," suggested Connell genially.

I begged off from the grand tour, since I hadn't come to Balangiga to shake the hand of every man in Company C. "If you'll excuse me, Captain Connell, I think I can be of more use scouting up the coast toward the north. I want to be off with Sergeant Jefferson and my Macabebe at once."

Longbottom seemed suddenly uncomfortable with the notion of me rattling about unattended in his future bailiwick. Indeed, indiscreet conduct on my part might have negative repercussions on his tenure as the commander of Company C, even though he had not yet been officially installed in office.

"Perhaps you ought to stay closer to the village for a few days, Fenny. You know, familiarize yourself with the terrain a bit before you decide on a plan to capture the Moro. I'm as anxious to take this Surlang fellow as you are, but in truth we don't even know if he is really in the area."

The last thing I needed, of course, was Longbottom's advice. I decided, however, to put on the face of pure reasonableness. "Perhaps you've got a point, Joshua. But since I rather think that time is of the essence, I'll split the baby as it were. I'll take along one of Captain Connell's men as a guide. Captain," I asked, turning to Connell, "can you oblige me?"

Connell nodded. "Why not take Sergeant Markley? He knows the area hereabouts as well as anyone."

"Sergeant Markley?" I echoed. The name was familiar. "Why, I believe I had the pleasure of meeting Sergeant Markley in Manila."

"Oh? Well, it's a small army, eh?" said Connell. Then he ordered a passing private to fetch the good sergeant, and in a few minutes Markley's large frame lumbered into view.

"Sergeant Markley, I believe you know Captain Travers?"

"Yes, sir. We got acquainted chasing after a Moro one fine morning."

I smiled at this, as did Captain Connell. "Well, apparently that Moro is still on the loose, and word has it he's coming this way."

"Surlang?" growled Sergeant Markley, suddenly tense. "Here on Samar?"

"Yep," I assured him gravely.

Captain Connell continued. "Captain Travers wants to go on a patrol to the north. Guide him along the main trails and assist him in any way you can."

Sergeant Markley seemed agreeable enough to this, but Longbottom looked as though he wanted to argue the point further. In the face of my determination and Connell's lack of concern, however, he went along peacefully when Connell steered him off for the rest of his tour.

I quickly brought Markley up to speed about Surlang and his depredations, mentioning that he had kidnapped two American ladies, which prompted an abrupt, "Goddamn, we should have mowed him down when we had the Colt machine gun trained on him."

"My thoughts, exactly," I concurred, "but that's all water under the bridge now. The only thing that's important is that we don't let him slip away again."

21

Balangiga, Samar
September 27, 1901

Markley quickly gathered his gear, and then we were on our way along with Henry and Bustos. I hadn't mentioned to either Connell or Longbottom the fact that I intended to stay the night in the bush. We crossed the river on a *barota,* as canoes on Samar were termed, and then headed north on foot. The countryside along the coast was a dizzying pattern of small rice paddies as far as the eye could see. To our right, about a mile from the coast, rugged hills rose at a steep angle to the narrow strip of cultivated land. Those slopes were heavily jungled, a natural haven for any lurking Pulajans. As we went, we passed sullen natives in their fields who eyed us indifferently and then went back to their drudgery. Their glances were a bit too indifferent, I thought, as though they expected we might be only temporary nuisances.

I quickly noted that most foot traffic through the paddies seemed to move along one central dike that ran parallel to the coast. This dike apparently served as the local thoroughfare, and we used it to explore the neighborhood. Careful to stay in extended order, and with a round chambered in our Krags at all times, we poked about from paddy to paddy and from hut to hut. In this manner we spent the hours until sundown, when Markley finally suggested that we ought to be heading back to Balangiga.

"We're not going back," I said flatly. I pointed to a wide spot on the main dike where it intersected a smaller dike that formed a boundary of a rice paddy. "We'll spend the night right there. I have a hunch that Surlang's lurking in this neck of the woods and he'll show his hand directly." Then, I thought grimly, I'd set Bustos on him like a bulldog on a burglar.

Markley didn't argue, for he had no love for Surlang. Together with Henry and me, Markley huddled under a section of mosquito netting in the dark as Bustos stretched out comfortably in the mud, oblivious to the horde of insects swarming over him from head to foot. Despite the cramped conditions, we all nodded off.

It was two hours past midnight when a nudge on my shoulder wakened me. "Whaaa . . . ?" I sputtered with a start, only to have a hand clamped across my mouth.

It was Bustos, who whispered tensely, "Surlang comes."

I nodded and he released me. I wakened the others and we quietly cleared for action, casting off the netting and leveling our Krags. To the north a small group was approaching along the dike. In the moonlight I could see the unmistakable outline of white capes flapping in the night breeze. Pulajans! I realized with a jolt.

I peered breathlessly into the dark and saw that near the head of the approaching column was a fellow wearing the khaki uniform of a Tagalog officer. This might be Lukban, Aguinaldo's lieutenant. More ominously, I saw that the figure directly ahead of him was sporting a turban; it could only be Surlang. By Christ, the precious map was almost within my grasp again!

I whispered for everyone to spread out and not to fire until I did. Bustos eased the *patok* from his belt and waited quietly by my side. When the approaching group was twenty feet from our position, it halted. The lead man had suddenly noticed the four dark shadows on the path before him.

"Take them!" I shouted, firing my Krag. Immediately the others followed suit, and a volley crashed forth. The leader toppled lifeless into the fetid paddy waters below the dike, and then we were on them. Henry seized Surlang just as he drew his kris; then Bustos rushed past me and lashed out with his *patok*. The blow fell on Surlang's turban, and although it failed to penetrate the dense matting of silk, it knocked the Moro senseless. With Surlang stunned, I bore in with sudden boldness and pinned him to the ground, while Markley vaulted past us to take the Tagalog.

"Stand, damn you!" cried Markley, but one of the Pulajans behind the Tagalog rushed forward to grapple with Markley. The startled Tagalog took to his heels with the rest of the Pulajans, leaving only Surlang and Markley's assailant behind. Markley threw his opponent to the ground, and fired two quick shots into his heart.

Meanwhile, Surlang had revived and was putting up a furious struggle.

"Sergeant Markley!" I called, as Henry, Bustos, and I held down the enraged Moro. "Give this bastard a butt stroke or two, will you?"

"Glad to oblige, sir," replied Markley calmly, raising the stock of his Krag and bringing it down with sickening force on Surlang's head. The frantic Moro shuddered, stiffened, and then went limp.

Then Henry scampered off in the direction the Pulajans had gone and came back carrying something. "Look at this, Fenny. I saw the Tagalog drop it as he ran."

It was an ornate Spanish ceremonial sword of the finest Toledo steel. Markley whistled appreciatively. "No peasant soldier carries a beauty like that. That fellow in the uniform was none other than General Lukban, Captain Travers. I think some big trouble is brewing."

I nodded somberly. "And I say the chief instigator is lying right here in front of us." I gave Surlang a savage kick for emphasis, and he let out a pained grunt. Then I quickly searched his prostrate form for my precious map, explaining to the others, "He might have more weapons, you see."

Although I searched everywhere on Surlang's person, even in the silver betel nut box he carried about his neck, the map was nowhere to be found. The bastard must have secreted it somewhere in his travels. Damn his hide, I concluded angrily, I'd have to make him reveal its whereabouts. Surlang was coming around now, and I gave him a few more stiff kicks to clear his head. Bending down, I tore off his turban and seized him by his topknot.

"We have a few things to chat about, Senor," I growled in Spanish.

The Moro merely glared back at me. "So, it is the white *capitán* from Zamboanga," he sneered contemptuously, his lips curling as he spoke to show his blackened teeth. I could barely suppress a shudder at the sight of him, for up close Surlang looked like a fiend straight from hell. "First you killed or captured my followers in Manila and stole what was mine. Then you followed me to Palanan to once more steal what was mine. Well, you failed—but I didn't. I tracked you to Zamboanga and stole what was yours!" he boasted, and then gave a revolting snicker.

By God! This cur had been stalking me in Zamboanga! I thought that Fiona and Alice had simply been unfortunate victims of a random slave raid. I had never imagined that the whole episode had been a carefully contrived campaign of revenge. Fortunately, neither Markley nor Henry could understand Spanish, so they couldn't fathom the grave accusations Surlang was leveling at me.

"Where are the women?" I demanded, shaken.

"You'll never see them again, not in this life," he hissed venomously, contempt dripping from each word as he spoke.

I slapped him hard, but the sneer stayed in place.

"Bustos," I commanded, "bind this animal. Henry," I added darkly, "start a fire."

"A fire, Captain?" queried Markley. "That's not very safe, is it? I mean there's more Pulajans out there than the ones we just ran off."

"They won't be coming back," I snapped. "They have no idea what our numbers are, and the fact that we feel secure enough to light a fire will convince them we're here in strength. Henry," I repeated firmly, "make that fire."

"Okay, Fenny," he said, "but I hope you know what you're doing."

"I do," I assured him. In a short while Henry, with the help of Markley, had a cheery little blaze going. When the flames were hot enough to sear the skin on my face, I turned to Bustos. Pointing to the Moro I ordered, "Find out from Surlang where the white women are."

"*Si,*" grunted the Macabebe with a ferocious grin. Surlang, who had kept his face in a contemptuous smirk up to this point, suddenly blanched. Bustos stuck the ax head of his *patok* into the flames until it glowed red hot. Then with an expression of pure bliss he faced Surlang and laid the hot steel along the side of the Moro's corded neck.

Surlang grimaced as the smell of burning flesh filled the air, and beads of sweat appeared on his brow. Yet he remained silent.

"My, God," said Sergeant Markley, appalled. "Captain Travers, don't tell me you intend to torture this man."

Henry too was looking at me nervously, for this wasn't exactly the sort of behavior one normally expected from an officer and a gentleman.

"Yes, that's exactly what I intend to do, Sergeant," I informed him grimly. "Do you recall that I told you this beast kidnapped two American women?"

"Yes, sir," replied Sergeant Markley.

"Well," I told him, "one of them was my fiancée and the other was Captain Longbottom's wife."

"I didn't know that, sir," stammered Markley, appalled. "I'm real sorry."

I brushed aside his condolences. "I plan to tear the location of Mrs. Longbottom and my fiancée from this animal even if I have to reduce him to a human cinder in the process. And then I plan to personally put a bullet in his brain so he can never kill again!"

Bustos plunged his ax head back into the fire. Now Surlang struggled at his bonds and began cursing a blue streak in his Moro tongue. Undeterred, the Macabebe gleefully seized the Moro's topknot and then gave the other side of Surlang's neck the same treatment.

Surlang let out a high-pitched yowl, like the shriek of a dog with its foot caught in a steel trap. "White pig!" he screamed at me. "Your whores are in Jolo, and they will stay there for the rest of their lives!"

I was jolted by his outburst. Alice and Fiona were in Jolo? Why, that meant they had been sold as slaves to the sultan of Jolo, just as Pershing had surmised. Which meant they were in the clutches of the single most powerful Moro of them all.

This information was alarming, but at least I knew where Alice was. I pulled my sword from its scabbard, for now it was time to turn to the subject of the missing map. With a tight little smile, I put the point on Surlang's Adam's apple and applied pressure.

"Now, you left-handed sidewinder," I hissed, "there's another little matter between you and me."

I saw the fear in Surlang's eyes as he realized I was quite prepared to kill him. It was then that a voice called out in the night. "Ho, the fire!"

Markley peered into the gloom. "It's Captain Connell," he announced, relief in his voice.

"Come on in, Connell," I called, putting up my sword reluctantly.

Connell came forward at the head of a squad. With him was Longbottom. "Sergeant Betron here," he said, indicating the platoon sergeant at his side, "told me you hadn't returned at dusk, Travers. It's way too dangerous for such a small group out here in the boondocks all alone. We've been searching for you for hours with no luck until we heard the gunfire. Thank God you're all right. . . ."

Then his voice trailed off as his eyes fell on Surlang, singed neck and all, and then on Bustos's glowing *patok*. "What the hell is going on here, Captain Travers?" he demanded stiffly.

"It's as I thought," said Longbottom disdainfully. "I told you that Captain Travers's methods bear careful scrutiny. It looks like we got here just in the nick of time."

"Longbottom, you dolt," I countered hotly, "this is the murderer who took your wife. Nothing's too harsh for him, as far as I'm concerned, and I'll tell you something else. I think that he's in league with General Lukban. I'm telling you the Pulajans have got their bowels in an uproar, and things will be getting hot real soon in Balangiga."

"You mean they aim to attack?" asked Connell.

"That's exactly what I mean," I retorted levelly.

"He's right, sir," spoke up Sergeant Markley. "I saw a Tagalog officer just an hour ago coming along this trail. We ambushed the group he was with and took the Moro. And Sergeant Jefferson found something else."

Henry handed over the Toledo blade. Longbottom and Connell eyed it and each other with concern. "Let's get back to town," Connell said hurriedly.

"Er, why don't you go ahead and take Sergeant Markley with you?" I suggested. "My men and I will be along shortly, as soon as we're finished here."

All I needed was another hour or so with Surlang and he'd be babbling as freely as a mountain brook. When I was done, I'd kill him, plain and simple, and with no regrets. Surlang was a mad-dog killer, and there was no doubt he would get me unless I got him first. Captain Connell, though, shook his head, for he had read my intent.

"We can't do that, Travers. The prisoner comes with me. He'll be treated fairly and then sent into a regular camp to be interned. I'm sorry about your fiancée and Captain Longbottom's wife, but that's the way it will have to be. Sergeant Betron, you and Sergeant Markley bring the prisoner along."

I raged impotently as they cut Surlang loose and then marched him off into the night. Furious, I motioned to Henry and Bustos to follow along. That's when I saw Surlang's kris lying in the mud. It was beautifully wrought, with an ivory handle and intricate blood channels carefully formed in the tempered blade. A hank of what I guessed was the hair of some unfortunate victim adorned the carved handle like a saber cord. I picked up the kris and studied the blade carefully in the moonlight. It bore seventeen copper fillings. My God, Surlang had killed nearly twenty men! I shoved the blade through my belt and tramped off into the night.

22

September 28, 1901

Once back in Balangiga, Surlang was put into the prisoner tent with his hands bound and then Captain Connell doubled the guard. That done, it was time to turn in. Sergeant Markley found a place for Henry and Bustos in the barracks above the tribunal; Longbottom and I turned in at the convent.

I passed a night of fitful sleep. My heart was heavy with fear that Surlang would somehow slip away in the dark. Several times I awoke to check with the sentries outside the prisoner tent, and each time they had produced Surlang, bound and glaring, for my inspection.

In addition to doubling the guard, Captain Connell responded to Surlang's presence by issuing orders to Mayor Abayan that at the crack of dawn parties of natives were to be set to work hacking back the shrubs that encroached upon Balangiga from every side, thereby interfering with clear fields of fire. "If Lukban comes for the Moro, we'll be ready," Connell assured me before he retired.

At first light, I was up and on the plaza. Reveille sounded and the troops slowly roused themselves. Soon the smell of frying bacon drifted to my nostrils from the field kitchen and I headed in that direction. Connell and Bumpus remained asleep, it apparently being their custom not to arise until after the troops had breakfasted. Longbottom snored right along with them.

I walked onto the plaza and studied the stirring village. Across the plaza toward the tribunal, groups of prisoners were gathering for the day's fatigue details in obedience to Connell's order. A sleepy corporal was handing out bolos to the workers, an act that made the hackles on the back of my neck rise. I for one disagreed with the notion of natives roaming about with ready access to bolos, but this evidently was the way Connell had run things before we arrived, and who was I to tell him how to run his business?

Here and there a groggy soldier could be seen heading in the direction of the field kitchen. Behind me the church bell began ringing, no doubt calling the faithful to worship. I turned and looked in the direction of the bell tower. It was Sanchez, the chief of police, pulling on the bell rope as though his life depended on it. Funny, I thought, I wouldn't have pegged that rogue as the religious sort.

Bemused, I turned to go. Suddenly pandemonium broke loose all around me as the docile prisoners abruptly raised their bolos and with shrill whoops attacked the stupefied soldiers!

In the rice fields north of the village, red-clad figures arose in the morning mists, all armed with bolos. From hundreds of throats erupted the dreaded battle cry of the Pulajans, *"Tad-tad! Tad-tad!"*—Chop! Chop! A chorus of conch-shell horns sounded, and the massed Pulajans advanced at a run. On they came, wave after wave of wild-eyed fanatics, their bolos gleaming viciously in the morning sun.

"Turn out the guard!" I bellowed. "We're under attack! Pulajans!" I started to run back to the convent where my Colt lay on my bunk, but I stopped in my tracks when a mass of Pulajans charged toward the stairs into the convent. They hacked down the overmatched sentry who tried to fend them off with bayonet thrusts, and then boiled up the stairs and in upon the sleeping officers. I stood rooted to the spot as the shrieks of dying men erupted from inside the convent. Then a window flew open and Captain Connell, still in his flannel drawers, hurtled through the air to the ground below.

Close behind him came Longbottom, with a nasty gash across his brow. Longbottom landed, arose unsteadily on a twisted ankle, and followed Connell straight for me. Several Pulajans, seeing the fugitives, headed to intercept them.

"Help, Travers!" screamed Connell, stretching out his arms imploringly as he came. He was calling on the wrong fellow, however, for tangling with mobs of maddened natives waving bolos just wasn't in my nature. I turned on my heels and sprinted for the tribunal, looking fearfully over my shoulder as I went. Connell's screams turned to shrieks as the Pulajans surrounded him, then he let out one high-pitched yip and fell moaning. By then I was at the tribunal. The sentry at the entrance was dead, his head nearly severed. Inside was a scene straight from a slaughterhouse, as stunned soldiers struggled with howling Filipinos.

One Pulajan turned as I blundered into this hell. He had a Krag, but the safety mechanism was engaged, and the miscreant had no earthly idea how to disengage it, which prevented him from gunning me down immediately. As he struggled unsuccessfully with the bolt, I lashed out in a blind panic, smashing him hard with a fist to the chin. The Pulajan grunted and sagged to floor, and I grabbed the Krag as he went down.

Almost insane with fear, I bolted back onto the plaza, gibbering and hooting for help. All I found was a frenzied Filipino who rushed upon me, bolo held high. My guts frozen with dread, I crouched and delivered a crushing butt stroke to my assailant's head just as he closed with me, the maple stock dropping him like a sack of oats.

Then, with eyes agog and spittle running down my slack jaw, I scanned the plaza. Connell was in pieces, his severed arms scattered about him so that he looked more like a scarecrow that had been ripped apart by a high wind than anything human. The Pulajans had Longbottom spread-eagled on the ground and were about to butcher him as well.

"Help! Oh, my God, help me!" screeched Longbottom piteously.

I immediately resolved to let the idiot fend for himself. He was clearly doomed, and why draw down lightning upon oneself in a thunderstorm, eh? But then Longbottom emitted such a heart-wrenching wail that I wavered, then thought, oh, what the hell, maybe I should at least make a try at saving the luckless bastard. Perhaps if I'd had my senses completely about me I would have scampered off straightaway. But I wasn't thinking clearly, you see, and that was probably why I disengaged the safety with my finger, threw the Krag to my shoulder, and sighted. The rifle roared and a boloman pitched over dead. I rather enjoyed that, so I worked the bolt and fired again, then again and again.

Four Pulajans lay dead before the fight was gone from the rest of them. The survivors ran jabbering for the convent, and Longbottom was on his feet hobbling to me as fast as his injured ankle would let him.

"What the hell's going on, Fenny?" he cried, panic written all over his face.

"Surlang's friends have come to set him free, damn you," I retorted. "I should have killed him last night when I had the chance."

"What will we do now?" gasped Longbottom, shock robbing his mind of any capacity to form a course of action. Behind me the screams and shots continued from inside the tribunal, especially the upstairs, which served as a barracks. I knew we'd have to find shelter somewhere, but where?

As my rattled brain cast about for a plan, I suddenly realized that the Filipinos seemed to have mainly bolos, not rifles, and that the greatest volume of fire was coming from behind the tribunal where the field kitchen was located. That meant there were Americans in that direction, and they were fighting back. Where there were numbers, there would be safety, I decided.

"Let's go!" I yelled, running along the front of the tribunal and around the corner, with Longbottom following as best he could.

In the yard between the field kitchen and the rear of the tribunal, a vista of utter carnage unfolded before my eyes. Dead soldiers lay everywhere; those still alive fought off their attackers with brooms, sticks, and even the wooden benches on which they had sat down to breakfast. One big sergeant careened by with a stiletto handle protruding from his ear and the tip of the blade extending from his throat. Blood streamed down his body, but he was swinging a club ferociously and rallying a small cluster of half-armed fugitives around him.

Safety! I thought with relief. I thrust myself into this tiny band as they fought their way to the nearest nipa barracks. The Pulajans yielded before the maddened soldiers as they worked the bolts of their Krags and blew a corridor through their tormentors.

"Pick up more ammo!" I screamed to Longbottom over my shoulder, petrified lest our protectors run dry in the midst of the foe.

Obediently, Longbottom pulled a Mills belt from a fallen soldier lying in our path and handed it to me. I passed it on to the fellows up front who were doing the actual fighting, careful to stay sheltered behind them all the while. Battling every inch of the way, we pushed forward to a nipa hut where soldiers were at all the windows pouring fire out upon their attackers. At the door was Sergeant Markley, waving us on.

"Come on, boys, come on! You've almost made it!" he cried.

Then we were in, and I was weeping with joy like a woman at a wedding and hugging a grizzled private when someone cried out: "It's Sergeant Betron, he's coming this way!"

I peeked through a window and saw it was true. Betron too had a knot of men around him and was smashing and stabbing his way toward Markley's nipa hut. The Pulajans could not stand before Betron, and parted their ranks until he was at the foot of the stairs outside the door.

"How many men do you have, Markley?" demanded Betron, as his men fended off the encircling Filipinos.

"Four, Betron," Markley shouted in reply.

"Armed?"

"To the teeth. We have extra Krags too," he added, motioning to rifle racks between the bunks behind him.

In an instant Betron knew what we had to do. "Pass out those Krags and then follow me."

"Where?" Markley asked doubtfully.

I chimed in too, none too eager to venture forth into the fray. "Now hold on, Sergeant Betron. Markley's got a fine little nest right here. I think we—"

Betron, however, had not struggled this far just to debate his salvation with me. "Just do it!" he roared, and the men hopped to. Betron had decided that unless we counterattacked instantly, nothing would be left of Company C except for dead men. The longer the Pulajans had free run of the town, the longer they would have to gather up Krags and figure out how to put them to deadly use, something he didn't have time to explain to me.

When the men were ready, Betron drew a deep breath and growled, "Let's go."

Still unconvinced of the wisdom of all this, I protested that I was an officer, by God, and would not be overruled by a mere platoon sergeant, when I was ejected by main force from the hut. Out the soldiers sallied, screaming like men possessed. A dozen bolomen immediately confronted them. The troopers loosed a volley and closed with their bayonets. That was more than this band of Filipinos could stand, and they flew for their lives.

"Let them go," ordered Betron. "We've got to clear the main barracks."

The area between the field kitchen and the rear of the tribunal was still choked with struggling figures. Betron realized that the fastest way in would be through the main entrance, which faced the plaza. He led his ragtag command at the double around the corner of the tribunal, cleared away a lurking boloman with a quick hip shot, and gained the main entrance. From the upstairs we could hear the sound of a tremendous struggle. Clearly, there were still soldiers alive above.

Betron halted and looked back at his men. "Ready?" he roared, for his fighting blood was up now.

Sweaty, pale faces nodded in response, and Markley added grimly, "Yep." I said nothing, for with my knees audibly knocking together, I found I had temporarily lost the power of speech. Longbottom, for his part, was beyond caring. His twisted ankle was swollen to huge proportions, and he had picked up so many bolo slashes along the way that he was tinted a gory crimson.

"Then let's get it done!" snarled Betron savagely.

He thundered up the stairs at a dead run, his Krag at the ready.

At the top of the stairs was an open orderly room, its floor strewn with dead bodies. A thick knot of bolomen was at the far end of the room, hacking at a wooden door. Right in the midst of them, shrieking bloody hell at the holdouts inside, was Surlang! The planks of the door were splintered, and through the gaps whoever was inside was fighting back with bolos of their own, thrusting the blades into the attackers as best they could.

"The arms room!" cried Markley. "If they get in there, it's all over!"

I for one didn't need to hear anything further; I fired my Krag into the crowd of Pulajans. A boloman shrieked and fell. Markley fired, and then a fusillade erupted from the soldiers around us. Undaunted, Surlang uttered a great oath and charged.

He leaped straight for me, but Markley blocked his way, meeting the Moro with a fierce upstroke of his rifle stock. The full force of the blow caught Surlang on the chin and rolled him across the floor, where he lay under a window, dazed. Then with a fierce yell, the soldiers were on the demoralized bolomen, who in the close confines of this fight couldn't raise their blades to swing in self-defense.

"Give 'em hell, boys!" I whooped from behind as they closed upon the Filipinos, their bayonet thrusts ripping through rib cages and bellies. "For the old Ninth!"

I was delirious with joy now that the tide had changed, and even got bold enough to jam the barrel of my Krag between struggling bodies to blast a Pulajan or two into eternity. Within a minute the uneven struggle for control of the room was over. A dozen natives lay in a bloody twisted heap at our feet. Then I turned to Surlang, intent on finishing what Longbottom and Connell had interrupted the night before.

But Surlang was gone! While we were distracted by the melee, he had slipped out the window into the yard below. Damn, I raged, but then the door to the arms room opened slowly and out stepped a grinning Henry.

"Am I ever glad to see you," he declared. Behind him was a glowering Bustos.

"Kill many Pulajan, si?" Bustos leered evilly.

"Si," I replied; but we weren't done yet, for Sergeant Betron bellowed above the din, "Everyone grab more ammo and as many Krags as you can carry."

The soldiers hurried to the rear entrance to the barracks. The wooden steps that formerly led down to the field kitchen had collapsed beneath the weight of soldiers and bolomen struggling up from the mess tents below. Sergeant Betron stood in the open door and had a bird's-eye view of the fight down in the yard.

"Let 'em have it!" he ordered, and the soldiers opened up. Regulars all, and hence crack shots, they mowed down the Pulajans. The beleaguered soldiers in the yard, given breathing room by our fire, rallied as we tossed down Krags and ammunition belts. Now the fire redoubled, driving away the Pulajans in a hail of hot lead.

Sergeant Betron raised his hand. "Hold your fire and follow me," he commanded. His stalwart band, now reinforced by Henry and Bustos, doubled back across the orderly room and down the stairs to the plaza. I clung anxiously to the tail of the group, not at all keen to be left anywhere in Balangiga by myself. Nor was Longbottom. Reviving now that the momentum was shifting to our side, he pleaded desperately for help, crying out for me not to leave him and clinging to my arm like a damned leech. Had we been on our own, I would have shucked him like a husk from an ear of corn, but there were too many witnesses for that. Instead I took him by the scruff of the neck and propelled him none too gently down the stairs. When we staggered forth from the tribunal we saw that the Filipinos were running for dear life everywhere.

"Let's finish 'em off," declared Sergeant Betron grimly.

He formed a ragged skirmish line and then marched it across the plaza, driving a crushed herd of Pulajans before him all the way to the riverbank. Many of them tried to save themselves by jumping in and swimming for the far shore. It was a turkey shoot, however, and not a single Pulajan made it. When it was over, Betron raised his hand for a cease-fire.

Behind us the sound of shots had tapered off from a barrage to scattered pop-pops, as enraged soldiers tagged the last few fugitives. Then all was quiet. A drum began to roll in the plaza, and from all corners of Balangiga soldiers dragged themselves and their slain comrades to the sound.

A squad was sent into the convent, where Lieutenant Bumpus's corpse and that of the company surgeon were found in their beds, sliced almost beyond recognition. None of C Company's original officers had survived the onslaught.

Sergeant Betron, as the ranking sergeant to survive the massacre, took the roll and then turned to face Longbottom and me. Now that Connell was dead, Longbottom was the commander by default. He, however, was in no shape to take the report. His crusted uniform gave mute evidence to the several pints of blood that he had lost, and he was almost unconscious with the pain from his ankle. A look of indecision went over Betron's face, and then he made up his mind. He reported to me.

"Seventeen men fit for duty, sir. Of them, twelve are lightly injured. There's also nineteen severely injured; most of them are real bad off."

I waited, but Sergeant Betron said nothing further. Why, that was only thirty-six men. There had been an entire company in this town yesterday! "And the rest . . . ?" I asked queasily.

"Dead, sir. Thirty-eight in all."

My knees bowed in shock. This was the worst bloodbath since Custer went down on the Little Bighorn. Nearly half a company swept away, and by an enemy armed with little more than bolos!

I looked over my pitiful command. There had been nearly four hundred attacking Pulajans, I estimated, but only about one hundred of them lay dead. Ominously, Surlang was not among them. More bodies had sunk beneath the waters of the river, and I guessed that another hundred Pulajan wounded had been carried off by their companions. That still left at least a hundred and fifty available for another go at us. With Surlang still alive, there was no doubt that he would make sure they did precisely that.

I was all for hightailing it to safety; Betron's somber report merely sealed my determination in that regard. "Sergeant Betron, gather up all the canoes you can. We're going to bury our dead and then we're heading for Basey."

Now Longbottom bestirred himself. "You can't let them scare us off like that, Travers," he moaned groggily. "It'll look like we're cutting and running."

"Damnit, Longbottom, the surgeon's lying yonder in three pieces!" I snapped whiningly. "Most of these men will bleed to death if they don't get help, and those Filipinos scampered away with armfuls of Krags and ammo! If they learn how to use those weapons in the next few hours, we'll never escape from here. Sergeant Betron, gather the boats!"

23

The journey to Basey was a torture that will ever burn deep within my brain. We'd gotten away in a small flotilla led by Bumpus's proa. An outrigger big enough to carry eighteen, the proa was under my command. It held the most seriously wounded, with Sergeant Betron, Henry, and a few stunned privates administering aid as best they could. Despite their best efforts, the bottom of the proa was three inches deep in blood, and the cries of the wounded were horrible to hear. As the injured soldiers lay helpless, clouds of insatiable, biting flies that had trailed us all the way from shore fed on their open wounds. There was little fresh water to slake the thirst of these poor wretches, and they suffered dreadfully as the heat of the day soared to nearly a hundred degrees.

The rest of our vessels consisted of *barotas* of various sizes and states of repair. The smallest, a two-man canoe, was manned by the redoubtable Sergeant Markley and a private. Our worst fear, thankfully, was not realized: The bolomen had no stomach for a general pursuit. Oh, a few boats did push off from the shore, but our Krags held them at bay. Careful to keep their distance, the Filipinos jeered derisively across the water as we fled. One Pulajan, more daring than his fellows, even rose to a precarious standing position in his *barota* and bared his backside to us. As frightened and dispirited as I was, the target was simply too tempting. I wrapped the sling of my Krag around my left arm for balance and support, sighted, and fired. The taunter hurtled off the *barota* and into the sea, to be seen no more.

That pretty much settled down the Pulajans, content now to let us be off and claim their victory, costly though it was. Our ordeal, however, was far from over. Now our enemy was the untamed sea. The worst of the wounded, of course, suffered the most, and more than once in those first few hours of flight a lifeless corpse was slipped over the side. On each occasion, fins appeared silently as we paddled on, then there was a thrashing of white water, followed by silence once more.

Leyte Gulf, calm at the start of our journey, was soon swept by a gusting west wind that whipped the placid seas into whitecaps. Initially we were grateful for the wind, for it chased off the flies and cooled the air. As it continued to increase unabated, however, our gratitude turned to consternation. No sails could remain unfurled under such conditions, causing all hands to strain at their paddles just to keep from being carried onto the shore. By sunset, it was evident that Markley's craft was the swiftest of all, and so over the shrieking wind, Betron called out, "Sergeant Markley, go ahead! Get word to Basey and we'll follow as best we can!"

Then the sun slipped behind the distant hills of Leyte and a desperate night settled upon us. One *barota* was able to stay near us in the dark, but two others disappeared. When we called to them, no answer came from across the windswept waves.

"There's a full squad we can't account for, sir," yelled Sergeant Betron against the gale. "Should we go on or turn back to see if they need help?"

In the dark I couldn't see a foot in front of my face, but I felt all of their eyes—Henry's, Longbottom's, and the others'—boring into me. Under the best of circumstances, I shied away from tough decisions like a mustang crossing paths with a rattler. Now my nerves were shot, I was battling a terrible case of seasickness, and the minuscule reserve of cool judgment I normally possessed was thoroughly drained. How could I be expected to shoulder a matter as weighty as this? In a fit of self-pity, I silently damned Betron for putting me on the spot. Why couldn't he just make all the decisions, as sergeants did anyway? I almost told him precisely that, but what came out instead was a gloomy, "No. They'll have to make it on their own. If this wind gets any worse, we'll be capsized ourselves. Push on, Sergeant."

And push on we did, through a night of incredible hardship. Around midnight a young private with a half-severed arm gave up the ghost, and we dropped him over the side. At this, a corporal with a badly gashed neck shuddered and began blubbering from fear that we'd heave him to the sharks as well. I was all in favor of doing so immediately to stop his blasted mewling, but Betron hurried forward over exhausted men and cuffed him sharply.

"Shut up, damn you! You're safe here as long as you're alive, but by God, if you cause a panic among these men I'll throw you into the brine myself."

The murderous edge in Betron's voice pierced the poor soldier's haze of fear, and somehow he got a grip on himself. "I'm . . . I'm sorry, Sarge, it's just . . ."

Betron put a hand on the fellow's shoulder compassionately. "I know, Corporal, we've all been through hell. Just hold on, and we'll get you some help. Just hold on."

The corporal nodded manfully, and Betron returned to the stern of the proa. For my part, I was convinced that the fellow's panic was fully justified under these harrowing circumstances. We were all going to die, and die horribly, weren't we? Yet not an hour later, the gale died down, and we were able to raise our sails again. They filled lustily, and soon we were clipping across smooth waters due north toward safety.

I must have drifted off, for a voice woke me with the cry, "Lights ho! It's Basey, boys! We made it!"

The lookout was right. The lights off the starboard bow could only be Basey! Within the hour we had docked and were safe once more among our comrades.

By dawn, troops of the 9th Infantry were gathering to avenge the slaughter at Balangiga. A reinforced Company G was mustered under its commander, Captain Bookmiller. Telegraph messages flew to the battalion headquarters at Calbayog, farther north on the coast of Samar, and to department headquarters at Tacloban. Once the wounded were cared for, the relief force boarded a refitted coastal steamer dubbed the *Pittsburgh*. As his men filed on board, Bookmiller studied Longbottom and me uncertainly. "Any volunteers for a return trip, gentlemen?"

Longbottom, wrapped in bandages from head to foot, looked like a farmhand who had fallen into a threshing machine. I felt no sympathy for the dolt, for his mangling was in my view simply his just deserts for interfering when I had that damned Surlang in my grasp. Yet despite his wounds, Longbottom nodded grimly at Bookmiller and gasped weakly, "The sooner the better."

Bookmiller studied Longbottom's glazed eyes and remained unconvinced. "No, Captain Longbottom, you had better stay here. The surgeons have told me you'll be needing a great deal of rest before you're fit for duty again. I'm afraid you're bound for the field hospital in Tacloban."

Then he turned to me. "Captain Travers? Are you game? I could use the insights of an eyewitness to this tragedy."

What? Go back to Balangiga? After having spent a day and night straining every muscle in my body to flee the place? Not on your life, thank you. I was about to explain reality to Bookmiller when Lieutenant Colonel Foote joined us, fretting over the last-minute details of the return expedition. He also brought news of another disaster.

"A wire just came in from Tacloban, gentlemen. Totally shocking news, I'm afraid. President McKinley has been assassinated." Gravely, he gave us the details. McKinley had been shot by an anarchist named Leon Czolgosz and, after lingering for eight days, had expired. Teddy Roosevelt had already been sworn in as president.

"Oh, my God!" gasped Bookmiller. I joined with a loud "Amen," not so much at McKinley's passing as at Roosevelt's ascension. Having Teddy as the chief executive of the United States was like handing a five-year-old the throttle of a locomotive. There was no doubt the thing would soon pick up speed; the only question was how long it would stay on the tracks.

That sad duty done, Lieutenant Colonel Foote turned back to the grim business at hand. "You'll be taking Captain Travers along, of course, Captain Bookmiller," he asserted, looking at me for what he expected to be ready confirmation. "I assured General Smith that Travers here wanted nothing more than to avenge the poor men of C Company."

Still nauseous from the perilous sea passage, my words of protest gagged deep in my throat. Instead I could only give a funny little bob of the head, the precursor of a swoon.

Foote took it for a yes. "Excellent, Travers," he exclaimed with a clap to my shoulder. "I knew the Ninth could count on you. Now get your men to Balangiga, Captain Bookmiller, and start putting this fiasco aright."

So Henry, Bustos, and I embarked on the *Pittsburgh*. By noon we were back at Balangiga, walking through the smoking ruins that once was Company C's encampment.

"Holy Jesus!" exclaimed Bookmiller as he surveyed the grisly scene. "I've never laid eyes on anything like this!"

Neither had I. Our dead, whom we had hastily interred yesterday, had been just as hastily disinterred. The desecrated corpses lay everywhere, carved up like so many sides of beef. Most of them had been gutted, with their entrails strewn about the streets of the town. Here and there a severed head leered obscenely from atop a stake. More than one body had been incinerated over a fire, and everywhere buzzed swarms of angry black flies. Oh, I shall never forget that horrid day, for the smell of putrefying flesh under the tropical sun was overpowering.

Bustos padded over to a hearth and sniffed tentatively at the smoking remains of one poor wretch, until a black look from me sent him scuttling from my sight. I thought again of that fiend Surlang, and how he'd been able to whip a sullen populace into a horde of murderous avengers so quickly that all our heads were spinning. I entered the convent where the officers had slept. The inside was a charnel house, with parts of human bodies strewn everywhere.

I went to the cot where I had slept and rummaged about in the blankets until I found what I was looking for—Surlang's kris and my Colt. I holstered the revolver and slipped the kris through my belt, swearing anew to see Surlang dead if it was the last thing I did. Then I went back onto the plaza and found Bookmiller still looking about with numbed disbelief.

"This calls for vengeance," he announced stormily, taking in the horrors around him with mounting fury until finally he was shaking with anger. In a voice choked with emotion he vowed, "Travers, I'm not a man to go to extremes, but if these people want war, then I say it's war they'll get."

"Amen to that," seconded an equally appalled lieutenant nearby.

Within a week, war on a scale never before imagined by the Pulajans came to Samar. General Jacob H. "Hell-roaring Jake" Smith, so named because of his stentorian voice, was ordered to Samar and given the mission of sounding the clarion call of revenge. From all points of the compass, troops flowed onto the island. Battalions of the 11th, 12th, 17th, and 26th Infantry Regiments arrived, together with artillery batteries, cavalry squadrons, and several companies of native scouts. When his force, designated the 6th Separate Brigade, was assembled, General Smith issued the dreaded General Order Number 100. It proclaimed that under the laws of war, any partisans found bearing arms were fair game. Then he unleashed the dogs of war.

My role in all of this started innocuously enough. I finished picking through the ruins of Balangiga with Bookmiller, and helped identify the corpses of Abayan and Sanchez, who had sided with the Pulajans in the uprising. I made myself generally useful as long as it didn't involve any strain on myself, nor any time in the field on the trail of the *insurrectos*. Meanwhile, Hell-roaring Jake put the ball in play, as it were. Throughout Samar, his brigade was on the move with fire and steel, and the result was pure hell. Churches were seized and used as depots, huts were razed, and fields were set ablaze. All livestock was slaughtered, and any bands of natives who failed to surrender quickly enough to suit Smith were killed. From one end of Samar to the other, Hell-roaring Jake spread death, destruction, and mayhem.

I rather expected that with a sizable portion of the American forces in the Philippines now on Samar, there would be no further need of old Fenny's services. In fact, I intended to book passage back to my billet at Zamboanga and recommence the search for Fiona and Alice, when fate took a nasty turn. A coastal tug, the *Mobile,* dropped anchor off Balangiga with a message for me. It was from Smith, ordering me to report forthwith to Catbalogan up on the coast north of Basey. With a hasty farewell to Bookmiller, I was off, finding myself deposited the next morning on a rudely constructed quartermaster wharf at Catbalogan. I was told to wait right there and Smith would be along for me straightaway.

As I cooled my heels, I eyed a warship that rode at anchor beyond the bar. It was the cruiser USS *New York.* I recognized her, you see, for the *New York* had been the flagship of Admiral Sampson, when he commanded the Atlantic Fleet back in '98. Indeed, the *New York* had escorted General Shafter and V Corps during the landings at Daiquiri that led eventually to the Battle of San Juan Hill and the capitulation of the Spanish in Cuba. I surmised that the *New York* was probably still an admiral's flagship, which meant that something portentous was afoot here in Catbalogan.

I didn't have long to ponder the mystery, for a gaggle of officers approached the wharf from the town. The leader was a brigadier general, clad in tropical whites, with his small peaked cap pushed far back on his head in the style of a carelessly dressed milkman. He was thin and short, with an enormous gray mustache as wild and untamed as its owner. As he neared, I saluted.

"You're Travers, right?" the general demanded with a voice that could have blown windowpanes from their frames at ten yards. The stern blue eyes locked on mine and I saw that this was a fellow with a fire in his belly; it could be none other than Hell-roaring Jake.

"Yes, sir," I replied, waving my message before me like a note to the schoolmarm. "I was told to report to you."

"Get in the boat, Travers" was his thunderous reply.

I looked about to where Smith was indicating a steam-powered launch manned by attentive bluejackets. I dutifully followed him as he clambered aboard and then we were off to the *New York*. I tried to hunker down unobtrusively near the stern, but at a gesture from Smith, his staff heaved me forward until I was at his side. Squatting beside Smith was a silent major, who eyed me appraisingly. On his collar was the insignia of a judge advocate.

Smith caught the direction of my glance. "This is Major Glenn, the judge advocate for the Department of the Visayas." Then he added enigmatically, "You two will be seeing quite a bit of each other."

Just what the dickens did that comment mean? I wanted to ask. But Smith continued, "Travers, what do you know about the marines?"

The marines? That was a damned odd question, but I merely stammered, "Er, not a lot, sir."

Smith gave a snort like a cannon blast at this. "Neither does anyone else. The problem is, though, the navy has a whole brigade of the rascals garrisoned at Cavite up near Manila. The best I can figure, their job is to guard the navy yard and throw drunken sailors in the brig."

Cavite? A marine brigade? Nothing Smith had said thus far made any sense to me. Mercifully, he decided to get to the point.

"Admiral Rodgers commands the navy's Asiatic Squadron in these waters. That's his ship yonder. Well, it seems that Rodgers heard about Balangiga and got all in an uproar. He went to General Chaffee whining that I should take on a battalion of his marines. As far as I'm concerned, marines are nothing but jailers who occasionally go to sea, and honest soldiers should have nothing to do with 'em. But General Chaffee, for reasons unknown to me, has decided to humor Rodgers. And that, Travers, is where you come in."

"Me?" I asked, flustered. "What have I got to do with the marines?"

"Why, you're going to ride herd on 'em!" guffawed Smith.

"Ride herd? Why, there must be some mistake, General. I'm not even assigned to your department. My orders place me under the command of General Davis in Zamboanga. I'm afraid there's been some terrible mistake."

"There's no mistake, Captain Travers," Smith countered flatly. He nodded at Major Glenn, who shoved a folded order into my hand with the speed of a seasoned process server. I opened it quickly and scanned its contents. By God, it said I was assigned on temporary duty to Smith's headquarters!

I looked up, confused. I had a hundred questions for Smith, but by then we were alongside the cruiser, and the helmsman made for a lowered gangplank straight ahead. Smith was up and scrambling for the cruiser's deck before I could get out a sound, then a bo'sun's pipe sounded and Smith's staff flowed up the steps after their chief. Reluctantly, I followed.

Once on deck, Smith greeted Admiral Rodgers and then, turning, called me to his side. I saluted Rodgers as Smith announced, "Admiral, this is Captain Travers. He'll be the army liaison to your marines. He's a decorated veteran and was in Balangiga when the rebels attacked. No finer choice for this role can be made."

"Thank you, General," replied Admiral Rodgers, who in turn cocked a finger toward a short, stocky, khaki-clad figure standing at stiff attention a few paces to his rear. This fellow took one step forward. I took one look at that arrogant face, with its supercilious cast of eye and the flaming red mustache with upturned ends, and recognized the hombre right off. Why, it was Maj. Littleton W. T. Waller! I had last seen Waller back in Tientsin when we were both campaigning with General Chaffee against the Boxers. In China, Waller had cemented a reputation for himself as a strutting peacock of a fellow who could fight well but who was vain, pompous, and very much dedicated to the eternal glorification of Littleton Waller. The silver oak leaves on his epaulets told me that things had gone well for Waller since China.

"General Smith, this is Brevet Lieutenant Colonel Waller," announced Admiral Rodgers. "He's the commander of the marine composite battalion. Colonel Waller has my utmost confidence and I'm certain you'll find his battalion a valuable addition to your brigade."

As Admiral Rodgers spoke, Waller eyed me sharply from beneath the brim of his campaign hat. Pinned jauntily to its crown was the globe and anchor, the insignia of the Marine Corps. The glint in those eyes said Waller had heard of me. "Captain Travers, you say?" he barked. "Not the same Travers who made the ride from Hsiku Arsenal?"

"The very same," I assured him, all of this going over the head of Admiral Rodgers. Waller quickly explained about my ride on the night that Admiral Seymour's column had been hemmed in from all sides by hordes of bloodthirsty Boxers. I had ridden unwillingly with that Prussian madman, *Hauptman* Von Arnhem, and together we roused the allied army in Tientsin to go to Seymour's relief. Although the truth of the matter was that the Hsiku ride was a shoddy affair marked by deceit and blunders, it had been seized upon rapturously at the time, and unearned laurels had been cascading down upon me ever since.

"So, the two of you are acquainted," observed Smith approvingly. "That's good, because you're going to be closer to each other than bugs in a blanket."

"And my area of operations will be where, sir?" asked Waller. His tone was brusque, almost impertinent. Hell-roaring Jake, however, always a bit short in the manners department himself, didn't seem to take offense.

"You're to range from Basey south all the way to Balangiga. The army units in that region will be withdrawn. You'll have a free hand within your sector, Colonel Waller."

Waller and Admiral Rodgers exchanged looks of evident satisfaction. I surmised that they had previously decided that Waller's marines should resist service under the direct operational control of an army officer. Smith's pronouncement had just handed them that desired situation on a platter.

In their glee, however, they failed to notice Smith's equal merriment. In a flash of insight, I knew the cause of it. You see, Smith planned to fling Waller's marines into the most desolate, implacably hostile region of Samar and then seal the door behind them. He'd let the marines out again only when they produced enough corpses to ensure that the insurrection on Samar was truly extinguished. The beauty of the arrangement was that, other than the destruction wrought to date, all the dirty work would be done by marines, not Smith's soldiers. If Chaffee or those damned anti-imperialists in Congress bleated, Smith could blame it all on the navy!

"General Smith, your proposal is completely satisfactory," Colonel Waller said, beaming. "Where should I put my battalion ashore?"

"Basey. That will be your headquarters, and you are to keep in constant communication with me at Tacloban."

"And my mission, sir?"

Here Smith paused, a sly look coming over him. "Let's just step off to the side, shall we?" he suggested. Smith, Waller, and Admiral Rodgers drew off several yards to where a lifeboat dangled from its davits. There they conferred in earnest whispers.

All this was damned odd, I thought. Oh, I had been involved in shenanigans from time to time, all right, but this was the first time I'd ever seen a commander get marching orders that couldn't withstand the light of day. Intrigued, I bent an ear in that direction. Fortunately, Hell-roaring Jake lived up to his nickname; his whispers would serve as conversational tones for anyone else. He had one hand on Waller's shoulder and with the other was poking a finger into the marine's chest for emphasis. Unknown to me at the time, Smith's words were to have awful consequences for him and Waller in the future. I've heard a hundred different versions of this fateful conversation reported since, but I can only relate what I heard, and that was enough to chill the marrow of any sane man.

"What I want you to do, Colonel, is to kill as many of these damned rebels as you can and then burn out the ones who are left behind," instructed Smith. "Kill and burn, do you hear me?"

Waller didn't seem particularly taken aback at this, but Rodgers started visibly. "Even civilians?" he challenged, aghast.

"Admiral, let me tell you something," declared Smith forcefully. "There are no civilians out here. At Balangiga, we found the mayor and the chief of police among the dead that the rebels left behind. Let me make myself perfectly clear: The more Colonel Waller kills and burns, the more he will please me. I've made General Chaffee a promise that I'll have Samar pacified by Christmas, and I aim to keep that promise. Any more questions?"

Hearing his instructions, Waller became excited, like a small terrier does in the presence of a caged rat. He was fairly quivering to begin the great adventure that Smith was outlining for him, and he had but one query: "How old does a native have to be before you consider him a combatant, General? Sixteen? Fifteen?"

"Ten," spat Smith. "They were that young at Balangiga with bolos in their hands. I say let them reap what they have sown."

Ten years of age? That seemed a bit young to me, and I had survived Balangiga. Oh, I'd seen armed youths there all right, but no babes the age that Smith was now laying on the altar of sacrifice. I looked to Waller for some show of distaste at Smith's order, but there was none.

"Ten it is, sir," Waller replied crisply, eyes alight at the prospect of the bloodshed to come. As an afterthought he asked, "Oh, and sir, what are your views on prisoners?"

"I want none, damnit. None of our men at Balangiga were given quarter."

At this, Admiral Rodgers blanched, looking as though he might be ill. But he wasn't; instead he spun on his heels and hurried off, evidently deciding it would not be advisable to hear another word of this infamous conversation. From the stricken look on his face as he swept past me, I could tell he was sorry he had ever suggested that the marines be sent to bloody Samar.

24

Basey, Samar
November 10, 1901
Waller set two of his four companies, together with his headquarters staff, ashore at Basey. Then he was off with General Smith and Admiral Rodgers to establish his two remaining companies farther south at Balangiga, under the command of a likable young fellow named Captain Porter. Porter relieved Bookmiller, who eagerly departed the shattered and haunted remains of that once-bustling barrio.

With his pieces on the chessboard, Waller soon got to work. His men commenced patrolling throughout the region and rounding up all likely insurgents they chanced upon. Those Samarans who resisted, or who took too much time deciding to go along peacefully or not, soon became "good Indians." Waller, you see, wasted no time in impressing himself firmly in the consciousness of the sullen natives.

As for me, well, I liaised, which to me meant swilling rum with the off-duty officers, and playing cards whenever I found a game where my credit was good for a few dollars. I had some success at the gaming tables, and even more at the cockfights to which the Filipinos were madly addicted. All in all, duty at Basey suited me just fine. I abated my revelries only long enough to wire General Davis at Zamboanga about my being shanghaied by General Smith, and to pass on that Surlang had let slip that Alice and Fiona might be on Jolo. I suggested that Davis might want to make inquiries in that direction and followed all this up with a formal report scrawled in my abysmal handwriting. I dispatched my report by transport with Henry and Bustos, telling them both to sit tight in Zamboanga until I got back.

Between drinking bouts, I occasionally wandered into Waller's headquarters just to take the pulse of his operations. On one visit, soon after landing at Basey, I noticed an order signed by Waller pinned to the bulletin board. It read like a prescription for murder and mayhem:

HEADQUARTERS MARINE BATTALION—SAMAR
U.S. FLAGSHIP NEW YORK
CATBALOGAN, SAMAR
23 OCTOBER 1901

Captain Porter with Companies F and H will garrison Balangiga. One 3-inch gun with six boxes of ammunition. The duty will be to scout the surrounding country to the Eastward, connecting with the Army at Quinapundan, Salcedo, and clearing out that part of the country; scouting then to the Northward and Eastward toward Pambuhan on the east coast; to the Westward & Northward, Westward to about half way between Balangiga and Basey. The country between the points named must be cleared of the treacherous enemy, and the expeditions, in a way, are punitive.

All rice and hemp are to be seized, and if practicable, brought in, if not, it must be destroyed. Bancas and boats of all kinds not painted red and registered or not showing proper papers must be seized, and, if not practicable to use them, they must be destroyed.

Rice must not be allowed to get into the interior. Unregistered bancas carrying contraband must be seized. Families may be allowed enough rice per diem to subsist upon.

Impress native labor for all manual labor as far as possible. Clear back the brush, keeping it down as far as possible.

Place no confidence in the natives, and punish treachery with immediate death.

All parties of any strength must be accompanied by a Surgeon. Natives will be utilized to carry provisions, and a few with long poles will precede the column to look out for pits and traps.

Men must be cautioned about these means of death.

Allow no man to go to meals, the sinks, or anywhere without his arms and ammunition. The same instructions apply to officers.

All males who have not come in and presented themselves by October 25th will be regarded and treated as enemies. It must be impressed on the men that the natives are treacherous, brave and savage. No trust, no confidence can be placed in them.

The Headquarters will be in Basey. Wire connections will soon be had between Balangiga and Basey. A company will be stationed at a point either between Basey and Balangiga or Basey and Santa Rita. Notice will be given of its locality when decided upon.

The utmost energy and activity will be observed in the suppression of the insurrection and the pacifying of all portions of the island, in order that we may soon proceed to the Northern part of the island.

The men must be informed of the courage, skill, size, and strength of the enemy. WE MUST DO OUR PART OF THE WORK, AND WITH THE SURE KNOWLEDGE THAT WE ARE NOT TO EXPECT QUARTER.

The latter fact will be told to the men after they are landed.

We have also to avenge our late comrades in North China, the murdered men of the Ninth U.S. Infantry.

> LITTLETON W. T. WALLER
> Major & Brevet Lieut-Colonel, U.S. Marines
> Commanding

I looked up when I'd finished reading. Waller's adjutant, Lt. J. Horace Arthur Day, was giving me an evil little smirk. I'd already pegged Day as the social misfit in the marine battalion, you see. He was quarrelsome, petty, vindictive, and an inveterate drunkard. In other words, he was rather like me, which was probably why I took an instant dislike to him. At the moment, Day's face was a bright scarlet and his eyes were bloodshot, for he was well into his daily ration of whiskey.

"I see Colonel Waller's signed the riot act," I smiled.

"That's right, Captain," scowled Day, for he was usually in a foul humor when he was in his cups. "He issued it right after he met with General Smith on the *New York*. It tells the men just where the colonel stands regarding the damned *gugus*."

"Oh, that it does," I agreed readily.

"We marines don't believe in halfway measures, Captain," Day assured me. "We heard all about Captain Connell's mollycoddling of those bastards. If he'd only had the guts to issue such an order, I think most of his men would be alive today."

I didn't necessarily disagree. What made my stomach turn, though, was the evident delight Day took in all of this. Here was a born killer, I told myself, a fellow who could cut a man down in cold blood for no reason at all and then go take his supper as calmly as you please. Oh, don't get me wrong; I'm not above killing, and I'd surely sent my share of varmints to the happy hunting grounds. But if I killed, there had to be some reason for it. Maybe not overwhelming provocation, mind you, but at least a reason. Day wasn't like that, though. No, he'd plug someone simply for amusement.

"Perhaps, Mr. Day, perhaps," I allowed. "All the same, I think Colonel Waller might want to be a bit more careful about his choice of language. Things like this might be misunderstood, you know." I was pointing to the part about punishing treachery with immediate death. "Narrow minds might think Colonel Waller was encouraging wholesale butchery."

Day snorted. "Colonel Waller's men are marines, Captain Travers. They're disciplined. The colonel knows they'll understand exactly what he means."

I let it go at the time, for in truth all of this was navy business; besides, even if I had wanted to set Waller straight, I saw damned little of him. From the very beginning he was a man consumed with a passion to destroy and conquer, constantly off with columns striking north and south from Basey, torching villages and destroying rice stores. The sheer violence of his onslaught had its desired effect, for the Visayans, formerly bold and insubordinate in these parts, were becoming increasingly scarce, while those who dared to venture into Basey kowtowed to us and rolled about in the dirt like Chinese peasants before Manchu lords.

This peaceful interlude led to some interesting opportunities for old Fenny. Immediately upon arrival, I took up where I left off with the charming Lenai, drawing her to my bed with all the ardor that a brush with death tends to arouse in a fellow. Soon I was so comfortably installed in my new digs that I had completely lost track of Waller's antics—that is, until the colonel came storming back from patrol late one afternoon in the middle of a tremendous downpour to seek me out.

I had set down stakes in a large tent equipped with a raised wooden floor, a lodging some distance apart from the converted convent that served as Waller's headquarters. This arrangement was deliberate, for my goal wasn't so much comfort as privacy. At the moment of Waller's arrival, in fact, I was doing the Manila waltz with the almond-eyed Lenai. Waller rapped sharply on the tent pole before entering, barely giving me enough time to hustle Lenai through the rear tent flaps and to toss her sarong after her.

"Captain Travers," he announced peremptorily as I hastily smoothed back my hair, "I've decided to strike inland. The Pulajans are holed up at a *cuartel* called Sohoton Cliffs on the Cadacan River. I aim to blast them out of there and finish this campaign pronto like General Smith wants."

I sat on my cot and pointedly swirled whiskey in the bottom of my tin cup, hoping that Waller would surmise that the liquor was the cause of my florid complexion. I digested his news as the heat of passion slowly drifted away. A *cuartel* was the term used to denote native forts in these parts. That meant Waller had found a mother lode, a major center of resistance.

"The Sohoton Cliffs, eh? Well, that's a new one to me, Colonel. I wish you all the best," I said blithely, fishing out a stogie from the metal ammunition box that served me as a humidor. "Cigar?" I offered.

When he shook his head impatiently, I bit the end off a Havana, lit it, and took a great pull. I could be saucy as I pleased, since no regular officer in the army viewed a marine of any rank as his superior, and I wasn't about to change that tradition. Marines were a lower social class entirely, you see, rather like tradesmen who weren't quite fit to be brought into the parlor for tea. No, the back porch would do fine for them. All of this meant that if Waller wanted to charge off to seize this *cuartel,* he could damn well do it without me.

My effrontery didn't go down well with Waller, however. "I'm not asking, Travers, I'm telling. You're the one who was with Funston. You know how to cross the hills on these damned islands. General Smith promised you'd help us, so get off your lazy backside and help!"

Oh, ho, I thought, so Waller bothered to find out a bit about what I had been up to since China. Well, it was time to teach him that my trek through northern Luzon with Funston didn't mean I was available for every harebrained hike he concocted. "General Smith sent me here as a liaison officer, Colonel, not a bush beater," I informed him languidly. "So, if there's anything you need from the army, just tell me. Bacon, beans, bullets—anything you need. I'll fire off a telegraph or ring over to Tacloban on the telephone within the hour. You may rely upon it."

I swilled down the rest of my whiskey and stared back hard at Waller; I was in the right and he damned well knew it.

Waller took off his rain-sodden hat and collapsed on a rickety camp stool. "Damn it, Travers, we need you," he pleaded. "We've run the bastards away from the coast, but now they've gone to ground. If we can smash this band, the others might come down from the hills and seek peace."

"Then why don't you simply march up to these Sohoton Cliffs and finish 'em?" I queried, taking another pull on my cigar. It seemed like a simple enough proposition to me.

"We can't, blast them," replied Waller resignedly. "The natives always seem to know where we go. It's like hitting air, I tell you."

"Then get some native scouts, Colonel. Use 'em like Apaches to sneak through the bush ahead of you."

"We've done that. The scouts are no more able to come to grip with the Visayans than we are."

"Are your scouts Visayans?"

"Of course. That's all there are on Samar."

I laughed dryly at Waller's denseness. "Colonel, you don't use a fox to catch a fox. You use hounds."

"What's your damned point, Travers?" he demanded testily. I could tell from the purple veins bulging from his forehead that he didn't take kindly to being ridiculed, especially by a captain who showed not the slightest appetite for field duty.

"Your Visayan scouts are useless to you," I explained pedantically. "They'll lead you around these hills on a merry chase for as long as you please, but they'll never turn their blood kin over to you. What you need are some reliable auxiliaries, like the Ilocanos from Luzon. That's what the army uses. Them or Macabebes."

Waller snorted in exasperation. "That would take months, Travers, and I don't happen to have months. Time's a wasting even as we speak. The biggest rebel band in southern Samar is at Sohoton Cliffs right now. They're gathered around their grand chief, a rogue named *Capitán* Verde."

I sat up at that. "*Capitán* Verde, you say? Why, that's Captain Green in English."

Waller nodded. "Our spies say that Verde was one of the master-minds behind the Balangiga massacre. If they're right, we could pay the bastards back in spades for what they did to your boys."

Maybe, but that wasn't what mattered to me. "Tell me more about this *Capitán* Verde, Colonel. Has anyone described what he looks like?"

"No, none of the spies I've sent close to Sohoton Cliffs has ever returned." Of course not, I thought wryly; they went over to the enemy.

"I've been told, however," continued Waller, "that this Verde hails from some island group other than the Visayas."

It could be, I mused, it just could be. I would have figured that Surlang was long gone from Samar, but on the other hand, perhaps he had decided to stay around and stir the pot a bit further. Maybe he wanted to ensure that there was a ready market for the next shipment of rifles he tried to slip past the American navy. Who could fathom that devil's mind? Perhaps he knew I was still on Samar and wanted another go at me. Hell, maybe this Verde character wasn't even Surlang, but whatever the truth of the matter, Waller's tale galvanized me into action.

"Colonel, we've got work to do," I announced.

Within the hour I was huddled with Waller and his staff studying the maps of the region around the Cadacan River. There was damned little detail to them, but we could glean that the cliffs were at a spot about fifteen miles upriver from the sea. Waller had summoned Captain Porter from Balangiga to help in the effort and added Capt. Hiram Bearss, another company commander, for good measure.

With the leathernecks huddled around me in the stifling heat of the Samar night, I pondered the situation. "Water is the easiest way to travel in these islands. Whatever the rest of the plan might be, we'll have to bring our heavy ordnance up the river. We can break down the Colt machine guns and the 3-inch cannons and lash them to bamboo barges."

Waller shook his head wearily, as if to say that he might have overestimated me after all. "Travers, we're not complete idiots, you know. Don't you think we already thought of that? Two weeks ago we started up the Cadacan but got so peppered by sniper fire from the banks we had to turn back."

Like their colonel, Porter and Bearss eyed me narrowly. Unabashed by their skepticism, I challenged Waller right back. "Did you use your scouts at all?"

Captain Bearss answered. "Of course, Travers. We had them shadow the boats along the shore. They couldn't do a damn thing about those snipers."

I fixed Waller with a hard stare. "Couldn't, . . . or wouldn't?"

The marines exchanged uneasy glances. When their eyes were back on me, now properly attentive, I continued. "Here's the way I see it, gentlemen. What you need to do is first secure the banks using marines, not native scouts. Also, spread the word among the scouts that you're going up the Cadacan, but not all the way to the Sohoton Cliffs."

"Lie to our own scouts?" protested Captain Porter indignantly. Waller's raised eyebrow told me he too disapproved of the notion.

"Absolutely," I assured them breezily. "If there's anything I've learned about the Filipinos, it's that they know everything you do, only sooner. Don't try to hide your movement, or they'll see right through you. No, let 'em know when you're on the move—just make sure they don't know where you're going. Gentlemen, it's time you stopped treating these natives like they're dumb beasts and realize they're cunning adversaries. Keep them at arm's length, I say."

"Okay, Captain Travers, we will," snapped Waller, not liking my condescending tone, and adding with a Parthian shot, "as long as you do the same with your harlot."

Porter and Bearss reddened at this, and I was taken aback. Waller was a bit sharper than I had estimated. I thought my fornication had been conducted with the utmost discretion, you see, but obviously I was wrong. Waller evidently had eyes back at headquarters when he was out ranging the hills. Who could it be? I wondered. Ah, yes, I concluded, that perfect little ass, Lieutenant Day. Well, this would require a repayment in kind at an appropriate opportunity.

"I'll see to it, Colonel," I blustered with a forced smile.

"You do that, Captain," rejoined Waller sternly.

Hoping to get beyond this awkward subject, I studied the maps intently. "Yes, this will do," I said, putting my finger on the barrio of Liruan, a small dot on the bank of the Cadacan about ten miles from the sea. "Let it be known that you intend to establish an advanced base at Liruan. Give hints to your scouts and *cargadores* that you don't have sufficient forces to assault the *cuartel* at Sohoton Cliffs right at the moment. Believe me, that word will get back to this *Capitán* Verde as reliably as if you had personally carried the message to him. That'll make the bandits relax a bit, you see, and not rush off in a panic when you draw near."

Waller was grinning from ear to ear now. "And instead of stopping, we rush forward and pounce on the bastards. I like it, Travers. I like it just fine."

25

Liruan, Samar
November 17, 1901

The operation went exactly as planned. On November 15, Captain Porter went up the Cadacan to Liruan with a small party and halted, looking for all the world like a timid patrol too hesitant to push any farther into the interior. On the same day, a second column of about fifty men under Captain Bearss went by water to the barrio of Odoc, a pigsty of a place about five miles downstream from Liruan. Bearss then marched toward Porter, burning everything in his path. Finally, on November 16, came the surprise. Waller, with a line of barges and *barotas* lashed together and towed by a sturdy steam launch from the gunboat *Vicksburg,* dashed up the Cadacan to join Bearss and Porter.

Our prevarications to Waller's scouts worked like a charm. No snipers lurked in the bushes, and no conch shells sounded on the surrounding hills. All was quiet, for the enemy had been gulled, by God. When dawn broke red and expectant over the Cadacan on November 17, Waller and I were standing on the bow of a barge; he was studying the looming Sohoton Cliffs through his field glasses and chomping at the bit in his eagerness to be on the Pulajans. He could smell victory—and possibly a further promotion—in the air.

"There it is, Travers!" chortled Waller giddily as he scrutinized the *cuartel*. "Let's just hope they haven't flown the coop."

"Right," I replied somberly, for I was not nearly as sanguine as Waller. What I saw before me was a position of immense natural strength. The cliffs were overhanging projections that soared two hundred feet above the banks of the Cadacan River where it narrowed into a defile about fifty yards wide. The cliffsides were honeycombed with caves, and everywhere the enemy had erected scaffolding of bamboo ladders and hemp cargo nets. In those cargo nets were hundreds of tons of boulders just waiting to be sent careening down on any boat foolish enough to try to force the passage past the *cuartel*. The Pulajans had picked the site of their bastion well; it would be a tough nut to crack. I saw no foe afoot, but there was no doubt they were watching us.

"Travers," ordered Waller, "take your place with Captain Porter's column on the shore. Remind him that he'll advance up the bank as I take the boats up the river. When I'm within range, I'll pound the caves with the 3-inch gun while Porter's men seize the cliff on their side of the bank and fire across to the far shore. When we've roughed 'em up a bit, I'll have my *barotas* carry Porter's men across the river to seize the opposite cliff. Now get going."

I hurried away, quite eager to be off Waller's boats if he planned on going anywhere near those cliffs. Being buried under an avalanche of boulders was hardly what I had in mind when I dreamed up this little excursion. I found Porter's men on the move already, the beaters to the fore hacking their way through *bejuco* vines and bamboo thickets so dense that a man could lean against them and not fall down.

I noted that the marines were in rough shape, most of them having been in the field almost continuously for the past month. Their uniforms were in rags and their shoes were coming apart at the seams. To compound their misery, the weather had taken a turn for the worse. The monsoon season was fully upon Samar, and the men had endured constant rain since leaving Basey. Yet their spirits were high, which indicated they were either tremendous fighters or morons.

"Okay, Porter, here's the plan one more time," I announced as soon as I landed. "You get to the cliffs on your side of the bank, then wait for Waller; he'll come up with the boats and plaster the place. Then you cross over the river under his guns and take the other bank. Got it? Bank, boats, then cross." I had learned in my short sojourn with the marines that it paid to keep instructions severely simple. The sea service did not seem to attract cerebral types among its officers.

Porter nodded. "Got it. Bank, boats, then cross."

He hurried to the van, eager to be at the hated Pulajans. That was the wonderful thing about campaigning with marines, you see. They had their bowels in such an uproar to be at the foe that they hardly noticed I hung to the rear, more than willing to let them take the bit in their mouths.

Within minutes the beaters stumbled upon a well-worn trail. The marines quickly pushed past them, following the trail warily and testing the path every few feet with long bamboo poles to detect hidden foot traps. The enemy now knew we were coming, for we found a crude bamboo cannon, its barrel crammed full of scrap iron, pointing down the trail in our direction, with its hemp fuse still burning. Whoever had lit it had scampered off just as the marines appeared.

"Let's get a move on," called Porter anxiously. "They might get away."

His men responded enthusiastically, pressing down the trail as quickly as possible but just short of a foolhardy rush. The marines burst out of the jungle foliage into a cleared area strewn with cooking utensils, small banana-leaf shelters, and bedrolls. Iron kettles were bubbling away on small fires, the rice in them still boiling.

"They were just here!" bellowed Porter. "It looks like they didn't expect us to come up the bank, men. Don't let 'em rally."

That was all the leathernecks needed to hear; soon things began taking on a momentum of their own. The marines were off in all directions, racing up and down the bank, routing out whatever Pulajans lurked about. They quickly secured the bank and stood about staring hungrily at the far shore. Nothing I saw there appealed to me, I can assure you. Dense crowds of jeering Filipinos manned rifle pits on the crests, and in the caves gouged into the cliff face I could see natives gripping spears and bows as they taunted the marines to cross over the river and fight.

"Get the Colt gun up here," directed Porter, and immediately a party of native bearers trotted forward and set up the weapon under the no-nonsense direction of Sergeant Quick. The marines loved Quick, a lean, leathery fighter who had earned the Medal of Honor in a landing at Guantanamo Bay in Cuba back in '98. Under Quick's supervision, the gun was soon trained on the cliffs; at a signal from Porter, it cut loose. Streams of bullets ripped into the caves, sending screaming Pulajans cartwheeling into the river, and lacerating the cargo nets holding the boulders. Their deadly loads hurtled down on the wounded Filipinos struggling in the current below.

"Whoo-eee!" I exulted. "Let 'em have it, boys!"

The marines, thoroughly into the spirit of the moment, trained their Krags on the enemy as they tried to flee the caves up rickety bamboo ladders that scaled the cliff face. Few of these fugitives made it, but now the Pulajans on the lip of the opposite cliff opened fire with rifles probably purloined at the Balangiga massacre. Soon bullets were zipping annoyingly our way, and I darted behind the Colt gun for protection.

"Blow them out of those damned trenches, Quick!" I ordered. The good sergeant dutifully had the crew raise their fire; soon bullets were snaking among the rifle pits, throwing up great puffs of dust as the 6mm rounds shattered the soft volcanic pumice on the crest. "That's it, that's it!" I cried excitedly.

As I watched the enemy run about in consternation on the far shore, I saw one figure stand in the open and attempt to rally them. He wore a green turban. At this distance there could be no doubt—it was Surlang, alias *Capitán* Verde. "There!" I exclaimed. "The son of a bitch in green. Let him have it, Sergeant Quick!"

Using a Colt gun as a sniper weapon is a daunting task, but the plucky marine gave it a go. Quick pushed the gunner aside and took the weapon himself, sending a burst straight toward Surlang. I saw a great cloud of earth erupt into the sky near where the Moro had stood only a second before, and when the cloud of dust dispersed, Surlang was gone.

"I think you got him!" I hooted, running now for the edge of the cliff on our side of the river. Porter was there, directing his men as they descended to the river's edge below. "Get your men to the far side," I urged him, "right now, before the Pulajans carry off their wounded." I prayed that Surlang had the map somewhere on his person; all I had to do now was search his corpse, and the prize of the *Jesus Maria* was mine!

Porter looked startled. "What about the colonel's boats, Travers? We're to wait for him, right? Banks, boats, then cross—just like you said."

I looked down the river to where Waller's riverine convoy was struggling forward against the strong current. They wouldn't draw near to us for another thirty minutes, a period of time that seemed to be an eternity in my sudden lust to lay my hands on that precious map once more. "Waller's stuck on shoals, Porter," I extemporized. "Why, just look at him. He's high and dry. We have to change the plan and cross the river ourselves."

Porter looked dubiously down the river. Some of Waller's men were indeed standing in shallows as they pulled at the bows of their *barotas* in a desperate attempt to get into the fight unfolding before their eyes. "Well, they are moving slow," he allowed.

"Slow? They're marooned, I tell you! Trust your own eyes, man. You have to strike while the iron is hot, Porter. Press on, man!"

With me egging him on and his own natural bent for action surging to the fore, Porter's better judgment yielded. "I suppose you could be right about those shoals," he conceded.

"Of course I am," I assured him bluffly. "Now, let's get going." We scrambled down our cliff side using the bamboo rails and ledges cut into the face by the industrious Pulajans. Soon we stood on the boulder-strewn edge of the swift-flowing Cadacan. There we found that the Pulajans had taken all their *barotas* to the far shore when they fled our onslaught.

"We need a damned boat!" bellowed Porter to the leathernecks crouched about firing up at the opposite cliff. That was all the direction these fellows needed; a wiry little private promptly dove into the water and struck out strongly for the opposite shore. Swimming through a hail of spears, arrows, and boulders, he managed, incredibly, to reach the far shore unscathed, pushed a *barota* into the river, and paddled back. In seconds a squad of his mates clambered in and pulled for the far shore. They splashed from the *barota* with their Krags flashing death. The *barota* came back again and again until Porter's column, including me, was across the Cadacan in force.

With Quick's Colt gun providing cover above us, Porter gave the command, "Up the cliff, men!"

As inflamed with greed as I was, those words struck a cold chill in my heart. The cliff face was straight up, and plenty of determined Filipinos still waited at the crest. The reaction of the marines, however, was one of pure joy. You would have sworn that Porter had just told 'em to be off for a three-day debauch in a Manila bordello and to send the chit around to him when they were done. Instantly, screaming leathernecks were on their feet, yelling themselves hoarse as they clambered up the bamboo ladders the Pulajans had foolishly neglected to draw up the cliff after themselves.

I stood below, amazed. "By God, yes, men, yes! That's it, straight at the little monkeys!"

Porter laid a rough hand on me as he rushed forward toward a ladder. "Officers to the front, Travers," he shouted gleefully, propelling me to the base of the cliff and all but booting me up a ladder.

The prospect of scaling that cliff was about as inviting to me as strolling through a tornado filled with nails. As men climbed ladders to my left and right, I protested over the din of battle, "Heights don't agree with me, Porter! I'll pass out, I swear I will!"

Porter, lost in his excitement, was deaf to my entreaties. "Get a move on, Travers, or the men will beat us to the top!" he urged, shoving me along so forcefully that my feet were skipping rungs on the way up.

"Let 'em!" I squealed, twisting on the ladder as a spear flashed past my shoulder, missing me by less than an inch. I whipped out my Colt and fired up at my assailant, toppling the villain from a crevice where he had been lurking.

"Nice shooting, sir," laughed a marine on the next ladder.

Ashen faced, I could barely nod my head in reply. By God, I was being dragooned to my death by a bunch of berserkers who thought close combat was the ultimate diversion. Boulders crashed down past us and arrows laced the air, but up we pressed, the marines in a wild battle frenzy and I in a near faint. Then, with the lip of the cliff only inches away, I completely balked. I gripped the ladder with whitened knuckles and refused to move, frozen with fright at the thought of what might await me above.

Porter had no such qualms. "We made it!" he roared, and using his head like a battering ram, butted me square in the seat of my pants and sent me flying from the ladder. I sailed over the crest and rolled in a heap on the gritty pumice. Clearing my head, I looked up in time to see an enraged Pulajan bearing down on me with his bolo raised for the kill. His battle cry was drowned out by my shriek for mercy, when suddenly Quick's Colt gun spoke. The Pulajan fell riddled with lead, and then the marines gained the ledge everywhere around me and sailed into the foe.

There, on the harsh volcanic stone of Sohoton Cliffs, unfolded one of the most savage hand-to-hand fights I've ever witnessed. The Pulajans, enraged by their casualties and the impudence of the daring Americans, surged forward in a last attempt to hurl their tormentors over the cliff. The marines, just as determined to prevail, met them with Krags and bayonets, thrusting past the slashing bolos with their own cold steel. After a desperate struggle, the Pulajans were slowly forced back, fighting every inch of the way as they were pushed through their extensive camp just beyond the crest.

"Look for the body of a devil in a green turban!" I yelled as I capered about excitedly behind the advancing marines. "He was their leader!"

I crouched low, dodging right or left to sidestep the occasional arrow or spear that passed my way. Then, between the shoulders of two marines lustily pounding a Pulajan to a bloody pulp with the butts of their Krags, I saw a flash of green. It was Surlang, and by Christ he was quite alive! Sergeant Quick had missed him after all.

"There he is!" I shouted. "Get him!"

Surlang was in the middle of a tight cordon of his followers, withdrawing in good order from the field. He saw me as I leveled my Colt at him, but he wisely stepped behind an unsuspecting boloman. I blew the fellow's brains out, and as he slid lifelessly to the ground, Surlang executed a disdainful little salaam to tweak me for having shot the wrong man. God, but that Moro was a cool one!

Seeing their target now, Porter's marines charged upon Surlang's entourage, cutting down the enemy on the fringes of the group. There were just too many Pulajans, however, and the marines were nearing exhaustion. Surlang's bodyguard withdrew stolidly to the edge of the jungle, charged the marines abruptly to gain breathing space, and then, at a command from their leader, turned and fled. They disappeared so suddenly into the jungle that, except for the carnage they left in their wake, it was as though they had never existed.

26

"Dad blame you, Porter, why didn't you wait for me?" Waller was stamping his feet in fury at being stranded below on the river while Porter was routing the enemy. Around him lay the blown marines, most of them in bare feet, for the pumice of the cliffs had ripped away the last of their shoe leather. All of them were low on rations, and it was evident that there could be no question of a pursuit. "We had a plan, didn't we?" demanded Waller peevishly. "I was to bring up the guns while you crossed over. Why, if the enemy had had more rifles, I'd be hauling all your carcasses out of the river this very moment."

"But, sir, Captain Travers said—" Porter tried to explain.

"Said what?" demanded Waller.

"That you were stuck in the shallows," quailed Porter miserably.

"I wasn't stuck, damn you!" ranted Colonel Waller. "I was slowed down a bit, but not stuck. We got here just fine in the end, didn't we?" He pointed to his little flotilla nestled at the foot of the cliffs.

"Well, yes, you did, sir," answered Porter despondently, giving me an imploring look.

I took pity on him and decided to defuse the volatile Colonel Waller. "Look at it this way, Colonel," I explained patiently. "Porter prevented the enemy from making off before your command could maul 'em, right? Why, just look around you. I see at least forty bodies, and Porter didn't take a single casualty. I'd say this is the sort of news that's going to play well in Manila, and when it does, the name on the bottom of the telegram will be yours, not Porter's."

Waller paused to consider this, then cracked a lopsided grin as he saw the truth in my words. "I suppose you're right, Travers," he admitted grudgingly, adding as an afterthought, "not, er, that Captain Porter and all the others won't get their due. No, I'll see to that."

And to his credit, he did. After the column endured two more rain-soaked days in the field, it stumbled back to the coast and took ship for Basey. Most of the men, racked now with fever, were immediately hospitalized. Not Waller, though, for he had more important things to do than be sick, namely to publicize his victory over the Pulajans. Oh, he was a whirlwind of activity. First, he dictated a telegram for the churlish Lieutenant Day to prepare for General Smith at Tacloban. And a masterful missive it was, singing the praises of his command and touting the skirmish of Sohoton Cliffs as the greatest clash of arms since Waterloo. Then Waller sat down to pen a lengthier report, preserving every detail of the engagement for posterity.

This done, and his exhausted command sheltered beneath rain-soaked roofs of thatch, Waller waited. Would his efforts be appreciated? Would his fondest ambition for renown both within and without the Marine Corps be realized? Was he going to parlay his time in this wilderness into something tangible? The delay played hell with his nerves, more so than the thought of meeting the enemy in battle ever did. Nervous and morose, Waller withdrew to his quarters and brooded.

I did the same, bringing the pretty senorita Lenai along with me as consolation for the escape yet again of Surlang. I had just settled down to a night of sweet bliss, in fact, when cheering from the direction of Waller's headquarters disturbed my tranquillity. "What the hell? Have those loco leathernecks found someone else to kill?" I muttered.

Curious, and a little annoyed, I threw on some clothes and a rain slicker and marched over to Waller's office. In the antechamber where Day rode his desk, I found Porter and Bearss. Day, happily waving a telegram, was so drunk he could hardly stand.

"Look, Travers," he gloated boozily, dropping the "sir" as he shoved the telegram in my face. "It's from General Smith. He's admitting that one marine is worth ten damned soldiers. What do you think of that?"

I snatched the paper from his fist. "I think you ought to have your backside kicked up a two-hundred-foot ladder once in a while, Day. Maybe then you wouldn't be so damned snotty. I was at Sohoton Cliffs and you weren't—remember?"

Bearss and Porter howled with mirth at this, causing Day to glower darkly. Wisely, though, he held his tongue as I read the message.

HEADQUARTERS SIXTH SEPARATE BRIGADE
Tacloban, Leyte, P.I., November 19, 1901

WALLER, Basey:

The brilliant success of your command—both men and officers—has my highest congratulations. It was not unexpected, however, and I know that in the future if they meet with cliffs too high to scale with ladders—that is, if necessary to surmount obstacles encountered—they will fly. There is nothing impossible for the American fighting men, and your work in the Sohoton Province is an additional proof of that fact.

Success by barefooted Americans began at Valley Forge, and I am proud to know that the same indomitable spirit that won in spite of obstacles over one hundred years ago has shown itself in Samar. Give your command the needed rest, and then touch up the enemy again. In your report mention the officers and men who especially distinguished themselves.

Smith
Brigadier General, Commanding

A nice little pat on the back but nothing more, I thought. In fact, I was heading out the door for a far more meaningful reward when Waller hurried in, having been roused by an orderly. He took one look at Smith's message and was transported into raptures.

"By God, this is glorious!" he rejoiced. "General Smith approves of our efforts. And look, look! He wants us to have another go at the enemy. Oh, this is marvelous, simply marvelous. Mister Day, have this telegram copied and posted everywhere for the men to see. It will mean more to them than anything!"

I rather thought that some dry clothes and shut-eye were what Waller's men were craving at the moment, but Day promised to have the message papered around Basey like some tawdry political bill before the night was out. Smith's flowery prose would greet the feverish leathernecks when they stumbled out of their sickbeds on the morrow.

Waller turned to me in his ecstasy. "Captain Travers, this is a turning point for this battalion. General Smith has given us his personal stamp of approval. Isn't it thrilling?"

No, it wasn't, but I avowed nonetheless, "Absolutely, Colonel." There wasn't anything in Smith's message that couldn't be found in a run-of-the-mill, postbattle proclamation. It was simply the sort of drivel one wrote on such occasions, you see, and any fool could see that Smith meant nothing by it. To Waller, however, Smith's telegram meant the world. I was beginning to see that Waller was the sort who simply lusted after approval, and Smith had just shown that he was prepared to dollop out the tripe by the wagonload. To Waller, Smith's accolade was to be savored as if it were the rarest nectar imaginable, for it promised martial renown and a chance for the marines to be recognized by the highest echelons of the army command. Oh, it was a happy group I left behind that night, patting each other on the back and dreaming of further opportunities to burnish their promising reputations.

The next few days simply heaped more fuel on the fire as messages of congratulations flowed in from everywhere. Admiral Rodgers telegraphed his kudos, which sent Waller tripping about his office in a paroxysm of delight. Then came the ultimate honor. I was in Colonel Waller's office discussing his need for a resupply of ammunition when Lieutenant Day entered, holding a sheet of papers before him so reverently that one might have thought it was a negotiable check equal to a year's salary.

"It's from General Chaffee, sir," he gasped, his voice almost breaking in emotion. Day deposited the document on Waller's desk and stepped back expectantly.

Waller read it, his eyes tearing with unrestrained joy. When he was able to speak, he croaked hoarsely, "Read it, Travers, read it. Ah, but wouldn't a soldier kill to receive a message like that from his commanding general?"

Obediently, I read the telegram:

Manila, P.I., December 1, 1901

Major Waller, Basey, P.I.

Have just read your message to General Smith dated 19th. Thanks
to officers and men. Assure each of my cordial regard and my
highest appreciation of the manly heart and soldierly spirit which
makes light of obstacles and is never daunted or satisfied while
service can be rendered to our country. I hope kind Providence
will guide the footsteps and take the part of marine soldiers battling
for peace in the wilderness of Samar.

Chaffee

I looked up. So what? I had known Chaffee back in north China
when I stood at his elbow as he ordered the assault on Peking. That
man was no emotional puss; he wrote this sort of twaddle only because it was expected of him as the department commander. If he was
here in Basey, in fact, he would probably rip into Waller about the
terrible shape of his poor boys and the chronic shortage of rations
in the field. Chaffee was about as unsentimental an hombre as ever
strapped on a pigsticker. The only thing that mattered to him was
getting the job done right and bringing back as many soldiers as possible
with whole skins in the process.
    Waller, however, saw none of this. He sat nearly speechless in his
chair, tenderly cradling the telegram in his hand and murmuring, "God
bless you, sir, God bless you."
    This caused me to eye Waller nervously; had the heat and constant
rain addled his brain? Just what was it about the runty marine that
made him so all-fired eager for praise? His carryings-on just weren't
natural, and the sight of him cooing to a piece of paper set my skin
to crawling.
    Waller caught my stare, and with an effort set the paper down on
the desk. "General Chaffee wants further sacrifices from my battalion, and by God, he shall have them. Look at this, Travers," he directed. He shoved a handwritten letter across the desk at me. I picked
it up and read. It was from Captain Ayer, General Smith's adjutant
general over in Tacloban. "Pay particular attention to the part about
the telegraph line General Smith wants," Waller admonished me.

I did. Smith's aide had written to say how happy the general was about the Sohoton affair and had added near the bottom, "As soon as your men are well rested he is desirous that you open up a trail to Hernanai on the east coast as he hopes soon to stretch a telegraph wire along that route."

I looked up. "Okay, I read it."

"That's what we'll do next," vowed Waller. "I'll get a column over to the east coast, probably to Lanang, and then scout inland from there. We'll find that trail General Smith wants and find it pronto."

The usefulness of a telegraph spanning Samar from east to west was obvious. That would allow us to shift forces back and forth between coasts as the situation dictated. The mission wasn't a problem; the condition of Waller's men, however, was.

"Look here, Colonel," I cautioned, "the message says to do all this when your command is well rested. Your men don't quite fit that description in my book. Why, most of them are walking malaria cases."

Waller brushed aside my objections. "They're marines, Travers. They'll rise to the occasion. I have no qualms about the men or their officers. We'll get that telegraph line laid out or die trying. Are you with me?"

"With you?" I asked, taken aback. "Er, what exactly do you mean, Colonel?"

"Are you ready to go with us, Travers? No white man has ever crossed Samar, and we'll be going through territory as rugged as any on this earth. You proved your mettle at Sohoton Cliffs, and I'd be honored to have a man like you at my side."

The probability that I would accept Waller's ludicrous proposal was, of course, slightly less than the odds that the carabaos in the nearby paddies would stroll about on their hind legs reciting Shakespeare. "You honor me greatly, sir, but I'm afraid that's not possible," I rebuffed him smoothly. "You see, I had a touch of fever when I was out with General Funston. I'm under strict medical orders not to go off to the hills for extended forays again. The expedition to Sohoton has just about done me in. I'm so very sorry." I'd fully recovered from my bout of fever contracted with Funston, of course, and waited tensely to see if Waller would call my bluff.

He didn't. Waller, it turned out, had a tendency to take officers at their word, an unfortunate proclivity that would eventually come near to ruining him. "A pity, Travers. I could have used you."

"Oh, I'll be much more help to you here, sir," I promised. Which was true, since in the field I'd only bolt down his rations and then bleat to be taken back to the coast and hospitalized for a few months. "I can make sure that General Smith in Tacloban receives all of your messages as they come in to Basey."

Waller liked that idea, as I knew he would, and so he put aside the notion of me accompanying him to the interior. He talked instead about his broad view for Samar. This generally involved him making war on an increasingly larger scale until he was breveted to full colonel and given a brigade rather than a battalion to command.

As soon as I decently could, I excused myself from the thickening fog of his imaginings and slipped out the door. In the antechamber sat Day at his desk, huddled over a scrap of paper with Captain Dunlap, another of Waller's company commanders, and Lieutenant Gridley, a likable youngster whose father was Captain Gridley, the old sea dog who had served so ably under Admiral Dewey in the Battle of Manila Bay.

"What have you got there, Day," I inquired, "another wanted poster from Major Glenn?"

Glenn, the judge advocate I had met in the launch with General Smith up in Catbalogan, had become active of late in his role as military commission. Glenn had taken it upon himself to interrogate suspected collaborators on Samar, and by all accounts he was remarkably skilled in that regard. Once he broke a suspect, he used the information gleaned to pen lurid wanted posters about other suspects, and then plastered them all over Samar. Lieutenant Day was predictably addicted to reading the damn things, and he was slowly coming around to the belief that there was an assassin lurking behind every tree in Basey.

Day fixed his beady eyes on me and answered with a hint of smugness, "No, it's a directive, Captain." He held it between his thumb and forefinger. "It's quite interesting. Maybe you ought to have a look at it."

I snapped the thing from his hands and glanced at it. In a flowing hand it stated, "The interior of Samar must be made a howling wilderness."

With a dismissive sniff, I tossed it back. "What's this, Day?" I taunted. "Are you writing poetry now?"

"No, I'm not," he countered archly. "I'll have you know that those are General Smith's express orders to Colonel Waller. He wants the country hereabout laid waste."

I laughed aloud at this nonsense. Oh, don't mistake me, I didn't doubt that such was Smith's desire, for indeed I'd heard him say as much. What I did doubt, however, was the authenticity of this paper. "Come now, Day," I chided him harshly, "use what few brains you've got, man, or they'll atrophy altogether. Can't you see that this note isn't a proper instruction? Why, it's not addressed to anyone and it's not dated. It's nothing, I say."

"That's not what I told Colonel Waller," he maintained stubbornly. "I got that paper directly from General Smith when I was over in Tacloban yesterday. It's written in his own hand, I tell you, and he gave it to me himself."

"Then why didn't he sign it?" I challenged. "I swear, Day, if you weren't so damned dim-witted you'd be dangerous," I declared and, with a wave of disgust, sailed out the door.

Were all marines daft? I wondered. That paper was as official as the etchings on a latrine wall. It deserved to be placed in a drawer somewhere and locked away until the middle of the next century.

27

Basey, Samar
December 24, 1901
"Bon voyage, Colonel!" I called through a veritable waterfall of sheeting rain as Colonel Waller clambered into the whaleboat that would carry him out to the gunboat *Arayat* lying at anchor just off Basey. Preceding Waller on board the gunboat were fifty marines and an assorted lot of scouts and porters. Waller had combed his fever-stalked companies for the fittest men to make what promised to be the most daring trek of the campaign. With them were Porter and Bearss, a Lt. A. S. Williams, and, of course, the intrepid Sergeant Quick.

Waller's plan was simple. The *Arayat* would carry his party over to Lanang on the east coast of Samar. Once landed, Waller intended to ascend the Lanang River by *barota* for as far as it was navigable. From there he would march overland, heading in the general direction of the Sohoton Cliffs. Waller had been told that somewhere between the headwaters of the Lanang and the Sohoton Cliffs lay an old Spanish trail that spanned the interior of the island. If it existed, Waller felt it would be an excellent track along which to string General Smith's telegraph wire. Waller meanwhile dispatched Captain Dunlap from

Basey to the Sohoton Cliffs area with supplies to await the emergence of Waller's column from the jungle and to assist in transporting it back to its home base.

As I watched Waller go—and mind you, I was positively elated to be left behind—two things about his plan struck me as ominous. First, he brought no rations with him. Instead, Waller intended to draw provisions from the army garrison at Lanang. That spelled trouble to me, unless the commander at Lanang was an unusually generous soul. You see, resupply on Samar was so erratic that few officers would voluntarily empty their larders for any but the closest of comrades. Waller, as a marine, had no claim of kinship on the army troops at Lanang.

Second, the weather was abysmal. Samar was wallowing in the monsoon season, and hardly a day passed without torrents of water pouring from the skies. Waller could not have picked a worse time to lead his exhausted command into the rugged highlands. But none of this threatened me personally, so I cheered lustily as Waller was rowed off to the distant gunboat, whereupon I turned on my heels to plan my Christmas entertainment.

I'd been a good boy this year, or at least not a completely malevolent one, and I deserved a treat, by God. Old Saint Nick saw to it, you might say, for lovely Lenai made herself available to share my humble abode all through the yule season, and together we rang in the New Year. I was so engrossed in these festivities, in fact, that I hardly bothered to leave my tent and brushed off all attempts by Day to pester me into performing any official duties. That's why I was surprised when my tent flap opened one sodden afternoon in early January and Day stepped unbidden into my little seraglio.

"Sir, Major Glenn's here to see you . . ."

He never finished the sentence. Instead his jaw fell open at the sight of my bronze maiden, buck naked, sprawled with me in the pile of linens that Lenai had cleverly fashioned into an oversized bed.

"My God, Day, don't you knock?" I thundered at him, but Lenai didn't seem embarrassed in the least. Instead, she showed an appalling lack of taste by winking at the dumbfounded adjutant.

Scandalized, Day stammered, "I'll . . . I'll wait outside," and hastily retreated.

"My dear, I beg your indulgence," I said, exasperated. "It seems the general's lawyer wishes a word with me." With a great sigh, I rose and drew on a pair of trousers. I popped my head through the tent flaps to see Major Glenn, ramrod stiff in his black slicker, fixing me with a withering stare. "May I be of service, sir?" I inquired calmly.

Fury wreathed Glenn's face as the sound of girlish tittering emanated from within my tent. Lenai evidently found great humor in the situation, you see. "Captain Travers, present yourself at headquarters in two minutes!" he snapped. Without another word he turned and stalked off in the rain.

Cursing Glenn, and Day for bringing Glenn to me, I dressed, knocked back a shot of whiskey from the bottle I kept in the footlocker by my cot, and sauntered after Glenn. When I arrived, I found him ensconced in Waller's office. He had his timepiece in hand.

"You're late, Captain," he announced acidly, eyeing his watch. Day, at his side, smirked, confident I was about to get my comeuppance.

Glenn clearly had a burr under his saddle about something, but whatever it was, I would be damned if I would dance to his tune. He was nothing but a legal officer, while I, by Christ, was a fighting man. At least that's what all my citations said, and I intended to act the part. "Then why don't you sue me, Major?" I countered, taking a seat without waiting to be asked.

Day took a step back in shock, aghast at my blatant insubordination. Glenn clenched his jaws in rage but said nothing. All this was just as I figured, you see. Glenn didn't want to antagonize me, because he wanted something; otherwise he wouldn't have come calling in the first place. So with a saucy grin on my face, I settled back to find out what was so all-fired important.

"Get out, Day," ordered Major Glenn.

"But sir," Lieutenant Day protested, "I'm Colonel Waller's representative when he's in the field. I have a right—"

"Get out!" exploded Major Glenn, and before the echoes died in the room, Day was gone from sight and the door was closed. When we were alone, Glenn observed contemptuously, "So, Travers, you've got a taste for the native women, eh?"

"I see Mr. Day has been talking out of school," I retorted, unabashed and not caring a whit for Glenn's sanctimonious attitude. Just what was this bird's game? I wondered.

"Captain Travers, did it ever occur to you that the local ladies might be spies?"

No, frankly it hadn't, but even if it had, I would not have been deterred in the least from my lecherous conduct. In fact, I would gladly have shared some meaningless bits of military gossip to lure a lovely woman to my bed. I didn't think this response would be appreciated by my inquisitor, however, so I said instead, "Come now, Major Glenn, I'm a lowly liaison officer. Even if there were spies lurking about, I would hardly be in a position to inadvertently let slip some important intelligence. I just don't have any, you see."

I sat back pleased at the compelling force of my logic, but Glenn's grim expression remained fixed in place. He slid a lengthy document across the desk. Looking down, I saw that it was entitled Circular Number 6 and was from Smith's headquarters, dated Christmas Eve. I scanned it quickly; it was a fulminating polemic by Smith warning the troops to suspect everyone and trust no one. One paragraph in particular stood out. After decrying the treachery of the Samarans in general, it proclaimed:

Under such conditions there can be but one course to pursue, which is, to adopt a policy that will create in the minds of all the people a burning desire for the War to cease; a desire or longing so intense, so personal, and so real that it will impel them to devote themselves in earnest to bringing about a state of real peace—that will impel them to join hands with the Americans in the accomplishment of this end.

I looked up with a smile. This rag was nothing more than another of Smith's bloodthirsty little rantings. "I see the general has dashed off a little note of Christmas cheer to the troops. How thoughtful of him."

Major Glenn was not amused. "Captain Travers, have you ever heard of the Katipunan Society?"

"Can't say as I have, sir. Are they Masons of some sort?"

"Hardly," sniffed Glenn. "Captain, the Katipunan Society is our real enemy in these islands. It's a secret society that was initially dedicated to ridding the Philippines of the Spanish. When we displaced the dons, the Katipunan Society declared war on us. Now, I understand you're acquainted with Emilio Aguinaldo."

"I've had that pleasure," I responded. "A downright friendly gent."

"And also the head of the murderous Katipunan Society," averred Glenn. "The society has tentacles in every barrio in the Philippines with the exception of Moroland. It forms a shadow government all around us, collecting taxes and enforcing laws, even in towns we control.

It was the Katipunan Society that decided to attack the Balangiga garrison, and I have reason to believe that it's planning another strike soon."

"What?" I squawked in alarm. "Another attack? Where?" My veneer of insouciance was gone; I was suddenly as skittish as a steer in a slaughterhouse.

"Right here in Basey, Captain Travers. The signs are all around you if you look."

"What signs?" I demanded fearfully.

"The sullen stares. The incomprehensible answers when we ask where the rebels went after we routed them from the Sohoton Cliffs. The ominous quiet all around."

"Hold on now, Major," I objected, "that's not very compelling evidence. After all, the natives are sullen and silent everywhere we quarter troops, including Manila."

Seeing my skeptical expression, Glenn asked, "Perhaps you've noticed the women coming into the town for the holy days?"

I'd seen a few, and I said so.

"I've made it my business, Captain Travers, to learn as much as possible about what happened in Balangiga. One thing I discovered, for instance, was that many of the weapons smuggled into that town were secreted under the dresses of the local women. Captain Connell had put out an order that females were inviolate, and so they were not searched. I don't think it's any coincidence that quite a few ladies are on the streets of Basey these days."

Damn, maybe he was right. I'd seen groups of women entering Balangiga when poor Connell had pointed them out to me. Still, I wasn't entirely convinced. Basey seemed a mite more secure than remote Balangiga had been. Maybe, just maybe, Glenn was suffering from an overactive imagination.

"Hmmmm, I don't know, Major," I demurred. "I've searched a few of those sarongs, and—"

"You've done what?" exclaimed Glenn.

"Er, that is, I've searched my mind," I corrected myself hastily, "but I'm not sure I see the same signs of impending doom that you do."

"Well, then consider this, Captain Travers. I'm told you know of an outlaw named Surlang. Is that correct?"

"That's right. I chased his backside from Zamboanga to Balangiga, where he personally hefted a bolo on that bloody day. Unfortunately, he escaped."

"I know," retorted Major Glenn crisply. "I am also aware that Surlang is known in these parts as *Capitán* Verde. Although he's a Moro, the Pulajans accept him for a couple of compelling reasons. One is that he's a charter member of the Katipunan Society."

Ah, I thought; that would explain why Surlang had been scuttling about with Aguinaldo up in Luzon. They were damned lodge brothers!

"Also," continued Glenn, "Surlang runs the guns from Borneo that the Pulajans are depending upon to keep the insurrection on Samar alive."

"I know all about Surlang's guns, Major," I said. "I was with Commander Henderson when he took Surlang's schooner off the coast of Leyte. I also saw Surlang at Sohoton Cliffs, although he got away before I could put a bullet in his brain. But what's the point of all this? So what if Surlang is in the hills? With the number of troops that General Smith has on Samar, Surlang'll be hounded from pillar to post until he either gives up or flees to Moroland."

"Oh? That's not what I've heard," Major Glenn countered darkly.

Something in his tone caused my heart to skip a beat in apprehension. "What have you heard then?"

"That Surlang is plotting at this very moment with some of the leading citizens of Basey, the *pudientes,* to let his band of cutthroats into town so that they can do to the marines what they did to the 9th Infantry at Balangiga. Also, Surlang plans to have gunrunners based in Hong Kong deliver Mausers to General Lukban to replace the ones that the navy seized off Taytay Point."

I was edgy now but still determined to keep up a brave front. "Oh, come now, Major. Basey isn't exactly Balangiga. After all, Waller has Colt machine guns in the streets and 3-inch cannons covering the plaza. And he doesn't let the locals stroll about with bolos in their hands. Aren't you being just a touch too jumpy?"

By way of an answer, Glenn opened a slim leather portfolio and withdrew a sheet of parchment, which he handed to me. Written in a flowery hand in Spanish, it was a report from a Filipino agent in Hong Kong. The letter stated that rifles were ready for shipment and that they would be released as soon as "Senor Harlock" was paid. The letter implored General Lukban to contact "El Moro" so that the necessary transportation could be arranged. My face was taut with fear when I returned the letter to Major Glenn.

"We don't know who this Mr. Harlock is," said Glenn, "but we suspect that he's a representative of a British trading firm that operates from the coast of China to Borneo."

I knew who Harlock was—and he wasn't British. He was an American, by God, and I had no doubt that he had access to all of the Mausers Surlang might need. Harlock had been collecting the damn things since the surrender of the Spanish back in '98 in Cuba, and he'd added to that collection after the collapse of the Boxer Rebellion in China. Hell, I'd even helped smuggle his wares out of Havana harbor, but I couldn't breathe a word of that to Glenn, of course.

"Yes, well, I'm sure you're right," I managed to gasp with a strangled knot in my throat. "This Harlock fellow is probably just what you say, some low-level transfer agent in Hong Kong. If I had to guess, I'd say that the key to containing this situation is to prevent Surlang from running a ship to Hong Kong and collecting the goods."

"I agree, Captain Travers," seconded Major Glenn, "and I think we can pretty much prevent him from doing that. If he has another signal success in Samar like he had at Balangiga, however, other Filipino nationalists, or Moro adventurers who are inclined to admire Surlang's depredations, might decide to ship the rifles for him. It's a big ocean, you know, and we can't patrol all of it. That's why it's important to keep Surlang from scoring any more victories until his followers give up."

"Er, assuming you're right, Major, shouldn't you be telling all this to Lieutenant Day? After all, he's the acting commander of the marines Colonel Waller left behind, not me."

"I have to admit, Captain Travers, news of your fraternization with the local jezebels has done nothing to inspire my confidence in you. However, Mr. Day's got no experience fighting this devil Surlang. Since you do, I charge you in Colonel Waller's stead to prepare this garrison to defend itself."

"From what?" I protested. "Major, you've shown me that some guns are ready in Hong Kong for delivery, and you've suggested that we have more than our share of ladies walking the streets. Well, to some folks the latter situation isn't necessarily bad, and the former seems just a bit too remote for any immediate concern. What I'm saying is, you haven't shown me any proof that Basey is ready to burst into revolt on an instant's notice. I mean, it's all well and good to be vigilant, but we can't go running about being scared of shadows in the night, now can we?"

Glenn didn't answer me directly. Instead he rose and put on his hat. "Follow me, Captain Travers," he directed.

Day joined us and together we trailed Glenn past the tribunal building, which also served as the crowded military prison in Basey, to where a nipa hut stood off by itself. In the hut was a squad of troopers, men whom I had never seen before. I took them to be Major Glenn's personal staff. Spread-eagled on the floor was a sputtering Filipino, water flowing from his mouth and nose. From his flushed face and disheveled appearance, it was obvious that he had been worked over for quite some time. I recognized the hombre the instant I laid eyes on him. By Christ, it was old Senor Jacosalen—Lenai's father!

"What the devil is going on here, Glenn?" I demanded. "This man is no more a confederate of the Pulajans than you or I. Why, he's the tax collector, and he's cooperated fully with Colonel Waller ever since our arrival here."

Major Glenn was unimpressed with my remonstrances. "Haul him to his feet," he ordered.

Instantly the soldiers pulled the quivering Senor Jacosalen to his feet, his eyes rolling imploringly from one hard face to the next. "Senor," commanded Major Glenn in fluent Spanish, "tell Captain Travers about the conspiracy."

"It is true, it is true!" sobbed the frightened tax collector. "The alcalde"—the mayor—"of Basey will lead an attack on the Americans. On the grave of my mother, I swear this is true."

"Take him to the guardhouse," ordered Major Glenn as I stood by in stunned silence. "Lieutenant Day, haul in the alcalde. Let's see what he has to say about all of this."

In due course, Lieutenant Day returned to the hut at the head of a squad. Dragooned between the files was the alcalde, babbling nonstop as he approached the site of inquisition. Like the born politician he was, the swarthy little scoundrel feigned complete surprise at this unsettling turn of events.

"Major Glenn! Lieutenant Day! I must protest. Colonel Waller has been assured of the unswerving loyalty of the populace of Basey. If there is some suspicion in your minds, please let me set it to rest! I beg of you, let us speak together on this matter so that our cordial relations are not damaged!"

Glenn was blunt in reply. "Senor Jacosalen has told us about the conspiracy, Senor. Do not trifle with us. I demand to know what arms are secreted about Basey. What intelligence have you sent to the rebels in the hills? What supplies have you sent them?"

"Arms? Supplies?" The face of the alcalde registered incredulity. "Major Glenn, there has been some monstrous mistake."

That was as far as he got. "Take him," barked out Glenn. His men stepped forward and seized the struggling mayor, hauling him into the nipa hut, where they threw him to his back and pinned him in place. A private who knew exactly what he was about forced a hose into the mouth of the struggling victim as another soldier pinched the fellow's nose closed. The hose was connected to a large metal can of water, and at a nod from Glenn the pouring commenced.

This was the water torture I had heard about when I served with Funston, and it was every bit as gruesome as advertised. The struggling alcalde swelled like a puffer fish as the water went in, his body convulsing and his face discolored as his oxygen was cut off. I watched his contorted visage and realized with horror that the poor bugger was literally drowning before my very eyes. When the can was emptied, the alcalde was rolled on his stomach and kicked and pummeled until he regurgitated the water. Then, gasping for air and in shock from the trauma, he was rolled over for another dose. It took only two repetitions of the process before he was squealing for mercy, promising to take Glenn to the arms cache, anything to stop the torture.

"That's better," Glenn said, grinning viciously. He nodded at his men to haul the sobbing alcalde to his feet. "Take us straight to the arms, Senor. If there is a single delay or misstep, you'll be right back in this hut so fast it'll make your head spin. Now march."

And march the fellow did, taking us directly to the jungle at the edge of town and down a worn trail that led into the interior. We went no farther than a hundred yards along the trail before he pointed into a thicket.

"There, Senor," he whimpered.

Soldiers and marines plunged in, hacking with bolos to clear the way. Then, suddenly, there was a quick movement as hidden natives bolted from the same thicket onto the trail ahead of us. As they flew down the trail like deer, I saw that there were three of them, two men and a woman. The soldiers had time only for a few hasty shots, and then the natives were gone.

"Anybody recognize 'em?" demanded Glenn.

"Nope," said Day. "All these natives look the same to me."

I was stunned; I recognized one of them all right—it was Lenai, my bed companion! "No, I'm afraid I never saw them before," I murmured. Oh, I properly damned her gorgeous hide as being a scheming plotter, but nonetheless she was a wonderful lover, and that carried a good bit of weight with me. Besides, I didn't particularly care to submit Lenai to Glenn's tender mercies.

"Let's find out what they were protecting," said Glenn.

We all pushed into the foliage until we located a pit covered with banana leaves. When the leaves were stripped away, we found a cache of bolos, spearheads, a few hundred cartridges, and several barrels of black powder. By Christ, the alcalde had told the truth—and signed his own death warrant.

Day was white with fury. "Good God, the *gugus* were plotting against us all the while. I'll see to it that they pay for this!"

Glenn looked at me in smug self-satisfaction. He'd been in town for only a few hours, yet already he had uncovered a plot that had probably been brewing under the noses of the leathernecks for a month. "Let's get back to town, Captain Travers," he fairly preened. "There isn't much time to put the defenses in order."

Hauling the cache with us, we hurried back. As we drew near the headquarters building, a rattled sentry hailed Lieutenant Day. "It's Colonel Waller, sir! Captain Dunlap just brought him in. There's been trouble, sir. Big trouble!"

28

Waller was lying on a litter in his office, his uniform torn and tattered and his eyes burning bright with fever. His feet were bare and swollen to the size of small watermelons. He was gaunt, almost emaciated, and red welts were visible on his legs and arms from the bites of leeches. Waller looked like a man who had just marched through hell.

"Day!" he gasped weakly as we entered. "The column's been separated. The march was more trying than anything I could have imagined. Our food gave out. We had only four days' worth of rations, and I put the men on half rations. They started to falter, dropping out along the way. I took Captain Bearss and the strongest men and went ahead to meet Dunlap. Porter stayed behind in the jungle with the main column of about thirty men. Dunlap and I tried to return for 'em, but we couldn't find their trail. Porter may have doubled back to Lanang, or else just gotten lost in the jungle. Whatever the case, we must get to them before they starve, or worse."

Day was bug-eyed with fear and alarm. "Worse?" he squeaked. "What could be worse, sir?"

"The natives are rising, I fear. One of my bearers, Victor, tried to steal my bolo along the march. I ordered Dunlap to throw him in the guardhouse. Poor Porter, however, has the bulk of the natives with him—and the weakest men. I'm worried sick that the churlish beasts may turn on my poor marines."

"They're mutinous here too, Colonel," asserted Day. "We just uncovered a cache of arms and powder. The mayor and the tax collector are in on the plot. The natives may fall upon us at any moment."

"Oh, my God!" lamented Waller. "How many able-bodied men do you have, Day?"

"No more than fifty," he answered.

"They'll have to do. Double the guard here in Basey, then get your gear and join me and Dunlap." Waller tried to rise but couldn't. An orderly helped him to his feet, and he stood rocking unsteadily.

Expecting an imminent attack on the headquarters, Day was perplexed. "Where are we going, Colonel?"

"Back into the jungle as soon as we've gathered some supplies. We've got to find Porter's column. We'll start from the area of the Sohoton Cliffs and march west." Looking at me, he ordered, "Captain Travers, I need you to travel to Lanang by boat. Alert the army garrison there. Have them send a column from the east. Perhaps that way we can locate the lost marines before they perish."

"I'm on my way," I assured him, more than grateful for an excuse to be gone from Basey.

I expected a protest from Major Glenn at this, since he wanted me here to rally the defenses, but in the face of Waller's dreadful tidings, the judge advocate merely affirmed, "Of course the army will do anything it can to assist your command, Colonel Waller. As General Smith's representative, I can assure you of that."

"Thank you, Major," smiled Waller weakly, exhaustion revealed in the lines on his face. "Then let's all be off. Men's lives are in the balance, I fear."

Waller was gone the next day, after having reported the fiasco to General Smith at Tacloban. Smith's adjutant general, Captain Ayer, arranged for the gunboat *Arayat* to carry me around the tip of Samar to Lanang. As for Major Glenn, the Torquemada of the Visayas, he wrapped up his visit to Basey in grand style. Sitting as a military commission, he sentenced the alcalde, Senor Jacosalen, and the local priest—whom Jacosalen had gratuitously implicated in the plot—all to be shot in the town plaza. Their bodies were still warm when Glenn and his squad of henchmen decamped for parts unknown.

When I arrived in Lanang, the garrison was already abuzz with news of the Waller disaster. Captain Porter, Sergeant Quick, and two privates, exhausted and almost dead from hunger, had stumbled into town just the previous day. I found Porter in the hospital tent being questioned by Captain Pickering, the army commander.

"Porter," I interrupted, "Colonel Waller made it to Basey. He had gone back for your men but couldn't find any sign of them. Where are they, for God's sake?"

Porter waved his hand feebly. He, like Waller, was on his last legs. "Back along the trail, Travers. The food . . . ran out. We found nothing to eat in the jungle. I hurried back with Sergeant Quick and two privates because we were the strongest. Lieutenant Williams was left in charge of the main body back on the trail."

With that Porter slipped into unconsciousness, and a medical officer stepped in to shoo everyone away. I left the tent with Pickering. "Damned foolish business," Pickering muttered as we went out. "When Waller was up here to start his hike, I told him not to try it. The interior is too rugged to attempt a passage in the monsoon season. Besides, I didn't have enough food to properly feed his column. This whole affair is pure madness, and if any of his troops die, Waller should be made to bear the consequences."

I didn't disagree with Pickering, but the first order of business was to save whomever we could, and I told him exactly that.

"I have a relief column ready to go," Pickering assured me. "As soon as the rain slackens so that the river ebbs a bit, it'll be off. Until then, all we can do is pray that those brave men don't die needless deaths."

The rains however, continued, flooding the Lanang River basin. Trees and debris washed downstream, forcing Pickering to postpone the rescue effort for a full day. When the weather broke long enough for the river to recede a bit, boats, soldiers, and native bearers hurried upriver.

We waited for days in Lanang. Finally a *barota* appeared, paddled by natives from the relief column. Lying in the bottom of the canoe were four starved marines. These poor wretches were bundled off to the hospital, more dead than alive.

"That's part of 'em," growled Captain Pickering anxiously. "Where the blazes are the rest?"

The answer came three days later. *Barotas* appeared in force, and the sentries alerted the garrison. Pickering and I, with Porter in tow, hurried to the wharf. As each canoe docked, soldiers rushed to lift the gaunt and feverish marines onto litters and hustle them off to the hospital. Captain Porter was in tears as he watched the wreckage of his men lifted from the canoes, all of them so weak they could not stand.

"My God, my God," he wept softly. Spying Lieutenant Williams, he cried out, "Williams, I only count twenty-three men here—there are ten missing! Where are they?"

Williams, unable to lift his head, could only gaze dully at Porter. "We left ten back on the trail, Captain," he murmured faintly. "They couldn't make it. No food. Too much fever. We couldn't. . . ." Here his voiced trailed off.

"You couldn't what, son?" urged Captain Pickering.

"We couldn't help them," Williams managed to whisper. "Just slipped away. Slipped away."

I exchanged a horrified glance with Pickering. Ten marines lost in the jungle? This was a disaster, all right. Oh, it was nowhere near the butcher's bill we had paid at Balangiga, but the difference was that this debacle had been totally avoidable. Williams, however, wasn't done relating his grim news.

"Captain," he wheezed to Porter. "The natives."

"The natives? What about them?" queried Porter.

Williams flexed his fingers but was too weak to lift his hands. All eyes went to the deep, suppurating gashes on his palms.

"Did the native bearers do that?" demanded Captain Pickering.

Lieutenant Williams gave a slight nod of his head. "Traitors," he murmured.

Captain Pickering looked down the length of the dock. He saw none of the natives who had originally been on the expedition. Only the ones taken upriver by the army relief column were present. "Where are the marines' porters?" he demanded.

The answer came from the army lieutenant who had led the relief column. "They're following, sir. Lieutenant Williams told us about their treachery during the march. They attacked him when he was too weak to defend himself. If we had arrived one day later, they would have murdered all the marines. We booted the lot of 'em back into the jungle, but then left one canoe on the riverbank for their use. As much as they might want to flee, they'll be along shortly. Believe me, there's absolutely nothing to eat out in that wilderness."

"By Christ, they'll pay for this," vowed Porter, trembling with fury. When his marines were bundled off to the hospital, he sat down on a hogshead to wait for the natives to arrive. Attending him was Captain Pickering and two squads of soldiers.

At dusk, a crowded *barota* bearing twelve apprehensive natives appeared around a bend in the river. The natives paddled quietly for the dock, casting worried glances at the assembled white men. The soldiers stood silently as the canoe docked and the natives clambered out. I eyed these hombres carefully. Compared to the marines, they looked pretty damned fit, causing me to wonder if they had secreted food from the unfortunate Americans. Only when the bearers attempted to file as unobtrusively as possible past the soldiers did Captain Porter speak.

"Clap these bastards in irons," he barked. "Haul them to the *Arayat*. I aim to bring them straight to Colonel Waller."

Two days later, the *Arayat* dropped anchor at Tacloban and immediately hailed the shore for assistance. Lighters pulled to her side, frantic to rush the sick marines to the well-equipped hospital ashore. Soon the story of tragedy and treachery was all over General Smith's headquarters. Porter ordered the twelve natives held below decks in irons until a boat could be arranged to carry them to Basey. Since that probably wouldn't be until the following day, Porter implored me to go over to Basey immediately to ready the jail for the traitors. He couldn't go himself because of his poor physical condition.

I had no desire to go, feeling much safer in Tacloban, but Porter was persistent, and besides, the poor bugger had suffered terribly. So in the end I reluctantly agreed. When I reached Basey, I found it a town gripped by a siege mentality. Rumors of imminent attack were everywhere, and the story of the perfidy of the natives, which had been telephoned ahead of my arrival from Tacloban, merely threw more wood on an already burning fire. Upon landing, I was met by Lieutenant Day and a corporal's guard of edgy marines.

"Captain Travers," warned Day, "be on your toes. The town is filled with spies and the villagers are waiting for the signal to rise. It could come at any moment now. The news about the ten men the natives killed on the trail with Lieutenant Williams is going around Basey from native to native."

I gave Day a quizzical look at this. "What in tarnation are you talking about, Day?" I demanded. "None of Williams's marines were killed by natives. Ten dropped out from hunger and haven't been found, but nobody's even hinted that they were murdered."

"You're mistaken, Captain," Day insisted querulously and, I thought, a bit too loudly. "A report came over the wire from Tacloban within the hour saying that ten were killed and ten died of starvation."

"Day, get a hold of yourself," I snarled back. Things were tense enough without him muddling up the facts into a hopeless jumble. "Ten marines are missing. Period. None were killed that we know of."

Day remained stubbornly unconvinced. "You're wrong," he insisted with a bull-like shake of his head. "The *gugus* killed ten and ten others are missing."

Was he mad? I wondered. A sudden whiff of alcohol told me the true nature of his delusion, however. Day was drunk, soused to the point of near insensibility. Here he was at the head of a band of armed marines, all the while drunker than an Irish lord. Deciding that there would be no reasoning with the fool, I asked instead, "Is Colonel Waller back yet?"

"Yep. He and Dunlap staggered in yesterday, more dead than alive."

"Then I need to see the colonel to make arrangements to receive the prisoners from Tacloban."

"There's no point in that, Travers," Day maintained blearily.

"No point? What the dickens do you mean, Day?" I demanded.

"I mean the colonel's nearly delirious with fever. He's been raving all night. He won't hear a damned thing you have to say."

"Then who's in charge here?" I asked uneasily.

The answer confirmed my worst fears. "Captain Dunlap, I suppose, but he's also feverish, so I guess I'm the only officer fit for duty."

That was a less than comforting thought; I was sitting atop a potential explosion of native rage, and the reins of command were in the unsteady hands of Day. "Listen, Mr. Day," I said carefully, "you mentioned there are spies about. What exactly do you mean by that? Have you caught any since Glenn left town?" If the answer was affirmative, you see, I'd turn right around and scurry back to Tacloban.

"Well, no," he admitted, then added mulishly, "but all the loyal natives say an agent was sent here to provoke an uprising just like the one in Balangiga."

"The natives say?" I snorted. "Come now, Day, don't tell me you're listening to tall tales from the locals. Yes, things are bad, and yes, we need to keep our eyes peeled, but we can't run around in a blind panic. Go post your men around all the avenues, and then get some rest. In the morning things will look better." Especially if you lay off the booze, I thought bitterly to myself.

Day fulminated a bit more about spies and partisans, but ultimately marched off woozily, with his small command following along obediently. I watched the drunken oaf stagger away, and then decided it might be wise to check Waller's condition personally. I was heading for Waller's office when I passed by an alleyway between two sturdy nipa huts. Suddenly, a brown hand shot out from the shadows, clapped around my mouth, and dragged me into the alley. I started to struggle, hoping to get off a yelp that might bring Day's men running, when the feel of cold steel at my neck stilled my struggles.

"Do not move, Senor," a husky voice said. "We intend you no harm."

Slowly the powerful grip was released. When I could speak once more I bawled fearfully, "Who in tarnation are you?"

My attacker did not reply. Instead, he turned to watch as a second figure stepped from the deeper recesses of the alley. A dim shaft of light fell on the newcomer's face, and I saw that it was Lenai! I felt dread and lust in equal measure and wondered whether I could make a dash from the alley before her friend could get his bolo into play.

As if reading my thoughts, Lenai hastened to say, "There is no need to fear, *Capitán*. If we wished you dead, you would be gone already."

"Then why did you drag me in here, Lenai?" I quavered.

"To save you" was the answer.

"To save me?" I echoed, flabbergasted. "I mean, I appreciate it, of course, but what precisely are you talking about?"

"You could have turned us all in to the judge, the one you call Glenn," Lenai explained. "We have no doubt that we would not have been able to remain silent under his torture. I do not know why you kept the secret of our identity, but you have done us a great service. In return, we shall do you a great service."

I struggled to absorb her words. Lenai's companion, I surmised, was one of the rascals who had been flushed from the bushes with her when Glenn uncovered the arms cache. If my numbed ears were hearing correctly, she was grateful and she aimed to show that gratitude. But why, I wondered, especially after what Glenn had done to her father? I had been present too. Didn't she hate all white men for that?

Lenai saw the question that was written all over my face. "No, *Capitán,*" she assured me. "You see, this Glenn is not a man with a soul. He is a beast whose heart is dead to compassion. Yes, you were there when my father was put to the torture, but I know it was not your wish. We too would be like beasts if we could not tell the difference between the innocent and the guilty, *si?*"

"*Si, si,*" I heartily agreed. This was the race we derided as savages, we who razed entire districts and dispossessed entire populations just to get at a few diehard *insurrectos?* By God, Lenai's words were resounding within my fear-crazed mind as the very essence of reason and sweet mercy. She wasn't going to have my throat slit right here and now. Oh, hallelujah! She was Florence Nightingale and Clara Barton all rolled up into one soft, deliciously formed body! When I got control of myself enough to stop my knees from knocking audibly, however, I found the presence of mind to inquire, "Er, Lenai, dearest, what exactly is it that you're saving me from?"

Her face was suddenly grim and her words were harsh. "*Capitán* Verde is in the guardhouse."

I jerked as though I had been hit with lightning. By God, Day's rumors had been true after all! "Surlang . . . er, Captain Verde? Here in Basey? How? Why?"

"He arrived in Basey today. He plans to lead a revolt, one that will free Basey. That is why he deliberately had himself thrown into the jail. He will rally the prisoners inside. Also,"—here she paused, and I thought I saw tears in those tender eyes—"he intends to kill you."

"But how do you know all this? And why are you telling me?"

"Never mind where I get my knowledge. The important thing is that his plan will fail. We cannot resist the power of the Americans any longer. Too many people have already died, but *Capitán* Verde does not care. He is not of our people. That is why I tell you this. Also, I say these things because . . . I love you, *Capitán.*"

"Oh, and I love you, my dear," I assured her fervently. If a profession of devotion was what she expected, by God, that's what she would get, for I was not unmindful that her companion's blade was only inches from my neck.

Lenai rushed into my arms and gave me a sudden, wild kiss, and then tore herself away. "I must go now, *Capitán.* We . . . we will never meet again."

Now the tears were running from the darling girl's eyes in earnest, and she dabbed at them as she jabbered to her companion. After warning me not to follow, they were gone, like two wraiths that had never really been there in the first place. Shaking my head as though awaking from a dream, I stumbled from the alley.

So, I thought, gathering my numbed senses, Surlang was in the Basey prison. I remembered that he had started the Balangiga massacre from inside the calaboose. Maybe the demon had decided that he had hit upon a winning tactic for dealing with the hated Americans. Slip into their compounds and unleash his special brand of hell from inside. Yes, that had to be it!

Suddenly I found myself screaming at the top of my lungs for Day. I found the dolt sprawled facedown across a table in the guard shack on the plaza before the prison. An empty brown jug was smashed on the earth at his feet. He had collapsed in a stupor just minutes after leaving me! "For the love of God, man, wake up!" I yelped, seizing him by his tunic and shaking him violently.

"Wha . . . wha' do ya want, Travers?" he mumbled groggily as he regained consciousness.

"You have a prisoner named *Capitán* Verde, right? He arrived only today."

Day shook his head, trying without success to get the cobwebs from his whiskey-dulled brain. "Naw, it ain't so. Just some *gugu* who wandered into town as bold as you please, asking for Jacosalen. I just happened to be around a corner with a patrol. I was all over him before he knew what hit him. He's a mean-looking brute, all right, but nobody said he was this Verde hombre."

Day hadn't been at the battle of Sohoton Cliffs, I recalled. That meant he had never set eyes on Surlang before. "Bring me to him," I demanded.

Day managed to pull himself erect. "Okay, okay. Just hold your horses, Travers."

I hurried him over to the guardhouse, where he peered through a barred window and pointed out a sinewy figure who sat on a rude bench, his back to me.

"There he is," avowed Day.

I looked in. The man identified by Day was fully half a foot shorter than Surlang. "That's not him, damn you!"

"Well, it ain't my fault. I told you before that all these *gugus* look the same to me," he protested whiningly. "How about that galoot over there?" He pointed to a far corner where a tall figure stood in the shadows.

A whisper spread among the other prisoners now, and slowly the figure stepped forward until the dim light illuminated his blazing black eyes. The glare of hatred that fell upon me was so powerful that I staggered back a step. It was Surlang!

"That's him!" I gasped. "You've done it, Day. You've done it! That's Captain Verde, all right."

Day's eyes went wide with pleasure, for even in his drunken haze he was aware that he'd managed to pull off a bit of a coup. "You want the bastard shot?" suggested Day with a wicked smile.

At first I blinked at him uncomprehendingly. "Shot?"

"Yep. Shot, gunned down, riddled. Do you want that damn'd *gugu* killed or not?"

The alcohol must have completely addled Day, I thought, for he was talking about executing Surlang as casually as one might speak of shining a pair of boots. "I'm not following you, Day," I said carefully. "Are you, er, volunteering for the job?"

He gave his thick head a firm nod. "You bet I am. Why, I helped kill those traitors Glenn uncovered, didn't I?" he bragged. "I see no reason why I shouldn't get rid of this one as well. Besides," he snickered, "I can use the practice to get ready for those killers who are waiting over in Tacloban. How about it, Travers? I'll tell the colonel, and if he agrees, I'll have this Verde fellow six feet under within the hour."

"Wait a minute, Day," I challenged him. "Didn't you say that Waller's raving with fever? How could he approve an execution?"

"Oh, he has his good moments," Day said vaguely. "Now how about it?" he repeated, nodding in the direction of Surlang.

Day's offer was tempting, but there was a big difference between finishing Surlang off in a deserted rice paddy and shooting him right in the middle of a bustling garrison town. Not that I didn't think that extermination wasn't just the thing for Surlang. The fiend had certainly earned death a hundred times over, and killing him could only confer a decided benefit on this benighted island. As for due process and a trial, those things were all well and good, but they just didn't apply to a varmint like Surlang. He was a wily snake that might slip away in an instant, so he had to be killed the moment he showed himself, and with no hesitation. No, the decision to kill Surlang didn't cause me a moment's pause, and Day was the right man for the job, no question about it. I just had to ensure that the thing was done under some veneer of authority.

"Er, could we step around the corner a minute, Mr. Day?"

He gave a hiccup and shambled along behind me as I went around the side of the tribunal building. When I was certain we were out of earshot of the nervous marine sentries, I put a hand on his shoulder. "Day, let me tell you something about *Capitán* Verde. He was in Balangiga the night before the massacre. Hell, he started the whole thing."

Day's head was lolling again, and I wasn't certain he was paying attention. He smelled as though he had been drinking steadily since I left for Lanang, and that was days ago. "Day, pay attention, damn you!" I growled, giving him a savage shake. "Captain Verde's poison, do you hear me? He's got to be shot and shot now. First, though, tell me if he was searched when he was captured."

"Searched? Hell, yeah," slurred Day. "I searched the bastard myself."

"And? What did you find?" I asked hopefully.

"Not a damn thing. He was as clean as a whistle. If he had any secret messages, they must've been stored in his head."

Blast it; I was stymied again. Surlang would never let me get near my precious map. That was a pity, but it also meant there was no reason to keep Surlang alive a moment longer.

"Day, get your besotted backside over to Colonel Waller and get permission to shoot *Capitán* Verde. I want this done all nice and proper. Round up some witnesses too, you idiot. Do you hear me? Tell Waller what I've told you, and get his blessing on this thing. As soon as you do, get the job done." I gave him a final shake for emphasis. "I want no delays, understand? That's the key here. Set your mind to the task and get it done."

"Sure," replied Day with a sloppy salute and then weaved off toward the headquarters building. I watched him go, praying that he got the message straight. But for the fact I had no desire to be publicly implicated in the events I had just set in motion, I would have gone to Waller myself. I could only hope that Day got the message across coherently, and that Waller was not lucid enough to put a stop to my scheme.

Whatever the outcome, I had no intention of staying around to see the job was done. No, I had had quite enough of Basey, thank you. Lenai and her *compadres* were still loose in the back streets, and just seeing Surlang in that cell reminded me all too clearly of those awful moments in Balangiga when I thought my life was forfeit a dozen times over. No, I couldn't face up to another nightmare like that. Porter's task was now banished from my mind, and Basey had seen the last of me until whatever evil Surlang might be plotting was thoroughly quashed.

I found the boat I had taken over from Tacloban waiting by the quay and ordered the tars manning it to carry me across the strait. We were about three hundred yards from shore when I heard the distant crack of a rifle. As the sound reverberated off the placid water, I allowed myself a faint smile.

Arriving at Tacloban, my vessel steamed slowly past the *Arayat*. On its deck for a breath of air were the mutinous porters whom Captain Porter had clapped in irons. Tomorrow they would be carried across the strait to Colonel Waller. Their mournful eyes told me they clearly realized that retribution awaited them in Basey.

29

Tacloban, Leyte
January 22, 1902
"What the devil does this mean?"

I looked up from the small desk I had commandeered in a corner of General Smith's headquarters to see Captain Ayer puzzling over a telegram that had just clattered in over the wire from Basey. I got to my feet and tentatively made my way across the room until I was in a position to read over Ayer's shoulder. What I read left me stunned:

IT BECAME NECESSARY TO EXPEND ELEVEN PRISON-
ERS, TEN WHO WERE IMPLEMENTED IN THE ATTACK ON
LT. WILLIAMS AND ONE WHO PLOTTED AGAINST ME.

S/WALLER, BREVET LIEUTENANT COLONEL

As I was reading, General Smith came out of his office. "Sir, you had better see this," said Ayer, handing the message to General Smith.

"Yes, what is it?" asked Smith distractedly, obviously preoccupied with greater matters. One look at the telegram, however, reordered his priorities. "Well, well," he beamed approvingly, "I see Colonel Waller's been busy."

"I'm not sure, sir," responded Ayer. "What does he mean by 'expend'?"

Smith wasn't listening, however; he was sauntering back to his office whistling a jaunty tune. I suspected that Smith knew damned well the meaning of "expend"; it meant that Waller had gone on a killing spree over there in Basey. He'd started with Surlang, thanks to me, and finished with ten of the porters. Although I was amazed that Waller had decided to shoot so many natives, the most important thing to me, of course, was that he had eliminated Surlang. With the Moro out of the way, there was no further reason to tarry any longer here under General Smith. It was time to return to Zamboanga and search for Alice.

My mind began casting about for ways to arrange for the transfer I now desired. Since Waller's battalion was undermanned, there was no way he would consent to me leaving. My eyes fell on the telegram Smith had cast aside. Yes, I decided, that would fit the bill nicely.

When Ayer turned to other matters, I palmed the telegram and went off to the room where the telegraph operators sat busily clicking out their messages to Smith's scattered units. I approached one young fellow and pronounced officiously, "General Smith has directed that this message be sent on to headquarters in Manila. See that it goes out immediately."

The youth looked no farther than the silver bars on my shoulder. "Yes, sir," he replied.

With that one wire, Waller's campaign on Samar came to a screeching halt. General Chaffee, stung by constant criticism from the anti-imperialist press at home and the antimilitary carping of Judge Taft at his elbow in Manila, was aghast at the news. He descended on Samar in a fury, launching an investigation into the affair using his own inspector general. What the inspector general found completely shattered Chaffee's confidence in Smith. Waller had executed eleven natives without a trial, nor even the cursory inquiry of a military commission! It was scandalous. How could Smith have stood by and let such an atrocity occur?

Following the investigation, an order came over the wire from Manila. The marine composite battalion was to stand down from duty on Samar and return to Cavite. The message was silent on the issue of the killings. Waller's exhausted marines dutifully assembled at Tacloban for a review by General Smith before embarking on the steamer that would carry them back to Cavite. Smith addressed the marines with flowing oratory, praising them for their efforts and wishing them godspeed, but he studiously avoided any private words with their anxious commander. It was only after the ceremony, when Waller stood waiting for his men to board their transport, that he spotted me. He hurried over and plucked worriedly at my sleeve.

"Captain Travers, you're close to General Smith. What's to become of this infernal investigation? Has he heard from Chaffee?"

Waller was clearly frightened to death that his career was going to be affected by the killings. In truth, though, Smith had been completely silent on the matter, almost withdrawing into himself from the moment Chaffee's inspector general had appeared. The bombast that had been the old fire breather's characteristic trademark had been absent ever since then.

"I'm afraid General Smith hasn't mentioned any of that to me, Colonel," I answered levelly. "You could raise it directly with him before you left, I suppose."

"No, no, that wouldn't do," fretted Waller. "The general's got too much on his mind to be bothered with my worries."

That seemed to be it then, so I said, "Perhaps you're right, sir. I guess I'll wish you a pleasant voyage. Fair winds and gentle seas, eh?"

Waller, however, was reluctant to leave, for he clearly had something to get off his chest. I hoped that my breezy demeanor would signal that I was not at all keen on becoming his confidant, but unfortunately the pest didn't take the hint. "This is an awful mess, Travers. Smith can't tarnish the reputation of my marines just because things got carried away over there in Basey. It would never have happened if I hadn't been out of my mind with fever. Damnit—I thought at the time I was doing what Smith wanted. I acted in good faith. But does he support me after the fact? No, he shuns me like I was a damned leper. It's insupportable, I tell you. If I had it to do all over again, when that fool Day came in with his tale about Captain Victor, I should have sent him across the strait to confer with Smith. I should have laid the whole mess squarely on his doorstep."

At first I thought Waller had misspoken. "You mean Captain Verde, don't you, sir?"

"No, not at all. It was a Captain Victor whom Day wanted shot. Definitely Captain Victor. And shot he was, the first of the eleven. Damn it all, I should have sent that oaf Day on his way."

Captain Porter chose that moment to signal that it was time to board the transport, and Waller hurried off, leaving me gaping in his wake. Either Waller was confused or Day had garbled my message—badly! Captain Victor was the common thief who had tried to steal Waller's bolo while the two of them were out in the jungle together. Had Day muddled Victor's name up with Verde's in his rum-soaked head and hauled the wrong native from the jail to be shot? The feeling of smug satisfaction that had enveloped me ever since I left Basey slowly drained away, leaving in its wake seething doubt. Could Surlang still be alive? No, that couldn't be possible, I told myself. Not even a drunken marine could have so completely botched such an easy job. Although my doubts lingered, it was a foregone conclusion that I was not going back to Basey to lay those nagging questions to rest, and in the end, I decided to have faith that even as big a fool as Day was, he could not have made such a monumental blunder. There simply was no way Surlang could have escaped me this time.

Putting the matter behind me, I made immediate arrangements to book passage back to Zamboanga, where, I had since learned, Longbottom had gone as soon as his wounds from Balangiga had healed. I suppose that Longbottom's concern for Fiona accounted in some measure for his haste to be off, but I couldn't discount the suspicion that he, like me, had seen all of Samar he could stomach.

Transport, unfortunately, was scarce, and I was placed on a waiting list. I had to cool my heels around Tacloban for the better part of a week before I was notified that Captain Ayer had tickets and orders for me. At the news, I fairly ran to his office to collect them. The somber expression on the adjutant general's face, however, alerted me that something unusual was afoot.

"What is it, Ayer?" I asked warily.

He handed over the bundle of documents before him. "Those are court-martial orders, Travers," he replied.

The bottom of my stomach fell to the floor. "Who's being tried?" I asked shakily.

"Colonel Waller. General Chaffee's decided to send him before a general court-martial for murder."

"Murder?" I cried in dismay, raw fear clutching at my guts. "What has any of that got to do with me?"

"Colonel Waller has made his choice of counsel. He's selected Major Glenn—and you."

"Me? A defense counsel at a court-martial?" I sputtered, astounded. "By Christ, there's been a terrible mistake, I tell you!"

"There's no mistake," countered Ayer firmly, showing me the order that appointed me as counsel for the defense. He was right; the damned thing was signed by Gen. Adna R. Chaffee himself.

30

Manila, Luzon
March 18, 1902
"All rise!"

At the bellowed command from the sergeant appointed as bailiff of the court-martial, Waller, Glenn, and I rose. To our right, the judge advocate—Waller's prosecutor, Major Kingsbury—also rose.

Yes, it was old Kingsbury, whom I had met when Surlang broke loose inside Manila when I first landed in these islands. General Chaffee, short on trained lawyers, had appointed Kingsbury, since he was good with details and seemed reliable enough. Kingsbury acknowledged me with a curt bob of the head, nothing more, and then in filed the members of the court, thirteen in all, led by the president of the court, Brig. Gen. William H. Bisbee. The court members, like the judge advocate and the members of the defense, were attired in dress uniforms. Even without his buttons and sashes, Bisbee would have been about as imposing a figure as could be imagined, and indeed, as he stood grimly to commence the trial, Bisbee looked like the very incarnation of doom.

Bisbee swore the judge advocate to his duties and then directed sharply, "Major Kingsbury, read the charge against Major Waller." For these proceedings, Waller's brevet title of colonel had been dropped, you see. Bisbee's dour expression turned positively bleak when Kingsbury obeyed. His eyes, along with those of the other court members, an even mix of army and marine officers, fixed straight on Waller. Holding the charge sheet before him, Kingsbury cleared his throat primly and read:

Charge: Murder in violation of the Fifty-eighth Article of War. Specification: In that Major Littleton W. T. Waller, United States Marine Corps, being then and there detached for service with the United States Army, by authority of the President of the United States, did, in time of war, willfully and feloniously and with malice aforethought, murder and kill eleven men, names unknown, natives of the Philippine Islands, by ordering and causing his subordinate officer under his command, John Horace Arthur Day, First Lieutenant, U.S. Marine Corps, and a firing detail of enlisted men under his said command, to take out said eleven men and shoot them to death, which said order was then and there carried into execution and said eleven natives, and each of them, were shot with rifles, from the effects of which they then and there died.

This at Basey, Island of Samar, Philippine Islands, on or about the 20th day of January, 1902.

When Kingsbury finished, the only sound in the room was the scratching of the matronly court reporter's pencil on her paper as she transcribed the events for posterity. The proceedings were under way, and Waller was on trial for his life.

"Be seated," ordered Bisbee, then he turned to Waller and demanded, "Major Waller, how do you plead?"

I held my breath, for I'd gone over this part of the court liturgy in detail with Waller and Glenn. Several days earlier, Glenn, an experienced barrister, had noticed a loophole in the law. Waller, it seems, had been cut loose by the army and returned to Cavite *before* the charge was served on him. To Glenn, that meant that the army had lost jurisdiction over Waller. Only the navy could try him, yet the navy had no jurisdiction in Basey where the murders took place. Check and checkmate, Glenn had reasoned to an attentive Waller. Merely raise the issue of jurisdiction instead of entering a plea and Chaffee will have to let you go, advised Glenn.

At the time, Waller had turned to me and asked, "Captain Travers, what's your view of Major Glenn's suggestion?"

I was no lawyer, and Waller damned well knew it. I'd made that very point loudly and repeatedly as soon as I had landed in Manila. Waller, however, had brushed aside my protestations, and indeed barely had a word with me before this conclave with Glenn. So I was understandably in an irritable mood, and I snapped in reply, "Colonel, the only way you're going to avoid going through a court-martial is to slip down to the dock and hop a tramp steamer to China. Glenn's motion isn't worth the breath it'll take to argue it."

"Hold on now, Captain Travers!" retorted Glenn hotly. "I have an obligation to offer Colonel Waller the very best legal defense possible. I would be remiss if I did not make this motion, and I don't mind telling you that I take exception to your butting into areas where you have no professional experience or credentials."

"Listen, Glenn," I scoffed, "we both know that you have an ulterior motive for making this motion, and it has nothing to do with my lack of credentials. The plain truth of the matter is that you're prepared to try any lamebrained scheme you can think of to get Waller off." It was an insolent tone I took with Major Glenn, all right, but one I could afford to take. As the military commission for Basey, he had quite a few skeletons to hide, and I just happened to know where a few of them were buried.

"Lamebrained scheme?" exclaimed Glenn, outraged.

"Exactly so," I maintained coolly, for I was right and I damn well knew it. "You see, I happen to know General Chaffee, Glenn. I was with him back at Peking when we took the Forbidden City. Chaffee was prepared back then to turn his guns on his Japanese and Russian allies when they impeded his way into the place. That tells me he's not the sort to be thrown off the scent by your piddling little plea of no jurisdiction. Your client's going to trial, come what may, and if you weren't so damned concerned about your own hide, you'd face up to that fact right now."

Glenn, his face crimson with fury, was on his feet now. "I resent your accusations, sir!" he almost screamed.

"Resent 'em all you want, Major, but they're true. I've only been in Manila a few days, but I've already heard that after Waller and Day are tried, you'll be next. Chaffee's inspector general nosed around Samar a bit after he was done with poor Waller here. He found out that you put half the officials on the island to the water torture, and shot anyone who was idiotic enough to confess to anything. That information got Chaffee's nose a bit out of joint, as you can well imagine."

"I was empowered as a military commission, damn you, Travers!" ranted Glenn. "I was within the authority granted to me by regulation to execute those mutinous dogs!"

I snickered at this. "Oh, that'll look great screaming from the front page of the New York *World*. I can see it now: 'Major Kills Townsmen—Lawfully.'" I shook my head with amusement. "No, my friend, Chaffee won't buy what you're selling. He'll let you tell your story to a court-martial."

This settled Glenn right down, and as he considered what lay in store for him, I turned back to Waller. "This jurisdiction argument is plain foolishness. It has about as much chance of prevailing as a clawless cat in a kennel."

"Then what do you suggest, Travers?" Waller's question was cold, almost condescending. I knew that he didn't give a tinker's damn for my opinion, but I gave it anyway.

"Tell the court what happened. You were sick, out of your head. Lieutenant Day came to you about shooting a native and you agreed. Maybe on a better day you might have mulled it over a bit more, but what's done is done. You just weren't yourself. Then, when the boatload of mutineers showed up from Tacloban, and your staff advised that ten of 'em be shot, well, you just kind of went along. Again, you were out of your head, temporarily loco. Under the unique and desperate circumstances that prevailed at the time, you can't be blamed for what happened. Nope, you did your level best, and when the smoke cleared, well, there just happened to be eleven dead folks lying around town. True, things got a mite out of hand, but it could have happened to anyone, eh?"

I'd ended with a huge smile, to show how compelling this tale would be, and the best part was, it was all true. Hadn't Waller told me himself that he had been half insane with fever, and if his head had been clearer he would never have listened to Day? It was a story the court might buy, and it had the added advantage of screening my role in egging Day on the way I did. And damnit, I deserved to slip through this net. When I had set Day on Surlang, I had never imagined that Waller would then go off half-cocked and shoot ten of the twelve *cargadores* implicated by Lieutenant Williams and Captain Porter without so much as a hearing. I hadn't wished any of those poor beggars ill, you see. I had only been aiming to rid the world of Surlang.

The icy stare Waller gave me in reply told me there was something about this situation I didn't understand, and he wasted no time in laying it straight out for me. "Travers, you really don't have half the brains of a tree frog. Do you actually think I would stand up in open court and confess that I had lost my mind, if only temporarily?"

The smile on my lips was slipping a bit, but I kept up a brave front. "Of course. It's that or face a possible death sentence, Colonel."

Waller cut me off with a wave of his hand. "The subject is closed, Captain Travers. I intend to command marine units after this trial. I can sustain some damage to my reputation and still accomplish that goal. The Marine Corps can be damn forgiving about certain things, but if there's one thing it never overlooks, it's weakness. Whatever happens here, I'll do nothing that might jeopardize my prospects for a future command. And I expect my *counsel,*" here he eyed me pointedly, "to follow the same line."

I sat back dumbfounded. For my money, Waller truly had a defense based on mental incapacity. Why, here he was facing the possibility of being fitted with a hemp necktie, yet his only concern was getting another command. If that wasn't insanity, then I didn't know what was. Waller did, however, unravel one mystery for me. That is, he had made clear why I had been selected as one of his defense counsels. I was the only one who had heard him admit that he was out of his head back there in Basey. Since such talk could ruin him if it were to come out in open court, he precluded that possibility by bringing me on board the defense team; I would be unavailable to testify, you see.

All this was going through my head again as Waller rose and, referring to himself in the third person, informed General Bisbee: "Sir, the accused enters a plea in bar to the jurisdiction of the court."

A murmur broke forth from the assembled court as Major Kingsbury shot to his feet, completely flummoxed. He had been sent by General Chaffee to try Waller quickly and with a minimum of fuss, by God. Kingsbury's role as judge advocate was supposed to be simplicity itself. He was to get Waller convicted by Bisbee, then bring the conviction back to Chaffee all wrapped in a neat bundle so that Chaffee could approve the recommended sentence. Nobody had warned Kingsbury to expect any legal legerdemain, and the staid old staffer hadn't the foggiest notion of how to reply to Waller's plea.

"Well, well, this is irregular, sir," he stammered out in protest. "Highly irregular, I say."

"I haven't asked for your thoughts yet, Major," observed General Bisbee bluntly. "Sit down!" at which Kingsbury sank like a stone and sat mute. Turning to the defense, Bisbee growled, "Please continue, Major Waller."

And Waller did, putting forth his argument just as Glenn had marked it out for him. He introduced orders into evidence showing his attachment for army service, and then orders showing his relief and return to Cavite. Then, citing some treatises that Glenn had dug up, he argued that no charges were pending against him at the time of said relief, which equated to a complete lack of jurisdiction over him by the army. So, if the court would be so kind, would it please inform General Chaffee that the game was over and the time had come for a complete withdrawal of the charge? Having delivered his brief masterfully, Waller sat with a flourish.

A glint of concern in his eye, Bisbee turned to Kingsbury. "Now, Major Kingsbury, what does the judge advocate have to say to all of this?"

Kingsbury was up instantly, squawking and blowing. "Begging the leave of the court, sir, the defense motion is inadmissible. Yes, improper and inadmissible. Can there really be an issue of jurisdiction here? No, I say. Why, look for yourself, sir. There sits Major Waller. If he's here, well, we've got him, don't we? I mean, seeing is believing, isn't it?"

Now Glenn rose. "I object, sir. The judge advocate makes a mockery of our plea. He seems to say that because General Chaffee ordered Major Waller to this place for trial, it follows that there's jurisdiction. Such reasoning is utter nonsense, sir."

Kingsbury was objecting now to Glenn's objection, and the two of them were fussing back and forth like two bluejays fighting over spilled seed corn, until General Bisbee thundered, "Stop it! Stop it, I say!" Once he had gaveled the chamber into silence, he said, "Major Kingsbury, the defense has offered assorted official orders and legal authorities to support its position. Do you have points and authorities in opposition?"

Authorities? Kingsbury didn't like the sound of that one bit. Wasn't Bisbee going to simply gavel Glenn and Waller down and get the proceedings rolling again? When General Bisbee's steely glare told him this court-martial intended to play by the rules, all fair and square, Kingsbury gulped uncomfortably.

"You wish authorities, sir? Why, well, I guess there's the authority of General Chaffee. He has ample authority, as you well know. Oh, and yes, we have the authority of the president of the United States. Indeed, the president has a great deal of authority." On Kingsbury went, hopeful now, invoking the name of every functionary between Waller and Teddy Roosevelt, including the commissary officer who doled out rations to the navy yard. Kingsbury picked up speed as he went, reciting the chain of command like a Hindoo mantra, oblivious to the fact that, to every objective observer in the room, his position was hopeless. He was steaming along much like a side-wheeler with its helm jammed over, you see. He made lots of noise and generated plenty of smoke, but in the end he did nothing except splash about in circles. It rapidly became evident to General Bisbee that the judge advocate hadn't the slightest idea of how to respond to Waller's surprise move.

Finally, General Bisbee could stand no more. "When I say authorities, Major Kingsbury," he interrupted savagely, "I mean legal authority!

Can you provide me with legal authority to refute the argument on jurisdiction made by Major Waller?"

That was it. Kingsbury was nailed down, and in the despondent voice of a small boy forced to admit he hadn't prepared his lesson for the day, he squeaked, "No, can't say as I can, sir."

"Then this court will retire to consider the defense's motion."

Within the hour Bisbee reconvened the court. When all was in order once more, he announced for the record, "The decision of this court is that it is without jurisdiction in this case. The record will be sent back to General Chaffee with the recommendation that the charge be dismissed." He banged his gavel twice and the court was adjourned.

Glenn was nodding smugly; as soon as the court withdrew, Waller swept him up in a huge bear hug. "You did it, Glenn, you did it!" exulted Waller. The two of them capered about the nearly deserted courtroom as the diminutive court reporter looked on in amazement. It was several minutes before they noticed me watching them with a look of bemused detachment.

"Travers, are you blind, man? We won!" whooped Waller. "We won!"

I sniffed at this. "You haven't won anything yet, Colonel. Chaffee didn't go through the trouble of hauling you before this court-martial only to see you slip off on the strength of Glenn's legal filibustering. No, this fight ain't over by a long shot."

Glenn threw me a look of pure contempt. How dare I question his forensic abilities? "This case is finished, Travers. When General Chaffee sees the force of our arguments, he'll withdraw the charge. The facts will admit no other outcome."

"I repeat, Glenn, you don't know General Chaffee. Mark my words, your motion won't deter him for an instant."

As things turned out I was wrong about the time; Glenn's motion stumped Chaffee for three days. Then messengers summoned all members of the court and the accused back to the hearing room, and Major Kingsbury stood to read a letter from General Chaffee. The language was well composed and quite proper in tone. Stripped of its veneer of civility, however, it said: Try Major Waller and be quick about it.

General Bisbee listened as the letter was read, then retired for a short deliberation. When the court reconvened, his face was a mask. He cleared his throat and announced, "The action of the court is that, after due consideration of the views of the convening authority, as expressed in his letter just read to the court and embodied in the proceedings, and of the documents considered and read, the court reconsiders its former decision upon the question of jurisdiction, and now decides that it has jurisdiction, and directs that the case proceed to trial."

He may as well have said to loose the hounds. Waller paled and sank back in his seat as Glenn frowned sullenly. Kingsbury, however, gave a satisfied little smirk, then stood up and piped, "The government calls Captain Dunlap."

Dunlap was sworn, and in his stumbling, repetitive way, Kingsbury elicted a flow of testimony from the witness showing that Waller's hastily conceived expedition had been set in motion at the worst possible time, and undertaken by men already weak from disease and hardship. With that established, Kingsbury got to the events in Basey on January 20. "Now Captain Dunlap, did you have some communication on the morning of the twentieth with the headquarters at Tacloban?"

Dunlap nodded. "Lieutenant Gridley was in Tacloban that morning. He told me over the telephone that our party—meaning Captain Porter's party—had arrived from Lanang on the *Arayat*. He had seen them, he said, and had talked to Captain Porter, Mr. Williams, and some of the men. He said that our men were in horrible shape, that he thought some of them were dying, and that they had evidently suffered a great deal. He went on further to say that he was going to send some prisoners to Basey, and that they had been very treacherous. He said he had been told this by Captain Porter and Mr. Williams. They had gotten food for themselves when our men did not know how to get it or where to get it. He also said that several of them had attacked Mr. Williams, who had several bolo wounds."

"Is that all Mr. Gridley told you?"

"No, he added that all of these fellows were scoundrels and deserved to be shot."

All of this helped Waller, not the prosecution, and both Waller and Glenn were smiling a bit as Kingsbury continued. "Now, did Sergeant Quick arrive in Basey in advance of the boatload of natives from Tacloban?"

"Yes, he did. Captain Porter sent him over to report to the colonel." This was news to me. I supposed that Porter had turned to Quick as an emissary when I failed to reappear after my harrowing trip over to Basey.

"Did you have occasion to speak with him? That is, did you personally engage in conversation with Sergeant Quick that morning?"

"Yes, while he was standing in the hall waiting to see Major Waller. I asked Sergeant Quick about the march and about the natives. Do you wish to hear the conversation?"

"Yes."

"Sergeant Quick said that they had a very hard trip in the interior and that the men had suffered a great deal. He said that some of the natives had been very faithful—and mentioned two of them. He also said that the others had been very treacherous, that they had succeeded in finding food for themselves while the men starved. And he said that the natives had been mutinous, that they would not do anything the men told them to do."

Kingsbury turned and walked toward the court members, his back to the witness. "Did Sergeant Quick tell you he knew these facts because he had personally seen the commission of them?"

Dunlap's face clouded, but he answered frankly. "He just told me about what happened. Whether he had seen the happenings or just heard about them, I cannot say. He simply told me the natives had done these things."

"You don't know where he got his facts?"

"No."

Now I saw the point of Kingsbury's questioning, and a damned clever maneuver it was. Sergeant Quick, although present on the doomed march, had returned to Lanang with Porter ahead of Williams's stricken party. Quick, therefore, had not been a witness to the events he related to Dunlap. Neither had Lieutenant Gridley, who had spoken by telephone to Dunlap. That meant Waller had acted without troubling to first talk to any eyewitnesses. He had ordered men to be killed based on hearsay alone.

His object now painfully clear, Kingsbury drove forward remorselessly. "Did you hear Major Waller give the order to kill these people?"

"I heard Major Waller give the order to Mr. Day to take out the prisoners who had been sent back under guard to be shot."

"When Major Waller gave this command, was it a deliberate command?"

"It was."

"Was Major Waller sick at this time?"

"He was."

"Was he lying down or standing up at the time he gave the command?"

"He was lying down, as I remember."

"Do you think Major Waller was in his right senses?"

At a sharp nudge from Waller, Glenn was on his feet. "I object to that question, Mr. President," referring to General Bisbee in the parlance of courts-martial. "The answer calls for an expert medical opinion on the part of this witness."

This set off another round of bickering, which Kingsbury finally ended by withdrawing the question. After some further less-than-incisive probings, he returned to his chair and sat down.

Ignoring the admonition that only a fool serves as his own lawyer, Waller rose diffidently to conduct the cross-examination. Why he took charge of his own defense in this manner I have no idea. Perhaps his inflated opinion of himself led him to conclude he was the best man for the job. Perhaps he was simply uncomfortable with Glenn. Whatever the reason, Waller was nervous and fidgety now that his motion had failed, and his questioning showed a less-than-sure hand. At the very conclusion of his cross-examination of Captain Dunlap, however, he did make one key point when he inquired, "Did you express any opinion to Major Waller about what should be done with the prisoners?"

"I did."

"What was your opinion?"

"I told Major Waller I thought they should be shot" came the firm answer.

"That is all," announced Waller, looking grimly pleased, and he took his seat.

31

The next day I sat apprehensively as Kingsbury called Lieutenant Day to the stand. Day, pending charges himself, was in essence a coconspirator, and all the court members eyed him damned narrowly as he took the oath. A sheen of sweat glowed on Day's florid brow, betraying his deep unease. Since Day was his witness, Kingsbury fired the opening salvo.

"Did you receive any orders from Major Waller, your commanding officer, regarding the execution of certain natives?"

"I did."

"Did you receive an order on January 19, the day before the vessel arrived with the native prisoners at Basey?"

"I did."

"That's a damned lie," hissed Waller at my side. "I didn't order him to shoot anyone on the nineteenth—or at least I don't remember doing so."

I was white with fear now. Where was Kingsbury going with this? The charge sheet said nothing about any shooting on the nineteenth! As far as I knew, there had been but one killing on the nineteenth, and that had been at my direct instigation. Good God, was Kingsbury going to ask Day where he got the notion to kill Surlang? If he did, I would be the next one served up with charges from Chaffee!

"Cut him off, damnit," I whispered anxiously to Glenn. "Waller's charged with killing people on the twentieth, not the nineteenth. Cut him off!"

Glenn, not appreciating the danger, started to argue with me, saying that a single day one way or the other didn't matter; but Waller, praise heaven, was in a contentious mood and rose on his own behalf.

"We object to that question!" he shrilled. "The charge specifies the alleged order was given on January 20, and the accused has knowledge of giving the order then. We are prepared to try this case only on that specification."

Kingsbury turned to Waller, unimpressed by the objection. "I direct the attention of the court to the language of the specification. It says 'on or about the twentieth day of January.' That gives me a degree of latitude, Major Waller."

All of this set off another catfight with Glenn, who at last, following Waller's lead, leaped into the fray and argued that if Kingsbury wanted to lump any killings on the nineteenth into the killings on the twentieth, he should have said so in the charge. Kingsbury countered by insisting he had leeway on this matter, causing Glenn to assert that Dunlap had spoken of killings on the twentieth, and now the prosecutor was stuck with that day.

Finally General Bisbee, fed up with both their antics, rapped his gavel and roared, "The objection is overruled, Major Glenn! Major Kingsbury, please proceed."

My insides were trembling like a Shaker with the raptures as Kingsbury repeated, "You have stated, Lieutenant Day, that you received an order from Major Waller on January 19, the day before the prisoners arrived at Basey. Will you state what that order was?"

Day looked right at me and paused. All eyes were on him, and nobody noticed the slight motion I made of drawing my index finger across my neck as I looked into his darting eyes. My message was clear: Spill your guts on me, Day, and I'll see you in hell.

Day swallowed hard and murmured in response to Kingsbury's question, "I should like to state that charges for murder have been preferred against me and I am to be tried. Some of the questions here might tend to incriminate me. I should like to have my counsel, Mr. Harrison, present while I'm on the witness stand."

This caused a great hubbub until Bisbee finally ascertained that neither party objected seriously to Day's request, so Mr. Harrison was let into the room. Harrison, a seedy old shyster clad in a rumpled white linen suit, cut in a style that might have been fashionable twenty years earlier, shuffled down the aisle to stand at his client's side. General Bisbee's nose crinkled in distaste at the tobacco juice stains on Harrison's lapels and the broken veins of the lawyer's near-flaccid nose. Day's attorney had the thoroughly disreputable look of a fellow who had spent the previous evening curled up behind the bar of some low-class cantina. I pegged Harrison for what he was, one of the broken-down barristers who flocked to the edge of army encampments to make a living by providing uneven and usually marginal defenses to soldiers charged by courts-martial.

After some hurried conversation with Day, Mr. Harrison turned to Kingsbury and announced with a great spray of spittle, "My client is prepared to proceed, Counselor," and trailed off with a huge wracking cough. For that announcement, I estimated, he would probably charge Day the better part of a month's pay, and the thought gratified me immensely.

Stepping back to avoid any contagion, Kingsbury repeated his question to Day. "State to the court, Lieutenant Day, what that order was."

"I can't recall the exact words, but the order was to take a native out and shoot him."

"This was on the nineteenth?"

Day looked at me before answering, and what he saw in my eyes must have unnerved him again, for he mumbled evasively, "Uh, I don't remember the date."

Kingsbury shot a look of exasperation around the room before asking in a peeved tone, "Was it a day previous to the arrival of the prisoners?"

I made a little cocking motion with my thumb and forefinger. Day flinched at the sight and stalled miserably, "I, er, don't exactly understand the question, sir."

Now General Bisbee was growing restive, and threw Day a withering look. Day shifted uncomfortably under that glare and turned miserably to his attorney for succor. He got none, for Harrison was busy ogling the spinsterish court reporter, who gave him a look of pure revulsion in return.

"I will put it a different way," offered Kingsbury. "Did you receive an order in regard to a native from Major Waller, the commanding officer, previous to the arrival of the launch with the prisoners and sick men?"

"I don't remember any launch arriving with any sick men," Day maintained elusively.

Kingsbury's patience with Day was nearing an end. "Well, a vessel!"

"I don't remember any vessel, sir. Do you mean prior to the arrival of the *Arayat* in Tacloban?"

"No, I don't mean that! I mean previous to the arrival of a vessel that brought a group of prisoners from Tacloban to Basey."

"Yes, I did."

Glenn jumped up at this. "You say an order was given prior to arrival," he said to Kingsbury. "Does that mean the order for the execution was given on that same day prior to the arrival of the launch? Your last question does not bring out the date."

Kingsbury rolled his eyes in frustration, for now he too was getting confused. Turning to Day, he tried again. "On the twentieth, on the very day that the boat arrived, with these prisoners. Before the boat arrived, did you receive an order in relation to a native?"

"I did."

"That was before the boat arrived?"

"Yes, before the boat arrived."

"Will you please state to the court what that order was, as near as you can recollect."

"To take the native out and shoot him."

I was lost now myself. What was Day talking about? I knew, of course, that Surlang had been shot on the nineteenth. I knew also that the other prisoners, the mutinous bearers, were shot on the twentieth, after they arrived from Tacloban. The exact number of these wretches was not clear, you see, for Waller had not bothered to have them counted before he ordered their executions. Judging from the charge sheet, and allowing for the killing of Surlang on the nineteenth, I would have guessed that the number of fatalities on the twentieth had been ten. Was Day now saying that earlier on the twentieth, before the arrival of the natives from Tacloban, some other native had been shot in Basey? If so, that made twelve dead, not eleven.

"Do you know what the name of that native was?" continued Kingsbury.

Day appeared to ponder the question mightily before answering, "I do not."

I was puzzled at his answer. Why would Day not divulge this fellow's name if he was willing to admit that such a shooting had actually occurred? There was nothing to be gained from lying on this point, was there? Then it occurred to me that perhaps Day wasn't being quite as deceptive as I thought. Maybe the alcohol he had imbibed on those fateful days had clouded his memory, and the damned fool truly couldn't recall the details of those horrible events.

Sensing that this line of questioning was proving to be a dry well, Kingsbury shifted his focus to the executions of the natives sent over from Tacloban, and I sat back as this tale unfolded. Day asserted he had been ordered to execute nine of those men—not ten—and by God, he saw to it.

Kingsbury culminated his questions to Day by asking, "Do you know whether any of the natives you had charge of that day had any trial?"

"No, sir, I do not know of any trial."

I waited tensely for Kingsbury to return to the events of the nineteenth, to straighten out those jumbled facts for the court. Instead, to my complete amazement, Kingsbury turned to General Bisbee and said, "No further questions for this witness."

Astonished and relieved, I sat there counting victims in my head. Day had owned up to killing nine natives sent over from Tacloban, and had hinted that one more had been killed earlier on the twentieth, before the arrival of the nine. That made ten, which, added to the killing on the nineteenth, made eleven deaths.

Waller stood and conducted what I thought to be a mild cross-examination—and for good reason, since Day was a smoking bomb that might explode if handled too roughly. Waller was so timid with

Day, in fact, that he failed to clear up any of the confusion that Day had created. When he was finished, General Bisbee had a look of puzzlement on his face.

You see, Bisbee's confusion stemmed from the fact that Waller was charged with killing eleven natives on the twentieth, but Day had seemed to testify that only ten had been killed on the twentieth, nine from Tacloban and one before their arrival. What was the truth of the matter? Bisbee looked up from a sheet of paper where he had made little scratches, each representing a victim, and demanded, "Now just how many men in all were executed to your knowledge, Lieutenant Day?"

"Eleven, sir."

"When were they executed?"

"Ten on one day and one on the previous day. I cannot recall the exact dates."

My guts slid wildly at this, and I felt as though I might vomit all over Glenn's carefully arranged folders. By God, Bisbee was hopping right back into that dangerous territory that I thought I had escaped! Waller fidgeted for his own reasons, convinced that he had ordered eleven men killed, but all of them on the twentieth. If he was right about that, and Day was also right about a killing on the nineteenth, then there had been twelve executions, not eleven.

"Ten prisoners executed on one day and one prisoner executed on the day previous, making a total of eleven prisoners shot on two separate and consecutive days?" General Bisbee asked by way of clarification.

"Yes, sir," affirmed Day, "but I cannot recall the exact dates."

I held my breath, dreading Bisbee's next question. Would he ask Day why this first victim was killed? If he did, I would be exposed for the culpable abettor I was. Instead, I was relieved to hear him growl, "You may step down, Lieutenant Day." Day did as he was told, and together with Mr. Harrison he withdrew.

Kingsbury was shaking his head as he counted murder victims on his fingers and then looked at the charge sheet, which clearly stated that eleven victims had been killed and all on the twentieth. Somewhere he'd lost one, but he hadn't a clue as to where that might have happened. All in all, I concluded, if Day's object had been to thoroughly muddy the record of the case, he had succeeded brilliantly. Why, now even Waller wasn't sure how many men he had ordered to be killed. It could have been ten, eleven, or twelve. There was no way of knowing, you see, for the man Waller relied upon to carry out the executions was none other than Lieutenant Day.

Making the numbers come out right, however, was not Bisbee's problem. He cleared his throat pointedly, causing Kingsbury to look up from his figuring and get on with the trial. The judge advocate responded by calling to the stand a succession of enlisted marines who had carried out Waller's and Day's lethal orders. The testimony of these boys—yokels with good hearts and suspect memories—filled up the rest of the week but served only to deepen the morass that Day had created. Some remembered a killing on the nineteenth at the order of Lieutenant Day, but they couldn't recall who might have been shot. They described the victim, though—a short runt of a fellow who had begged piteously for his life. Others remembered that there were two separate shootings on the twentieth. The first was a native called Victor—which, ominously, tended to confirm what Waller had told me as he embarked for Cavite—whom Day had hauled out of the jail at Waller's order. The second shooting they remembered was of the group of natives sent over from Tacloban. A cook named Kresge remembered that one of these latter had bolted, and after a short chase had been caught and shot.

Once finished with the testimony about the actual executions, Kingsbury loaded the record with testimony from the officers and men who had made the perilous trek across Samar with Waller. These included Captain Porter and Sergeant Quick, who made their statements in clipped, professional tones. It was evident from their demeanor that they wanted to help Waller as much as possible, but being decent fellows they were unable to slant their testimony too far from the truth. As a result, the earlier picture painted from Dunlap's testimony that had shown Waller's trek to be foolhardy and reckless, and undertaken with an almost criminal disregard for the condition of his men, was strongly reinforced. Then, after nearly ten mind-numbing days, the prosecution ground mercifully to a halt.

Finally, it was Waller's turn. He commenced his defense by immediately recalling Captain Porter to the stand. "Did you have an occasion, Captain, to be present at a conversation between General Smith and Major Waller?" he asked, referring to himself again in the third person for the record.

"Yes, when the battalion arrived at Catbalogan," replied Porter.

Waller then produced his order of October 23, 1901, entitled Circular

Number 6, which stated, "Place no confidence in the natives, and punish treachery with immediate death." Waller read the entire order into the record and then asked Captain Porter, "Does that message fairly capture the instructions you heard General Smith impart to Major Waller?"

Captain Porter fixed his jaw and averred, "It did not go as far."

I nodded my head in agreement, for I had been there. Smith had told Waller to kill and burn, and the more the merrier. Why, next to Smith's verbal instructions, Waller's missive had been a model of rectitude. That, of course, was the main point Waller wanted from Porter, and it was a telling one. For the first time the court was on notice that Waller had not been running a renegade operation in Basey. To the contrary, he was following General Smith's express desires. When Waller was done with Porter, and Kingsbury finished a wholly ineffectual cross-examination, General Bisbee questioned the captain.

"Captain Porter, back in Catbalogan when your battalion first arrived at Samar, what did General Smith instruct Major Waller to do should he encounter treachery among the natives?"

"He was instructed to punish treachery with death," replied Porter firmly.

General Bisbee sat back to digest this, casting a searching glance at his fellow court members as he did. That ended Porter's time on the stand, and Waller next called poor Lieutenant Williams. His testimony was heart wrenching in the extreme; when Kingsbury rose to cross-examine, he merely reinforced the horror that Williams's tale had created in the minds of the court members.

"Now, Lieutenant Williams, isn't it possible that the natives you thought were being treacherous simply didn't understand the extremely dire straits of your men?"

Williams shook his head in emphatic disagreement. "No, there was no misunderstanding. On the day of the attack on me, the men were completely exhausted. We had crossed a stream and pitched tents, unable to walk any farther. The natives hung back in a sullen and mutinous way. The men needed fires to dry off, and I thought that one native had crossed the stream to our side. I went and searched for this man, and about a hundred and fifty feet from the camp I found, on a little knoll, a round shack made by placing some banana leaves against the side of a tree. I pulled some of the leaves apart and shouted to the natives to come out. One of them did. I told him to stand aside, finding that there were others in there. I ordered them to search for firewood; that was my object in getting them. A second man came out holding a bolo. He looked pretty savage, so I pulled my revolver, not with the idea of shooting him, but more to intimidate him, you see. As soon as I did this he grabbed the pistol with his right hand on the barrel, and my right hand in his teeth. A third man then came out, and he pushed my legs from under me. I fell down with my head lower than my feet. The second one to come out had dropped his bolo when he took hold of my revolver. He told the third man to take the bolo, which he did; then he knelt down by my left side and commenced stabbing me. I thought every stab was going through me, and I let go of the revolver and seized the bolo. Finally, I wrenched it away from him, and prevented him from stabbing me through. When I stopped him, and as the other man was monkeying with the revolver, the third man got some heavy twine that he had around his pack. That's when I started to yell for help. In a minute or so my men came crawling up, the first one too weak to work the bolt of his rifle. The natives ran away the instant before the men arrived."

This bit of graphic drama shocked the court. Noticing the growing fury on the faces of the court members, Kingsbury asked hopefully, "Might not these natives have thought that you were going to shoot them, and were merely trying to prevent you?"

"I hardly think so," Lieutenant Williams maintained staunchly. "The second man was up like lightning to seize my pistol. Nothing I did in ordering them out of their hut would have given them the notion that I intended to shoot them."

Kingsbury fuddled around a bit after this, but the damage was done. Glenn saw the opportunity for some more gain; he hurriedly scribbled down a few questions for Waller, who studied the note briefly, nodded, and then was on his feet for a redirect examination.

"How would you characterize the conduct of the natives, Mr. Williams?" he asked.

"It was most mutinous."

"Did they disobey orders?" queried Waller, eyeing the court, not Williams.

"They disobeyed direct orders."

"More than once?"

"More than once."

"Nothing further, sir," oozed Waller smugly as he resumed his seat.

All of this was extremely good for Waller, except for one important point. Arguably Williams would have been justified in shooting the treacherous natives when and where the mutiny occurred. Was Waller, however, who had not been present and was certainly not confronted with mutiny on January 20, when the shackled natives were brought before him, justified in summarily executing them nearly two weeks after the fact? That was the issue that would decide his fate, and both he and the court knew it.

At Glenn's urging, Waller recalled Captain Dunlap as a defense witness. Glenn, you see, was agitated about the native whom Day had testified had been shot by Waller's order on the nineteenth. Dunlap assured the court that he had heard no order given by Waller on the nineteenth to shoot anybody.

Kingsbury, however, now under the firm impression that ten men had been shot on the twentieth and one on the nineteenth, demanded of Dunlap on cross-examination, "Captain, how can you reconcile your testimony with that of Lieutenant Day, who said he shot a man on the nineteenth at the order of Major Waller?"

Dunlap shrugged. "I can't, sir, other than to say that if an order had been given on the nineteenth to shoot anyone, I would have known about it."

Kingsbury, now completely baffled, looked as though he wanted to keep after Dunlap, but then shook his head in resignation and took his seat. For my part, I fought hard to keep a wide grin from wreathing my face. Why, this was better than I had hoped for; not only was Day unwilling or unable to implicate me, but now Dunlap was insisting that no shooting had occurred at all on the nineteenth. I was off scot-free, by thunder, and if Surlang had been sent to his Muslim heaven as I intended, then it had been the perfect crime!

General Bisbee, however, bewildered anew by the conflicting testimony regarding the events of the nineteenth, tried to straighten matters out. Happily, he fared no better than Kingsbury. "Captain," he asked gravely of Dunlap, "what was your duty in Basey on the nineteenth?"

"I had no particular duty that day, sir. I was merely assisting Major Waller because he was ill. I was ill myself, and together we were trying to do our best."

"Well, what was your duty on the twentieth?"

"I had no particular duty, sir."

"No particular duty? Why, that's extraordinary. Wasn't there an officer of the day, Captain?"

"No, there wasn't, sir," explained Dunlap. "Ordinarily, yes, that would be the case. But you must understand that on the nineteenth and twentieth, the entire battalion was virtually unfit for duty. Everyone was sick, and most of the men were in their bunks completely worn out. Posting ordinary rosters just wouldn't have made sense."

Undeterred, General Bisbee pressed, "What I want to know, Captain Dunlap, is whether there was an officer in Basey responsible for checking the prisoners' identities as they were executed. Were any of those executed not on the expedition with Major Waller and Captain Porter?"

I saw where Bisbee was going. Day had said he killed a man before the boat arrived from Tacloban, arguably a man who had not been on Waller's hike.

"I can't say, sir," replied Dunlap.

Bisbee eyed Dunlap thoughtfully. The witness was being candid; he simply had no idea who was shot on the twentieth beyond what he had already testified to. The central problem, you see, was that no roll of the doomed had ever been taken. The marines hadn't bothered to keep any official track of their victims, and now they were having the dickens of a time accounting for the carnage they had wrought. It was farcical, almost unbelievable, but there it was. All of this made the marines look like complete fools in the eyes of General Bisbee and the other army officers, but I cared not a whit about that. No, the only important things were that Surlang was dead and the deep mystery about the nineteenth remained.

"You may step down, Captain," Bisbee sighed at last.

After several inconsequential witnesses were called to show the court the general truculence of the populace of Samar, Major Waller announced that the defense would call himself to the stand. I expected this, for Glenn had told Waller that there was no way this court would acquit him unless he explained his own story under oath. It hadn't been a hard sell, for the little martinet was just dying to set the record straight, or at least the record as he knew it. I sat back in my chair to listen, for Waller had been maddeningly reticent with me up to this point. This would be the first time I heard his recollection of the events in question, and I reckoned it would be damned interesting indeed. As things turned out, I was not to be disappointed on that score.

First, under questioning from Glenn, Waller admitted that he had indeed ordered a native named Victor executed on the morning of the twentieth. Victor, explained Waller, had been a bearer in the expedition across Samar. When Waller had forged ahead, leaving Porter behind with the main group, Victor had accompanied Waller's small party.

"What occurred on this march that made you suspect this Victor of treachery?" asked Glenn.

"The day after we left Porter, we rested in the jungle for the night. I bedded down with my back to a tree with Captain Bearss. My bolo stuck into my side, so I loosened it and put it down by my side. This freed my body from the pressure. After some time I felt that the bolo was gone. I woke Bearss and told him that. The night was rainy, and in the rain the grass and leaves glowed because they're phosphorescent. Anyone who's been up in those hills knows about the phenomenon. Well, by this light, I saw a dark shape on the far side of the tree from Bearss and me. I reached for that shape; it was a native, this Victor fellow. I put my revolver to his head and demanded my bolo. He had it right in his hand, you see."

Glenn waited for the import of this incident to sink into the minds of the raptly attentive court members. "What impression did this incident make upon your mind as to the intention of Victor?"

The answer was as forceful as a cannon shot. "I thought perhaps he intended to kill one of us." Then Waller added something that shook me to the core. "I later found out, you know, that Victor was in reality 'Captain Victor,' that notorious and infamous captain of the *insurrectos*. He was present at the Balangiga massacre, I've been told, leading a contingent from Basey during that bloodshed. Had I known any of this before, I can assure you I would not have allowed him to accompany my expedition."

What the devil was Waller babbling about? I wanted to shout. How had he so totally confused Victor's name with that of Captain Verde, Surlang's nom de guerre? Then I felt a wave of nausea sweep over me, for I saw it all too clearly now. Yes, there had been a blunder, one of massive proportions. Day had indeed hauled the wrong fellow from the jail on the nineteenth. He hadn't gotten Surlang, but instead some innocent dupe, probably the short runt some of the marines had testified about. This wretch had been pushed through the door by Surlang and promptly shot by the inebriated Lieutenant Day. It all fit into place, for hadn't Day told me twice that he couldn't tell the natives apart?

Then, the following morning, the twentieth, with the monikers Verde and Victor completely jumbled in his fevered mind, and with no recall of the killing he had ordered the day before, Waller acted again. He ordered this Victor, a lowly and unoffensive footpad, hauled out and shot, convinced that he was rightfully executing the grand Jacobin of Samar. Surlang, meanwhile, seeing that the executions escalated when the prisoners arrived from Tacloban and that the marines were especially vigilant against attack, craftily decided to make his break. He must have slipped into the group from Tacloban, and it was he who made the break that the cook Kresge testified about.

Kresge testified that the escaping native had been run down and shot, but I was certain now that the man Kresge tracked and killed was not Surlang. No, the wily Moro had slipped his pursuers, and they had shot instead some startled villager who instinctively took flight at the sight of a gang of wild-eyed Americans waving Krags.

Shaken as the full realization of what had occurred struck me, I had but one thing to be grateful for: The botched orders, the incomplete memories, and the stark inconsistencies on the record in this case were so layered one upon the other that no court could ever untangle the truth of the matter.

Unmindful of the sudden dampness on my brow, Glenn turned next to the touchy matter of Day allegedly killing a man the day before the prisoners from Tacloban arrived in Basey. "Did you ever order Lieutenant Day to execute a prisoner on the nineteenth?"

"No, I did not," Waller avowed stolidly. "Why, I had not even heard of such a thing until this trial commenced."

There it was; Waller had decided what his fevered memory was, and by God, that settled the matter for him. When he was done with his testimony, Waller looked defiantly around the courtroom. General Bisbee eyed him thoughtfully, but I couldn't read the message in those flinty eyes. Was he in favor of acquitting Waller or of throwing him deep in some military jail and tossing away the key? I couldn't say, but if this had been a prizefight rather than a trial, I would have called the contest a draw at this point.

With a deep bow to the court, Major Glenn announced augustly: "Sir, the defense rests."

"Will there be rebuttal?" General Bisbee inquired of Major Kingsbury.

Sensing that his case needed buttressing, Kingsbury rose, nodding his head vigorously. When he spoke, his words were the most potent yet uttered in the course of the trial. "Yes, sir, there will be rebuttal. I have sent a letter to General Chaffee requesting that he make available in this courtroom General Jacob Smith."

A gasp went up from the spectators, and several reporters jumped up and scrambled out the doors, heading for the telegraph office. Glenn leaned toward Waller and whispered worriedly, "We're in the soup now! Kingsbury's going to hammer at our contention that you operated within Smith's directions. If he cuts that line, you'll sink for sure!"

32

April 7, 1902
"Do you swear to tell the truth, the whole truth, and nothing but the truth, so help you God?"

"I do," boomed General Smith in the resounding bass that had earned him the sobriquet Hell-roaring Jake.

"Please be seated, sir," said Major Kingsbury.

Smith took the witness chair, looked grandly about the chamber, and then turned back to Kingsbury. His expression was one of detached majesty, as though he were above the tawdry matters under discussion herein, but quite willing to pull the brawling parties apart long enough to set the record straight before he retired once again in glory to Mount Olympus.

Waller, on the other hand, was as keyed up as a rooster at a Tagalog cockfight. His toe was tapping and he drummed out an agitated tattoo with a pencil on the table. Smith's testimony would determine his fate, and he damn well knew it. Glenn, too, watched Smith intently, while I watched Glenn. After all, Glenn had been Smith's judge advocate on Samar, and I couldn't help but wonder what dirty little secrets the two of them shared.

With Smith ensconced in the witness chair, Kingsbury had a smile on his face for the first time in a week. Here was a witness who would clarify the limit of Waller's authority in a crisp, understandable manner. After establishing a few preliminaries, Kingsbury drew himself up to his full height and commenced what he hoped would be the finish of this troublesome case. "General, I will read you an order that was issued by Major Waller, and published to his command." Thereupon he read Waller's bombastic missive of October 23, the now-familiar Circular Number 6, which spoke about placing no confidence in the natives, and punishing treachery with immediate death. "Did you ever see that order before, sir?"

"Never while I was in command of the brigade," replied Smith firmly. "I saw it last night for the first time."

"Now, General Smith, did you ever in any conversation with Major Waller give him, or anyone else, the impression that the instructions in this order were not severe enough in the conduct of affairs on Samar?"

The question was so garbled that Smith did a double take to see whether Kingsbury was fully in control of his faculties. Why, hadn't Smith just stated that before last night he had never seen the damned order? What was Kingsbury trying to do, impeach his own witness? I stifled a belly laugh as the flabbergasted Smith waggled his head from side to side, looking for Kingsbury to rephrase the question. To no avail, however, for the judge advocate stood with his back to the witness, awaiting the reply with grave dignity. Smith, in a pickle and with nowhere to turn, finally decided to answer the question he had been told to expect.

"No, sir, I would have cut out portions of that order had it come to me."

Court members shook their heads in puzzlement at this exchange, and I could read their expressions. They were wondering, you see, if Smith had come here to tell them what truly happened on Samar, or whether he was just a carefully rehearsed puppet for the judge advocate. Kingsbury, expecting just the answer that Smith had given to the badly fumbled question, and not noticing the quizzical looks he was getting from the court members, sailed on serenely.

"Now, sir, did you have a conversation upon the arrival of Major Waller's battalion on Samar?"

"Yes, I did."

"In that conversation, or any other, did you ever give any instructions to Major Waller in regard to what you thought was meant by the provisions of General Order Number 100?"

"Yes, sir. I gave instructions that treachery must be looked out for. I said that we must have no more Balangiga affairs. But I stressed that treachery under all circumstances must be governed by the provisions of General Order Number 100."

Smith was being crafty, you see. General Order 100 allowed the summary execution of armed partisans taken in the field; it allowed no such treatment for unarmed prisoners.

"Sir, did you in any conversation with Major Waller indicate to him that, as district commander, he had the power of life and death over unarmed and defenseless prisoners that at any time might be turned over to him by his subordinates?"

"By Christ, Glenn, object!" demanded Waller under his breath. "That's not rebuttal evidence, that's new evidence! Kingsbury has hauled Smith in here because his case is so weak that he needs new evidence to convict me!"

Intensely aware that Waller's fate was on the line, Glenn was up as though his seat had springs. "We object, Mr. President!" he fairly shouted. "This witness is here to rebut, not produce new evidence. There is nothing in the defense's case that this line of inquiry could possibly rebut."

Completely intent on Smith's words, General Bisbee was startled by this outburst from the defense. "What? What? Explain yourself, Major," he demanded.

"The defense has never contended that the executions at Basey were done at the order of General Smith," explained Glenn. "They were done on the authority of Major Waller in his capacity as a subdistrict commander. Circular Number 6 is in the record, without objection, but the defense in this case does not rest with showing that General Smith ordered these killings."

This made Waller shift uncomfortably, since he rather fancied that such was exactly his defense, at least by implication. Glenn had just pushed him off from shore in a leaky boat with no oars.

"May it please the court," interjected Kingsbury, "the issue of what authority was granted to Major Waller by General Smith was indeed addressed in the testimony of Captain Porter. I say this rebuttal is entirely proper."

There was more scratching and clawing between the two of them, but it was evident to me that Bisbee was thoroughly intrigued by what General Smith had to say on the subject. "The objection is overruled," he quickly decreed.

Much gratified, Kingsbury turned once more to his witness. "I repeat, General Smith, did you in any conversation with Major Waller indicate to him that, as district commander, he had the power of life and death over unarmed and defenseless prisoners who at any time might be turned over to him by his subordinates?"

Smith answered sharply. "No, sir. I had no such authority myself, and could not delegate any authority I did not have."

Waller snorted incredulously at this, drawing a peeved look from Kingsbury and a frown of disapproval from General Bisbee. With a dismissive glance in the direction of the defense table, Kingsbury continued his examination. "Did you ever indicate to Major Waller that as sub-district commander he had special powers not given to your other subdistrict commanders?"

"No, sir."

"If charges of treachery against prisoners had been forwarded to you, would you have ordered a court to try them?"

"I should have ordered a military commission, and had them tried." Here Smith flicked a look at Major Glenn, whose eyes were suddenly hooded and unblinking.

"Had you a military commission in your command at that time?" inquired Major Kingsbury.

"I had, sir—one at Tanuan, one at Catbalogan, and one at Calbayog."

"Sir, was there ever a telegram received at your headquarters in regard to the killing of the natives at Basey?"

"There was," confirmed Smith, pulling thoughtfully on his flowing mustache. "It was received about January 22, this year. I did not see it, however, until a few days ago."

Eh, what was this? I happened to have been in Smith's headquarters when that very telegram came in. Smith had read it straightaway. Just what was he trying to pull here? Oblivious to my startled look, Smith continued, "That telegram was from Major Waller, saying that he had expended eleven natives. My adjutant general informed me after that dispatch came that it had been received, but he did not understand it, as it stated that Waller had expended prisoners. I never received a message reporting the killing of any prisoners."

"In regard to this matter of natives being expended, did you take any action on it?"

"About January 22 or 23—probably the twenty-third—General Chaffee came on shore at Tacloban. While we were in the military ambulance I used for transport, he turned to me and said, 'Smith, have you been having any promiscuous killing on Samar for fun?' Well, I did not understand what he meant. I knew nothing of it. I said, 'No, sir.' He

said, 'Well, I understand that at Basey they have been killing some
people over there.' I knew nothing of it until General Chaffee told
me of it, and immediately I had the matter looked into. I started an
investigation, you see."

General Bisbee eyed Smith coldly at this, and Hell-roaring Jake,
catching that look, seemed to actually fidget on the stand like a lowly
private. You see, Basey was only seven miles across the strait from
Smith's headquarters, and if Chaffee had heard of the shootings all
the way up in Manila, how could they have possibly escaped Smith's
immediate notice in Tacloban? Bisbee had expected Smith to stride
into this courtroom and shoulder sole responsibility for the entire tragedy
at Basey. Instead, here he was dodging questions like a common thief
hauled up before the town magistrate. Why, it was shoddy practice to
say the least, and damned near conduct unbecoming an officer. Major Kingsbury, more intent on getting all his questions asked than on
noticing the effect that Smith's answers were having on the court, picked
up none of these signals. Confident that Waller was being demolished,
he forged blithely ahead.

"Did you, at any time during your command on Samar and Leyte,
ever have any confidential relations with officers to warrant their thinking
that you would sustain them in treating prisoners in any way except
in the way prescribed by the laws of war?"

Aware that his testimony was not going over well at all, Hell-roaring
Jake responded in a shy little squeak, "Not one."

"Horseshit," I muttered loud enough for Smith to hear and look my
way. His eyes opened wide as he recognized me from that day on the
launch heading out to the *New York*. Now he knew there was a fellow in court who could put him on the dock for perjury, and that thought
set him to trembling.

Kingsbury, essentially done now, concluded quickly and turned the
witness over to the defense. As Waller stood gravely for the cross-
examination, Smith had the devil of a time tearing his eyes from me.
"General Smith," began Waller, "you stated that you had a conversation with Major Waller on the subject of treachery by the natives."

"Yes, we did."

"And you ordered that treachery be punished summarily by death,
did you not?"

"No, sir," Smith maintained desperately.

"No?" echoed Waller, surprised.

"I said punished summarily. The part about death wasn't in there. I meant punished summarily under the provisions of General Order Number 100."

That was a lie and Smith knew it, but it was his testimony now, and the determined set of the general's jaw told Waller he would never budge Hell-roaring Jake from that position.

"Well, then, sir, since you mentioned General Order Number 100, is it not true that you never curtailed the rights given Major Waller by that general order? In other words, you never told him he had no authority to do certain things?"

Smith thought a moment about this, not certain where Waller was going. "Er, no, I did not curtail Major Waller in any way under General Order Number 100 or under the laws of war."

That, you see, was all that needed to be brought out to sustain the defense that Glenn had outlined to the court—that is, that Waller had killed the eleven natives under his own authority and made no claim of acting under the orders of General Smith. Satisfied with this admission, Glenn was urging Waller in whispers to cut it off and sit down, but I hurriedly scribbled a few notes on a scrap of paper and shoved it at Waller.

"Ask him about this," I hissed.

Waller walked to the defense table, glanced at the paper, and then marched back toward Smith, who watched him advance with the same cold stare a cobra might give an approaching mongoose.

"General Smith," inquired Waller, "what did you think the word 'expend' meant in the telegraph sent by Major Waller?"

"Why, I spoke to my adjutant general, Captain Ayer, about that very thing. He told me he did not understand it. I said that I didn't either. Why, if General Chaffee had not come down to Samar, I never would have understood it."

"Have you never heard the word used before?" pressed Waller.

"I never heard the word used as meaning that something wrong had been done, no," insisted Smith. "Nor did I believe that such was the meaning at the time, sir. It never occurred to me, or Captain Ayer. Neither of us had the least idea."

This was complete balderdash, of course, and it was now abundantly clear that General Smith had come into this courtroom with only one thought in mind: to save as much of his own professional hide as possible. If that meant tossing Waller to the wolves, well, so be it. Waller saw this too, and the realization infuriated him. Perhaps he should have left well enough alone and taken his seat at that point, but now his blood was up and he pressed on.

"When Major Waller ordered that eleven natives be killed on January 20 in Basey, did he disobey any specific order of yours, or did he just interpret General Order Number 100 and the laws of war in a way different from you?"

It was both a simple and a superb question. It in fact encapsulated the very essence of the defense case. Had Waller acted within the scope of his lawful authority or not? In his impetuosity, Waller had blurted out the key query upon which the outcome of the trial would hinge.

A simple question deserved a simple answer, but Smith, weaving wildly in his attempt to avoid any telling blows against himself, was now incapable of veracity. His mewling, pathetic reply brought looks of dismay and consternation to the faces of the watching officers. "I really don't know what Major Waller did over there, sir, about which you ask me. I don't know what he did. I don't know now, with the investigation—the investigation being taken from me—that there was some act committed there."

Smith paused here to see how his evasive response was being received and was met with stony glares from all quarters. Sheepishly, he finished his answer in an awkward half whisper. "It was taken out of my hands, and the inspector general was sent over and made a confidential report, and I don't know what it said. I don't know what Waller is being tried for." Eyebrows shot clear to the ceiling at this, and a smothered guffaw sounded from somewhere back where the reporters were seated. "I've been down there where I can't get mail, and I have not learned things."

The courtroom was wrapped in a thick shroud of embarrassed silence now, for Smith had completely abased himself and cast in doubt the candor of all his testimony. Even Kingsbury, finally aware of how badly his rebuttal had miscarried, was carefully studying his boots, too chagrined to meet the eyes of the stricken General Smith. Then someone coughed, papers rustled somewhere, and slowly life returned to the stilled chamber.

The damage done, Waller handed Smith back to Kingsbury, who performed a halting redirect examination of his thoroughly chastened witness. After a few desultory questions from the court, Smith was mercifully released. He fled the courtroom like a scalded dog, and none who saw him go expected he would ever again be placed in command of troops.

The defense then put Waller back on the stand to insist that Smith had told him unequivocally to burn and kill, and to take no prisoners. Why, Waller asserted, Smith had even sent over a handwritten note via Lieutenant Day directing Waller to reduce Samar to a howling wilderness. Captain Porter also took the stand in surrebuttal to state the same thing, and then the defense rested. After closing arguments, General Bisbee announced solemnly, "This court will be adjourned," and he and his fellow court members filed out to determine Waller's fate.

Glenn, Waller, and I retired to the waiting room down the corridor from the courtroom. As Waller and Glenn paced nervously, I tilted back on a wooden chair and puffed placidly at a fresh Havana. I could afford to be in a jolly humor, you see, for whatever the outcome of this trial, I was in the clear. That was why, as Waller and Glenn huddled together to agonize over every bit of key testimony, I idly mused about Waller's fate and couldn't help reflecting on what I'd learned of the marines over these past few months. Oh, they were first-rate fighters, all right. No, I'd never seen finer, but God almighty, were they dumb! Why, a crew of leathernecks could bollix up a simple order beyond all recognition in seconds, and a complex order was an impossibility. And were they excitable? Why, jackasses in a blazing barn were more capable of cool reasoning than Waller and his boys. So it was no wonder that I was chuckling quietly at the foibles of these lethal buffoons from Cavite, and had just sent my third halo of blue smoke to the waxed ceiling when in strode a familiar—and unwelcome—figure.

It was Lieutenant Colonel Quinlon, and from the set look on his weasel face, he was looking for me. "Captain Travers," he hailed. "I'm glad I caught you on a recess, lad."

"It's a bit more than a recess, Colonel," I informed him suspiciously. "The court is deliberating at this very minute. Colonel Waller here," I said, poking my cigar in the direction of my anxious client, "is waiting to hear whether he's to be executed for murder."

"A pity," mouthed Quinlon perfunctorily and then got down to business. "Travers, I've heard some talk at Chaffee's headquarters that Fee is off on some island called Hobo."

"Jolo," I corrected him, remembering the telegram I had wired to General Davis from Basey.

"Whatever," Quinlon said breezily. "My point's this lad: Do you figure that an expedition might be launched to rescue the poor colleen?"

"Well, I suppose that notion might occur to General Davis," I allowed. Then I added warily, "What's your reason for asking?"

"Oh, I was just wondering, Travers," he grinned slyly. "After all, I'm a grieving father, you know."

Quinlon's protestation of parental concern notwithstanding, I had long ago learned the fallacy of ascribing altruistic motives to the old reprobate. In fact, I was about to ask none too gently just what the hell his game was when we were suddenly joined by the bailiff.

"The president sent word to return to the courtroom immediately!" he announced tensely. "The verdict's in!"

The verdict was in? By God, that was record time for a two-week trial! Waller gave Glenn and me a despairing look, and then led the way back down the hall with a trudging gait. I had barely enough time to snuff out my smoke and join Waller at the defense table when the court members filed in behind a grim-faced General Bisbee.

"Major Waller, please rise," ordered General Bisbee.

Waller rose pale and shaking, but then with an effort drew himself together and faced the president manfully enough. I had to admit, although Waller was a sycophantic bungler and an insufferable blowhard, there was nonetheless steel in the little fellow's backbone.

"Major Waller, this court finds you of the specification, guilty, except of the words 'willfully and feloniously and with malice aforethought,' and of the excepted words, not guilty. Of the charge, not guilty. You may be seated."

Waller's bottom hit the chair as though he had been poleaxed. "What the hell did he say?" he cried.

"Beats me," I rejoined with a shrug. "As I've already told you nine ways from Sunday, Waller, I'm no lawyer." This being my first court-martial, I hadn't a clue about what all that hocus-pocus meant.

Glenn, however, was radiant. "You're free, Waller!" he exulted. "They've just acquitted you, by God!"

Glenn was right, for now marine members of the court were surging forward to shake Waller's hand and to damn Smith's irresolute hide. Oh, it was over for Waller, all right—and for Samar. That unfortunate island was a desolate wasteland, a place of death and grief. General Lukban was in chains in an army prison, his resistance movement completely and utterly broken. And the human price of this campaign of terror? Well, no one could reckon it exactly, since many of the dead were never counted, nor indeed were they even buried. So complete was Smith's campaign of annihilation, however, that he was known thereafter throughout the army as "Howling Jake," and his gory deeds were discussed only in guarded whispers.

Officers who had served in the islands, however, and who had faced the bolos of fanatical Pulajans, paid homage in their own way to those who followed Howling Jake on his wild death ride. When such an officer thereafter entered a mess, all mess members would rise with the proclamation: "Stand, sir, for he served on Samar!"

It was not only the officers who were changed by the Samar campaign. The troops who came down from those hills, no matter how hardened they might have been when first they came to the island, knew they had wallowed in blood beyond their darkest nightmares. They avoided one another's eyes, and were only too glad to board the transports when they departed Samar's crimson shore.

After Waller's trial, Lieutenant Day went to the dock. Claiming that he had only followed orders, he too was acquitted of all charges. Then Glenn was tried, but he put up an able defense and suffered no more than a reprimand. Finally General Smith himself was court-martialed for conduct prejudicial to good order and discipline. Not surprisingly, he was convicted, but he was sentenced to a mere admonishment. Enraged, or perhaps embarrassed, President Roosevelt intervened, ordering that Smith be retired from the active rolls. Howling Jake, a broken shell of a man, lived out his days with the dreadful memories of the ghosts of Samar.

As for me, I saw enough murder on Samar to last me a dozen lifetimes. Yet the one thing I yearned most to see—Surlang's lifeless body—had eluded me. When the destruction of Samar came to a smoking, bloody end, I was left with but one galling conclusion. Surlang, the archfiend who had launched Samar down the path to hellfire, had escaped yet again!

33

Longbottom and I stood before General Davis's desk as he studied us searchingly. "Explain this all to me again, Captain Longbottom," insisted General Davis. "Especially this part about needing a company of native scouts."

"Not just any native scouts, sir," Longbottom corrected him. "I need Macabebes. Specifically, I want the men who normally follow this fellow Bustos."

"And you want to take them to Jolo? To meet with the sultan?" asked General Davis, shaking his head skeptically.

Undeterred, Longbottom nodded. "That's right, sir. As Captain Travers's telegram informed you, Surlang let his guard slip long enough to tell us that he had somehow arranged for Fiona and Alice to be taken to Jolo. I'm willing to bet that they're still there."

"And you, er—correct me if I misunderstand you, Captain Longbottom—want to buy them back?"

"Exactly, sir. That's why I want you to get permission from General Chaffee in Manila to have the paymaster give me ten thousand dollars in gold."

"This is very irregular, Captain Longbottom," demurred General Davis, turning to stare out his window as he pondered the extraordinary request.

Suddenly a noise from the antechamber outside the general's office interrupted his ruminations. "I tell you I'm going to see the general, damn ye!" came a high-pitched voice. "It's my daughter who's been taken!"

By God, it was Lieutenant Colonel Quinlon, I realized—and then remembered his peculiar visit to the courtroom where poor Waller had been awaiting sentencing. What the dickens was the old bag of wind doing here? Before I could speak, however, General Davis stamped angrily to his door and yanked it open.

"What's the meaning of this commotion?" he demanded sharply.

"General, I've come to see about me daughter," insisted Quinlon, shaking off frantic orderlies as he spoke. "I want to know what's being done to rescue her. She's been gone for months now."

General Davis raised his hand, and the orderlies stepped back. "Do I know you, Colonel?" he asked icily.

"No, sir. I'm Lieutenant Colonel Quinlon. I'm down from Manila to see about me daughter."

"Your daughter?" echoed General Davis, perplexed. The two missing ladies, you see, were Miss Brenoble and Mrs. Longbottom. There was no Miss Quinlon abducted, as far as General Davis knew. Bewildered, he looked to me for some explanation.

I wanted to seize Quinlon by the neck and shake him until he divulged whatever his scheme was, but that wouldn't do at the moment. Instead, I managed, "Sir, this is Mrs. Longbottom's father." Then I added with honeyed insincerity, "Colonel Quinlon, how good to see you."

"Sir, welcome to Zamboanga," added Longbottom, once he overcame his mortification at his father-in-law's sudden appearance and unforgivably boorish behavior. One never arrived at a general's office unannounced, you see.

Upon seeing Longbottom, Quinlon bawled emotionally, "Joshua! I know how ye must feel, son!"

"Er, thank you, sir" was all Longbottom could muster in reply, as he took the old fellow's hand reluctantly and glanced at General Davis with trepidation.

I couldn't have given a damn about Longbottom's chagrin, but I was more than a little concerned about Quinlon's presence. What the blazes could the old villain want here in Zamboanga? Certainly his appearance was occasioned by more than a desire to free Fiona, for unquestionably the army had better men than he for that job. No, he had an angle, I was sure, but I couldn't quite discern it. Which only added to my anxieties, for at that moment I had been listening slack jawed as Longbottom tried to sell General Davis on a proposition so bizarre that I could scarcely credit my ears upon hearing it.

You see, when Longbottom had arrived back from Samar bandaged from head to foot, General Davis had been very solicitous to the dolt, what with word of the disaster at Balangiga and the subsequent Samar campaign being on the lips of every officer on Mindanao. Of course, for my money, Longbottom should have been branded as the officer who started that entire debacle by preventing me from dispatching Surlang when I had the chance. But Davis, knowing nothing of this, instead lent an ear to a string of loco ploys that Longbottom concocted, all designed to recover Fiona and Alice.

First, Longbottom had convinced General Davis to send out native emissaries to Jolo. Ominously, none had returned. Then he convinced Davis to have the navy steam threateningly close to the shore of Jolo as a show of force. This merely resulted in a *juramentado* appearing on the town plaza of Zamboanga and skewering two startled sentries before being cut down by the victims' enraged comrades. The dried blood of these wretches was still being washed off the walls of their sentry shack, in fact, when I landed from Manila. Had I needed any encouragement to steer clear of Longbottom's ill-advised machinations, that would have been it. Needless to say, I stoutly resisted his immediate attempts to enlist me in his addlepated cause.

At least, that was, until this morning, when an officious young lieutenant greeted me as I stepped from my billet and hustled me directly to Davis's office, where I found Longbottom pitching his latest plan. And a godawful stratagem it was, dreadfully flawed if not completely suicidal. I was just on the verge of telling General Davis exactly that when suddenly Quinlon barged in upon us.

Seeing no polite way to get rid of his unwelcome interloper, General Davis made the best of an embarrassing situation. "Well then, Colonel Quinlon, since you've traveled all this way, you may as well come in," he relented, the frost still evident in his voice. "Captain Longbottom was just mentioning to me a plan of his, albeit a tentative one, to rescue your daughter."

"I must be part of any such rescue," insisted Quinlon adamantly. "I'm Fiona's father, and I must be afforded an opportunity to get her back."

General Davis didn't take kindly to demands from mere lieutenant colonels, of course, but he was astute enough to know that many officers were quite well connected politically. As unprepossessing as Quinlon might appear, Davis couldn't be sure what contacts this fellow might have in Washington.

Seeing Davis's hesitation, and not at all liking the idea of being saddled with Quinlon under any circumstances, I took immediate countermeasures. That is, I cleared my throat and said delicately, "Colonel Quinlon, do you think that's wise?"

"Wise? Of course it is, Travers, and besides, what business is it of yours?" squawked Quinlon, taken aback. He had imagined that as the aggrieved father, he would be handled with kid gloves, and the command in Zamboanga would give in to any demand he might make. He hadn't, however, figured on running into me.

"Sir," I smiled unctuously, "I mean no disrespect, but there's no telling how long the expedition might last, and certainly your duties as a general's aide in Manila won't allow you to be away for long."

"Why, I've got all the time in the world," Quinlon countered irritably. "Since General MacArthur handed over the reins to General Chaffee, I've been told that I'm to make way for new aides."

Aha! So that was it, I thought. Without Longbottom in Manila to look after him, Quinlon had been cut loose from headquarters. If he didn't locate meaningful work soon, he just might find himself run out of the army because of his congenital incompetence.

"Be that as it may, sir," I continued, unfazed, "the, ah, expedition that Captain Longbottom is proposing to General Davis promises to be, well, a demanding one"—I didn't want to come right out and say desperate or futile, you see—"that will require young bucks at the peak of physical conditioning. I say this with great personal esteem, Colonel, but I don't believe you've seen action since you led the 71st New York in Cuba."

"*The* 71st?" rumbled General Davis, scrutinizing Quinlon narrowly.

Quinlon reddened under his gaze but gamely stuck to his guns. "There's more to that story than is commonly known, General," he retorted heatedly. "My men were subjected to the heaviest artillery fire of the war. Besides, the army never leveled any charges against me. . . ."

I raised my hand soothingly, satisfied with the damage I'd inflicted. "You mistake my point, Colonel Quinlon," I oozed with my sweetest smile. "I only wanted to note that you haven't seen battle in more than three years. That means you're not at your usual razor edge, sir. In fairness to Fiona, shouldn't you leave her rescue to fellows who are?"

I looked to Davis for support and got it. "There would be hell to pay in Washington if we didn't exert our very best effort to rescue those poor young ladies," confirmed General Davis with finality. "Colonel, this will have to be Captain Longbottom's operation. I know how you must feel, but that's my decision on the matter."

The wind left Quinlon's sails at this. Davis put a hand on his shoulder sympathetically and guided him to a chair, where he collapsed in resignation. Then General Davis turned his full attention to Longbottom. "Now, Captain, let's get back to this expedition to Jolo that you're proposing. You believe the ladies might still be there, do you?"

Quinlon's interruption had given me time to collect my thoughts. One glaring weakness in Longbottom's reasoning crystalized in my hitherto paralyzed brain. Before Longbottom could reply, I interjected pointedly, "That belief, sir, is based on information that comes from a questionable source and is months old. Why, for all we know, the women may have been spirited off to Borneo by now. We can't just go poking around the wide Pacific without some assurance that we'll find them at the end of our search."

"Borneo?" exploded Quinlon anew. "Is that where my darling girl has been carried off to?" he wailed.

"Get ahold of yourself, Colonel," ordered General Davis, his sympathy for Quinlon rapidly evaporating.

Seeing the doubt on General Davis's countenance that my mewlings had just planted, Longbottom struck back. "What Captain Travers says is true, sir. The information is dated, yet I feel it to be nonetheless accurate. The main point, though, is that there's really no option other than acting on this intelligence."

"Eh? How's that?" sputtered General Davis. "You speak as though I have no say in the matter, Captain!"

The general's tone was ominous, but Longbottom acted as though he had a strong hand and, damn him, he played it coolly. "Sir, I'm merely saying that you put your finger on the main point when you said there'd be hell to pay if we didn't exert our very best effort to rescue these poor ladies." Then he added a subtle rapier thrust straight through General Davis's vitals. "I know you were thinking of the War Department when you spoke—but I'm thinking of the press."

"The *press?*" exclaimed General Davis nervously, the idea that the fourth estate had any role to play in this drama having escaped him until this very moment.

"Yes, sir," Longbottom assured him. "Both you and General Chaffee would be crucified by the American press if it were to come out that you had passed up any opportunity to pluck two American ladies from the clutches of a pack of Moro slavemasters."

This prospect caused General Davis to give a little shudder, as though he had just envisioned a headline announcing his own unexpected retirement. After all, there was some truth to Longbottom's words. The papers from home were filled with fulminations against Waller and Smith regarding Samar. The last thing Davis needed was for the slavering American dailies to turn their attention to Mindanao. Also, unbeknownst to me, Davis had been ceaselessly bombarded with telegrams from George Duncan in New York demanding action to recover his beloved niece, Alice Brenoble. Duncan was too powerful a gent to ignore for long. Weighing all this, Davis turned and faced Longbottom.

"Explain to me again why you need the Macabebe scouts," he said.

"Because we can't take American troops to Jolo, sir. They would simply upset the delicate political entente we have with the sultan of Jolo. So, we'll take native scouts, and if any of them should turn up in the clutches of the Moros, well, they're Filipinos, not Americans, right? I suggested Macabebes because Captain Travers here knows them and their leader, Bustos. In fact, Bustos happens to be right here in Zamboanga."

"Very well, gentlemen," pronounced Davis with finality. "I understand and appreciate the great service you've both given on Samar and the personal loss you've both suffered in this matter. I might say it's been more than any man should be expected to bear." Longbottom, the insufferable twit, nodded manfully at this, as did I, thankful that Davis had no inkling it was I who had started Surlang's vendetta back in Manila when I relieved the blasted Moro of his precious map. "This is what I'm prepared to do," General Davis continued. "I'll arrange for the Macabebes, as you ask. That should be no problem."

What he didn't say was that General Chaffee too had been receiving Duncan's telegrams and would be quite predisposed to any scheme, no matter how half-witted, that showed he was making some progress in the case.

"As for the money—"

"The money? What money?" demanded Quinlon, surging suddenly back to life now that we were speaking his language.

"Colonel," roared General Davis, his patience with Quinlon now gone, "sit there quietly or get along your way! Do I make myself clear?"

Quinlon nodded, chastened at last. "Yes, sir, very clear."

"Good," growled General Davis. Calming down, he turned to Longbottom and continued, "As for the money, well, it's an extraordinary amount, Captain Longbottom, but I plan to secure your personal signature for the funds. And yours," he added, eyeing me sternly.

I gulped and stiffened under that glare, but Longbottom piped up cheerily, "Of course, sir."

"If you come back with the ladies, but not the money, the funds will be deemed to have been expended in the public interest, and you'll be relieved of all accountability. If, however, you return without the money and without the ladies, well, then I'm afraid you both must be held personally liable for the full amount. I know that's harsh, but there's just too many possibilities under these circumstances for malfeasance of official funds. I'm sorry, but those will have to be the terms."

Longbottom didn't flinch at Davis's conditions. "That's acceptable, sir," he replied. I merely gave a wary nod, the thought of paying back the better part of three years' salary not exactly warming the cockles of my heart.

"And there's one more thing, Captain Longbottom," added General Davis.

"Sir?"

"The sultan of Jolo is currently at peace with us. While you and Captain Travers were on Samar, Captain Pershing commenced operations on Mindanao with a view toward penetrating and pacifying the Forbidden Kingdom."

I knew all this, since Pershing had told me about his expedition before I left on the trail of Surlang. But I was uneasy now, not quite certain where all this was leading. Davis didn't keep us guessing for long.

"The point is this, gentlemen: As much as I sympathize with your plight, if you do or say anything on Jolo that breaches our peaceful relationship with the sultan, I will personally draw up charges against both of you. Do you understand that?"

Davis's voice was all business now, and there was no doubt in my mind that he would sacrifice either of us as a balm to the sultan in the blink of an eye.

Longbottom cleared his throat nervously and replied, "I understand completely, sir."

34

Then we were dismissed. Outside Davis's door Quinlon commenced to pester us about how much money we were to receive, and how we were to use it, and on and on. He was such a nuisance that finally I rounded on Longbottom and snarled, "He's your father-in-law, damnit! Take him in charge until we're ready to sail!" Then I turned on my heel and left the two of them gaping in my wake.

I repaired forthwith to the officers' mess to drink bourbon and ruminate about the impending doom waiting for me on Jolo. As for the preparations for the journey, hell, I left them up to Longbottom. He had dreamed up this circus, and he could damn well get the show on the road himself. Predictably, he did, for the fellow had an amazing flair for organizing things. Longbottom arranged with Commander Henderson for the use of his three cutters, and General Davis contacted headquarters in Manila to have the Macabebes brought to Zamboanga. After a fortnight of feverish work and planning by Longbottom, and ceaseless bourbon swilling by me, all was in readiness. On a quiet evening Commander Henderson's flotilla slipped once more from Zamboanga's harbor, this time heading due east into the untamed Sulu Sea.

Longbottom had secured enough information about Jolo to form what might loosely be called a plan of action. Once we were under way, he gathered me, Henry—yes, Henry, for I refused to budge without him, you see—Bustos, and Henderson around and spelled it out. "Jamal-ul-Kiram's *cotta* is our target," he announced almost triumphantly.

Bustos, in the dark up to now, gasped. "He is sultan!"

Longbottom nodded with a grim smile. "He's the only lord on Jolo likely to have enough wealth to buy two white women, or at least that's my bet."

Pershing had long ago surmised exactly that, of course, but still the notion of tangling with the head Moro damn near bowed my knees. I hoped the others thought my sudden rocking motion was due to the pitch of the cutter.

"Where do we find this Jamal-ul-Kiram?" asked Henderson.

"He'll be in Maimbung, on the southern shore," replied Longbottom. He turned to the chart of Jolo spread out across an ammunition case before him. "About here," he said, pointing to a spot two miles inland from the southern coast.

"There's no anchorage off that beach," observed Commander Henderson tersely.

Longbottom nodded. "You'll have to put us ashore over the surf, and then hold your position until the landing party returns."

"It should be possible if the sea and weather cooperate," Henderson allowed.

"Good. Once ashore, we'll strike inland and let the Macabebes scout the way to Jamal-ul-Kiram."

Bustos looked at Longbottom with doubt etched all over his scarred face but held his tongue. It was just as well, for what he didn't say was that, other than large parties of heavily armored Spaniards, no raiders had ever landed on Jolo and lived to tell the tale.

Catching Bustos's look, I asked queasily, "What happens if and when we get to Maimbung, Longbottom?"

He pointed to the two canvas sacks stacked against a nearby bulkhead, each one stamped with a bold "U.S." Inside each sack was five thousand dollars in twenty-dollar gold pieces, good old American double eagles. "We find Jamal-ul-Kiram and offer to trade the gold for the girls. If we strike a deal, we hustle the girls back to the cutters and leave as soon as possible."

"And if the sultan refuses, sir?" asked Henry quietly.

It was a question Longbottom clearly didn't want to hear. He gave a strained little chuckle and insisted, "No native can resist that much gold. The sultan will take it, all right."

I rolled my eyes heavenward and Henry clamped his jaws tight with worry. We did not have long to ponder the problem, however, for by late the following afternoon Jolo was in view. As the blood red sun sank into the western sea, Commander Henderson dropped anchor three hundred yards from a secluded white strand.

"The surf's low, thank God," he said as the Macabebes, armed with new Krags and bandoliers of ammunition, took to the longboats. "There'll be no problem in staying right here until you return."

"Good," I said tensely, not at all certain that we would be returning.

The normally garrulous Macabebes were quiet as we rowed ashore, fully aware that they were entering the domain of some of the most feared warriors in all of the Philippines. In the fading light, I could see them quietly working the bolts of their Krags and fingering the sharp edges of their bolos. God, I thought, if these insensible beasts were jittery, what has Longbottom gotten us all into?

Then the boats were on the beach; the landing party disembarked in silence and filed inland. The hunt for Alice and Fiona was under way in earnest, but I felt no exhilaration. If the Moros turned nasty, they could overwhelm us long before we made it back to the boats. That realization settled around me like a cloak of lead. Bustos ordered out a scouting party, which quickly found a broad path. We followed this for two miles or so, passing small *cottas* along the way where we could hear family groups within settling back for dinner. We gave these places a wide berth, and continued undetected until the thick palm groves opened into a spacious sandy area about the size of a baseball park.

In the center of this clearing stood a formidable wooden stockade, its portal fashioned of huge teak tree trunks painted a garish scarlet. In the growing dusk I could make out the spire of a minaret soaring above the *cotta*, and from within came the sound of many gongs and cymbals, as though a celebration was under way.

"Maimbung," whispered Bustos.

I nodded as I studied the forbidding battlements. I could see groups of guards armed with spears walking the defenses. Fortunately, they didn't seem particularly alert. "Now what?" I hissed nervously to Longbottom.

"Well, we proceed as planned," he whispered back.

"What the devil does that mean, Longbottom? Your plan didn't cover this part, damnit," I retorted skittishly. "You said to come here and give the gold to the sultan. You never discussed how we were supposed to get inside his digs."

I could see Longbottom pondering in the growing gloom, and realized with an awful feeling that he was groping his way along as he went! By God, if that wasn't a recipe for disaster, then I didn't know what was.

Finally Longbottom announced uncertainly, "You stay put with the Macabebes and the gold, Travers," and he set the two canvas bags at my feet. "I'll slip in to get the lay of the place and to make sure Alice and Fiona are here. If they are, I'll come back and we'll announce our presence to the Moros and parley with them."

I didn't like it, but since he was the one venturing forth, that calmed me a bit. "Okay," I croaked hoarsely, and watched as he carefully went off, darting from palm to palm in the dim light. He had gone no more than twenty feet, however, when he suddenly plunged into a hole covered over with huge banana leaves and gave out a stifled cry.

"Christ, I'm wounded!"

I hastened forward with Bustos and Henry to find Longbottom's foot in a hole two feet deep. Protruding from the top of his foot was a sharpened bamboo stake.

"*Belatic*," muttered Bustos, which I guessed was the Moro term for foot trap.

"Son of a bitch, he did it again!" I fumed as I coldly eyed Longbottom writhing in agony.

"Did what?" whispered Henry at my side.

"Went and got himself mangled, just like he did at Balangiga! That's how I wound up serving with that maniac Waller for the most nightmarish few months of my life. Now he's gone and done it all over again. Why, I have half a mind to shove a stake through his other foot. It would serve the clumsy bastard right."

"Damn you, Travers, don't talk like that," Longbottom moaned, not certain that I wasn't completely serious.

But I couldn't stop ranting and raging at the bumbling fool, until, that is, I finally realized I was doing no good and that we couldn't stay here on the edge of Maimbung for long. I considered retreating to the cutters and pleading Longbottom's incapacity as a reason to call off the whole demented venture. Henry, however, wouldn't hear of it. He insisted that we carry on, arguing that if there was any hope of rescuing the damsels in distress we should, and generally appealing to my sense of compassion. That, of course, was about as productive as hawking moonshine at a Southern Baptist picnic, but when Longbottom recovered from his pain long enough to join Henry's entreaties, I finally held up my hands in resignation.

"Okay, okay! We'll go on with it. Does that satisfy the two of you, damnit?"

Sullenly I set about the business of approaching the stronghold of the mysterious Moro sultan. First, I arrayed the Macabebes into a defensive position from where they could cover the massive gate should trouble erupt. Longbottom, now bandaged but still in great pain, was left with them. Then, when all was in readiness, I turned to Henry and Bustos. "I guess it's time to go," I said glumly.

Together, the three of us crept forward to the *cotta*'s log palisade and halted in the shadows, searching for some way over the obstacle. Bustos saw it first. Handholds had been chipped into some of the logs, perhaps as a way to let scouts and messengers back into the citadel in times of emergency. To me, it looked like a pathway straight to hell, and every fiber in my body screamed to cut and run while we still could.

"Er, Henry, why don't you lead the way?" I suggested faintly.

Perhaps sensing that I was nearly at the end of my tether, Henry gulped but replied gamely, "Sure, Fenny."

Up he started, with Bustos on his heels and me bringing up the rear, ready to leap to the sand below should an alarm sound in the dark.

There was no outcry, however, and the three of us slipped undetected over the parapet onto a wide firing step, where we paused silently in the shadows on the far side. As the gongs and cymbals continued unabated from below our perch, I rose carefully to a crouch and looked about.

The nearest guards were over by the main gate, talking in low tones and laughing among themselves. In the dark I could see a red glow as they shared a massive cheroot. Within the palisade stood a collection of nipa huts laid out in a circular pattern around a central mosque and an adjacent building constructed of sturdy timbers. This latter structure was a sprawling hall, ornately festooned with wooden carvings. It was, I determined, the palace of Jamal-ul-Kiram. From the main gate, a wide avenue ran all the way to the mosque, and it was on this avenue that most of the inhabitants of Maimbung were gathered. From the many bonfires and the gay dancing that was everywhere evident, I surmised that we had stumbled upon a Moro festival of some sort.

"Now what?" I whispered.

"We poke around and see if the ladies are here," asserted Henry.

Venturing farther into the Moro sanctum seemed like sheer madness. Why, they'd flay us alive if we were taken. "Can't we just try to spot 'em from here?" I whined.

"Fenny," reasoned Henry, "we can't parley with these fellows until we're sure the goods are here, right? Now, if the ladies are in Maimbung, they're probably under lock and key somewhere. If I had to guess where, I'd pick that big building over yonder. I say we ought to go see."

"And I say we ought to get out of here," I quailed miserably, painfully aware that the guards in the distance were well within spear-throwing range.

Henry, however, had no intention of coaxing me every step of the way. "Let's go!" he said sharply.

With that he dropped from the firing step to the ground below. Bustos followed, and not wishing to be left alone, I leaped down after them. Careful not to stir up any stray mongrels, we made our way to the side of the village farthest away from the front gate, and then approached the palace from the rear. We crept to within fifty feet of the edifice and paused again. Up close I could see that the carved timbers were lashed together with hemp, and the whole thing was roofed over with the ubiquitous nipa thatching.

Fortunately, large windows were everywhere, making it easy to scout the place. The structure had a main wing, which I took to be a chamber dedicated to state functions and such. This wing then branched off into several lesser wings, which I guessed were the living quarters. It would be in one of these smaller wings, I concluded, that we would probably find the sultan's seraglio.

"Follow me," said Henry softly. We made our way to the first wing and peered through a window. Inside were low tables set on a floor of gleaming mahogany. Around the tables were scattered ornate carpets of obvious great value. This was evidently a dining hall, and it was empty. Signaling us with a wave of his hand, Henry crept forward to the next wing in line, moving through low shrubbery to avoid detection. There was a lighted window up ahead, and Henry guided on it. Halting under cover of the foliage, we stared within.

I saw movement, a gliding shape, and then another. Were my eyes playing tricks on me? I wondered. Could it be? Yes, by God it was!

"You two stay here," I gasped, sudden boldness coursing through me. "I'll handle this myself."

Henry looked at Bustos dubiously. "Are you sure, Fenny?" he murmured. "I mean, you didn't seem so all fired eager just a moment ago."

"Oh, that was just a small bout of night blindness, Henry. Nothing more, really," I whispered in reply, already advancing as I spoke.

The window ledge was about five feet above the ground, and I rose carefully to take a good gander at the interior. No, my eyes had not deceived me; what they detected was a sight that few, if any, westerners had ever before beheld. It was Jamal-ul-Kiram's harem, and everywhere were preening women in various states of undress!

The harem was built around a central fountain, skillfully carved from hardwood, which rose straight through the floor and around which ladies arranged themselves as they went through their intricate toilettes. From the serious attention they were giving to this matter, I guessed that they were preparing themselves for the honor of their master's attention at the conclusion of the evening's festivities.

With no conscious intent, I was suddenly climbing through the window, heading straight for the tantalizing femininity arrayed before me. Oh, I couldn't have stopped myself had I wanted to, for my limbs were not mine to command. I was being driven on not by any deliberate thought in my head, but rather by a more primal urge—

my enflamed loins. Paradise lay before me, by God, and I would not be denied!

I stepped from behind an ornate Chinese screen as stealthily as a weasel in a rookery—so quietly, in fact, that the milling lovelies were at first unaware of my presence. My eyes bulged from their sockets as I feasted on the voluptuous display of distaff charms all around me. Slender Malay gals were everywhere, each one of them either naked or clad in gossamer harem pantaloons, which concealed nothing from the eye. Intermixed with them were Chinese wenches, and even a Hindoo or two. Oh, it was too much to bear, I tell you. I was startled from my trance by the strangled sound of my own voice gurgling, "Oh, Lord, thank you. Thank you!"

Instantly, every woman in the room froze. Then they turned to me as one, expressions of pure horror on their faces. You see, I had violated the highest taboo on Jolo; I had defiled the sanctity of the sultan's love nest! Some gave little shrieks; others fled to the far side of the chamber like a flock of pigeons in a city park startled by the antics of an impetuous child rushing into their midst.

Aghast at my predicament, I feared there might be a panicked stampede from the room. Just then, however, a perky little miss, as naked as a jaybird, advanced boldly from the huddled herd.

"Senor," she asked in dulcet tones, "our master, are you from him sent?"

Her Spanish was atrocious, and at first I didn't understand her point. Then it dawned on me that no sane person would venture into these hallowed halls without the sultan's express blessing, and the little vixen was trying to determine whether or not I had membership rights in this particular club. If she was asking, I figured, then that meant she didn't know. So I doffed my campaign hat with a smooth bow and promptly assured her, "Si, Senorita. It is the will of Jamal-ul-Kiram that I be here. I trust that causes you and your lovely companions no distress?"

She hastened to assure me that such was not the case, and then turned to explain my bogus status to her friends. After a moment of rapid-fire conversation, and several pointed looks at my strange garb, the mood of the room suddenly softened. The assembled sisterhood decided I must be an emissary from some strange kingdom whom their master desired to be wined and feted. Why else would I be there, eh? In an instant I found myself treated as an honored guest, shown to a seat, and offered sweets and fruits of all sorts.

A lovely Chinese girl with skin the color of gold mixed with ginger put her round bottom in my lap and fed me juicy grapes from a bunch she held coyly over her charming breasts. A Malay beauty produced a tortoise-shell comb and began arranging my locks, as yet others began chanting a soft tune for my enjoyment. Oh, it was delightful, a dream come true, a veritable earthly Eden. I never wanted to leave this chamber, and indeed all thoughts of my purpose for being here in the first place had been completely banished from my mind—until I glanced toward the window through which I'd crept to see Henry, bug-eyed and furious, gesturing at me to be about my business.

"Oh, damn it all," I muttered, coming slowly to my senses like a drunk throwing off the effects of a debauch. Turning to the gal who spoke a smattering of Spanish, I asked, "Are there white ladies here? ¿Comprende? ¿Las senoritas blancas?"

I pointed at the white skin of my face and then at her, but only produced a round of tittering, and then all the ladies started poking and tickling me.

"No, you don't understand!" I cried. "White ladies, you savvy?" I pointed at a gold platter nearby. "Hair like gold, si? Is there a lady here with hair like gold?"

Now my interpreter started to nod. "Ah, si. There are Spanish ladies. Two."

Spanish ladies? I wondered. Perhaps to her, I reasoned, any Caucasian might be called a Spaniard. "Yes," I said, "bring me to the Spanish ladies."

Smiling agreeably, she took me by the hand and led me from the hall down a narrow corridor from which branched off smaller rooms I presumed were sleeping chambers for the harem ladies or pleasure rooms for Jamal-ul-Kiram and his cronies. We stayed in the corridor, pushing past barrier after barrier of silken curtains. Their purpose, I assumed, was to muffle sounds and to divide the sleeping quarters into cozy little private nooks.

We pushed through the last of these drapes and suddenly entered a large chamber, not as big as the first, but roomy enough. Across the way from where I stood was a large double door that went clear to the ceiling. That, I surmised, was the main entrance to the harem. Here and there were more ladies, every bit as comely and unclothed as the ones I had first encountered. As we entered the chamber, all eyes turned our way. Disappointingly, however, everywhere I looked I saw naught but black hair and dark eyes.

That is, until my guide pulled aside a curtain across the entry to an alcove to reveal two light-skinned beauties! One, a blond-haired siren, stood before a small fountain wearing nothing but a little velvet jacket as she put on her earrings. At her side sat a nude Athena, arms upraised to comb her flowing auburn tresses. I recognized those locks at once.

"Alice!" I blurted out.

Alice turned, and her mouth fell open in stupefaction. Then she screamed, "Fenny, oh Fenny! Get me out of here!"

The blond turned too, and by God, it was Fiona! "Fenny, save us, please!"

Now the rest of the women found their voices too and a chorus of outraged shrieks went up anew to the heavens. My companion, however, set about silencing their outcry and explaining my presence as I flew to Alice's side. "Quickly, my dear," I said, scooping Alice into my arms, "we must go. I have a company of native scouts waiting beyond the walls, and if we can get to them you'll be safe."

"But, Fenny," protested Fiona, "what about the sultan? Does he know about this?"

"Not yet, Fee, but he will soon," I promised her. The outcries I had provoked had probably not gone unnoticed. "Now put some clothes on and let's get out of here."

"I'm not going anywhere without my jewels," Fiona insisted with a little stamp of her foot.

"Your jewels?" I asked, looking to Alice for some explanation.

"Jamal-ul-Kiram has a particular fondness for white ladies," Alice explained. "He's showered us with gifts since we arrived. I wouldn't take a thing, but Fiona here, well. . . ."

"So, Fee," I smiled with a shake of my head, "you've finally found a man who can keep you in the style you require, eh?"

"Joke if you want, Fenny," Fiona sniffed, "but that sultan knows how to treat a lady. Those jewels are mine, and if I'm going, they're going with me."

"Damn, Fee, there's no time for that," I remonstrated. "If I get caught in here, we'll all be buzzard bait."

"I'm taking the jewels with me and that's all there is to it!" shouted Fiona angrily, and with that she turned and rushed off. I let her go, knowing from past experience it was useless to argue with Fiona when she had her mind set on something.

Waiting impatiently with Alice warm and trembling in my arms, I breathed, "Alice, I've missed you madly. Are you all right? Have you been mistreated?"

"I'm fine," she smiled bravely. "I must admit that I was very frightened when Surlang first took us. Fiona and I were not at all certain that we wouldn't be killed. But after we survived the first few days, I came to think that we'd be just fine. After a while, Surlang met another Moro ship on the sea, and that's where we parted company with him."

"Another Moro ship?"

Alice nodded. "It was one of the sultan's ships. Ali Rashid, the sultan's counselor, was on board, and he led us to understand that Fiona and I were to come with him to Jolo. As you can imagine, we were quite anxious to leave Surlang behind, so we eagerly went with Ali Rashid. He paid for us, you know."

I mulled over this information in my mind. That would explain how Surlang disposed of his precious cargo, yet was able to sail east from Zamboanga, not west toward Jolo. He must have arranged the sale of his captives well in advance of seizing them—a fact that made me fear more than ever the diabolical intrigues of his twisted mind. I said nothing of this to Alice, of course, but instead smiled and inquired, "Tell me, how much was my lovely worth to the great sultan of Jolo?"

"About twenty small jars of opium, as best I could see," she responded.

"Hmmm. A king's, or rather I should say a queen's, ransom."

"Perhaps, Fenny, but it's hardly flattering being bought and sold like some prize cow. Well anyway, Ali Rashid took us to Jolo, and eventually we wound up here in the sultan's harem."

I pondered how to put my next question to Alice, so I went about it indirectly. "And how did Fiona bear up under all of this strain?"

Alice's face clouded over. "At first she cried all the time, and asked to go back to her father, or . . . to you."

"Me? Why ever would she say that?" I asked innocently.

"I asked her the same thing," replied Alice, "and she said that you made her feel safe like her father."

"Silly girl," I tut-tutted lightly. "I must say, though, she certainly seems back on her feet tonight."

"Oh, she is," Alice assured me emphatically. "You see, once we were settled in the harem, Jamal-ul-Kiram paid special attention to Fiona and me."

Oh, but I bet he did, I thought grimly.

"His other wives were very jealous, but Fiona didn't seem to care. She cozied right up to him, and"—here Alice hesitated a bit before going on—"Fenny, that woman showed no shame at all! I mean, she danced the Moro dance of love right in front of the sultan, with me and the other wives looking on!"

"Come now, Alice," I gently chided her. "Where's the harm in a little dance?"

"Little dance?" she snorted. "The love dance—or *magloonsy* as the Moros call it—is performed *naked,* Fenny! That woman cavorted before us without a single stitch of clothing on! Well, I couldn't believe my eyes. You wouldn't think this was the same demure army wife I first met back on the ferry to Zamboanga."

Oh, but I would believe such a thing, for you see I had seen Fiona in action back at Tampa in '98 when the army was staging for the invasion of Cuba. She was a howling bitch in heat when her fancy turned to lovemaking, bestowing her favors liberally to all likely comers. I said nothing of this to Alice, but instead screwed up a suitably shocked expression at her revelation and then changed the subject back to her by asking gently, "And you, my dear? Were you treated, well, gently?"

Alice flushed red at this and looked away. When she turned back to me, her face was downcast and there were tears in her eyes. "Well, it is a harem, Fenny. You see and do certain things here, you know. Just be assured that in this world, I love only you."

I hugged her close and she laid her pretty head on my shoulder. "I know that, dear. I know that," I assured her gently, all the while musing about all the new amorous skills Alice must have acquired. She had been an energetic lover before she was taken—but now she was a certified courtesan, trained by masters in that art! Oh, call me insensitive or call me just plain depraved, but whatever my faults, a lack of the ability to turn life's unexpected twists to my advantage wasn't one of them. That was why my imagination and my loins stirred at the thought that inevitably I'd cajole Alice into revealing to me the full extent of her newfound knowledge of Moro culture. Perhaps I'd even convince her to perform the *magloonsy* for me!

Just then Fiona rejoined us clutching a red leather pouch, which I took to be her recently acquired hoard. "I'm ready," she announced. "Let's go."

At that very instant, however, an immense gong sounded in the hallway beyond the great doors. "Er, are you ladies expecting company?" I squeaked with disquiet.

Before either of them could answer, the massive doors swung slowly open. Standing beyond the threshold was a band of Moro spearmen. The warriors took one look at me and charged, screaming hideously as they came on.

"Let me out of here!" I yipped, darting for the far side of the chamber, where the corridor led back toward Henry and Bustos.

"Fenny, don't leave us!" shrieked Alice, while Fiona uttered her battle cry: "Touch my jewels and I'll gouge your eyes out, you beasts!"

Perhaps I should have turned and made my stand by Alice, lived or died by her side. That's what any real man would have done, you might say. Well, perhaps so, but one doesn't change the habits of a lifetime in a split second. Instead, faced with overwhelming force, I bolted like a rabbit flushed from cover. Trying to salvage some dignity as I went, I yelled over my shoulder, "I'll be back with reinforcements, Alice. I swear I will!"

That bit of bravado cost me a second, letting one of the fiends close to within slashing distance. The tip of his kris parted the air just a fraction of an inch from my neck, sending me scampering even faster in retreat. I reached the corridor of the thousand drapes, plunging past the first one and throwing it hard at my pursuers as I went. I did the same with the next and then the next. The Moros, coming forward in a solid body, were slowed by the delicate material, and I could hear them cursing and slashing behind me. Reaching the first chamber that I had entered, I turned and pushed a sturdy divan across the floor, then set it on end and jammed it into the constricted passageway as a barrier to stem the pursuit.

"Henry! Bustos!" I cried in desperation, but from beyond the window through which I had entered I heard only Moros' screeches, and then a distant popping noise. Those weren't fireworks, I knew. It was gunfire, and that could only mean that the Macabebes had been discovered and were fighting back. Then the Moros burst through the last curtain and slammed into the divan I was sheltering behind.

"Good God almighty!" I wailed as krises whistled around my ears and pieces of divan flew in the air as though the thing was being fed bodily into a whirling buzz saw. Thoroughly unmanned, I dashed for the window, passing cowering harem girls who threw up their slim arms in despair and cried for mercy as I scuttled past. Reaching the window in four strides, I launched myself out into the night. I hit the ground hard, rolled once, regained my feet, and ran off into the dark, desperate to lose the Moros who were sure to follow.

"Henry!" I called urgently as I went, as loudly as I dared. "Bustos!"

My calls were met by silence. They were gone, by thunder, probably driven off by furious Moros responding to the invasion of the harem. I was on my own now. Spooked badly, I ran as quickly as I could in a wide circle back through the thoroughly aroused village toward the main gate. The irate citizenry, fortunately for me, was thronging around the palace looking for the intruders, which left all the byways between the nipa shacks clear for my escape.

Or so I thought until I neared the gate and three Moro warriors stepped from the shadows to bar my path.

35

Jolo Island
April 21, 1902

For an awful second they stood there in silence, hefting their krises and scowling wickedly.

I drew my Colt. "Get out of my way. I'm warning you!" I blustered, edging for the gate as I spoke. It was wide open, and I guessed that the Moros had sallied through it to engage the Macabebes. The three Moros didn't budge, so I cocked back the hammer. "Last chance, hombres," I promised them. By way of an answer, they leveled their spears and charged!

Immediately my Colt roared. The first one I caught full in the mouth, and he went down howling; the second I drilled through his head, throwing him back on the third. With four shots left, I fired into the chest of the survivor. This last Moro sagged, straightened with an effort, and then amazingly sprang forward again.

I fired once more, but on he came, screaming his war cry with his kris raised for the kill. Again I squeezed the trigger, and a geyser of red sprang from his forehead. Stunned by the impact, he faltered, then, incredibly, raised his kris anew.

I had one bullet left, and I realized there would be no chance to reload before this wild man was on me; my last shot had to count. I aimed for his forehead again and squeezed the trigger. The big Colt roared, and a chunk of gore blew from the rear of the Moro's skull. Then I saw a tiny blue hole in his forehead beside the first one I'd put there, and he collapsed into a tangled heap at my feet.

My way clear now, I started for the gate when a booming voice in perfect Spanish rooted me to the spot. "You will go nowhere!"

I turned to see a sight that chilled me to the marrow. The main avenue was empty of revelers now, and in their place stood a thick battle line of heavily armed Moros, some even clad in antique breastplates and morions their ancestors must have captured from luckless conquistadores. A hundred snarling faces fixed on mine, each Moro ready to do mortal combat. Behind the battle line, slaves and retainers bore great torches that lit the night with garish hues of red and yellow. By the flickering flames I discerned two figures advancing from the phalanx of warriors.

One, a portly rascal about thirty years old, was decked out in silk robes and a turban encrusted with jewels and festooned with gaudy feathers. The other was an old gnome of a fellow, barely four feet tall, wearing a simple white turban and a loincloth. He looked to be a hundred if he was a day, but his beady eyes seemed keen enough, and at the moment they were riveted right on me.

The younger of the two, I knew instantly, must be Jamal-ul-Kiram. General MacArthur had called him a degenerate, and for my money he was right. Jamal-ul-Kiram had the dissipated look of a wastrel hopelessly addicted to opium and women. Why, I hadn't set eyes on a facade this corrupted since I was introduced to the mayor of New York upon my triumphant return from Peking. Yet whether he was debauched or not, Jamal-ul-Kiram's blood was up at the moment, and he was screaming unholy murder, no doubt calling for my immediate execution. But who the devil was the old codger at his side? I wondered warily as I fought to contain my growing panic.

As if reading my thoughts, the ancient one spoke. "I am Ali Rashid, *wazir* to the sultan, his exalted majesty, Jamal-ul-Kiram."

At the utterance of the sultan's name, a reverential rumble went through the ranks of warriors that sounded like "ooh-wahh!"

Ali Rashid? I thought. Why then, this runt was the fellow who had gone to sea to exchange opium for Alice and Fiona. What had Alice called him? The sultan's counselor—yes, that was it.

Ali Rashid continued to eye me flintily. "You are an *americano, si?*"

"*Si.* Captain Fenwick Travers, United States Army," I replied hopefully. Maybe these beasts respected American power, I prayed, and would send me along my way with no further interference.

"You have no authority on Jolo," Ali Rashid spat icily, his tone quickly disabusing me of any notion that I might escape this fix without paying a price. "This fact is known to your leaders. Why do you come unbidden to our shores?"

A damned good question, of course, and I knew my life depended upon giving a damned good answer. Instinctively, I thought about lying. I could spin some cockamamy tale about coming to Jolo to establish good relations with Jamal-ul-Kiram, but I realized despairingly that events had moved dramatically past the point where my dissembling would be in the least credible.

Deciding that matters could not get worse if I told the truth, I replied, "I came for the women. The white women. They were sold to His Majesty by Surlang, the pirate."

A buzz went up at this, and the ranks of warriors parted. A familiar figure stepped forward, a figure in a green silk turban. By Christ in heaven, it was Surlang! At his side stood Fiona and Alice, both of them nude and bound at the wrists. In spite of the fact that I was facing imminent annihilation, the flickering light reflecting off their milky white breasts raised thoughts of passion in my fear-crazed mind.

Ali Rashid pointed to Surlang. "Do you say Surlang stole these women from you?"

I nodded. "I so accuse him. The one with the golden hair is the wife of an American officer. The other, the one with the hair the color of polished mahogany, she is my betrothed. Surlang stole them from me through trickery, and I have come to reclaim them."

Ali Rashid considered this. Woman stealing was hardly an indictment against Surlang; indeed, in these parts, it was a positive character reference. All this I understood, and in fact it explained why Surlang had been admitted back into the presence of the sultan. As an outcast from Jolo, he probably hoped to use the obvious charms of Alice and Fiona as tickets to buy himself back into favor at the sultan's court.

That was why I was puzzled when Ali Rashid glanced at Jamal-ul-Kiram, who in turn flicked a baleful glare in the direction of Surlang. I had only an instant to interpret these looks, but it appeared that although the sultan was fully prepared to endorse slave raiding as a general principle, he was annoyed that Surlang had been so artless as to allow me to learn the identity of the current owner of my womenfolk. That meant that Surlang's bid for readmittance into this pirate's fraternity had gone amiss. Whatever the outcome of this night's events, I was certain that Surlang was destined to be banished once more.

"Take them away," Ali Rashid ordered, and the guards led the protesting girls off, Alice begging for my life as she went, while Fiona caterwauled that someone had pinched her jewels, by God, and there'd be hell to pay when she caught the culprit.

When Ali Rashid turned his hard eyes back to me, it was clear that I bore the onus of explaining my intrusion into the sacrosanct precincts of the sultan's harem. "Even Americans know about the customs of the Moros," Ali Rashid said scathingly. "We hold slaves in our households by the power of our arms. If you wished to reclaim your women, you were within your rights to challenge the sultan's warriors in battle for their return. You had no right, however," he added darkly, "to trespass into the sultan's harem."

I gulped. I was on trial now, and I could guess at the outcome. Unless I started talking, and convincingly, I was a goner. "My government sent me to talk to the sultan, not fight," I stammered. "I merely wanted to ensure that the white women were in Maimbung, that's all. What I intended to do was to announce myself properly to his majesty, and then offer to pay for the women."

"Pay?" laughed Ali Rashid scornfully.

"Yes, pay. In gold pieces. Ten thousand dollars, American."

Ali Rashid threw a guttural command over his shoulder, and a slave hurried forward with the two sacks of gold. He laid them at the old man's feet and then withdrew. "Is this the gold of which you speak?"

I stared dumbfounded. The Moros must have driven off the Macabebes so quickly that they left behind the bullion. God, but they were ferocious devils, I thought with a shudder.

"Yes, that's it," I said numbly when I found my voice again. "My superiors wish your master to have it, as a sign of our love and respect. All we ask is that you turn over the ladies, undamaged, of course."

Ali Rashid was less than impressed. "You would pay a ransom for your women rather than fight?"

His question was biting, and I suspected that I had shown weakness. I tried to backtrack in a hurry. "Er, let me explain, Ali Rashid. As I said, my government wants peace with the sultan, not war. I was told to arrange this transaction with as little aggravation as possible to all parties concerned. It's the way we Americans do things, you see, and—"

Ali Rashid cut me off with a wave of the hand. "Ransom on Jolo is paid by the defeated. If you wanted to have the sultan's esteem, you should have come to fight for your women."

I gulped again, for the stormy look on Ali Rashid's ancient visage told me that a clash of arms was in the offing. I was right; the sultan raised his arms to the heavens and then screeched out a frenzied diatribe. A ripple of excitement went through his warriors, who raised their krises and began howling and stamping their feet in unison.

Ali Rashid then confirmed my worst fears: "You are to fight the sultan's champions, infidel dog," he commanded.

I reached into my cartridge pouch for ammunition. This infidel dog had no intention of committing suicide by meeting Moro krismen in single combat. I'd feed them hot lead instead, by God.

Ali Rashid, however, saw my movement and stayed me with a gesture of his hand. "This must be settled with bare steel," he declared adamantly.

My hand lingered at my revolver until I noticed a body of archers twenty strong standing in the shadows with their drawn bows trained at my heart. Slowly I eased my hand away; making a move for my Colt would plainly result in instant death.

Seeing my grudging compliance, Ali Rashid motioned to a nearby warrior, who immediately padded forward at a trot. This ruffian carried a coiled silver chain that terminated in a single shackle. As he advanced, the warrior uncoiled the chain until he reached me, whereupon he bent down and snapped the shackle about one of my booted ankles. I yanked back in alarm, only to be restrained by the chain, which was fastened to a huge wooden stake driven deep in the ground twenty feet away. Dashing back to Ali Rashid, the warrior turned to me and tossed a sword through the air, which landed at my feet. I holstered my Colt with dread and picked up the blade. It was heavier than the elegant Moro kris, and had more the look of a meat cleaver.

"That is a barong," announced Ali Rashid. "Use it well, infidel," he added with disdain.

I hefted the barong tentatively. Like a bolo, it was a single-edged blade, and seemed sturdy enough. But would its weight be sufficient to offset the slashing quickness of the krises I was bound to face? I had no intention of finding out.

"Ali Rashid," I pleaded forlornly, "surely you can't be serious! I'm no swordsman. Besides, if you kill me, you'll face the wrath of the white chief in Manila."

"There is only one power I fear," countered the old *wazir* coldly, "and that is Allah. *Capitán,* your time has come to fight."

"Wait, I say!" I wailed, but it was too late, for Jamal-ul-Kiram pointed to a stalwart Moro of his guard who promptly bowed stiffly and pranced forward. He cut the air viciously with his drawn kris as he came on, baring his fangs as he did. Then with a bloodcurdling cry, he charged— at thin air, as things turned out, for I was careening about like a scalded dog at the end of a leash.

"Get away, you brute!" I screamed as I flailed wildly all about me. The watching Moros roared demonically at my antics, while above the cacophony I heard the shrill screams of Fiona and Alice. I had thought they were gone, you see, but they must have found some vantage point from which to watch what promised to be the final chapter in the sordid tale of their poor Fenny's life. "Ali Rashid!" I implored. "Call him off, I say! Call him off, for God's sake!"

Oh, it did no good, for in my fear I was gibbering in English, not Spanish, and the Moros to a man thought I was bawling out my war cries. Insane with terror, and unable to run farther on my tether, I turned on my antagonist. Seeing me stand, he leaped at me with a slashing blow. I pulled my head back just as his strike seemed about to cleave my skull. Then with reflexes born of mindless desperation, I gave a great cry and hacked him across the neck with my barong just as the force of his swing carried him about.

Unfortunately, he was nimble, and he whirled lightly to counter me so that my blow, rather than being fatal, merely caused a nasty gash. Then, with a speed I could scarcely credit, the Moro hopped back a step and in the same instant slashed for my face. I ducked the singing kris by no more than a hair's breadth, stabbing out desperately as I did so.

My move completely surprised the Moro, for in his experience the barong was employed only to slash, never to stab. The tip of my barong plunged deep into his exposed abdomen. When I withdrew the heavy blade with a twist, it virtually eviscerated my opponent. His intestines spilled onto the sand before him, and for the first time, I saw shock on the face of a Moro. I took advantage of his consternation to step back and swing mightily.

The blade severed the Moro's head as cleanly as a melon from a vine. The severed head sailed through the air to bounce in the sand at Ali Rashid's sandled feet. The old counselor merely glanced at the horrible thing, the truncated neck of which oozed forth a stream of gore. He nodded at me—approvingly if I wasn't mistaken—but Jamal-ul-Kiram was furious. He unleashed a barrage of maledictions in my direction, and another fighter sprang forward. I noted with dismay that this one, unlike the first warrior, was protected by a jerkin of carabao armor.

"Not again!" I bleated in protest. "Goddamnit, this ain't fair! Ali Rashid, please listen! You can't keep me chained here all night to be slaughtered like a dog."

My remonstrances fell on deaf ears, however, as the second challenger advanced. He came on more cautiously than his luckless predecessor, for he had just witnessed a Moro cut down in hand-to-hand combat with an infidel, something unheard of before tonight. It was an article of faith among the Moros, you see, that no foreigner armed with only cold steel could stand before them. Clearly this strange American did not know the rules. So my new assailant advanced gingerly, hefting his kris warily in one hand, and drawing a long dagger from his sash with the other. If I wanted to stab instead of slash, well, he would accommodate me.

Trembling with a fear that bordered on insanity, I watched disbelievingly as this Moro stalked to within striking range. I was mumbling aloud now, and my bladder emptied of its own accord as I desperately tried to remember some shred of prayer I might invoke to deliver me from this nightmare. None came, but the Moro seemed suddenly shy in the face of my odd quivers and twitches, appearing to want to react rather than to force the action. As he paused uncertainly before me, I suddenly noticed that the Moro's foot was planted in the middle of a coil of the chain attached to my ankle.

Oh, don't ask me how I picked out that detail when my mind was otherwise befogged in a red haze of dread, and don't expect me to recall how I summoned up the will to act, when only the instant before I had been a pathetic column of quivering pudding. No, don't ask me any of these things, for I couldn't answer them other than to say I saw my only chance for survival and I took it.

At the very instant all of this came together in my brain, I yanked my foot back hard, catching the Moro in the snare formed by the tautly drawn chain. His foot swept out from beneath him as cleanly as if it was chopped away by an ax, and he hit the ground with a thud. Before he could recover his senses, I was on him. With a strangled cry that sounded for all the world like a ruptured sheep coughing up a wad of chewed grass, I raised my barong and brought it crashing down as though it were a battle-ax.

And missed—for the Moro, with the innate speed of his kind, rolled away before my blow could land! Then he was up, calmly parrying my berserk swings, all the while holding his dagger at the ready for a killing stab. He balanced lightly on the balls of his feet, legs spread, ready to respond to my every move. All except one, that is. With a vicious kick, I drove the boot on my unfettered foot straight into his crotch below the bottom edge of the carabao armor.

The force of the blow lifted the Moro off his feet, and he landed heavily on his knees in the sand. For an instant he was paralyzed, his only visible muscle action being to blink away his tears of pain. Then, desperate to save himself, he tried to raise his weapons. He was too late. My barong whistled downward like a bolt of lightning; there was a spray of blood, and another Moro head rolled in the sand.

As the headless cadaver slumped to the ground at my feet, the whole line of angry warriors stepped forward as one. They could have put an end to this maddening infidel in one rush, and I gaped at them with unbounded fear, knowing I would stand no chance against all of them. Then, to my utter amazement, Ali Rashid saved me once again by raising his hand to halt their assault. Jamal-ul-Kiram continued to yammer away with an insane fury, but Ali Rashid remained calm. He motioned for another champion to step forward.

A gorgeously attired Moro did so. He bowed to his sultan and then faced me. This, I knew instantly, was a *datu,* a lord, and this peacock would be even fiercer, if that was possible, than either of the two foes I had already dispatched.

But I was beyond fear now, you see, having slipped over the border to insanity to escape the awful reality that I was going to die in this hellhole, probably a slice at a time. I shook and trembled, and my eyes rolled up into my head until nothing showed but their whites. My face was so contorted by fear that my lips were drawn back tightly, and I bared my fangs through frothing saliva at the astonished Moros.

As I howled and grunted and waited for death in that awful arena of doom, I heard an awed whisper spread through their ranks: *"Amok! Amok!"*

And *amok* I was, all right, stark raving mad and fit to be tied. With all reason now banished, and yowling like a crazed sailor in a street brawl, I uttered a savage whoop and charged the startled Moro *datu* with my barong raised. His kris deflected my blow, and the air rang with the sound of steel on steel. Although the Moro was able to block my strike, the force of my frenzied blow was enormous, and the impact jarred the kris from his hand. He darted away to recover his blade, but not quickly enough, for now I had the speed of the wild-eyed lunatic I had become. Once more my barong sang out, and once more a headless body toppled in the sand. This time the sultan was utterly silent.

At this the warriors erupted in a paroxysm of fury, each one demanding the honor of being the next to challenge me. Gongs were beating wildly all around, and the rhythmic drumming gave the torch-lit scene a phantasmagorical air. Ali Rashid turned to the sultan now and was speaking rapidly as I staggered back and away toward the yawning gate. Whatever Ali Rashid had said was something the sultan didn't want to hear, for suddenly there was a violent argument between the two of them, with warriors joining the fray on either side.

This unexpected respite allowed me to regain my breath, and as I did so my faculties slowly returned to me. I became aware of the fact that none of the Moros were looking my way, so engrossed were they in the bickering about my defeat of their paladins. As they shrieked into each other's faces like stockbrokers in a financial panic, I stood there for some minutes before it finally occurred to me that absolutely nobody was paying the slightest bit of attention to me any longer.

I also noticed something else, something that brought hope and sanity surging back to me. When I had struck at the second Moro on the ground but missed his head, I had nonetheless hit the chain. Quite cleanly as things turned out, for the links about three feet from my ankle fetter had been completely sundered by my chopping blow.

Quietly, expecting a spear in the back at any moment, I turned, slipped through the gate, and made for the trees. All thought of rescuing Fiona and Alice was banished from my mind. There was only one skin that mattered any longer, and that was mine.

36

Hopping madly like an escapee from an Arkansas chain gang, I hurried through the darkness heedless of obstacles in my path. Along the way I saw several corpses, no doubt those of Macabebes not swift enough to escape the sudden Moro sortie. I found the route to the shore and, holding the length of chain in my hand so that it did not whip out and wrap about every tree I passed, I redoubled my speed.

Over the noise of my labored breathing, however, I thought I heard footfalls behind me. I had gone no more than four hundred yards when it was unmistakable; runners were definitely on my trail. The Moros must have stopped their bickering long enough to realize I'd flown the coop, and they evidently wanted me back. What was more, they knew every dip and bend between me and the shore. I had no doubt that they'd have my head unless I threw them off the scent somehow.

But how? My fevered brain raced wildly, seeking an answer, and then it hit me! What was it Pershing had said that Moros feared? Yes, that was it—the *bal-bal!* The werewolf!

I didn't have a *bal-bal* readily at hand, of course, so I made do as best I could. Halting on the path, I turned and cupped my hands to my mouth. Back at Fort Grant in Arizona many years ago, I'd sat on my bunk and listened to the yipping coyotes in the chaparral. Coyotes made as noisome a racket as one could imagine, so I used their cry as my guide. I commenced to yap and bark, then snuffle and grunt. Oh, I lowed and bellowed, long and hard like an ox in rut, then threw in a few cackles and quacks for good measure. My clamor was preposterous to my ears, but it immediately hit a nerve with the Moros. The sounds of pursuit lessened, and then stopped entirely. I heard a few nervous calls in the dark, the sound of Moros trying to buck up each other's courage, and then nothing.

I'd shaken the chase, by God! I exulted in silence, then took to my heels in relief. I clanked past the smaller *cottas* that we had skirted on the way to Maimbung, this time running right by their front gates looking for all the world like the ghost of Christmas past as the startled residents gawked out into the shadows. These Moros did not pursue me, although they could have taken me had they done so. No, they too had heard the call of the awful *bal-bal,* and they huddled by their hearths in dread.

Soon I was at the beach, where just beyond the line of white surf I could see the cutters at anchor. The last of the landing party was just clambering over the gunwales, and I could hear the sounds of a heated argument in progress. In particular, I caught Longbottom's querulous tones wafting across the water.

"Travers isn't coming," Longbottom was insisting forcefully. "The sultan's got him by now, and if we linger too long he'll get us too."

Commander Henderson spoke up in reply. "I'm sorry, Captain Longbottom, but I'm not budging. We still have a few hours before dawn, and we'll be safe here until then."

Then I heard Henry's voice. By the blazes, he was still alive! "Yes, don't leave Fenny, suh. You mustn't."

I put an end to the discussion by hallooing from shore. Soon Henderson had a longboat splashing back for me, and in no time I was on the deck of the *Jackson*.

"Weigh anchor, Commander," I said dourly. "We've been thwarted, I'm afraid."

Longbottom, propped on a blanket with his foot wrapped in a blood-soaked bandage, rounded on me furiously.

"Travers, what happened back there was inexcusable. We were under direct orders not to disturb the peace of the sultanate, and by God, the first thing you did was wade into Maimbung and provoke a riot. I intend to bring charges against you for disobeying General Davis's direct order and for dereliction of duty as soon as we return to Zamboanga. Commander," he added, turning to Henderson, "I'll expect you to back me up on this."

Damn his hide, I raged; Longbottom saw an opening to ruin my career and he intended to use it to the hilt, notwithstanding the fact that I'd just about lost my head in a vain attempt to deliver his wife from slavery. Before I could speak in my own defense, though, Commander Henderson intervened.

"Back you up, Captain Longbottom? I don't see how I possibly could. All I saw was the landing party go ashore with the ransom, as agreed to by General Davis, and then I saw the landing party return, unfortunately without the ladies. That must be the sum total of my report, Captain. I fail, therefore, to see how I can help substantiate any charges you might wish to bring against Captain Travers."

It was I who finally put an end to Longbottom's ill-tempered recriminations. "Let's get something straight here, Longbottom. General Davis said we were to do nothing to provoke hostilities, and we didn't. All we did was slip into the stockade for a quiet little look around when the Moros swarmed over us like hornets from a smoked-out nest." Henry, who had seen me in the harem fondling the sultan's lovelies, eyed me dubiously at this but held his peace. "We couldn't have reasoned with 'em had we tried. And don't forget, Longbottom, the only reason I took over command was because you stumbled into a foot trap like an idiotic greenhorn. You were on Samar, partner, and you damned well should have known that no column should enter enemy territory without a man out front with a long pole to probe for such traps. So if you want to make a report to General Davis, make sure you tell him how you incapacitated yourself through sheer incompetence. I'm certain he'd be quite interested to hear it."

That put things in a light that Longbottom could understand, and so after some more angry rumblings he finally got up and hobbled off to watch the *Jackson*'s bow cut through the phosphorescent night seas.

Upon our return to Zamboanga, General Davis was not at all pleased with our tidings. Alice and Fiona were still in captivity, the money was gone, and the Moros were in a decidedly ugly mood. Davis reminded us none too gently that he had warned us about returning without the gold, and that by God he had meant what he'd said. Something in Longbottom's crestfallen expression must have tugged at his heartstrings, however, for despite all his blowing and puffing, General Davis pulled in his horns after a bit and allowed as how he could wire Manila for further instructions about the missing funds. Perhaps there was some obscure provision in the regulations that could be cited to relieve us of liability. With that, he deferred action on the matter and we were dismissed, cut adrift to fretfully await the call from Davis that would decide our fiscal fates.

About the only good news of any note on our return was that Lieutenant Colonel Quinlon was gone. He simply disappeared, and I hadn't the energy or interest to inquire where he might have repaired to. When the expected summons from Davis came, however, things took an unexpected turn. Longbottom and I hurried to the general's office to find him seated at his desk holding a telegram. The grim look on his face spoke volumes. "This is very bad news, gentlemen," he intoned gravely.

"My God, I'm bankrupt!" moaned Longbottom.

"No, it's not about the money, Captain Longbottom," General Davis assured him. "No, it's that fiend Surlang. He's on the rampage again."

Eh? What was this? I was all ears now. General Davis continued, "This is an urgent telegraph from Cotabato, a small port on the west coast of Mindanao. Three days ago a band of Mindanao Moros ambushed a certain Lieutenant Forsyth of the 15th Cavalry and seventeen cavalrymen under his command. One trooper was killed, several were wounded, and all their horses were stolen. Lieutenant Forsyth has stated positively that the leader of the attackers wore a green turban."

A green turban? There could be a hundred hotheads on Mindanao sporting green turbans, but I knew instinctively that General Davis was right. This could only be the handiwork of Surlang.

"Captain Travers," Davis asked, turning to me, "if I understand correctly, the last time Surlang was spotted was on Samar."

I cleared my throat carefully and answered, "Yes, sir, that's right." Of course, I had been as vague as possible when I reported to General Davis upon my return from Maimbung. With Longbottom silenced by my ire, I had been able to sell General Davis a bill of goods about what had transpired between me and the Jolo Moros. I'd led him to believe that I'd no more than set foot in the Moro town than the crazed heathens erupted into a frenzy of violence, hacking down our men for no reason and sending us packing for the coast. Conveniently, I had omitted any mention of my sojourn in the sultan's harem, nor had I breathed a word about seeing Surlang in Maimbung. You see, I feared that Davis might note a pattern in Surlang continually crossing my path and ask awkward questions about why that might be.

To my relief, Davis had bought my yarn lock, stock, and barrel, agreeing with me that the great sultan of Jolo was as mad as a March hare and wasn't fit company for civilized men. Thus, the breach of the peace on Jolo couldn't be laid at old Fenny's doorstep. Because of my prevarications, of course, I had understandably needed to keep General Davis in the dark about the fight in the sultan's *cotta* and how my visit to Jolo had transformed Surlang back into a persona non grata as far as Jamal-ul-Kiram was concerned. That was why I was the only one in the room who understood the true import of Davis's telegram: Having been driven from Luzon, Samar, and now Jolo in turn, Surlang had fled finally to the one sanctuary remaining to him. That was the wilds of Mindanao, the heart of Moroland. I was certain that Surlang would attempt to lure me deep into the fastness of the Forbidden Kingdom and there settle his vendetta with me once and for all. If that was his game, I'd have no part of it, thank you. I'd hunker down right here in Zamboanga and wait until the crazy bastard expired of old age.

"Well, then," concluded General Davis, "it's obvious that Surlang has somehow managed to escape our net on Samar"—here Longbottom cleared his throat guiltily and stared at the floor—"and has relocated right here on Mindanao."

General Davis went to the wall where a map of his division hung and pointed to the coast of Mindanao where the Moro Gulf pinched the island into a narrow waist. "The attack took place here, near Malabang," he said, pointing to a coastal town in the shadow of the Butig Mountains. "At the time of the onslaught, Colonel Baldwin was nearby at Cotabato. I ordered him to gather all the troops at Cotabato and Malabang, mostly companies of the 27th Infantry, and pursue the bandits. He was to proceed from Malabang and follow the assailants to wherever they might flee." Then General Davis added portentously, "I expect that they'll retreat to the Lake Lanao area."

"Colonel Baldwin?" I interrupted, dismayed. "Is he, well, I don't know quite how to put this, sir. Is he the right man for the job?" I had taken Baldwin's measure already, and I could see that he was cut from the same cloth as Howling Jake Smith on Samar. To an old Indian fighter like Baldwin, the only good Moros were dead Moros, and he was certain to avenge Forsyth's defeat with fire and sword.

General Davis fixed me with a level gaze, and I could see that he too was worried. He was not anxious to follow Waller and Smith into the dock, you see. "Baldwin was the closest senior officer available" was all he said.

What rang loudest in my brain, however, was what General Davis didn't need to say: that Baldwin undoubtedly had thundered and blown to get an independent field command, and that in the end General Davis just didn't have the gumption to say no any longer. He'd sent the fiery colonel off into a powder keg that was just waiting for a spark like Baldwin to blow it sky-high.

"Baldwin's men will move north," continued General Davis with forced equanimity, "sweeping the area between Malabang and the southern shore of Lake Lanao."

"Er, won't that cause Captain Pershing some difficulties, sir?" I asked with growing disquiet. "After all, if I understood Pershing, he believed himself to be undermanned for the task before him as it was. With

Colonel Baldwin rampaging up from the south, won't all the Lake Lanao Moros rise up in arms too?"

Davis looked at me and pursed his lips, but then he admitted reluctantly, "That's my chief concern, Captain Travers. Colonel Baldwin has informed me that the southern Moros, those around Cotabato and Malabang, hail from the Manduindanao tribe. They're weak from a pure military perspective. If we can keep them isolated from the other Moros in the Forbidden Kingdom, who all hail from the Maranao tribe, we can bring the killers to justice with little effort."

"The Manduindanao may be weak, sir," I observed fretfully, "but the Maranaos aren't." I remembered Pershing telling me that they were the dominant tribe on Mindanao. "Isn't it possible that the Maranaos will take offense at a horde of infidels invading their backyard to thrash their fellow Muslims?"

"Possibly, yes, Travers, but not very probably, according to Colonel Baldwin," countered General Davis. "He believes that the Maranaos won't raise their hands to save Moros from a different tribe."

But they're all Muslims, aren't they? I wanted to scream. And Baldwin planned to lead an infidel host to the very shores of the Maranaos' beloved mountain lake, the very core of the Forbidden Kingdom, didn't he? I smelled big trouble here. I said as diplomatically as I could, "I suppose Colonel Baldwin might be right, sir, but if there's one thing I've learned about Surlang, it's that he's a master rabble-rouser. He was on Samar for less than a month before he had the Pulajans howling for our blood—and they were Christians. What's more, the ambush of poor Forsyth proves that Surlang was able to whip the Manduindanaos into a frenzy in a short time too. I have no doubt that he'll have the same effect on the Maranaos. After all, Surlang's a Moro Muslim just like they are."

"I don't entirely disagree, Captain Travers," replied General Davis. "That's why I want you to get to Malabang as quickly as possible and join Colonel Baldwin's column. Try to warn him against entangling the Maranaos in this affair. Urge him to make Surlang his main target, not the Mindanao Moros."

Me? Now, just hold on here a damn minute, I thought. I'd done my bit, hadn't I? I mean, I was on Samar when the place got torched around my ears, and I'd just returned from a none-too-pleasant little visit to Jolo. With Davis gazing at me expectantly, I knew I couldn't actually say any of this, so I took an indirect tack with him.

"Sir, you honor me with your great regard for my persuasive skills. I'm sure this is a mission that will require the utmost adroitness, and if it succeeds, the fortunate officer you send will be clearly marked for future favor." I'd set the trap, you see, and I gave a sideways glance to see if Longbottom would blunder into it. He did.

"Sir, I volunteer to go," he almost shrilled, for he found the prospect of his name in a citation to headquarters an irresistible lure.

"Thank you, Captain Longbottom," acknowledged General Davis, "but your foot is not healed properly. I would be remiss if I were to send you into the field in your condition. No, it must be Captain Travers here."

"And I'm ready to go, sir," I assured him smoothly but added wistfully, "if only . . ."

"If only what, Captain Travers?"

"If only my fever goes down, sir. It's been with me since Palanan, you see. It comes and goes, and I never really know when to expect it. It certainly seems to be coming at the moment."

That excuse had worked well with Waller, I thought smugly, and there was no reason to believe it wouldn't stymie Davis as well.

"Hmmm. That's a pity, Travers, for if you had been able to manage this affair as I desire, I was quite prepared to unequivocally recommend that your and Captain Longbottom's indebtedness to the government be remitted."

"I'm going!" I exclaimed. Then catching General Davis's astonished look, I added sheepishly, "Er, that is, I'm going to get some quinine powder, sir. To see if I can shake my fever, you understand. Perhaps I can be on my way soon—maybe within the hour."

37

Pandapatan, Mindanao
May 2, 1902
Before the day was out, Henry, Bustos, and I were on a fast steamer bound for Malabang across the Moro Gulf. As the vessel plowed through the shimmering waters, my thoughts turned to the confrontation that lay before me. Clearly I had unfinished business with Surlang. He had placed me in the line of imminent destruction so many times that now

I was losing count, and he had whisked my fiancée off to a preparatory course for aspiring houris. God alone knew how long Alice and
Fiona would be forced to endure lives of bondage. All that was bad
enough, but the real gravamen of my grudge against Surlang was that
he still had my damned treasure map. Yes, I considered it to be mine,
for after all, my claim to it was as good as anyone's, and certainly
better than Surlang's. As I pondered this, I realized that General Davis
had handed me a rare opportunity. I would be in just the right place
to ensure that Baldwin's troops ended the fiend's sordid career, and
if I was nimble enough, I just might be able to retrieve my property
at the same time. As seabirds wheeled lazily overhead, my thoughts
turned to the exquisite pleasures I could purchase with the lost treasure of the *Jesus Maria*.

Although the voyage lasted little more than a day, when I landed I
found that Baldwin's expeditionary force—several infantry battalions
supported by cavalry, artillery, and a contingent of native scouts—
had already commenced the campaign. With my guts churning in their
usual manner whenever I neared any combat zone, I requisitioned two
horses and a burro from the garrison at Malabang. The burro was for
Bustos, who to my surprise was frightened of horses and would only
consent to straddling an inoffensive burro. Thus mounted, we set out
along the muddy gash that marked Baldwin's advance to the north.

As I hurried past burned nipa huts and dead bodies rotting in the
brutal tropical sun, I could see that I had been right about Colonel
Baldwin. He envisioned his thrust into the Forbidden Kingdom as another
march through Georgia. His plan was evident; he'd destroy everything
in his path and merely hope that among the slain might be the attackers of Lieutenant Forsyth's party. Such indiscriminate killing, however, clearly was not the way to intimidate a proud foe like the Moros.

When I finally spied the rear of Baldwin's column, it was closing
in on a *cotta* called Pandapatan near the south coast of Lake Lanao.
As I galloped up to the colonel and saluted, one thing was abundantly
clear: Baldwin had not yet brought any Moros to decisive battle. This
made me uneasy, for Pandapatan was only five miles from the sacred
waters of Lake Lanao. All of General Davis's worst fears might yet
come to pass.

"Sir, General Davis sent me from Zamboanga to see if I could be of
any assistance. He's very, well, concerned about this Forsyth incident."

"I'm well aware of the general's concern, Travers," retorted Baldwin sharply. "That's why he sent me here to settle accounts with these villains. And in two shakes of a lamb's tail, I aim to do exactly that." Here he pointed toward the *cotta* where his troops were just now taking up positions on all sides of the place.

I studied Pandapatan carefully; it was essentially a log stockade, less palatial than Jamal-ul-Kiram's abode to be sure, but an imposing defensive position nonetheless. The *cotta* was surrounded by a ditch about ten feet deep and thirty feet wide, and it had but a single gate of heavy timbers. A rickety bamboo footbridge, wide enough to let only a single person pass at a time, ran from our side of the ditch to the gate. The footbridge was the sole access route into the *cotta*. I had no doubt that the approaches to it would be covered by the fire of Moros crouched on the far side of the parapet above the heavy gate. As primitive as the place appeared, it was a sturdy fortification, much more formidable than anything I'd ever seen on Luzon. Around the parapets I could see turbaned heads moving hither and yon, while from a pole affixed to the battlements a huge red banner hung limply in the still air. It was the red war flag of the Moros, and it meant that the warriors trapped within Pandapatan were determined to die fighting.

"How many Moros are in there?" I asked uneasily.

"Two, maybe three hundred," replied Baldwin, letting fly with a big cud of liquified chaw. "A few of them have old flintlocks, but the bulk of them are armed with spears and krises."

That was welcome news; the fewer guns in the hands of the Moros the better. "What about Surlang?" I asked. "Is he with them?"

Baldwin nodded. "If he's a big, strapping ox of a fellow in a green turban, the answer is yes. I saw him hang out that damned red flag with my own eyes." If the presence in the *cotta* of one of the most cunning Moro guerrilla fighters troubled Baldwin, he showed no evidence of it, for he gave me a yellow-toothed smile and hooted triumphantly, "We've got him cornered at last, son!"

Maybe, I thought, but a cornered rat can do some real damage unless you handle the varmint just right. Now was the time for the ultimate question, so I put it to Baldwin as delicately as I could. "I guess in view of these fortifications, Colonel, the best course would be to starve the little beggars out, eh? Maybe palaver a little and then separate them from Surlang?"

Baldwin shook his head sternly. "Not on your life, Captain. That's not what I had in mind at all. No, I plan to sweep these works with cannon fire and then carry them with the bayonet."

"Won't that just work into the Moros' hands?" I asked worriedly. "I mean, fighting at close quarters is their stock-in-trade, you know."

Baldwin merely snorted at this. "I find the fighting reputation of the Moros to be a bit overblown, Captain Travers. After all, on the march up here from Malabang, we put them to flight at every turn. No, I don't see that these rascals will stand up to cold steel driven home by trained soldiers."

I could see that arguing with Baldwin would be futile. He had it in his mind that a successful campaign was one that ended with the most possible enemy blood spilled. It never occurred to him that the reason for the weak resistance put up by the Manduindanao Moros during their retreat was that they wanted to link up with their stronger Maranao brothers before being heavily engaged.

Pondering a way to make the colonel see reason, I was startled to see a familiar figure canter up and report to Baldwin. By God, it was Quinlon! "The troops are in position, sir!" he bellowed. "Permission to open the assault?"

"Quinlon, what the devil are you doing here?" I demanded, adding as an afterthought, "sir."

Quinlon grinned broadly at the astonishment evident on my face. I'd known that he had disappeared from Zamboanga after I left for Jolo, but I had assumed that the old rogue had hied himself back to Manila. Never in my wildest dreams had I expected to find him here in the field.

"Colonel Baldwin's graciously allowed me the honor of serving as his second in command," Quinlon beamed. "A bit of combat duty can't hurt one's career, now can it, lad?"

So that was his plan. A nice neat campaign to bolster his lackluster record, and then off to Manila to lobby for a plush position like the one he'd held under MacArthur. Well, Quinlon was about to find out that the Moros weren't likely to cooperate in his quest to polish his résumé. At the moment, however, all I could think to say was an uneasy "Well, that's true, I suppose."

"Permission granted, Colonel Quinlon," snapped Colonel Baldwin crisply.

With that, Quinlon waved a gauntleted hand in the direction of a nearby bugler, who put his instrument to his lips. A staccato call carried through the heavy air and echoed off the silent walls of Pandapatan. No sooner had the notes died away than a cannon roared, then another, and then an entire battery. The shells slammed into the heavy walls near the *cotta*'s gate, tossing splinters and showers of dust high into the air. The defenders instantly dove for cover behind their breastworks as the artillery pounded the *cotta* mercilessly.

When the cease-fire was sounded, it took several minutes for the smoke to swirl away from the battered walls, revealing the scene of the battle. Amazingly, the fragile footbridge was still standing. The heavy gate beyond was chipped and splintered in places but still intact, and for all the pounding it had taken, the stockade looked quite serviceable.

"That ought to do it," announced Baldwin firmly when he had surveyed the place through his field glasses.

I blinked at him in disbelief. "You aren't thinking about charging over that bridge, are you, sir? Any troops caught on it would be helpless targets for the Moros."

"That's exactly what I intend to do, Captain," chortled Baldwin confidently. "Right now the only thing on the minds of those Moros is how to get out of Pandapatan with whole skins. They won't stand, Travers. You can depend on it."

"But, sir," I protested, "that gate is still on its hinges! A mere handful of Moros can thwart your attack from behind it."

"That's just my point, Captain—they won't. Why, just look at that parapet. There's nary a Moro to be seen. They've skedaddled, I tell you, and the place is ours for the taking. All my troops need to do is scale the wall and we've won."

True, the *cotta* looked deserted, but looks could be deceptive. Besides, I'd seen Moro warriors up close. They didn't frighten easily, and I was certain they were simply lying low to gull us into a stupid move. Before I could protest again, Colonel Baldwin made one.

"Order the charge, Colonel Quinlon."

Quinlon cackled with glee and pounded off. This was his moment of glory, by God, the opportunity to put to rest the shame he had endured since the Battle of San Juan Hill. He reined in before a nearby body of infantry, dismounted, and clumsily drew his saber. Tensely, the troops gripped rough-hewn ladders that had been hastily fashioned to scale the gate. Satisfied that all was ready, Quinlon signaled the bugler once more.

As he did so, I recognized two men in the front rank with Quinlon. It was Lieutenant Vicars and Sergeant O'Bannion, who had been with me in the fight off Taytay Point. They both saw me too and grinned weakly; the hopeless nature of this fool's errand was apparent to both of them. Unfortunately, it completely escaped Baldwin and Quinlon.

The bugler blew the charge, and drums began to beat. A roar went up from the waiting infantry, then a wave of cheering "goddamns" rushed the bamboo bridge. Quinlon scampered along with them, screaming at the top of his lungs and waving his sword as though he knew how to use the damn thing. At the bridge the assault column narrowed, for only one man at a time could step onto the structure. As their fellows stood on the edge of the ditch peppering the palisade with a hail of bullets, a thin file of khaki-clad attackers, lugging a ladder with them, edged across the bridge toward the ominously silent gate.

Quinlon, desperate for distinction, was the first man in the column. Behind him was Lieutenant Vicars and trailing farther behind was Sergeant O'Bannion and a few stouthearted privates. The assault party was only ten feet from the massive gate when their quarry suddenly reacted.

A rank of Moros armed with flintlocks materialized on the battlements directly above the gate, while on the gate itself hidden shutters flew open to reveal small firing ports. Through these ports were run the barrels of several *lantakas,* the crude small-bore cannons used by the Moros. At a screamed command, the Moros fired with everything they had.

38

A blast of flame erupted, riddling the American assault. Sergeant O'Bannion was among the first to fall, blown into the ditch, to be impaled on the *belatics* that had been planted there for exactly that purpose. The surviving privates scrambled as one for the safety of the rear. In their haste to be off, they left poor Lieutenant Vicars thrashing about on the bridge where he'd fallen.

Quinlon, amazingly unhurt despite the hot lead flying around his ears, tried to rally the flying troopers. "Don't abandon me!" he implored frantically. But before anyone could react to his plea, a sinewy figure leaped over the parapet like a man shot from a circus cannon and landed lightly on his feet astride the bridge. He ran along the span toward Quinlon, hefting a huge two-handed Moro fighting sword, called a *campilan,* as he came. The *campilan* was a beheading weapon, I realized instantly. At the same moment a shock of recognition coursed through me at the sight of the advancing Moro: It was Surlang.

Quinlon took one look at the death in Surlang's eyes and made his decision. "Holy Mother of God!" he wailed and leaped off the bridge onto the wicked *belatics* below. That left Surlang's path to the helpless Lieutenant Vicars clear.

"Oh, my God!" exclaimed Baldwin, appalled at what he was witnessing.

Vicars writhed as Surlang closed upon him, and then the awful *campilan* flashed. The lieutenant's head toppled slowly from his shoulders, then the headless corpse gave a mighty tremor and lay back on the footbridge.

In a flash Surlang was darting back for the safety of the gate. Horrified soldiers shouldered their Krags and loosed a few shots, but they were hurried and poorly aimed. The gate opened a crack and Surlang slipped inside just as a fusillade beat futilely against the scarred wood, then the gate was closed once more.

All that was left was Quinlon in the moat bleating like a frightened sheep. "Help me, men!" he begged piteously. "Oh, for the love of God, don't leave me! I'm half dead, I tell ye!"

Henry stirred at my side. "We have to save him, Fenny!" he exclaimed.

That certainly wasn't the way I saw things, of course, so I countered hotly, "We'll be killed if we go out there, Henry."

But Henry's mind was made up. "Think of poor Miss Fiona. Hasn't she been through enough already? We can't just let the Moros kill her father, can we?"

Sure we could, for I knew Quinlon well and by all rights the old meddler richly deserved such a fate. Henry had set me to thinking of Fiona, however, and the instant I did, a vision of her white breasts and firm hips popped unbidden into my mind. If she was ever rescued from Jolo, there might yet be an opening for me to enjoy the pleasure of her company again. Fiona would never forgive me, however, if she learned that I had left her dear pater to the tender mercies of the Moros. So with my bowels sliding queasily, I muttered grudgingly, "Okay, let's go get the old fool."

Tied to my saddle was Surlang's kris, the one I'd taken on Samar. I unstrapped it and shoved it into my belt. Then we were off our mounts and running. A blistering fire from the Krags to our rear pinned down the Moro defenders as we bolted to the edge of the ditch, and then damning myself for being a sex-addicted maniac, I leaped down lightly among the sharp *belatics.*

"Fenwick, lad," gasped Quinlon in relief as I dropped beside him. "I knew ye wouldn't leave me!"

"Let's go," I ordered gruffly, seizing him by the tunic and giving a tug.

"I can't, son, I'm pinned, I tell you!" he squealed.

I looked down to see a sharpened bamboo stake jutting up through the top of his boot. Quinlon was skewered as neatly as Longbottom had been on Jolo. I reached down and seized his ankle, but he cried out in pain and tried to shove me away.

"Hold still, damn you!" I roared back in the face of his hysterics, and then with a great effort pulled his foot free over the point of the *belatic.*

"Oh, sweet Jesus," he yelped, "I'm killed!"

"Shut up or you will be!" I swore, for his antics were drawing the attention of the Moros from behind the gate. I could see muzzle flashes now as the Moros blazed away in our general direction. Only Henry's withering fire from above me prevented them from drawing an accurate bead on us, but I knew he couldn't hold them too much longer. Once I had Quinlon free, I swung him over my shoulder like a sack of oats and called to Henry, "Help me up!"

Henry fired once more at the *cotta,* threw open the bolt of the Krag for safety's sake, then lowered the stock down for me. "Grab it, Fenny," he cried. "I'll haul you out!"

I seized the stock in one hand and with the other held the blubbering Quinlon. Henry pulled while I kicked mightily. Our muscles strained almost beyond endurance, but we were getting nowhere. Then suddenly Bustos was there, reaching down for my wrist and pulling vigorously. Together he and Henry gave one great heave and swung us out of the moat. Now other soldiers swarmed forward to succor Quinlon, who was suddenly in a dead faint. Henry drew me to my feet and we beat a hasty retreat as musket balls smacked into the earth all around us.

An abrupt lull then fell on the battlefield. But for the grotesquely impaled bodies at the bottom of the ditch, Vicars's headless cadaver sprawled obscenely on the bridge, and the moans of the wounded filling the air all around me, I would not have believed what my eyes had just witnessed.

Baldwin was both stunned and furious. "Why those, those . . . damned savages. Those filthy heathens. How dare they? How *dare* they?"

How dare they? I thought with amazement. Why, Baldwin thought it a social gaffe for the beleaguered Moros to fight in their time-honored ways. Apparently he expected them to play the role of demoralized primitives and meekly stretch their necks out to receive the edge of his sword. Well, if Baldwin thought that tangling with Moros would be as easy as pushing cowed Plains Indians onto a reservation, he was sadly mistaken. He had badly underestimated his foe, and now he was reduced to stuttering impotence.

"Sir, there's a party coming up from Lake Lanao," called an aide as Quinlon, bleeding and unconscious, was carried off to the rear.

All eyes turned in the direction the aide indicated. Henry squinted a bit and sang out, "Some of them are Moros."

"Moros?" queried Baldwin nervously.

Now I was jittery; was this some sort of Moro relief column on its way to Pandapatan? I carefully surveyed the approaching group.

"There's an American with them," I said, then stared some more and announced, "It's Pershing."

"Pershing?" repeated Baldwin, eyeing his aide with confusion. The aide merely shrugged, nonplussed like the rest of us. What the dickens was Pershing doing here? His jurisdiction lay on the north shore of Lake Lanao. And who were these Moros with him?

Pershing cleared up the mystery in a hurry. He trotted up on a fine hunter and fired a salute to Colonel Baldwin. "Sir, I received word from the Maranao Moros that your column had come to the shore of Lake Lanao." Here Pershing gestured at his heavily armed companions, who to a man scowled fixedly at Colonel Baldwin. "These gentlemen are a deputation of *datus* of the Maranao Moros. May I introduce Ahmai-Manibilang, sir? He's the sultan of Madaya."

At the mention of his name, a white-haired old ogre, whose arms and face exhibited the scars of innumerable kris wounds, glared at Baldwin and then shouted out a fearsome harangue.

Pershing interpreted for Baldwin. "Ahmai-Manibilang wants you to know that he has three thousand krismen at his beck and call, and that nearly fifty *cottas* on the lakeshore pay homage to him."

I recognized the name of Ahmai-Manibilang. He was the Moro who held dominion over Marahui, the proposed terminus of Pershing's road from Iligan. Pershing and his Moro friends must have heard Baldwin's guns and come running.

Baldwin was a pure bullhead, of course, but he wasn't hopelessly dense. He realized that Pershing's Moros wanted a declaration of friendly intentions, and if they didn't get it pronto they just might lay into Baldwin's troops.

"I'm here only for the bandits who ambushed Lieutenant Forsyth," announced Colonel Baldwin. "Tell them that, Pershing, and tell them that I also intend to seize that pirate Surlang. Once I accomplish those goals, I'll withdraw to Cotabato."

Pershing relayed all this to Ahmai-Manibilang, who fired back an angry blast, which Pershing in turn translated loosely for Colonel Baldwin. "Ahmai-Manibilang says the Maranaos were not overly concerned about your campaign against the Manduindanao Moros. They've had their own run-ins with the Manduindanaos over the years. When you advanced to Pandapatan, however, all that changed. The Maranaos now think your campaign against the Manduindanaos is just a ruse to bring your army to the shores of Lake Lanao. They think you intend to reduce Pandapatan and then march clear around the lake to subjugate the Forbidden Kingdom. They think that you're on a giant slaving raid."

"But that's ridiculous, Pershing," protested Baldwin. "You know that's not true. Tell them we have no quarrel with the Maranaos—at least not yet."

Pershing merely raised an eyebrow archly at this. "That's not exactly so, sir. You see, inside those walls are both Manduindanaos and Maranaos."

"What?" gasped Colonel Baldwin, aghast. "You say Maranaos are inside Pandapatan? But how could that be?"

"You charged up from Cotabato so quickly that you ran bands of Maranaos together with the Manduindanaos," explained Pershing. "Had you advanced in a measured way and announced your intentions carefully to Ahmai-Manibilang, this situation could have been avoided. But now. . . ." Here Pershing's voice trailed away.

Baldwin stood pale and shaken. His headstrong onrush had brought about exactly the predicament that General Davis had hoped to avoid at all costs. With a great effort, the colonel fought to steady himself in the face of this disastrous intelligence; in desperation he lashed out at Pershing, the bearer of bad tidings.

"Blast you, Pershing! Don't just stand there telling me what I've done wrong! Talk to those monkeys inside the walls. Tell the Maranaos to come on out and they won't get hurt."

Pershing shook his head. "That's not the Moro way, Colonel. Once you start a fight in the Forbidden Kingdom, you must finish it. You've made this into a battle against all the Moros in Pandapatan. Now I'm afraid you're stuck with things as they are."

Rebuffed, Baldwin grew increasingly truculent. "What was I supposed to do, Pershing?" he snarled. "Let a band of bushwhackers off the hook just to appease the savages on your side of the lake? I don't think that would have been received very well in either Manila or Washington, do you?"

Pershing held his ground fearlessly, completely composed in the face of his superior's outburst. "I daresay that such a decision might have been better received than the possibility of war across the whole of Moroland."

Baldwin's raging anger got the better of him now, and he exploded, "Oh, come off your high horse, Pershing! There's nothing to fear from the Moros. If we crushed the Tagalogs, we can crush the Moros too. I think your main concern here is that I not cross into your little bailiwick on the north shore of the lake. If I did, then I'd eclipse you in the dispatches to higher headquarters, and that would be the end of dear Captain Pershing's career aspirations. All your maneuvers to become General Davis's pet would have been for naught, wouldn't they?"

Oh ho, I thought! Now the underlying motive for the suddenness of Baldwin's campaign was evident; he wanted to steal some of Pershing's thunder by becoming known as the conqueror of the fierce Moros. Baldwin's need for a quick, decisive victory, moreover, explained his insistence on the disastrous assault across the bridge.

Pershing, however, would not be baited by Baldwin. Instead, he looked silently toward the ditch where the bodies from the assault party lay. Then he gazed at Ahmai-Manibilang and his followers, who were also eyeing the bodies of the Americans and were beginning to mutter among themselves.

Pershing turned and his eyes met mine. I nodded imperceptibly, for I too had sensed the Moros' thoughts: Ahmai-Manibilang had accompanied Pershing to ward off a blow by what he thought was an invincible, all-conquering force. The dead bodies in the ditch, however, put the lie to that notion. Not only could the Americans be killed, but they were being fought to a draw by a force composed in large part of Manduindanaos, a tribe of second-rate warriors in the eyes of the haughty Maranaos.

"Whatever your motives for opening this fight, Colonel," said Pershing tautly, "it is imperative that you end it soon on the best possible terms for us. If you don't, the lesson taken away from your campaign by the Moros is that resistance to the American government is quite possible."

Pershing was right. The only thing that would answer now was the eradication of every warrior behind that palisade. Baldwin too had seen the direction of the sullen glances of Ahmai-Manibilang and his *datus*.

"Don't you think I realize that, Pershing?" Baldwin retorted. "The problem is that damned *cotta*. Artillery seems to have no effect on those walls."

"That's hardly surprising," replied Pershing. "The Moros are clever engineers. Their *cotta* walls are ten or more feet thick, and consist of log forms filled with heavy stones. You could pound away at them all day to no avail."

"Then what do you suggest?" demanded Baldwin irritably.

Pershing raised his gaze to the heights behind us and then studied Baldwin's battery of artillery. After a minute of consideration, he spoke. "The solution to this problem seems to lie in placing indirect fire on the defenders, so that our shells pass over the walls and burst on the inside of the *cotta*."

"How about that hill, suh?" asked Henry from my side. He was pointing to an eminence about a quarter of a mile to the rear of Baldwin's headquarters.

Pershing eyed Henry approvingly. "Yes, Sergeant, that might just do. Colonel Baldwin, you should move your battery back to that height at once. Have the shells lobbed over the parapet and then attack the wall under cover of the barrage."

"You mean charge across that bridge again?" queried Baldwin uneasily.

Now I piped up. "There's no need to hit the wall at that spot, sir," I assured him. "That gate's not going to be blown off its hinges, no matter how hot your fire; besides, with its firing loops, it's well nigh impregnable. What you ought to do is have your men cut branches and tie them into bundles with hemp or rawhide strips or whatever you've got. While the artillery fire pins down the Moros, we can throw the bundles into the ditch against one side of the *cotta* until it's completely filled. Then, with the artillery still firing, the troops can advance on a broad front toward one of the walls. Once there, you can signal the guns to cease fire, and the infantry can go over the wall. The only thing left to be done is to have the cavalry standing by to saber any fugitives escaping over the other walls."

Pershing voiced ready agreement. "Yes, that'll work, Travers." Turning to Colonel Baldwin, he asked expectantly, "How about it, sir?"

Baldwin hemmed and hawed a bit, but ultimately it was the muttering of the nearby *datus* that moved him to swallow the bitter gall of admitting that he needed help, and from two insufferable underlings. "Very well," he sighed finally in resignation.

"One more thing, sir," added Pershing. "Captain Travers's plan will work only if your troops are led by a seasoned officer. I therefore suggest that you allow Captain Travers to head the assault."

Me? Why, that hadn't been part of my plan at all, and by God, I wasn't shy about saying so. "Well now, Pershing, I could do that, but remember this isn't my show. What's more, Colonel Baldwin has plenty of officers on hand. I don't want to thrust myself in where I'm perhaps not wanted." My protest sounded painfully lame, but Pershing didn't see through it.

"That's damned considerate of you, Travers, but the truth is that none of Colonel Baldwin's officers have anywhere near your battle experience. I'm sure he'll be glad to have your services. Am I right, sir?"

To my utter dismay, Baldwin agreed. "I suppose that next to someone like Travers, they're as green as June corn, the whole lot of 'em. I'll put a company at your disposal, Captain Travers." And before I could give further voice to my protest, he declared: "Captain Pershing, give the necessary orders."

39

Immediately we scattered to set our plan in motion, and within the hour all was ready. Pershing made sure that Ahmai-Manibilang and his *datus* had front-row seats, for this exhibition was going to be largely for their benefit. He gave them to understand in no uncertain terms that what they would witness was a display of the American way of war.

Then at a signal from Colonel Baldwin, a semaphore flag flashed and the artillery opened fire from the hill behind us. Shells crashed into the interior of the *cotta,* and thick geysers of dirt and splinters flew skyward. Smoke began to rise as the rattan huts within caught fire, and soon the air above Pandapatan was filled with a sooty pall.

After ten salvos, Pershing gave me the signal. I glanced anxiously at Henry and Bustos, both of whom had stayed close to my side even though I never said they had to make this charge with me. I drew my pistol shakily and trod morosely over to where the company I was to lead stood in massed ranks, each soldier carrying a bound bundle of faggots.

I was trembling like a leaf now, certain I was going to my death. You see, it was one thing to draw up a plan of attack as I had, and quite another to execute it. Had I known that things would come to this pass, I would have kept my damned mouth shut. I stalled and fidgeted as the men looked on expectantly. Colonel Baldwin made little shoo-ing gestures to me with his hands much like one would to a child who was reluctant to be on his way to school in the morning. It was clear I could balk no longer.

In desperation, I turned to the captain of the company and asked, "Do we have men here who have seen service in Cuba?"

"That we do," he assured me.

"Get them to the front. They're just the boys we need."

A tough sergeant and ten veteran privates moved to the fore. "Men," I told them, "you know what to do. I want you to show these other fellows how we did it back at Santiago. Go straight for the bastards, eh? Can I depend on you?"

They raised a great cheer in response and in excited voices assured me they were up to the task. With their yells ringing in my ears, I shouted, "Okay, let's go, men!"

Then we were off, the veterans surging forward as I had hoped, and me hanging back to where things might be a little safer. We reached the ditch and heaved the bundles into the yawning gap. Soon it was filled with a pile of branches twenty feet wide.

"Over we go," I called out, and a hundred goddamns edged across the bundles, treading carefully since the faggots shifted precipitously with each step we took. The artillery continued its barrage, the covering rifle fire pinned down the Moros, and we reached the far side of the ditch without casualties. Here the wall was ten feet above the faggots; if we couldn't see over it, at least it shielded us from any Moro musketeers within.

Now would come the most critical phase of the attack, the moment when the artillery fire stopped and the infantry went over the wall. In that instant, we would be most vulnerable to a sudden Moro counterattack.

"Get ready!" I bellowed anxiously to the men, and looked back across the ditch to where Pershing stood with Colonel Baldwin. "Cease fire!" I called, while waving my Colt.

Pershing nodded vigorously. He motioned to a semaphore flagman, who in turn signaled up to the hill. Immediately the artillery fire slackened and then stopped. For an instant the eerie silence filled my ears, and then I ordered, "Over you go!"

I stood cheerily on the faggots with my arms folded, a bit to the side so that I wouldn't be in the way. You see, I wasn't going anywhere. Instead I fully expected the troops to scale the wall behind the intrepid veterans and settle matters with any Moros lurking on the far side. Only then would I advance—in triumph.

Before a single man could react to my order to advance, however, the Moros struck back. Thirty of the devils appeared above us with cauldrons of boiling grease and torches!

"Look out!" someone shouted. The warning was still hanging in the air when the cauldrons emptied down upon the hapless troops. Then the Moros hurled their torches into the branches, and immediately great roaring flames shot up everywhere. The searing grease scalded several soldiers hideously, these wretches immediately throwing down their arms and fleeing with howls of agony to the rear.

Feeling the searing heat and sensing the sudden hopelessness of our position, I bawled to Henry, "Let's get out of here!"

The note of panic in my voice was all the men needed to hear; immediately the company and its officers bolted for the rear en masse, carrying Bustos along with them.

"We can't go back!" cried Henry, pointing to a sheet of flames behind us. It sealed us off from the route of retreat taken by the troops and threatened to cook us if we didn't move away promptly. What was more, we couldn't stay huddled helplessly under the wall for long; the Moros were bound to see our plight and finish us off. "We have to go over that wall, Fenny!" Henry insisted forcefully.

"That's crazy!" I resisted. "We'll be killed for sure."

"We'll fry if we don't! We have no choice," Henry maintained flatly, and from the set look in his eyes I could see there was no talking him out of it. I waved wildly to Pershing, who was busy heading off the retreat before it turned into a rout. When I had his attention I pointed frantically up to the hill behind him, and he nodded. Soon the semaphore flags were waggling excitedly, and the artillery boomed out anew. The crashing shells forced the Moros off the wall, and Henry sang out, "Now's the time!"

He formed a stirrup with his hands and boosted me up and over the top of the palisade. Then he handed up his Krag, and I extended my arm down, caught his hand, and swung him up. Together we hunkered down in our exposed position to take stock of the situation unfolding around us. A catwalk ran completely around the interior wall of the *cotta*. This was where the Moros had stood when they poured boiling oil onto our heads. No live Moros were in sight at the moment, for they had gone to ground after frying their attackers. Looking around, I saw that the *cotta* was littered with corpses, body parts, and abandoned weapons. This cheered me up, for the shelling had had its intended effect—the Moros had taken a fearful pounding.

Then Henry pointed along the catwalk. "Look! The gate's unguarded. If we can get it open and hold it that way long enough, Colonel Baldwin can throw a column into the fort."

Of course, there was a much more sensible course of action. We could wait for the flames below to die down and then hop back over the wall and scramble to safety, claiming that the Moro fire inside the *cotta* was too hot to stand. Who would call our bluff on such a tale? Not Pershing, for he could barely see us now and hadn't the foggiest notion of what we were going through. There was only one reason for not turning tail, and he was lying right beside me taking his air in great gasps. Yep, it was Henry. I knew he wouldn't skedaddle, and I didn't have the pluck to run off alone, being too fearful of a spear in the back from some hidden Moro. So kissing my common sense goodbye, I resigned myself to Henry's reckless plan.

"Oh, let's do it," I sighed disconsolately. Gathering my flagging courage, I rose shakily and crept along the catwalk, gingerly stepping over fallen Moros as I went. I had just traversed one ugly brute when Henry yelped from behind me, "Fenny, look out!"

I turned to see the "dead" Moro rise, his kris at the ready. He had been playing possum, by God, and without Henry's warning, I would have been a goner. I brought up my big .45 Colt and fired straight into his face just as Henry cut loose from behind with his Krag. The Moro jerked convulsively but did not fall.

Holy Jesus, they're indestructible! I thought fearfully. I fired again, and this time the Moro slumped, his kris point lowered to the ground as life drained from his body. I gave him a swift boot to the midsection, which hurtled him off the catwalk to slam into the hard-packed earth below.

I had no time to savor my victory, for Henry called yet another warning. "Behind you again!"

I whirled once more to face the direction of the gate. Many Moro "corpses" were now on their feet, advancing menacingly.

"Aim between their eyes!" I called to Henry. "Anywhere else is a waste of bullets!"

And fire we did, one shot after the other as the krismen came on, each determined to kill or be killed for Allah. Pershing, seeing our peril now that we were on our feet, redoubled the artillery fire. As the shells crashed all about us, we fought our grim fight, cutting down our attackers as fast as they came on. When my revolver was emptied, Henry stepped to the fore and worked his Krag until its five-shot magazine was emptied, whereupon he sheltered behind me as my Colt did deadly execution. Covering each other in this fashion, we fired until our barrels glowed red.

"It's a slaughter!" exulted Henry. As fast as the Moros advanced we mowed them down. With my natural marksmanship backed up by Henry's impressive aim, we soon piled Moros three deep around us on the catwalk. How long could they stand this fearful contest? I wondered anxiously, knowing that our ammunition was bound to run low soon. No sooner had I formed that thought in my mind than our bullets were gone!

There were six Moros left on the catwalk, while at their feet lay a score of their brethren. "Get ready, Henry," I warned fearfully. "Beat 'em off with your fists if you have to, for there'll be no quarter from these beasts."

Then something occurred that never before had been witnessed by Christians—the Moros suddenly broke and ran! At first I could scarcely believe my eyes, but then I found my voice: "They're hightailing it, Henry!" I whooped.

"Yep, we whupped 'em proper!" crowed Henry in return.

"Quick!" I said. "Jump down and get to the gate before they change their minds. I'll signal over to Baldwin's men."

Henry nodded, then flew down a ladder to the ground and scampered to the gate. He threw off the great teak timber that had served as a bar, pulled aside a cluster of dead Moros propped up against the inside of the gate, rolled the *lantakas* out of the way, and then slowly swung the great portal open.

I hustled along the catwalk to a point above the gateway and shouted and hallooed until a watching sergeant spied me. The sergeant nudged a captain, who, taking in the situation at a glance, waved his sword and called out orders to his men. Then a full company was on its feet and making a beeline for the now-yawning gate.

"Here they come!" I called happily to Henry, pivoting as I did so. What I saw at that moment turned the very blood in my veins to ice.

"Surlang!" I hissed. The demon had stalked me, disdaining to join the flight of the demoralized defenders.

"*Si, Capitán,*" he sneered. "I have come to take your head so that you may accompany me to paradise as my slave on this very day."

I gulped, my throat suddenly dry and my hand clammy on the grip of my Colt. "Well, partner," I said slowly, readying myself for what promised to be a savage fight, "if I have anything to say about it, your next stop won't be paradise—it'll be hell!" How I was going to arrange that wasn't exactly evident at the moment, and I rather hoped that Surlang would just move along peacefully now that help was on the way.

With the instincts of a wolf, however, Surlang sensed my fear. "Empty words," he snarled, leveling his murderous *campilan,* its blade still dripping blood. "But before I kill you, I wanted to let you know that I had both of your women, the blond one willingly, and the other one with the mahogany hair"—here he gave a sinister snicker—"against her will. Her struggles made the conquest all the more memorable."

His words burned into my soul. I had expected there might have been some hanky-panky between the ladies and the sultan of Jolo, but I had never imagined that this fiend had taken liberties with his victims before he sold them into slavery. Oh, I had no doubt Fiona might have taken readily to Surlang. After all, she was accustomed to a steady parade of swains trooping through her boudoir. But the very thought of Surlang pawing sweet Alice fired me with a rage bordering on madness, and I turned my now-empty Colt to use it as a club. Yet despite my anger, I had the presence of mind to remember that there was other outstanding business between Surlang and me.

"Where's my map, you son of a bitch?" I rasped, stepping forward as I spoke.

Surlang readied his *campilan* and crouched, a tight smile contorting his mouth. "Oh, now it is your map, eh, *americano* pig? Well, it's right here in my sash." He tapped the bolt of saffron cloth wrapped around his middle. "If you want the riches it shows, why don't you come and take it?" At this he gave a snarl like that of a hungry jackal.

What? The map was right in front of me? All I had to do was kill Surlang to enjoy the wealth of the ages? My fear evaporated as my avarice surged wildly to the fore, and with Surlang's challenge still ringing in my ears, I suddenly struck! I hurled the empty Colt with my full force, striking Surlang flush on the forehead. Caught flat-footed by this tactic and stunned by the impact, he swayed once and stepped back. This gave me just the opening I needed to sweep his kris from my belt.

Surlang's eyes flew wide as he recognized his own cherished blade, but if he was galled to see it in my hand, he never let it show. "So, you wish to cross steel with me, infidel?" he mocked, holding his free hand to the trickle of blood appearing on his brow.

Not really, for I'd rather have shot him and been finished with the matter, but I roared out a hearty, "Yes!" and leaped forward with a huge sweep of the kris. It slammed into Surlang's hastily raised blade, the power of my blow knocking him back farther. Seeing him off balance, I pressed my advantage, moving toward him with a torrent of strokes, any one of which would have detached his head from his shoulders had it landed cleanly.

Surlang, however, was a consummate bladesman, and he retreated before my assault with the aplomb of a seasoned dueler. Then, when my exertions began to tell, he suddenly counterattacked. Now his *campilan* was slashing for my throat, and I desperately warded off his cuts with the lighter kris. Emboldened, he drove me back, over dead bodies and piles of debris, straining with every lunge to force me off balance so that he could bury his blade in my Christian guts.

"Help, Henry!" I screamed as Surlang pressed me closely. I was blown now, and there was no doubt in my mind that the end to this fight was coming soon, and when it did I was going to be on the short end of the stick. "Do something, for God's sake!" I pleaded.

Henry looked about hastily for a rifle or pistol, but there was none to be found. Then he saw it lying on the ground—a heavy lance, what the Moros called a *simbilan,* topped with a wide metal head. It was a weapon admirably suited for hunting wild boars—or men.

Henry seized the lance, hefted it once, measured the distance up to the catwalk where I desperately staved off Surlang's frenzied onslaught, and then cocked his right arm. With a huge grunt he brought his arm forward violently and released the *simbilan.* It flew true to its mark, its head transfixing Surlang just below his rib cage and slamming into the timber behind him.

Surlang convulsed at the impact, then let forth a great howl, which brought a bloody froth to his lips. His rantings did him not a whit of good, for he remained spitted as neatly as a slab of beef at a Texas barbecue. Realizing he was hopelessly pinned, Surlang glared at me like a trapped wolverine, great rivulets of perspiration now cascading off his brow.

"Surrender, Surlang!" I demanded. "Drop your sword and I'll get aid for you. I promise." It was all a lie, of course, for if Surlang dropped his *campilan,* I'd cleave his skull in twain and reclaim my map, the corner of which I could now see poking tantalizingly from his sash.

Surlang, not at all unexpectedly, spurned my offer with a scowl of indignation. "Surrender to an infidel?" he scoffed through the blood that bubbled up in his throat and threatened to choke him. "I would rather walk on scorpions than surrender!"

"Suit yourself, amigo," I intoned menacingly. Then as Surlang watched with his mouth agape in shock, I dodged past his blade to where the haft of the lance extended from his flank facing Henry. I stepped high, caught the shaft with my boot, and drove it to the catwalk. Surlang shrieked in pain as my maneuver tore his insides apart, and then jerked sideways as I swung my kris for his head again and again. I had fixed the bastard in place by stepping on the shaft of the *simbilan,* you see, and with Surlang thus immobilized, I could hack away with impunity until his strength failed from loss of blood and he finally succumbed.

Surlang, however, was not done quite yet. A warrior from a long warrior line—and a proud Muslim determined not to shame himself in front of an unbeliever, to boot—he did what I would never have believed possible. Holding my flashing kris at bay with his sword arm, and with his free hand grasping the shaft of the lance, Surlang *pulled himself over the length of the shaft until he was free.* Loose at last, he stood there for an instant with his lifeblood literally gushing from his side as I fell back, stunned amazement all over my face.

Immediately, however, I rallied, for I knew that showing any fear to Surlang, even as grievously wounded as he was, would be a grave mistake. "Nice trick," I glowered bravely. "But you just finished yourself, Surlang."

He knew the truth of my words, for now as I came on once more, he retreated before me, his glazed eyes looking desperately from side to side for some avenue of escape. There was none; Baldwin's battalions were flowing through the gate held open by Henry, and the last of the wretched Moros were going over the far walls in a desperate attempt to escape their encirclement through the high cogon grass.

"It's over, Surlang!" I snarled grimly. "Give me the map, damn you. If you do, I'll kill you with one clean blow. It's all you can rightfully expect and you know it."

I backed Surlang all the way down the parapet to where the assault across the bundles of branches had come in, where the blaze in the ditch was roaring with unabated ferocity. Surlang looked from the flames to me and back to the flames.

"Now, infidel, you will see how a son of Allah dies," he vowed. So saying, he mounted the parapet and tottered uncertainly from exhaustion and loss of blood.

"No, damn you!" I screamed. "You're not going over with my map!"

I charged for the madman, tossing aside the kris and trying to grab his legs, but he was toppling now, and his feet were in the air. My hands closed on nothing, and with a look of serenity on his savage face, Surlang tumbled into the inferno and was seen no more.

My map was gone! As his last living act, the bastard had jumped into an inferno just to spite me. By God, I was penniless!

"Burn in hell!" I seethed as I looked into the raging holocaust below.

40

"Captain Travers, that was the boldest feat of arms I have ever witnessed," gushed Colonel Baldwin. "Without your gallant effort, my attack would have failed at great costs. I for one was not pleased when you showed up on my doorstep, Travers, but by God, I know a fighter when I see one. You can rest assured that I will mention you in dispatches to both General Davis and General Chaffee."

I nodded silently in the face of Baldwin's effusive praise, for my mind was completely preoccupied by other matters. I was devastated by the thought that Surlang's pigheadedness had cost me the riches of the *Jesus Maria*. After the flames in the ditch were extinguished, all that had been found of Surlang were his charred bones. His clothing—and my precious map—had been completely incinerated. The treasure was lost for good. Being mentioned in Baldwin's dispatches was damned small compensation for such an incalculable loss, so a clipped, "Why, thank you, sir. That's awfully good of you" was the best I could manage in response.

Even the normally reserved Pershing was moved to praise by my prowess. "Travers, there is no instance of a westerner besting a Moro in hand-to-hand combat. That was absolutely first-class fighting. I must also say that the Maranao *datus* were impressed as well. Ahmai-Manibilang went away from here determined to have peace with us at all costs. For that we have you and your valiant Sergeant Jefferson to thank."

I nodded absently. "Thanks, Pershing. It means the world for me to hear you say that."

It seemed like the sort of drivel he expected to hear, and I was right. He responded with a hearty slap on my back and a firm shake of my hand. "There's a promising future for you in the army, Travers," he predicted with a warm smile.

On that less-than-remunerative note, the campaign concluded. Colonel Baldwin settled his troops into a cantonment he constructed near Pandapatan, which he dubbed Camp Vicars. From there he could safeguard the hard-won peace on the south side of Lake Lanao.

Pershing, for his part, decided to travel with his Moro clients by boat across to the north shore of the lake. He planned to dwell there with Ahmai-Manibilang for a while to solidify the prestige and authority the fight at Pandapatan had brought to American arms. From Ahmai-Manibilang Pershing could secure mounts to carry Henry, Bustos, and me to the coast at Iligan, from whence we could book passage back to Zamboanga, and he offered to do so. Still in a foul humor at the manner of Surlang's demise, I accepted Pershing's offer with as much good grace as I was capable of mustering. When we gained Ahmai-Manibilang's *cotta* at Marahui and said our good-byes, Pershing took me aside for a private farewell.

"I've no doubt that General Chaffee will be most impressed by your actions at Pandapatan, Travers. I wouldn't be surprised if he arranges to have you posted back to the War Department, where you can add some more luster to what is already a glittering career."

"Well, we'll see about all of that," I replied vaguely, torn between my desire to shove my way aboard the very next ship leaving these shores and my anxiety to have Alice returned all safe and sound—by someone else, of course, for I had had my fill of Jolo, thank you. In fact, of the two competing impulses, the former was so strong that the notion of playing the attentive toady to some overweight fossil of a general in the War Department was actually quite appealing at the moment.

"Look me up when we're back in the States together, Travers," added Pershing in conclusion. "I can always find a place for a soldier who knows how to fight."

I thanked him politely, intending never to have anything to do with Pershing again for the rest of my life if I could help it, and then took my leave. And a very morose departure it was, for I had lost a potential fortune, Alice and Fiona were still captives, and I was most likely off to be a damned glorified clerk in the War Department and was actually looking forward to it! By God, the despair and ignominy were almost beyond bearing.

Yes, I was in a bleak state of mind as I followed the local guide Pershing had provided for us down the boulder-strewn trace that wound to the coast. Despite our best efforts to stay together, we frequently lost sight of one another as we picked our way through the incredibly thick jungle foliage. I was right behind Henry, with Bustos taking up the rear. The scowling Macabebe was last in line because he kept falling off the burro that Ahmai-Manibilang had provided for him.

We were bumping along in this fashion when something very odd happened. My listless pony, which up to that time had given no sign of independence and had merely followed in the footsteps of Henry's nag like an automaton, suddenly raised its head and gave a little whinny.

"Someone there," grunted Bustos from behind, pointing to a copse of towering banyan trees right in front of me.

"Of course there is," I retorted irritably. "Henry's there, just around that bend. You just saw him go that way with your own eyes."

"No," insisted Bustos. "Not Henry. Someone else."

"Oh, come now, Bustos, you're not seeing ghosts, are you?" I chided him.

By way of an answer, his burro brayed and then reared, dumping Bustos full on his backside onto the trail. The sight of the old headhunter sprawled in the mud struck me as uproariously funny, and I started to laugh—but my guffaws died in my throat when armed Moros suddenly stepped from the shadows. There were at least twenty of them, and probably more just out of sight.

"Big trouble," growled Bustos unnecessarily. He instinctively went for his bolo, and a dozen krises hissed from their scabbards.

Bustos wisely froze in place.

"What do you want?" I demanded boldly in Spanish. "I'm an American. We are at peace with the Moros, all Moros. What do you want?"

A diminutive figure strode onto the trail. "Have no fear, *Capitán*."

By God, it was Ali Rashid, from Jolo!

"Ali Rashid, what's the meaning of this? And what are you doing on Mindanao?"

Ali Rashid gave an avuncular chuckle and advanced upon me as two retainers hastened to keep him shielded from the sun with immense parasols. He was richly garbed in exquisite silks, and his turban glittered with precious emeralds and rubies. I had to admit, the little runt looked the very image of a powerful Moro *wazir*. "So impatient, so impatient," he clucked. "Are all of your kind so impatient? Come, dismount and join me here."

He squatted down on the path and motioned me to a spot close by his side, but I shook my head defiantly. I liked it just fine where I was, for in a pinch I could probably spur my pony through the Moros and down the trail after Henry. "No, thanks," I started to respond, "I'll just stay right—"

That was as far as I got before I was rudely dragged from my saddle and deposited where Ali Rashid had indicated. Shaking off his warriors, I concluded that his words had been more in the nature of a command than a request. Ali Rashid then barked something else at his followers, and Bustos was quickly hustled off out of earshot. When all had been arranged to Ali Rashid's satisfaction, he motioned to a retainer, who produced some tinder, lit a small fire with it, and set a silver vessel onto the flames.

"We will have tea together, *si?*" proposed Ali Rashid, smiling so widely that all his pointy teeth showed.

Surmising that this too was not a mere suggestion, I answered uneasily, "*Si.*"

When the tea was poured, Ali Rashid snapped his fingers and a servant stepped forward with a jewel-encrusted betel box. The old fellow reached into it with his spindly fingers, selected a sizable hunk of his chaw, and put it into his mouth. Then he offered the box to me.

"Betel?" he asked pleasantly.

"No, I don't care for . . . ," I began to say, but the words died on my tongue when I saw the menacing looks on the faces of Ali Rashid's guards.

"That is, I don't mind if I do. Thanks so very much," I corrected myself hastily, dipping in my fingers with forced gusto and putting a big wad of the disgusting stuff between my cheek and teeth. I took a few tentative chews and was rewarded with a taste somewhere between coal oil and boot leather.

"Marvelous," I managed to croak with a forlorn smile.

Ali Rashid nodded vigorously, thoroughly pleased. "You like, *si?* Jolo betel is the finest in the whole Sulu Sea."

I grinned, sipped, and chewed along in this fashion for what seemed an eternity, until I felt my jaws would break, when Ali Rashid suddenly clapped his hands together and rose.

Here it comes, I told myself; the party's over, and now it's time to send the guests along their way to Moro paradise. I was convinced, you see, that Ali Rashid was bent on revenge for all the Moros I'd slain on Jolo. That's why I was furtively studying possible escape routes, when to my utter surprise a lackey handed Ali Rashid an ornately embroidered Koran. The desiccated gnome opened the book and promptly began reading aloud. The Moros all about me bellowed exuberantly with each passage, and when Ali Rashid was finished, he handed the Koran back to its bearer.

"Arise, amigo," he smiled.

Warily, I stood up.

Ali Rashid undid a brightly hued scarf from about his scrawny neck. Taking my hat from me, he wrapped the scarf around my head to form a turban in the Moro fashion. Then he clapped me forcefully on the shoulder and all at once the Moros raised their krises and sent a great hallooing into the heavy canopy of leaves above our heads, driving a flock of startled parrots into panicked flight.

"*Orang Kaya Kaya!*" the Moros proclaimed thunderously.

"My warriors call you great man, Travers, for now you are a *datu,*" announced Ali Rashid dramatically.

I did a double take at this. "What? Me?" I gasped, astounded. "A *datu,* you say?"

"*Si,*" confirmed Ali Rashid. "This is the will of the sultan of Jolo. When you fought his guards on the very threshold of his *cotta,* you became a warrior of legend in our eyes. It was decided then that you would be a *datu,* the first infidel ever to have this honor. When I arrived on Mindanao, runners brought word of the Pandapatan fight. They say you conquered Surlang with only Moro steel in your hand. Only a true *datu* could do such a thing."

"Well," I stammered, "you must extend my thanks to the sultan. This is, er, certainly unexpected."

Ali Rashid smiled. "Will you not come to Jolo yourself to pay him homage?"

I tensed at this, since I seemed to be rather a bad judge as to when the old boy was giving a nonnegotiable order and when he was merely making a friendly suggestion. "That might, uh, be a little difficult right now," I hedged. "My general, that is my sultan, wants me to go to Zamboanga. *¿Comprende?*"

"Oh, *si,*" replied Ali Rashid with surprising good grace. "Duty I can understand. Then I will set you along your way, but not until you receive a token of the sultan's great esteem for your warrior prowess."

My ears perked up at this. "Token of esteem, did you say?"

Ali Rashid nodded and clapped his hands together sharply once more. A minion shuffled forward with a canvas sack. On its side were the stenciled letters *U.S.*

I realized immediately what it was. Ali Rashid watched craftily as he saw the light of avarice begin to glow in my eyes. By God, it was one of the sacks of gold we'd hauled to Jolo! It was crammed full of twenty-dollar double eagles. For some reason Jamal-ul-Kiram was splitting his haul with me. But why? I wondered. Reading my befuddlement, Ali Rashid didn't keep me in the dark too long.

"This is half of the ransom you offered for the release of your women. It is the pleasure of the sultan Jamal-ul-Kiram that you should have this to buy the slaves and arms with which a *datu* should always be surrounded."

My throat was dry now and my legs were trembling, and not from fear. No, it was the proximity of lucre, you see, for it always had a profound effect on me. Maybe I would get over the loss of my treasure map much sooner than I ever dreamed!

"Well, ha-ha," I tittered giddily, "this is truly generous of the sultan."

Then a thought intruded upon my bliss. General Davis had entrusted these funds to me with the clear understanding that they would either be paid in ransom or else would be returned to him. By all rights, any gold that the sultan of Jolo disgorged should go straight back to Uncle Sam's treasury.

I looked at Ali Rashid and saw in his calculating eyes his aware-
ness of the competing emotions that were racing through my brain.
He screwed up his wizened face and asked benignly, "Is there a problem
with the sultan's gift, Datu Travers?"

In that instant I realized that the gold was a test. The wily old Moro
had taken my measure as a fighter and found me truly impressive. Enough
so to be accorded the highest honor that his people could offer. Ali
Rashid was quite convinced that I was the foremost warrior among
all the Americans. Why else would I have been sent to Maimbung to
do battle? Now he wanted to gauge me in a different way, one that
would determine the extent to which these puzzling Americans dif-
fered from the insufferable Spanish dons. Were the Americans truly
superior beings? Were they driven by pure motives and an unswerving devotion to duty?

If such was the case, then they would be much more dangerous to
Moro culture than the easily corrupted Spanish had ever been. So
dangerous, in fact, that unbeknownst to General Davis or me, the sultan
of Jolo was considering making a submission to Manila. If, however,
Captain Travers, the American paladin, could be bought, then the
Americans were not so much different from the detested Spanish—
and the Jolo Moros would react accordingly.

The fate of rulers and empires teetered upon the outcome of my
test, you see, and instinctively I knew all this. That was why, as I looked
from the gold to Ali Rashid and back again, I thought of General Davis's
bond of trust. I thought also of the honor of the American army, and
I thought too of dear Alice. In her eyes, I was beyond all petty and
selfish needs. What would she think if her gallant knight-errant was
compromised by the savage Moros?

All these thoughts went through my mind as Ali Rashid waited, one
hand cocked on his bony hip in the attitude of a fishmonger haggling
with a difficult customer. Finally I saw my course of action clear before
me, and slowly I drew myself up erect. A sudden look of concern passed
over Ali Rashid. Had he gone too far? Had he insulted this strange
foreigner who fought like a man possessed? Although the *wazir* kept
his aged features perfectly immobile, his trepidation was visible in those
coal black eyes.

That was why, when I reached up and undid the scarf he'd knotted
about my head, the old goat just about wet himself in alarm. A buzz
of concern swept through his warriors, until I silenced them all with
a single raised hand, then smiled roguishly at Ali Rashid. "Please inform

your sublime master that I am forever in his debt, and that I shall always remember this gesture of Moro goodwill."

Oh, for a brief moment I considered refusing the gold. As soon as the notion entered my mind, however, I banished it as total nonsense. Beyond any niggling scruples or moral principles—things that had never weighed particularly heavily on me in the past and certainly didn't now—was the plain fact that, by God, I had earned this gold with the edge of my blade. I was entitled to my share of Jamal-ul-Kiram's spoils by right of conquest, wasn't I? What was more, General Davis had never said anything to me regarding kickbacks for services rendered. No, I was quite certain the point had never been raised, which meant that the issue of this gold being remitted to me secondhand from Jamal-ul-Kiram was a matter of first impression. To me that meant I could use my judgment, and my judgment told me to take the gold and run.

Moreover, I was a *datu* now, a Moro lord, by God. Why, the Moros themselves were saying so, and who should know better than they, eh? And by the blazes, if Ali Rashid was insistent on me being a *datu,* I'd damn well act the part. If something took my fancy, that was the thing I'd have, and at the moment, I had a damned strong urge to take the bag of coins he was dangling under my nose.

Beyond all these very compelling considerations, however, there was an overriding imperative. You see, Ali Rashid might mistake any hesitation on my part for ingratitude, and that, I suspected, was a dangerous thing to show to a Moro.

Vastly relieved by my receptive attitude, the calculating little *wazir* bowed back vigorously at my glowing tribute to his sultan's largesse and, leering like a Cuban whoremaster on payday, ordered that the gold be affixed to the pommel of my saddle.

Clearing my throat pointedly, I insisted instead, "Put the gold *inside* the saddlebag, if you please, amigo, and cover it with this." I handed the scarf to the lackey. "We don't want any prying eyes beholding the sultan's kind gift, now do we, gents?"

With the gold stowed, I figured that the festivities were concluded, and I was about to take my leave when Ali Rashid surprised me once more. He yammered out a new command, and I blinked in disbelief as retainers emerged from the jungle leading two fine Spanish mares. As the horses approached, I saw they each bore a veiled rider, clad in gauzy silks from head to foot and festooned with bronze bangles. Their forms were definitely feminine, and I wondered if Ali Rashid wasn't sweetening the deal by throwing in a few harem ladies on the side. Then, a soft puff of wind shifted those veils just an inch, and the sun reflected off blond tresses, and mahogany ones too. Why, those weren't Asian gals! No, it was Fiona and Alice, by God, all hale and fit!

"Fenny!" cried Alice, leaping from her mount and running to my arms. "My love, I knew you wouldn't rest until you found me. I just knew it!"

She was sobbing and laughing at the same time, and trying to kiss my lips as she did. I kissed her passionately right back, and made room as Fiona jumped to the ground with a squeak of joy and ran to my embrace as well. They were thanking me profusely, and asking how I had managed to force the Moros to release them. In return, I was kissing them with abandon and telling them to hush for now, silently vowing to come up with a suitable yarn in due time, one calculated to ensure their undying devotion.

With all this uninhibited bussing, hugging, and squeezing, our little reunion had the makings of a grand soiree, and it was only with the greatest reluctance that I pulled away and demanded of Ali Rashid, "Are the women free to go?"

"*Si,*" he assured me. "It is a gesture of friendship from my master. The sultan grieves at this parting, and has nothing but the fondest thoughts of both your ladies."

Of that I was sure. I hastily explained to the girls that they were at liberty to go, that I had men with me to protect them, and that they'd be back in civilization by nightfall. This brought forth more squeals and kisses; I heartily wished the Moros would clear out and let me have a private session with these two exceptionally grateful beauties. The expression on Ali Rashid's face, however, told me there was yet further business.

"Let the ladies prepare to travel, *Capitán,* while you and I say farewell," smiled Ali Rashid.

At his signal, the Moros got Fiona and Alice mounted again and drew them off to where Bustos waited, both of them giving the scarred and mutilated Macabebe frightened looks that said they weren't quite certain whether they preferred his company over that of the ferocious Moros. As all of this transpired, Ali Rashid reached into his robes and produced a red leather pouch. I recognized it at once; it was the jewel pouch Fiona had been separated from on the night of the ill-fated rescue attempt back in Maimbung!

"Jamal-ul-Kiram wishes me to deliver to you these gifts for your ladies." He loosened the drawstring and opened the pouch. I peered in to see a small fortune in pearls, rubies, and emeralds twinkling back at me. Why, there was enough loot there to equal another two bags of gold!

"These are the jewels he gave to the golden-haired one, and also the jewels the fiery senorita with the mahogany hair refused. My master wishes you to tell the ladies that he offers these gifts to honor them for all the pleasures they have given to him during their stay at Maimbung."

Licking my lips, I managed to reply, "Well, that's most generous of the sultan." Damned generous indeed.

"Since you are the lord of these women, I am to entrust their jewels to you. The sultan knows that on your honor as a *datu* you will vouchsafe their property."

I saw his reasoning in a flash. Moros, damned slippery rogues when it came to dealing with the world at large, were models of rectitude within their kin groups. It was unheard of for a *datu* not to ensure the welfare of his followers and womenfolk. In the eyes of Jamal-ul-Kiram, nothing could be safer than to place this bounty in my custody. As I considered all this, I stole a glance to where Alice and Fiona sat their mounts, each of them carefully studying the treetops in a pained effort to avoid eye contact with Bustos's single orb. I didn't think they'd seen Ali Rashid produce the pouch, but it paid to be careful in such matters, so I inquired softly, "Er, do the ladies know of your master's princely gift?"

"No, it is a surprise. The sultan has left to you the decision as to when to make known this sign of his affection."

I nodded with suitable graveness, and stretched out my palm to receive the goods. "Tell Jamal-ul-Kiram that I know of the perfect occasion for doing so," I assured him.

Ali Rashid handed over the jewels and I pocketed them with a fluid movement that even a seasoned cutpurse could not have helped but admire.

"And when might that be, Datu Travers?" the old rascal queried with a canny smile.

I looked him hard right in the eyes, and then raised my hands high, fingers spread wide to the tropical sky above. Ali Rashid craned his skinny neck back and gazed heavenward, wondering whether I might be invoking the Christian God. Hoping he might be thinking precisely that, I proclaimed sanctimoniously: "When the winds of the far north blow, and the cold rain falls on Manila!"

That, I reckoned, was about as close as I could get to explaining snow to a Moro.